Avon Books are available at special quantity discounts for bulk purchases for sales promotions, premiums, fund raising or educational use. Special books, or book excerpts, can also be created to fit specific needs.

For details write or telephone the office of the Director of Special Markets, Avon Books, Dept. FP, 1350 Avenue of the Americas, New York, New York 10019, 1-800-238-0658.

Laura Kinsale

The Shadow and the Star

AVON BOOKS ◆ NEW YORK

THE SHADOW AND THE STAR is an original publication of Avon Books. This work has never before appeared in book form. This work is a novel. Any similarity to actual persons or events is purely coincidental.

AVON BOOKS
A division of
The Hearst Corporation
1350 Avenue of the Americas
New York, New York 10019

Copyright © 1991 by Amanda Moor Jay
Inside cover author photograph by Constance Ashley, Inc., Photographer
Published by arrangement with Hedgehog, Inc.
Library of Congress Catalog Card Number: 91-92037
ISBN: 0-380-76131-9

First Avon Books Printing: October 1991

AVON TRADEMARK REG. U.S. PAT. OFF. AND IN OTHER COUNTRIES, MARCA REGISTRADA, HECHO EN U.S.A.

Printed in the U.S.A.

RA   10   9   8   7   6   5   4   3   2   1

Mother, Daddy, Cindy, Ubba, Grandma, Grandad, Elva, Tootsie, Bud, Frances, Sue, Georgia, Auntie, Christine—

Okage sama de: I am what I am because of your kindness.

No alien land in all the world has any deep strong charm for me but that one, no other land could so lovingly and so beseechingly haunt me, sleeping and waking, through half a lifetime, as that one has done. Other things leave me, but it abides; other things change, but it remains the same. For me its balmy airs are always blowing, its summer seas flashing in the sun; the pulsing of its surfbeats is in my ear; I can see its garlanded crags, its leaping cascades, its plumy palms drowsing by the shore, its remote summits floating like islands above the cloud rack . . . in my nostrils still lives the breath of flowers that perished twenty years ago.

MARK TWAIN

E lei kau, e lei ho'oilo i ke aloha.

Love is worn like a wreath
through the summers and the winters.

The Shadow Warrior

❖

1887

In a place of dark and stillness he suspended thought. He let the vast chatter of humanity slip away, let the sound of the light wind in the curtains fill his mind. He stared at his dim reflection in the mirror until the face there became a stranger, a set of features without expression in the silver eyes and impassive mouth . . . and then less than a stranger, only an austere mask . . . then something beyond even that: not human, but elemental shapes. Only a spectrum of dark and light, substance seen and unseen.

With reality before him, he set about transforming it to his own purpose. To conceal the gold of his hair, he borrowed a prop from the *kabuki* theater, the black hood worn by *kuroko* as they slipped furtively into a scene to change the set. To shroud his face, he rejected paint or soot as inadequate: too difficult to remove quickly, too flagrantly illicit should he be perceived. He tied a mask across his face instead, covering all but his eyes with cloth the color of charcoal shadows, a soft, supple fabric like the loose coat of deep midnight gray that he belted around his waist. Within his dark clothing he carried the means to scale a wall, to hurl a lightning bolt, to escape or wound; to kill. He chose pliable *tabi* in place of shoes, in order to walk silently and close to the earth.

Earth . . . water . . . wind . . . fire . . . and the void. He sat cross-legged on the floor. With his ears, he listened to the soft wind that no man was mighty enough to hinder. With his bones, he felt the vast heavy strength of the earth below him. With his mind, he accepted emptiness. Immobile, he blended with the night: unseen in the mirror, unheard in the breeze.

With locked fingers entertwined, he invoked the power of his intention to change the world as it existed.

He rose to his feet and vanished.

One

Leda came awake suddenly in the depth of night. She had been dreaming of cherries. Her body made the jerk of transition, an unpleasant startle that sucked in air and twitched muscles and left her heart pounding as she stared into the dark and tried to get her breath—to make sense of the difference between sleep and reality.

Cherries . . . and plums, had it been? Cobbler? Pudding? A receipt for cordial? No . . . ah—no . . . the bonnet. She closed her eyes. Her brain swam dreamily over the question of whether it would be the cherries or the plums to trim the ready-made, gable-crowned Olivia bonnet that she could buy directly, at the end of the week when Madame Elise paid out for the day work.

She felt instinctively that the bonnet was a much safer and more agreeable topic for contemplation than the one that she knew she ought to be contemplating—which was her dark room and the various even darker corners of it, and what disturbance it might have been that had woken her from a sound and much-needed slumber.

The night was almost silent, except for the tick of her clock and the soft breeze that flowed into the attic window, carrying the scent of the Thames tonight instead of the usual smells of vinegar and distilling. Queen's weather, they were calling this early summer. Leda felt it on her cheek. The celebrations of Her Majesty's Jubilee had made the evening streets noisier than usual, what with the crowds and commotion of the entertainments, and perfectly out-

3

landish foreigners from every corner of God's earth walking about, wearing turbans and jewels and looking just as if they'd got right down off their elephants.

But the night was quiet now. In the open casement, she could just see the outline of her geranium, and the cloudy pile of pink silk that she'd finished at two A.M. and laid across the table. The ball gown was to be delivered by eight, tucked and ruched and the embroidery in the train completed. Leda herself had to be dressed and at Madame Elise's back door before that, by six-thirty, with the gown in a wicker basket so that one of the workroom girls could try it on for faults before the porter whisked it away.

She tried to regain her precious slumber. But her body lay stiff and her heart kept thumping. Was that a noise? She wasn't certain if it was a real sound she heard or only the pump of her own heart. So, naturally, her heart just beat all the harder, and the idea, which had been floating nebulously at the edge of admission, finally took full control of her brain that there was someone in the small room with her.

The shock of alarm which Leda experienced at confronting this notion would have made Miss Myrtle snort. Miss Myrtle had been of a courageous disposition. Miss Myrtle would not have lain frozen in her bed, her heart pounding. Miss Myrtle would have leapt to her feet and taken hold of the poker, which would have been placed in a conveniently handy position next to her pillow, because Miss Myrtle had made it a point of habit to plan ahead for just such an emergency as not finding oneself alone in one's own room in the dark.

Leda was not made of such stuff. She knew she'd been something of a disappointment to Miss Myrtle in that respect. She did have a poker, but she'd forgotten to arrange it close by before she went to bed, being ever so weary, and the daughter of a frivolous Frenchwoman.

Unarmed, she had no choice but to take the next logical step and convince herself that there was most certainly no one in her room. Decidedly not. She could see most of it from where she was, and the shadow on the wall was only her coat and umbrella on the hook where she'd hung them a month ago, after the last cool weather in mid-May. She had a chair and a table with her rented sewing machine; a washstand with a bowl and pitcher. The shape of the dressmaker's dummy by the mantelpiece gave her a momentary start, but when she squinted more closely, she could look right through the open weave of the torso and skirt to the square shape of the fireplace grate. She could see all of these things, even in the dark; her bed was pushed up to the wall in the little garret, so unless this intruder was hanging from the ceiling beam above her like a bat, she must be alone.

She closed her eyes.

She opened them again. Had that shadow moved? Was it just a bit too long for her coat, fading down into the obscurity near the floor? Was not that deeper darkness the shape of a man's feet?

Nonsense. Her eyes were gritty with exhaustion. She closed them again, and took a deep breath.

She opened them.

She stared at the shadow of her coat. And then she threw back the sheet, scrambled up, and cried, "Who is it?"

Nothing but silence answered this comprehensive inquiry. She stood in her bare feet on the cool, rough wood, feeling foolish.

With a sweeping circle of her pointed toe, she passed her foot through the deep shadow beneath her coat. She took four steps backward, toward the fireplace, and groped for the poker. With that instrument in hand, she felt much more the mistress of the situation. She moved the poker in the direction of her coat, jabbing the iron rod all round in the fabric, and then waving it into each deep corner of the room and even under her bed.

The shadows went perfectly empty. No hidden intruder. Nothing at all but vacant space.

Her muscles went slack with relief. She put her hand on her breast, said a little prayer of thankfulness, and checked that the door was still locked before she returned to bed. The open window was safe enough, backed up on the sludgy canal, and accessed only from the steep rooftop, but still she kept the poker close by her on the floor.

With the much-mended sheet pulled up to her nose, she settled back into an agreeable dream in which a stuffed finch, very pretty and genteel, so much in the correct mode that one might be persuaded it was superior to both the plums and the cherries as an elegant trim for an Olivia bonnet, took a prominent role.

The Jubilee drove everything and everyone to a mad pace. It was barely full light when Leda trotted up the back stairs in Regent Street, but the girls in the workroom were all bent over their needles under the gaslights. Most of them looked as if they'd been there all night—which they likely had. This year, the annual rush of the Season accelerated: the parties, the picnics, all the pretty girls and stylish matrons in a tide of engagements and amusement for the Jubilee. Leda blinked her tired lids and blinked again, as she and the first hand among the seamstresses unfolded the vast puff of fabric from her basket. She was exhausted; they all were, but the excitement and anticipation were infectious. Oh, to wear something like it, the lovely thing! She closed her eyes again and stepped back from the ball gown, a little dizzy with hunger and agitation.

"Go and get a bun," the first hand told her. "I'll warrant you didn't finish this a moment before two in the morning, did you now? Take tea if you will, but hurry along. There's an early appointment. They've a foreign delegation to arrive at eight sharp—you're to have the colored silks ready."

"Foreign?"

"Orientals, so I believe. Their hair will be black. Mind you, it won't do to bring out the sallow in their complexions."

Leda hastened into the next room, gulped down a sugary cup of tea along with her bun, and then ran upstairs, greeting the resident hands as she whisked past them. On the third floor, she ducked inside a small room and slipped out of her plain navy-blue skirt and cotton blouse, bathed in lukewarm water from a tin bucket and porcelain sink,

and went trotting down the hall in her chemise and drawers.

One of the apprentices met her halfway. "It's the tailor-
made they've selected," the girl said. "The plaid silk—in
honor of Her Majesty's affection for Balmoral."

Leda gave a little cry of vexation. "Oh! But I—" She
caught herself up on the verge of making the very vulgar
admission that she could in no way afford the new outfit.
But it was to be the uniform of the showroom for the
remainder of the Jubilee; she would be obliged to have the
cost taken out of her wages.

With Miss Myrtle gone everything was really very difficult. But Leda would not cry about it, no indeed, she
would not, no matter how lowering it was. It was only
that she'd had so little sleep, and rested uneasily, and
woken late and cross. She felt more inclined to kick than
to weep, for Miss Myrtle had planned so carefully for the
future, and left a proper will and testament, in which the
lease of her little Mayfair house where Leda had grown
up was left to a nephew, a widower just shy of eighty, on
condition that Leda was to be allowed to stay on and manage it for him, with her own bedroom to remain hers if
she so wished, which she very much did wish.

The widower had agreed to it particularly, and in the
solicitor's office he had even said it would be an honor to
have Miss Myrtle's young lady hold house for him, and
just when everything was settled to their mutual satisfaction it was painfully unlucky of him to walk into the path
of an omnibus, leaving no will or heirs or even an expressed opinion on the matter.

But there, that was a man for you. A rather foolish sex
when all was said and done.

The Mayfair house had gone then to some distant cousin
of Miss Myrtle's who couldn't see her way to living in it
herself. Nor to keeping Leda on for the new tenants. Leda
was too young to be an acceptable housekeeper; it was not
done. No, not even if Cousin Myrtle, a Balfour, *had*
brought up Leda in South Street. An ill business, that, to
take a girl out of the gutter and put her above her natural
place. The cousin wondered at it, she did indeed. But then,

Cousin Myrtle always had been peculiar—the whole family knew it—never mind that she had once been engaged to a viscount; she'd stepped out with *that unspeakable man* instead, and put herself quite beyond the pale, and hadn't even had her marriage lines for her trouble, had she now?

Nor could the cousin quite see any possible way to keep Leda on in any other capacity, not for any amount of work or plain and fancy sewing, nor bring herself in conscience to write a character so that Leda could apply as a typist. The cousin was very sorry, she was sorry indeed, but she didn't know a thing about Miss Leda Étoile except that her mother had been a Frenchwoman, and where was the good of writing something such as that in a referral?

And indeed, as Leda had quickly found, it seemed that there were only two sorts of houses where a young lady of genteel manners and dubious French background would be welcome, and the showroom of a fashionable dressmaker was the mentionable of them.

Leda took a deep breath. "Well, we shall all look the veriest Highland fling in the plaid, shan't we?" she said to the apprentice. "Is mine made up?"

The girl nodded. "I've only to tack up the hem. You've an eight o'clock appointment. Foreigners."

"Orientals," Leda said as she followed the white-aproned girl into a room where stray scraps of material in all colors and patterns littered the carpet and one long table. While Leda tightened her corset and adjusted the wire hoops of the *tournure* behind her hips, the girl shook out a heap of green and blue plaid. Leda lifted her arms to allow the dress to fall over her head.

"Orientals, are they?" the girl mumbled around the pins in her mouth. She plucked them out and tacked deftly. "Them ones who wrung chickens' necks in the Langham Hotel?"

"Certainly not," Leda said. "I believe it was a sultan who—ah—precipitated the unfortunate incident of the poultry." Wringing chickens' necks was not a subject suitable for mention by a lady. Conscientiously, she made an effort to improve the girl's mind. "The Orientals are from Japan. Or Nippon, as it is properly called."

"Where't that be, then?"

Leda frowned, a little uncertain of her geography. Miss Myrtle had been a strong proponent of female education, but lacking necessary equipment—a globe, for instance— some of her lessons had made only a rather vague impression.

"It's difficult to describe," she temporized. "I would have to show you on a map."

The girl's needle flashed in and out of the silk. Leda wrinkled her nose at the reflection of the plaid dress in a cracked pier glass. She didn't care for these strong patterns, and worse, the stiff silk didn't drape well over the *tournure*. "See how it protrudes at the back." She plucked disconsolately at the generous fall of material behind her hips. "I look suspiciously like a Scottish hen."

"Oh, 'tisn't so bad, Miss Etoile. The green's nice enough with your eyes. Brings out the color. There on the table's the cockade you're to wear in your hair."

Leda reached over and swept up the decoration, tucking it into the dark mahogany of her hair at several different angles before she was finally satisfied with the effect. The cockade's dark green plaid was almost lost against the deep color of her hair, so she arranged the ornament with a rakish tilt. Miss Myrtle would have taken one glance and pronounced the effect rather too coquettish for elegance. She would then have found occasion to mention that she herself had once broken off an engagement with a viscount—a most imprudent action, she would admit—but girls of seventeen could frequently be counted upon to be foolish. (Here there always followed an expressive look at Leda each time the story was told, whether Leda happened to be twelve years old or twenty.) Miss Myrtle herself inclined to a genteel understatement of effect. That this refined inclination accorded conveniently with a very limited wherewithal to purchase vulgarly excessive trimmings and fashionable frivolities was a fact kindly overlooked by Miss Myrtle's intimate circle: delicately bred ladies of similar circumstances who found themselves in complete agreement on the point.

But Miss Myrtle was passed away, and however much

honored in Leda's memory, such simple tastes were not in vogue for a showroom woman on the premises of Madame Elise, by Special Appointment dressmaker to H.R.H. the Princess of Wales. The tailor-sewn plaid it was to be, and the price of the elegant, tasteful Olivia bonnet Leda had been dreaming about (ready-made, with the chaste addition of a stuffed finch) was undoubtedly half gone in the cost of the golden medallion on the plaid cockade alone.

Mrs. Isaacson, present force behind the pseudonym of the long-vanished Madame Elise, came quickly into the cutting room. She handed Leda a set of cards, wordlessly looked her over, and nodded briefly. "Very nice. I approve of the hair ornament—well-placed. Help Miss Clark to arrange hers as jauntily, if you will. The girl is drooping." She flicked her finger toward the cards. "There will be some English ladies with the foreigners. I believe that Lady Ashland and her daughter are also dark. Daylight and candlelight, the complete trousseau. Concentrate on the jewel-tones and perhaps pink—not a hint of yellow in anything, mind you—although ivory might do; we shall see. It's a large party by the time they all arrive—six or seven at once. It's my understanding that they may all wish to be advised together. You'll be required to step forward if I need you."

"Of course, ma'am," Leda said. She hesitated, and then forced herself to add, "Ma'am—might I speak to you in private, if you have a moment?"

Mrs. Isaacson gave her a shrewd look. "I've no time to be private with you just now. Is it about the new showroom dress?"

"I'm living out, ma'am. At this time—it is . . ." Oh, how awful it was to be forced to speak like this. "I'm in difficult circumstances at present, ma'am."

"The cost can be subtracted from your wages, naturally. Six shillings a week was the amount agreed upon in your contract."

Leda kept her eyes lowered. "I cannot live upon the remainder, ma'am."

Mrs. Isaacson stood silent a moment. "You are obliged to dress yourself appropriately to your position. I can't permit an alteration in the contract, you understand. The terms were clearly stated to you when you came to us. It would set a precedent I cannot afford to set."

"No, ma'am," Leda said faintly.

Another little silence passed, barely endurable. "I shall see what can be arranged," Mrs. Isaacson said at last.

Relief flowed through Leda.

"Thank you, ma'am. Thank you." She sketched a curtsy while Mrs. Isaacson lifted her skirt and turned away.

Leda looked down at the cards. As was becoming standard practice in this year of exotic visitors, someone from the Foreign Office had sent along helpful etiquette tickets. Below the date were the scheduled appointments.

Japan party—8.00 A.M.

H.R.H. the Imperial Princess Terute-No-Miya of Japan. To be addressed *Your Serene Highness*. No English.

Imperial Consort Okubo Otsu of Japan. To be addressed *Your Serene Highness*. No English.

Lady Inouye of Japan. As daughter and representative of Count Inouye, Japan Minister of Foreign Affairs, to be addressed per diplomatic usage *Your Excellency*. Fluent English, educated in England, will interpret with no difficulty.

Hawaiian (Sandwich Islands) party—10.00 A.M.

H.M. Queen Kapiolani of the Hawaiian Islands. To be addressed *Your Majesty*. A very little English, will need interpreter.

H.R.H. Princess Liliyewokalani, Crown Princess of the Hawaiian Islands. To be addressed *Your Highness*. Fluent English, will interpret with no difficulty.

Lady Ashland, Marchioness of Ashland and her daughter Lady Catherine. Presently resident in the Hawaiian Islands. Intimates of the Hawaiian queen and princess.

Leda flipped back and forth through the tickets, memorizing the titles while the apprentice finished her hem. This was Leda's element. Miss Myrtle Balfour had been zealous in her mission to bring up Leda in the proper etiquette to be observed by those received in good society. And truly, Leda had been received very cordially by the widows and spinsters of South Street. The aura of pleasant scandal that Miss Myrtle still retained from the days of *that unspeakable man,* in spite of some forty-odd years of living quietly retired in her parents' house, was a passport to any number of odd fits and starts. A Balfour was to be allowed, even encouraged, to have her eccentricities—it gave a sweet tinge of adventure and daring to the demure little society in South Street. So the South Street ladies had bridled up and given a pretty direct snub to anyone who might question Miss Myrtle's sense when she'd taken the notion to shelter the little daughter of a Frenchwoman in her home, and clasped Leda quite to their well-bred bosoms, so she had grown to womanhood among the faded flowers of Mayfair aristocracy, counting the elderly daughters of earls and vintage sisters of baronets as her close acquaintance.

All these Majesties and Highnesses were a bit grander than what she was accustomed to, however, and very kind and attentive of the Foreign Office it was to clarify the various relationships in advance, so as to avoid any threat of uncomfortable lapses. It would all pass off perfectly well, as it had when the Maharani and the Siamese ladies and the female mandarin had come last week.

With her hem finished, she went to select fabrics, carrying bolt after heavy bolt of brocades and velvets and silks to pile behind the counters in the showroom, where the tall, mirrored panels reflected back the rich pattern of the violet and amber carpet in the huge room. Other showroom women were doing the same, preparing for the press of regular clients, most all of them appointed for much later and more civilized hours of the day. She'd just laid the last bolt of striped silk atop the pile when the footman ushered Their Serene Highnesses of Japan into the showroom.

Madame Elise *cum* Isaacson hurried to curtsy and scrape before the four delicate Oriental ladies who stood like frightened fawns just inside the door. They all stared at the toes of their Western-style shoes, keeping their hands flat against their skirts. The partings in their jet-black hair stood out in straight lines, as white as their porcelain faces. Madame Elise bade them a formal welcome in her best French accent, and asked if they would please to follow her.

She backed away. After three steps, it was clear that none of the Japanese ladies were going to follow. They stood there silently, staring at the floor.

Madame Elise glanced at the footman, and mouthed, *Lady Inouye?* with her eyebrows raised. The footman shrugged almost imperceptibly. Madame was put to the extreme expedient of saying aloud, in plain unaccented English, "Lady Inouye—may I presume to have the very great honor, Your Excellency?"

No one spoke. One of the two Japanese ladies standing half-hidden behind the others made a faint motion with her hand toward the figure just in front of her. Madame Elise moved a step toward the lady. "Your Excellency?"

The Japanese girl put her fingers to her lips. She smiled behind her hand, and then broke into a shy giggle. In a pretty, girlish voice, barely above a whisper, she said something incomprehensible, sounding rather as if she were trying to sing around a mouthful of water. She bowed slightly, pointed back out the door, and bowed again.

"Oh, dear," Madame Elise said, "I thought Her Excellency was to speak English."

The girl repeated her hand motion out the door. Then she put her fingers to her throat, bent over, and gave a theatrical cough. She motioned out the door again.

Everyone stood dubiously silent.

"Madame Elise?" Leda ventured. "Is it possible that Lady Inouye hasn't come?"

"Not come?" Madame Elise's voice had a tinge of panic.

Leda stepped forward. "Her . . . Ex—cellency," she said, slowly and clearly, and then put her hand to her throat, coughed as the other girl had, and motioned out the door.

All four of the Japanese ladies bowed, their salutes varying in degree from a deep bending at the waist to just a slight bob of the head.

"Oh, dear," Madame Elise said.

Another moment of silence passed.

"Mademoiselle Etoile," Madame Elise said suddenly to Leda, "you may see to these clients." She took Leda by one elbow and pulled her forward, presenting her like an offering, and then curtsied her way backward, out of range.

Leda took a breath. She had no idea which ones were the princess and imperial consort, but her best guess was that they were the two who stood in front, who had just barely nodded instead of bowing. With an opening sweep of her arm, she tried to motion them all toward the seats prepared around the largest counter.

Like an obedient little flock of geese, they walked with tiny steps toward the chairs. Two seated themselves, and the other two sank gracefully to their knees on the floor, eyes downcast.

Well, surely the two in the chairs must be the royalty, and the other some sort of attendants. Leda took a fashion book from the counter. Not certain which lady, between a princess and a consort, took precedence, she offered it to the one who appeared the oldest of the two.

The lady drew back with a negative motion, passing her palm like a fan in front of her face. Leda apologized and curtsied deeply to the other, offering the book there.

That one, too, declined to take the plate-book. As Leda stood with it held between her hands, she looked in desperation at the two on the floor. Surely not . . . would the lower position be superior in their country? She saw no choice: she offered the book to the nearest of the kneeling ladies.

It was the one who had pantomimed Lady Inouye's indisposition earlier. Now, she held up her hand, refusing the book. She turned and spoke softly to the younger of the two ladies in the chair, who whispered in return. Leda stood helplessly while they mumbled back and forth. The kneeling girl turned back, bowed her forehead to the floor, and said, "San-weesh."

Leda bit her lip, and then quickly composed her features. "San-weesh," she repeated. "Fashion?" she added, holding out the book again.

It was firmly refused. Leda curtsied again and went behind the counter. She lifted two bolts of velvet and brought them out. Perhaps they wished to start with the fabric first.

The attempt was a failure. The Japanese ladies stared at the velvets without attempting to touch them. They began to speak softly among themselves.

"San-weesh," the kneeling attendant repeated to Leda. "San-weesh aye-ran."

"I'm so sorry," Leda said helplessly. "I don't understand." She tried a lime-green silk. Perhaps they were looking for lighter-weight fabrics.

"San-weesh aye-ran," was the soft, insistent response. "San-weesh aye-ran."

"Oh!" Leda said suddenly. "Do you mean the Sandwich Islands?"

The kneeling girl clapped her hands and bowed. "San-weesh!" she repeated gaily. All of the Japanese ladies giggled. The older woman had blackened teeth that made her mouth seem a vacant space when she opened it—a very strange and somewhat disconcerting effect.

"You wish to wait for Her Majesty of the Sandwich Islands?" Leda asked.

The attendant responded with a stream of Japanese. Leda curtsied and stood uncertainly. The ladies put their small pale hands in their laps and cast down their eyes.

For two hours, until the ten o'clock appointment of the Queen of the Sandwich Islands, they all remained so, with Leda standing escort over the small group as they sat patiently, looking neither right nor left, but occasionally whispering among themselves. The only break in this exquisite torture was when Madame Elise had the presence of mind to send in a tray of tea and Savoy cakes, which the ladies enjoyed with dainty enthusiasm and more giggles. They seemed like smiling dolls, small and shy.

The big showroom was quiet enough that everyone could hear the carriage when it stopped outside at last, and the English voices at the front door. Leda felt so relieved that she forgot her aching back and curtsied deeply. "The Sandwich Islands," she said hopefully, indicating the windows.

All of the Japanese ladies looked up and smiled and made their various bows.

In a few moments the Hawaiian party was at the door. A stately, slow-moving woman entered the showroom first, dressed in an excellently fitted purple silk morning dress which her ample bosom filled magnificently. Behind her was an equally large and graceful lady, a little younger and prettier, brown and broad-cheeked and regally composed.

Madame Elise moved forward and curtsied deeply. The second of the formidable pair said, "Good morning," in pleasant, perfectly understandable English. She nodded toward the woman in the purple silk. "This is my sister, Her Majesty Queen Kapiolani."

With an audible breath of relief, Madame Elise plunged back into her French accent. "Ze humble house of Madame Elise is honored by Your Majesty's presence," she purred, ushering the ladies forward.

Behind the Hawaiians, the rest of the party had paused on the threshold. Leda looked up, and for a bare instant forgot her manners in a gaze of open admiration.

Together in the doorway stood the two most beautiful women Leda had ever in her life beheld in one place at the same time. With the same high cheekbones and exquisite skin, the same glossy dark hair and wonderful eyes, mother and daughter made an arresting picture. They dressed simply, Lady Ashland in deep blue modestly draped over an insignificant dress-improver, avoiding the exaggerated poultry-like profile that Leda's plaid gave her. The daughter—Lady Catherine, the etiquette ticket had named her—wore a debutante's pale pink, her half-crinoline a little more fashionably expansive.

Madame Elise was still occupied trying to bring about communication between the Queen of the Sandwich Islands and the Japanese ladies, so Leda went forward to welcome Lady Ashland and her daughter.

Lady Ashland smiled in a friendly way, showing sun lines at her eyes that her daughter didn't have. "How busy you must be," she said comfortably. "We won't burden you for long—the queen wished to have one morning dress especially from Madame Elise. She has asked us to tell you it needn't be rushed through."

Leda immediately desired to put the business of any friend of this pleasant lady's before all others. "It is an honor and a pleasure to serve Her Majesty, m'lady. And we will be most pleased to help Your Ladyship in any way that you desire. There's no trouble to us at all."

Lady Ashland laughed and shrugged. "Well, I am no fashionable fribble, but perhaps—" She looked inquisitively at her daughter. Leda could see scattered strands of silver in her raven's-wing hair. "Won't you consider something, Kai?"

"Poor silly Mum," Lady Catherine said in a lively American accent. "You know I love a corset as dearly as you do." She tilted her head and smiled confidingly at Leda. "I just can't *tolerate* the awful things."

No corset? Lady Catherine was blessed with the sort of figure that would appear elegant in a flour sack, but no corset? Leda could hear Miss Myrtle turning in her grave. "We have a lovely rose-pastel swiss," she said. "It would make up into a morning frock. Very comfortable and light, but so smart."

The younger woman looked up beneath her lashes, a subtle spark of interest that Leda recognized instantly. She smiled and held out her hand toward the counters.

"Lady Tess?" The Hawaiian princess' sweet, low-pitched voice interrupted their progress. "There seems to be a difficulty with the imperial party."

All hopes that the Queen of the Sandwich Islands could communicate with the Japanese ladies seemed to have fallen flat. Madame Elise looked harassed as she stood among the alien group, where several of the Japanese had been sketching vague shapes in the air that appeared to mean nothing to the Hawaiian queen or her sister.

"We've no interpreter," Leda explained to Lady Ashland, "but they seem to be very determined on some idea which none of us can manage to fathom."

"Samuel!" Lady Ashland and her daughter said in unison.

"Has he left yet?" Lady Catherine cried, running to the window. She threw open the sash and leaned out. "Samuel!" she shouted, in most unladylike tones. "Manō Kane, wait! Come here!" Her voice dropped to a burble of affection. "We need you, Manō, to come and get us out of a spot again."

Lady Ashland merely stood by, not making any move at all to curb her daughter's wild display. Lady Catherine turned back from the window. "Caught him!"

"Mr. Gerard can translate," Lady Ashland said.

"Oh, yes, he speaks fluent Japanese." Lady Catherine nodded encouragingly at the Oriental entourage. "How lucky that he should have brought us this morning."

Indeed, it seemed to Leda a remarkably fortunate circumstance, since she supposed there couldn't be many people with such a singular talent as speaking fluent Japanese who happened to be escorting ladies about London dressmakers just at that moment. But Lady Ashland and her daughter lived closer to Nippon, of course.

At least, Leda supposed they did. She wasn't entirely certain about the location of the Sandwich Islands either.

She turned toward the hall, expecting one of those mustachioed Yankee businessmen who seemed to have trekked everywhere with their prosperous waistcoats and overloud voices. The footman moved into the room, and in the portentous timbre that Madame Elise insisted gave the proper majestic effect, uttered: "Mr. Samuel Gerard!"

The room full of women went uncharacteristically silent as Mr. Gerard appeared in the door . . . a collective intake of feminine breath at the sight of him—a golden, slightly wind-blown Gabriel come down to earth, minus nothing but the wings.

Two
〜〜〜〜〜〜
The Boy

⬩

Hawaii, 1869

Just to one side of the gangplank that thumped and creaked under the feet of the other departing passengers, he stood on the dock, silent. People pushed past him and ran to other people and congregated in laughter and tearful reunions. He shifted his feet, hurting in the new shoes that had been saved since London for this moment. He wanted very much to chew his finger. He had to keep his hands in a tight ball behind his back to prevent it.

He saw women in bright full robes of scarlet and yellow, with long loops of dark leaves hanging around their necks, and men with nothing on at all but breeches and a vest or a straw hat. Amid the crowd, girls sat bareback astride horses: dusky, laughing girls with long black hair around their shoulders and crowns of flowers on their heads, their brown legs dangling, calling and waving at the gentlemen in carriages and the ladies with their parasols. And behind it all were the green mountains rising up to mist and a double rainbow that spanned the entire sky.

On the ship he'd been afraid to leave his cabin. For the whole voyage, he'd stayed in his own snug space down where the steam engines throbbed and stank of coal and the steward brought him all the food he could eat. He'd hidden himself there until this morning, when they'd come and told him that he'd best put on his fine clothes, because the ship had rounded Diamond Head and put in for Honolulu Harbor.

The air smelled good here, with a strange, fresh scent,

clean as the sky and the trees. They were odd trees, like none he'd ever seen before, with strange plumed tops glistening and swaying on tall, bare trunks. In his whole life, he hadn't smelled air so clean, nor felt sun so bright and warm on his shoulders.

He stood there alone, trying to be inconspicuous and conspicuous at the same time, and terrified that he had been forgotten.

"Sammy?"

It was a soft voice, like the wind that ruffled his hair and blew its golden strands into his eyes. He turned around, reaching with a quick hand to wet his fingers and shove the offending lock back into place.

She stood a few feet away, holding a tumbling coil of gay flowers over her arm. He looked up into her face. The incomprehensible shouts and chatter of native children filled the air. Someone brushed past him from behind, shoving him a half-step toward her.

She knelt in her wide lavender skirts, holding out her hands. "Do you remember me, Sammy?"

He stared at her helplessly. Remember her? Through all the lonely days and hated nights, in all the dark rooms where they had tied his hands and done what they pleased with him, in all the days and weeks and years of silent misery, he had remembered. The one bright face in his life. The one kind word. The only hand raised to shield him.

"Yes'm," he whispered. "I remember."

"I'm Tess," she said, as if he might not be sure. "Lady Ashland."

He nodded, and found his fist pressed against his mouth. With a quick, awkward move, he made himself lower the rebellious hand. He locked it behind his back with the other.

"I'm so glad to see you, Sammy." Her open arms still offered an embrace. She looked at him with those pretty blue-green eyes. A huge lump in his throat made it hard to breathe. "Won't you let me hug you?"

Somehow his feet in the pinching shoes took him forward, a step, and then a run, and he fell into her arms with a clumsy force which made him feel stupid and hot with shame. But she was pulling him close with a small glad cry, tossing the wreath of flowers over his head, pressing her smooth cheek to his. There was wet on her face. He felt it as she squeezed him, and the swelling in his throat hurt and throbbed as if something was trying to get out that couldn't.

"Oh, Sammy," she said. "Oh, Sammy. It took us so long to find you."

"I'm sorry, mum." The words were muffled against the flowers and the soft lace at her collar.

She held him away from her. "It wasn't your fault!" Her voice laughed and cried at once. She gave him a little shake. "You're worth every minute of searching. I only wish those hateful detectives could have found you sooner. When I think of where you've been—"

He just looked at her, knowing nothing of detectives or searches and wishing she had no notion of where he had been. He ducked his head. "I'm sorry," he said again. "I didn't know—I didn't have nowhere else to go."

She closed her eyes. For a miserable moment he thought it was disgust, and he deserved it. He knew he must deserve it. He shouldn't have let those things happen to him; he should have done something; he shouldn't have been helpless and afraid.

But she didn't turn away from him. Instead she pulled him close again, a warm, hard hug that smelled of wind and flowers. "Never again," she said fiercely. Her voice caught, and he knew she was crying. "Forget it all, Sammy. Forget everything before today. You've come home now."

Home. He let her hold him against her and hid his face in the cool flowers and heard dumb little noises come out of his own throat, little whimpers that would have shamed a baby. He tried to keep them back, and tried to say something like a grown-up, like he ought to be—eight years old, or even nine, maybe, and he ought to be able to say something right. Her tears wet both their cheeks and he wanted to cry at least, but his eyes were dry and his throat just kept making those stupid little noises . . . *Home*, he wanted to say, and . . . *Thank you, oh, thank you. Oh, home* . . .

Three

◈

Leda was staring.

She caught herself in the middle of it, but not before
Samuel Gerard had looked straight at her, an instant's lock
of glances: hers paralyzed, his silver and burning beautiful, utterly stunning in a face of masculine flawless inhu-
manity . . . perfect . . . perfect beyond the perfection of
mere marble art, beyond anything but dreams.

It was the strangest moment. He looked at Leda as if
he knew her and had not expected to find her there. But
she did not know him. She had never seen him.

Not him. Never before.

His glance skimmed past her. Lady Catherine was coming forward, speaking to him in an easy, familiar voice,
as if it were the most ordinary thing in nature to converse
with this archangel come down to walk among mortal men.
His mouth curved faintly, not quite a smile at Lady Catherine, but suddenly Leda thought: *He loves her.*

Of course. They made a pair that almost tempted fate,
so perfectly matched they were. A dark beauty and a bright
sun-touched god. Meant for one another.

Ah, well.

"Now tell us—what *are* these poor ladies trying to
say?" Lady Catherine demanded, drawing him forward
with her.

He let go of her hand and bowed formally to each of
the seated Japanese ladies in turn. The morning sun sought
him through the tall windows as if to confer a special
favor, burnished the deep gold of his hair, slid light into
the depths of it. When he straightened, lifting his eyes—

and really, such handsome lashes as he had, thick and long, much darker than his hair—he spoke in the strange, clipped syllables of their language, bowing again with a courteous deference before he finished the brief speech.

The younger of the ladies answered with a flood of words and gestures, tilting her head once, very slightly, toward Queen Kapiolani with a timid smile.

He questioned her again. She giggled and made a fluid shape in the air, sweeping her hands wide around her own torso and then down toward her feet.

Mr. Gerard repeated his bow when she had finished. He looked toward the queen and her sister. "It is a question of a fashion, ma'am. A particular dress." Like Lady Catherine's, his accent was more American than English, and he spoke as gravely as if the fate of nations hung in the balance. "Her Majesty Queen Kapiolani has worn a white dress at court, ma'am? Heavily embroidered?" He made a slight motion with his hand: a vague, awkward, male sort of copy of the Japanese princess' descriptive movement. The color rose in his neck a little. "Loose? With no—ah—"

"No corset," Lady Catherine said wisely.

Mr. Gerard turned quite a deep crimson beneath his tan. He shifted his glance. All the ladies, of all nationalities, began to smile. Really, men were so charmingly absurd.

"Yes," the princess intoned. "The *mu'umu'u* of Japan silk." She spoke to her sister in yet another language, this one more liquid and lovely than the Japanese.

Mr. Gerard smiled. "Japanese silk, is it?" He spoke to the Oriental ladies again, and received pleased nods and eager chatter. He looked back at the others and translated. "They wish to thank Your Majesty for the honor to their country."

A series of courtesies were exchanged on this point, leaving everyone highly pleased with everyone else. Madame Elise clapped her hands, settling back into her overblown French manner.

"Of course, ze flowing robe of white brocade, cut in ze Hawaiian mode. I see it describe in a page of *Ze Queen* periodical." She fluttered obsequiously. "Perhaps Their

Serene Highnesses wish it to be copied, if Her Majesty should be zo gracious as to permit?''

It seemed that this was the case. Her Majesty showed herself perfectly satisfied to extend the favor to her estimable royal sisters from Japan. A footman was dispatched to escort the gown in question from the hotel; in the meanwhile, the fabric must be selected: it must be a pale brocade, and poor Mr. Gerard, as translator, was well and truly caught in the net of international fashion diplomacy.

Leda hurried off to discover what the storeroom had to offer. She returned carrying five bolts of white and blond silk piled to her nose. As she stepped into the showroom, Mr. Gerard moved next to her, lifting the ponderous weight all at once from her arms.

''Oh, no, please''—she was panting a little—''don't trouble yourself, sir.''

''No trouble.'' He spoke softly as he laid the bolts of fabric across the counter. Leda lowered her eyes, pretending to busy herself with the silk. She glanced up beneath her lashes. He was still looking at her.

She could not fathom what was in his face. The moment she caught him at it, he turned away, and she could not decide if his interest was more than her hopeful imagination. Not that she wished him to take an interest: not here—never here; she could not bear that—not the kind of regard a man would have for a showroom woman. It was all mere whimsy, just an amazingly beautiful man—a splendid sight that she could not but admire.

Still . . . he seemed, in a curious way, to be familiar to her. And yet that faultless masculine face was unforgettable; even the way he moved was memorable, with a controlled and concentrated grace in his dark, conservatively cut morning coat and winged collar. His broad shoulders, his tall stature, those remarkable dark lashes and gray eyes: already he was burned indelibly on her mind. She could only suppose she'd seen some illustration of a shining hero once, in a book, Prince Charming on his white steed—and here he was in Madame Elise's showroom, standing with pensive composure, surrounded by colorful silk and chattering women.

The other showroom girls were taking whatever excuse they could find to come into the room. Word of Mr. Gerard had spread. As Leda unrolled an ivory brocade over the counter, she intercepted a downcast smirk from Miss Clark, who was making herself inordinately busy straightening up a counter that did not need straightening.

Leda tried to check her by ignoring the smirk. Miss Myrtle had felt men to be something of an imposition on the world, not quite acceptable as topics of civil conversation, with the sole exception of *that unspeakable man,* who had evidently contained, entirely in himself, a complete repository of all the various and assorted incarnations of depravity to which the human soul was capable of sinking. *That unspeakable man* was therefore perfectly suitable as a conversation piece, and had in fact been abused for Leda's benefit and instruction with vigorous regularity in Miss Myrtle's drawing room over the years.

Leda was a little wary of men. But finally she could not help giving a tiny grin back at Miss Clark.

He was just too tremendous. He truly was.

Each time Leda spread out a new bolt for view, he pulled the previous one out of her hands as she began to roll it, and turned the fabric back onto the bolt himself, hefting the unwieldy weight easily. And he didn't make a fuss over it, either; he just kept up his translation from the Japanese to English and back again as he worked alongside her, while Madame Elise held each fabric up to the window and explained its properties and how it would show by candlelight and gas.

When Leda dropped her silver scissors, he picked them up for her. She accepted them with a mumble of thanks, feeling painfully bashful, as scatterbrained as a fluttery old maid when his bare hand brushed hers.

Leda was so absorbed in surreptitiously watching him that she started when the footman murmured in her ear from behind. She looked down and saw in his gloved hand a monogrammed letter sealed with a coronet.

"For Mademoiselle Etoile." The servant held it out to her.

Everyone glanced toward her except Madame Elise, who

went on talking without a pause. Leda felt her face go to a scalding color. She plucked the letter from the footman and held it behind her, wishing desperately for a pocket.

Madame Elise's phony French voice droned on, but suddenly she raised her eyes and stared directly at Leda for a moment. Leda dropped the letter to the floor behind her, standing so that her skirt covered it. She swallowed and looked down, fumbling blindly at the fabric on the counter.

She had no need to open the missive. She'd no need even to look closely at the coronet. It made no difference to which peer the seal might belong—such a note could mean only one thing, and have but one end.

This was how Mrs. Isaacson was to "arrange something." Leda felt appalled and humiliated, furious with Mrs. Isaacson, and then chagrined to think that perhaps it was what her employer had thought she was requesting. Many of the girls did walk out with men . . . but no . . . no—it did not have to be done this way, in the showroom, in front of the other girls and the clients.

She was publicly branded—her position made crystal-clear. Sold for the price of a silk plaid showroom dress and cockade.

Business had gone on around her. When she found the nerve to look up, the Japanese ladies were engaged in appointing a time for the first hand to go round to their hotel for the measurements. In the midst of it, Mr. Gerard translated. He would have seen the letter, too. They had all seen it, but of course no one was paying any attention to the affairs of a dressmaker's showroom woman.

The Japanese ladies rose to leave. Leda had no choice; she was forced to move away from where she'd dropped the letter so impetuously and attend to the Hawaiian party while Madame Elise ushered the others to the door. Mr. Gerard went with them out to the carriage. Before Leda could discreetly retrieve the letter, Lady Catherine called her name, eager to begin her own choices. Leda had just produced the rose swiss for her and an emerald glazed silk for Queen Kapiolani when he returned.

"Now do tell us, Manō." Lady Catherine spread the

swiss across her throat and struck a coquettish pose. "How does this take your masculine fancy?"

As he crossed the room, he had to walk right over the stretch of carpet where the letter lay. He did not glance at it, or at Leda.

But Lady Catherine just then had noticed, and pointed out his omission to him. "I believe Miss Etoile has mislaid her note." Her sociable American smile at Leda held nothing but innocence. "Won't you retrieve it for her?"

He turned and bent down. In misery, Leda accepted the envelope. He gave it to her with the face up, though the coronet had been showing clearly where it had fallen.

She could not even thank him. She could not look up. When Lady Catherine gaily drew his attention to the rose swiss again, Leda wished herself deceased and beyond humiliation, hidden beneath a nameless headstone in some obscure churchyard leagues away.

But she determined to do nothing so coarse as to expire of shame in company. She put her head down and calmly aided Queen Kapiolani in her decision on the emerald glazed. She helped Lady Catherine and her mother choose a suitable pattern for the morning dress. She listened to the easy talk between Mr. Gerard and all the ladies from Hawaii, who would not let him go now that he was in their power. It was obvious that they knew one another as well as any family: even the large and elegant Hawaiian ladies treated him with a motherly air, smiling indulgently when the others scoffed and rode him for his masculine discomfort at voicing aloud his opinion of the fashions. And in an amiable, teasing way, Lady Catherine took his verdict as law, discarding any pattern that he did not approve.

In love, Leda thought. *Of course. Why not?*

Leda stood by, providing fashion books, changing dresses on the stuffed model, showing Lady Catherine to a fitting room when the girl declared in her stout Americanish way that it was nonsensical to trouble a first hand to go all the way to her hotel "at her convenience," when she was right here to be measured. And then suddenly it was all over, and Leda was curtsying as Mr. Gerard took

Her Majesty's arm and escorted her into the hall. The princess and Lady Ashland followed.

Lady Catherine paused a moment, laid a hand on Leda's arm, and said, "Thank you. Indeed—I've always said that I hate going to the dressmaker's, but this has been quite fun!"

Leda nodded and forced a smile, in terror that this naive girl was going to push a tip into her hand, as if she were a gamekeeper or a chambermaid. But Lady Catherine only pressed her arm in a friendly way and let go, hurrying out after her mother.

Leda turned back to the counter, snapped up the coronetted letter, and hammered upstairs all the way to the empty dormitory hall before she stopped, panting, and tore it open.

> *My Dear Mademoiselle Etoile:*
> *I admired you from afar at the ball Tuesday last, as you laboured in company with Madame Elise to make your busy repairs to the ladies' gowns. But such a one should have her own pretty toilette, I believe, and I would be honored if you would allow me to serve you with the same, in the way of a dress worthy of you.*
> *Devoutly at your command,*
>
> *Herringmore*

Leda crushed it in her fists and ripped it apart. She would not bear this; she would not be insulted so—"admired from afar"—oh, the indecency of it! She did not even know who this "Herringmore" might be, and most certainly had no wish to be introduced. The common, wretched vulgarity of it, to be ogled as if she were some loose servant girl!

She should have become a typist. All the ladies of South Street had been against it, as being a forward and pushing occupation, unsuitable for a gently brought-up female. But typists were not forced to abide *this*, surely!

Admired from afar, indeed! The insolence!

She drummed down the stairs, tossing the shreds of the note out the open window on the landing. In the bathroom, she pulled the cockade out of her hair and almost twisted her back in her haste to get at the buttons and remove herself from the hateful dress.

In her own skirt and blouse, she marched back to the showroom to confront Madame Isaacson-Elise, that false, revolting hussy—and blow up all bridges sky-high behind her.

The walk from Regent Street to Bermondsey was long enough that Leda had always taken an omnibus or the railway when she was in funds. Her neighborhood now was dreadful, on the outer edge of what she feared she might find was a very great rookery slum if she had ever summoned up the courage to penetrate a few streets farther. But she had counted herself fortunate to find a single room there after she'd discovered that on two pound ten a month, which had seemed a very good wage initially, she was far too poor for the parlor flat she'd taken first in Kensington. It had required a certain amount of time for the reality of her new situation to press in upon her.

For now the attic room in a clump of ancient houses hanging over a tiny canal off the river, with tipsy awnings and broken shutters, was hers—at least until the end of the month, she judged. She paid upon every application, so the landlady approved of her and promptly mended windows and locks, but Leda had the foreboding that she would not be such a favorite if the woman discovered that she no longer had employment.

The situation would not last for long, of course. Leda would visit her ladies in South Street. They would give her the character reference that Madame Elise had denied, and Leda would start over—as a typist this time, which was what she should have done to begin with.

She chose to walk now, until she could unlock her account book from its little tin box and reckon up her situation precisely. Not wishing to arrive too early and arouse suspicion in the landlady's heart, she stopped in the Strand at an A.B.C. Tea-shop for Ladies, where she drank a dish and ate a cucumber sandwich. Then she bought an extra bun, lingering at her table beneath the cheerful lace curtains as long as possible on the strength of threepence. There was no wicker dress basket to lug today, so she tucked the uneaten bun into her purse as she walked along the embankment by the river and joined the flood of pedestrians, canvas-covered wagons, and cabs across London Bridge and into the malodorous industrial districts south of the river.

Here she preferred not to dally at an idle pace, but picked her way among the crowds and delivery vans with vigor. It was awkward to be walking unaccompanied; she wouldn't like to be taken for a lady of questionable character. But Miss Myrtle said that quality would always speak for itself, so Leda kept her chin up and her pace elegant, ignoring, for the most part, the scarecrow figures who lounged in shadowed doorways and lingered at the coffee stalls.

The first wave of odors beyond the bridge was pleasant and interesting: orris root, tea, oil of rosewood and pine from Hay's Wharf, the intermingled scents of the whole vast world come to breathe in a London warehouse. An old man with a queer, blank expression sat huddled against a lamppost. Next to him, a skinny half-grown pup lay panting, staring round with bright canine alertness at the passing flow of shoes and trousers. Leda walked past. Two yards on, she turned suddenly, rummaging in her purse. She marched back, thrust the bun in the old man's hand, and turned to walk on as he mumbled something after her. She could hear the pup whining in eagerness.

A train came roaring past on the line into London Bridge Station, the same rumble that woke her every morning at five, as regular as an alarm. Here the smell of vinegar overwhelmed the neighborhood, but she supposed there might have been worse odors in an area of industry—she had had whiffs of the tanneries now and again when the wind was in the east, and subtle, sickening waves of chloroform drifted sometimes from the hospital. Gutter children shouted at her halfheartedly as she passed, but she ignored them, and they left off to scratch at their bare toes and stare.

In her own street, the children were better kept. Indeed,

the dictatorial couple in the house next door operated an orphanage of sorts, and took in a few children from the workhouse sometimes, and kept them ferociously neat and pretty and well-behaved, never allowed them out-of-doors into the dirt, and tried to find sponsors and make arrangements for them. One beautiful little boy had been taken up by a benevolent gentleman and adopted away last month, just like Oliver Twist in Mr. Dickens' story.

Until that had happened, Leda had actually fancied that perhaps really it was a house like that one in the book, where the children trained as pickpockets. She'd considered mentioning her suspicions to the police, but had been a little afraid that they would laugh at her. Or worse, that her landlady would not appreciate the civic nature of her interest. Miss Myrtle would never have quailed at such a reservation, of course, but Leda had found that what seemed principled and self-evident in South Street was not always so clearly appropriate in Crucifix Lane or Oatmeal Yard or the Maze.

When she passed the wrought-iron door of the police station at the corner, she stopped to bid the night-inspector a good evening. But it was before her usual time, so Inspector Ruby had not come in yet. She left her compliments with a young policeman who touched his helmet very respectfully with his big hand and promised to convey them.

She turned down a street only an alley's width, with plastered houses as ancient as Queen Elizabeth overhanging the muddy pavement. She closed her mind to it and occupied herself with thoughts of a sleek brand-new typing machine, managing to penetrate as far as the foot of the lodging-house stairs before Mrs. Dawkins shambled out of her tiny parlor. The landlady stood in a thread of anemic light that fell across the banister and the first three stairs, the only illumination in the murky depths of the hall.

"Now then, what's this?" She propped a meaty elbow against the parlor door frame and looked at Leda with eyes pallid blue and protuberant, the slow, mechanical blink of a baby-doll. "Come in early, miss?" She bobbed her curly head as she spoke, her cheeks shaking. Mrs. Dawkins was always deferential toward Leda, but she had a way of looking out one side of her eyes when she cast them down that was most unpleasant.

"Yes," Leda said. "A bit early." She started up the stairs.

"Have ye left your basket?" Mrs. Dawkins asked. "Your basket w' the pretty dresses? Can Jem Smollett help you carry it up, miss?"

Leda stopped and turned. "I'm sure he could, if I had brought it. But I have not. Good evening."

"No basket!" The landlady's voice had a sharp warble. "They'll not have turned you off, then, eh?"

Leda put her foot on the next step and turned onto the landing. "Of course not, Mrs. Dawkins. Some of us have been given an afternoon to rest, before the greatest rush is anticipated. Good evening to you," she repeated, and hurried on up the stairs with the landlady's quavering mumble following her.

That would not do at all. Mrs. Dawkins knew her boarders—no doubt any small change in habit was cause for suspicion of a change in circumstances. Leda lifted her skirt and bit her lip, turning the last landing onto the narrowest set of stairs. At the top, she unlocked her own door and slipped inside, closing it behind her.

The little whitewashed garret seemed almost homey when she thought of what might become of her if Mrs. Dawkins put her out. Without employment, the only shelter she could obtain would be at one of those horrid boardinghouses, where the inmates were packed together in common rooms and her small savings would vanish at fourpence a night with a bed, and threepence without.

She had a desperate thought of laying her circumstances before the South Street ladies, but Miss Myrtle would never have sunk so low as to beg for assistance, by word or by deed. To make a civil morning call and mention that she now found it convenient to seek a more suitable position—that was acceptable. To admit that she was close to living in the street—no, she could not. She would not.

She opened the leaded-glass casement to let some of the

stuffy closeness leave the room. The odor of vinegar lay heavy in the neighborhood, mingling with the humid scents rising off the canal. It wasn't even dark, but she changed into her nightclothes and lay down, ignoring the complaint that was beginning to grow in her middle. One cucumber sandwich did not stick long to the ribs, but she was tired and feeling exceptionally impoverished, and a creeping sense of panic at what she had done. Sleep seemed so blissfully mindless.

As she closed her eyes, she thought of Lady Catherine and her mother, and how they should always wear jewel-tones to compliment their coloring. Drifting amid vague and whirling fancies of silk and foreign voices, she started awake with the room gone to darkness around her. It confused her a moment, for she felt she'd hardly slept a minute, instead of hours passing.

Her heart was pounding again, filling her ears in the dead silence. Far away, the thin whistle of a train rode on the night, disembodied from itself.

Her eyes slid shut, impossible to keep open. Lady Catherine seemed to be smiling somewhere, that frank, pretty smile, laying her hand on Leda's arm. Miss Myrtle urged her to wake up. There was someone in her room. She must wake up. *Wake up; wake up; wake up*—but she could not open her eyes. She was so tired; she would sleep in the street. It didn't matter. Silver scissors glittered in the gutter. She reached down to pick them up . . . and a man's hand intercepted. He was here, really here, right in her own room. She must wake up . . . she must . . . she must . . .

In the dream he caught her wrist and pulled her near, held her close against his chest. She wasn't afraid. She couldn't see him; she simply could not open her heavy eyes. But she felt so safe, cradled in his hold. So safe and comfortable . . . so safe . . .

Four

Manō Kane

Hawaii, 1871

It was a big house, but he was becoming accustomed to big houses. He loved them, the airy, empty rooms with their woven *lauhala* mats beneath his bare feet, the white pillars and broad porches called *lanai*, the way voices echoed back from the tall ceilings and the sound of the ocean was always in his ears.

He wore shoes today, going as he was on a visit with Lady Tess, and a white sailor's suit with navy-blue and red braids. It was so clean that he was reluctant to move. He did not want to spoil it. He had lots of clothes, but he preferred that they stay untouched and perfect in the wardrobe or chest. It was nice to look inside and see them neatly folded, so pure and crisp.

He sat in a chair with his eyes on the beautiful crisscrossed weave of the floor mats while Lady Tess talked with the grand Hawaiian lady Mrs. Dominis. Their conversation drifted past him, adult talk, of no particular interest. Lady Tess had asked him if he wouldn't rather stay home and play, but he hadn't. He wanted to be with her. That was what he always wanted. The very best was when she swept him up in her arms and hugged him, but he also liked it if she held his hand, or if he could just keep a fold of her dress in his fist.

Today, she'd brought Master Robert and little Kai, too. The Hawaiian lady enjoyed seeing them, Samuel could tell. He wondered if Mrs. Dominis had another name, in her own language, instead of the name the foreigners called her—the one she'd gotten from her bearded Italian husband. When he'd asked Lady Tess, she'd said Mrs. Dominis' Christian name was Lydia. That was all right, but he would rather have heard her true one. All the Hawaiians had strange and lovely names. She was a gentle lady too, with a low, rich voice and the golden-brown skin of the islanders. When she bent down to gather Robert and Kai close into her large embrace, they both seemed very pink and small.

Samuel himself had held back behind Lady Tess when Mrs. Dominis had wished to hug him. He didn't know why, because he was quite certain he would have liked it. But Robert and Kai were Lady Tess's real children. Samuel didn't have a proper last name. He felt a sham in his fine clothes.

Little Kai snuggled in Mrs. Dominis' lap and laid her cheek against the broad expanse of the Hawaiian woman's bosom. Robert fussed at being left out until she gave him a kukui-nut *lei*. The four-year-old sat down at her feet and applied himself to unraveling the knots between the black, polished nuts.

"Have you been fishing, Samuel?" Mrs. Dominis asked.

He nodded. The American and English ladies never spoke to the children in the drawing room, but the Hawaiians always wanted to know what he'd been doing, as interested as if they were children themselves. He said, "I caught a *manō,* ma'am."

"A shark! A big one?"

He rocked from side to side in his chair. "Pretty big, ma'am."

"As long as my arm?"

He looked up as she held out her fingers. Her arm was plump and soft, not as slender as Lady Tess's. "A little longer."

"Did you kill it and eat it?"

"Yes, ma'am. I hit it with a paddle. Kuke-wahine helped me to cut it up."

"We had it sauced for dinner last night," Lady Tess said.

"Good." Mrs. Dominis smiled at Samuel. "To kill and eat it will make you brave."

He looked at her with interest. "It will?"

"Certainly. *Manō kane*. A shark-man, afraid of nothing in the sea."

Samuel sat up a little, struck with the idea. He considered it, imagined himself as a shark, gliding in the dark depths of the ocean. Fearless. Biting anything that threatened him, with terrible sharp teeth.

"I'll sing you a song about sharks," Mrs. Dominis said, and began to chant in her own rich language. It wasn't even like a song, really; it didn't have a tune, but she tapped her fingers in her lap in rhythm. He listened to the flow of syllables, fascinated.

When she was finished, Lady Tess asked her to sing something else. Mrs. Dominis stood up, still holding Kai, and sat down at the piano. For the rest of their visit she played regular English songs, with Lady Tess and young Robert singing along, and Kai clapping her baby hands out of time.

Samuel sat still in his chair. He did not join them. Beneath all the more melodic tunes, he listened in his mind to the deep and rhythmical song of the shark.

Five

◈

"You should be married, my dear," said Mrs. Wrotham to Leda. The older woman did not, unfortunately, amplify on how this desirable object might be achieved, but sat perched on the edge of her bobbin-turned chair. "I don't care for typing." She tapped her blue-veined fingers gently together. "Only think how very dirty one's gloves must become."

"I don't suppose I shall wear gloves, Mrs. Wrotham," Leda said. "At least, perhaps I shall take them off when I'm working on the machine."

"But where will you put them? They will collect dirt, my dear—you know what gloves are." She nodded slowly, and the silver rolls of hair at her temples bobbed in time beneath her little bonnet, as coyly as a girl's of long ago.

"Perhaps there will be a drawer in my desk. I'll wrap them in paper and put them in there."

Mrs. Wrotham didn't answer, but still nodded in her slow way. Against the pale rose-pink walls and fading curtains of apple-green, she looked fragile, as delicate and antique as the garlands of Georgian plasterwork that adorned the ceiling and mantelpiece.

"It makes me very unhappy," she said suddenly, "to think of you at a desk. I wish you will reconsider, Leda dear. Miss Myrtle might not have quite liked it, do you think?"

This reference, made in a voice of tender reproach, touched Leda sorely. There was no doubt that Miss Myrtle would not have liked it at all. Leda bent her head and said rather desperately, "But only imagine how interesting it must be! Perhaps I might copy a manuscript written out by an author the equal of Sir Walter Scott.''

''Very unlikely, my dear,'' Mrs. Wrotham said, nodding more emphatically. ''Very doubtful indeed. I do not think we shall see the like of Sir Walter again in our lifetimes. Would you like to pour tea?''

Leda rose, conscious of the honor done to her with this request. It was very good of Mrs. Wrotham to ask, since Leda could see that her hostess was a little ruffled at the idea that an author might someday be born who could equal her favorite.

As they ate their thin-sliced bread and butter, the cockney maid announced Lady Cove and her sister Miss Lovatt. For a moment there was the eternal complication at the door, as Miss Lovatt tried to hold back and allow her sister the baroness to take precedence, and Lady Cove wavered and motioned helplessly and wished her elder relation to proceed first. It was resolved as it always was: m'lady finally preceded her sister meekly into the room and looked up gratefully at Leda as she placed chairs for them near the tea tray.

It was just like olden times as Miss Lovatt settled her wiry frame into a chintz-covered chair and demanded of Leda exactly what she thought she had been about to keep herself away from her friends for so long. As Leda struggled to explain without causing the ladies undue distress by too exact a description of what it meant to be employed for wages, Lady Cove saved her by saying in her soft voice that it was very good of Leda to come whenever she might honor them. Leda smiled at her, thankful for the reprieve.

With this addition to the party, the conversation passed to other matters, including the tenants in Miss Myrtle's house. ''Coarse-featured,'' Miss Wrotham said sweepingly of the new mistress. 'You can see her nose beyond her bonnet. We have not called.''

''He is an animal merchant,'' Miss Lovatt said.

''An animal merchant?'' Leda echoed.

''He deals in animals,'' Miss Lovatt amplified, with an enigmatic lift of her finger. ''Deceased. On a large scale.''

There was no more to be said to that. Whatever the

gentleman did with deceased animals on a large scale was better left to the imagination. A moment of respectful, melancholic silence passed, as everyone contemplated the sad fate of Miss Myrtle's house, and Leda thought of her snug bedroom with the velvet Brussels carpet and *irisé* wallpaper patterned in dark blue on shades of pink and red.

"Have you made any improvements to your new flat, dear?" Lady Cove asked Leda.

"Oh! Improvements?" She cast about for an appropriate answer, something to deflect further inquiry into the parlor flat that she hadn't been able to keep. "I have not decided yet what improvements to make. I don't like to be hasty."

"Very wise," Miss Lovatt said, nodding. "You are always such a steady girl, Leda. We have worried about you, but I believe you shall do very well."

"Oh, yes, ma'am."

"Leda tells me that she wishes to become a typist," Mrs. Wrotham announced. "I must allow that I don't like it."

"Indeed not!" Miss Lovatt set down her teacup. "No, we all agreed that a typist was not suitable. The couturiere is the preferred choice."

"I was—that is—you see—I find I am not quite comfortable at Madame Elise's," Leda said.

"Then you must change your situation," Lady Cove said in her kind, whispery voice. "What can we do to help you?"

Leda looked at her gratefully. "Oh, Lady Cove—it would be a very great compliment to me if I might have a character—" She broke off, aware of the inelegant abruptness of the request. "—a sentence only—really, I fear Madame Elise won't—if it would not impose—your good nature—" She bit her lip on the tumble of words.

"We shall consider," Miss Lovatt said. "It isn't that we are not happy to recommend you, Leda dear, you understand. But perhaps you should not be too previous about leaving Madame Elise to become a typist."

"But, ma'am—"

"You must listen to wiser council, Leda. A typist is not suitable. It is an occupation for strong-minded females."

"You will dirty your gloves," Mrs. Wrotham added.

"But she needn't wear gloves, need she?" Lady Cove asked timidly.

"Of course she must wear gloves, Clarimond. There will be persons of a common class involved in such a post. Runners. Shopboys." Miss Lovatt's nostrils flared. "Actors, perhaps."

"Actors!" Lady Cove squeaked.

"Perhaps she might be required to type their parts. I myself have seen an advertisement for the Ladies' Typewriting and General Copying Office, offering to copy actor's parts and documents for solicitors."

The three ladies all looked reproachfully at Leda. She lowered her eyes in disgrace and took a sip of tea, having no defense to make. She would very much have liked to eat several more of the paper-thin slices of bread and butter, but that would have been gauche.

"We shall consider," Miss Lovatt said—meaning, of course, that she would consider and the other ladies would listen humbly to her discourse and conclusion on the topic. "We want the best for you, Leda my dear. Miss Myrtle would wish us to take every care for your future. You must come back Friday next, and we shall see about it then."

Leda spent the rest of the day sitting in the anteroom of Miss Gernsheim's Employment Agency. Her interview with Miss Gernsheim did not go smoothly from the moment that lady understood that Leda would have no written character from her former employer. Typist, Leda was given to understand, was a most sought-after position, generally given to those with prior training and experience. Without even a character . . . Miss Gernsheim tapped her fountain pen against the side of her inkwell and looked grave.

Leda mentioned her South Street connections.

"I have not heard of Lady Cove," Miss Gernsheim said unencouragingly. "Is the family listed in Burke's?"

"Certainly," Leda said, stung. "They have held the

barony since 1630. And Lady Cove is a Lovatt on her maternal side.''

"Indeed. You are related, then?''

Leda looked down at her gloves. "No, ma'am,'' she murmured.

"Ah. I thought perhaps an ancestral connection would account for your command of the family tree.''

"No, ma'am,'' Leda said again, and was silent.

"I believe 'Etoile' is also an unfamiliar name to me. What district does your family inhabit?''

"My family is no longer living, ma'am.''

"How sorry I am,'' Miss Gernsheim said in a businesslike tone. "But what are your origins? In a case such as yours, with little experience and a history of resignation with prejudice, prospective employers will wish to know who you may be. There is all sorts of trouble these days; all sorts of disagreeable persons are known to be at large. Socialists. Housemaids who murder their mistresses. The dangerous classes. You've heard of Kate Webster, of course.''

"No, ma'am,'' Leda said.

"Have you not?'' Miss Gernsheim raised her thin eyebrows and looked candidly surprised. "It was in all the papers. Richmond. Some years ago, now. The maid of all work—the one who cut up a poor old widow and boiled her in her own copper. And then there was Madame Riel—throttled by her woman right in her own house in Park Lane. This sort of thing makes employers most suspicious. You are not Irish, I hope?''

"My origins are French, ma'am,'' Leda said steadily.

"Can you be more specific, Miss Etoile? How long has your family been in England?''

Leda began to find the little office stuffy. "I'm not certain of that, I am afraid.''

"You seem to be more conversant with the history of the Lovatt family than your own.''

"My mother died when I was three. Miss Myrtle Balfour of South Street took charge of my upbringing at that time.''

"And Mr. Etoile? Your father?''

Leda sat helplessly silent.

"Are you a relation of this Miss Balfour's, then? Can she not supply a character?"

"No, ma'am," Leda said, and was horrified to hear a tiny flutter in her voice. "Miss Balfour passed away a year ago."

"And you are not yourself a relation of the Balfour family?"

"No, ma'am."

"You were adopted?"

"Miss Balfour took me into her home."

The other woman looked impatient. "I cannot call this an auspicious background, Miss Etoile. Perhaps we would do better to seek positions for you that do not require the most stringent qualifications. Have you considered the shops?"

Leda spread her gloved hands against one another. "I would prefer not to engage in shop trade, ma'am, if you please."

"Come, come—this is too nice. You don't suppose your breeding puts you above it?"

"I would prefer something more respectable than a shop, ma'am," Leda said stubbornly. "I really wish to be a typist."

"If that is the case, you will have to present me with a strong letter of character from a high source. Lady Cove at the very least."

"Yes, ma'am."

Miss Gernsheim was making notes. "I understand correctly that Etoile is your mother's name, then?"

"Yes, ma'am." Leda's voice had gone to a whisper.

"She was not married?"

Leda gave a little speechless shake of her head. Miss Gernsheim lifted her eyes from the paper, regarding Leda with a frown, and then wrote. "What is your present direction?"

"Mrs. Dawkins at Jacob's Island, ma'am. Bermondsey."

"Jacob's Island!" She closed the notebook and laid down her pen. "You are something of a challenge, Miss

Etoile. It's most unusual for sensible girls to look above their background. When you return with your character, we shall see what we can do. Will Monday a week be convenient?''

"I believe that I can bring the letter earlier than that," Leda offered.

"You may bring it by as soon as possible, Miss Etoile, but it will be Monday at best before I have reviewed the openings to find what might be appropriate to your circumstances. Close the door gently behind you, if you please. My head quite tortures me today."

Leda, too, had the headache. She left the office in a gloomy mood. She would have somehow to manage to find Lady Cove at home when her sister Miss Lovatt was not there, a formidable task in itself, and then coax the timid baroness to write a character which Miss Lovatt had plainly hinted was not to be written, including a line expressing clearly that Leda hadn't the temperament of a murderess . . . just the sort of thing that would excite a conversation on the topic of sanguinary servants, and end by putting Lady Cove into a tremble over the possibly evil designs of her butler, a quavery-voiced, stoop-shouldered man who had been employed in her home for thirty-five years.

And to have to wait for more than a week just to hear of openings! Leda mentally totted up her accounts and trudged grimly onward.

It was late dusk when she reached her neighborhood. The night-inspector was just stepping up to the station-house stairs. He stopped when he saw Leda on the walk behind him and held open the gate. "You're early again, miss! Heard you was by early yesterday."

"How do you do, Inspector Ruby? Have they left everything properly in order for you?"

"Certainly have, miss. Certainly have." This part of their exchange was a ritual. Leda asked after his wife and children and what his supper had been, and offered to pass along Miss Myrtle's receipt for ox tongue.

"Thank you kindly, miss. Come up then and I'll put it into my memorandum book, if you're not in a hurry."

Leda climbed the stairs and went through the iron wicket door that he held open for her. Inside the stuffy station room, the Inspector's podium stood alone in a pool of gaslight, like a pulpit in the gathering dusk. A woman lay full-length on the floor inside the single cell, a dark heap mumbling and moaning softly to herself in the shadow, while a policeman jumped to his feet off the outer bench and saluted his superior.

Leda felt it would show a vulgarly prurient curiosity to examine the woman in the cell too closely, so she sat down on the bench and leaned against the whitewashed wall, taking the inspector's book into her lap to write. In spite of the sultry atmosphere, the reserve policeman began to stoke up the coal beneath a copper kettle on the hob grate, apologizing to the inspector for not having his tea at the ready.

The inspector grimaced. " 'Tis no nevermind; you brew the bitterest cup o' stable muck I ever did drink, Mac-Donald.''

"Sorry, sir,'' MacDonald said. He straightened up, looking as if he couldn't think what to do with his big, freckled hands. He hooked them in the webbing of his white belt and popped the shiny buckle, giving Leda a shy glance. "Never have got the way of it. Me sis always does the honors at home.''

Leda put the book aside. "Let me make your tea for you, Inspector. I'm quite practiced.''

"Why, that's capital of you, miss.'' Inspector Ruby rubbed his mustache and smiled. "I'd be obliged to you, I would. Nothing like a lady's touch.''

Leda crossed the stark room and busied herself with the kettle and the fire. From the corner of her eye, she saw the female figure in the cell roll over and shift about on the floor, as if trying to make herself more comfortable. The woman made a low moan. As she turned over onto her back, her swollen shape made it obvious that she was very much . . . ah . . . in a condition of imminent fructation, as Miss Myrtle would have put it, speaking in a whisper behind her hand.

"Oh, dear," Leda said, straightening up from the little stove. "Are you quite well, ma'am?"

The woman made no answer. She was breathing heavily, arching her back. Behind Leda, Inspector Ruby gave an inquiring grunt. "Mac? What have we here?"

"Book says disorderly, sir." Sergeant MacDonald cleared his throat. "They took her up on the afternoon beat. Turned away from Oxslip's in the Island, she was. Made a row. Scratched Frying Pan Sally's face."

Leda turned round in surprise, in time to catch the men exchange glances. "Oxslip's?" she asked. "In my street? That's where they take in the orphan children."

Inspector Ruby gave her a queer frown. He chewed his upper lip, pulling at his mustache with his teeth. Sergeant MacDonald looked nonplussed.

"Orphanage," Inspector Ruby said roughly. "Yes, that's right, miss."

She watched the prisoner clutch at her back and groan. When Leda looked closely, it was easy to see that the woman really was little more than a clear-skinned girl, barely out of her middle teens. "Perhaps—Inspector Ruby—I believe—" Leda hesitated to put forward an opinion, knowing nothing of midwifery, but the girl was making some very significant noises now. "Should a doctor be called?"

"A doctor, miss?" The inspector peered at the girl. "You don't mean—Lord help us—she's not about to—"

The prostrate figure in the cell interrupted him with a moan on a rising note, then broke off suddenly into a whispered torrent of profane words.

"MacDonald," the inspector snapped, "send to find if the medical officer is still abroad. She won't have money enough for any doctor."

"Yessir. I'll see to it right away, sir." MacDonald sprang into a quick salute and disappeared out the wicket door with admirable haste.

"MacDonald!" the inspector bawled after him. "*Send*, I say—you're not to go! There, the great stupid lump of a fellow; a pox on him, he heard me plain as day. Frightened of female things, he is." Inspector Ruby grinned at her. "Sweet on you, miss. Asks after you every day. Hardly could contain himself that you spoke to him last evening." He took off his jacket with the bright buttons and began to roll up his sleeves. "And what d'you think of this poor girl, then? I suppose we shall have to take a closer look at her."

Leda backed up against the wall, hesitating as he opened the cell and motioned her in. "I'm afraid I don't know much about it," she admitted. "She seemed to be in affliction, and I thought perhaps a professional man ought to be brought in."

"Bless you, miss, we don't see professional men down here, you know. Not for this sort. Perhaps the medical officer will send a midwife . . . perhaps not." He went into the cell and knelt beside the girl. "Here now, what's to be done, little lady? Are you having your birth pains? How long you been hurting?"

Leda couldn't hear the girl's mumbled answer, but the inspector shook his head at the answer. "All day, is it? Silly child—why'd you not speak up?"

"I don' want it," the girl panted. "I don' want it comin' yet."

"Well, it's coming, for all that. Your first?"

The girl made a whimper of assent.

"Why'd you go to Oxslip's? You wasn't hopin' to be brought to bed there?"

"Me girlfriend . . . she asked around for me . . . give me to expect they'd take the babe." The girl swallowed and rolled her head to the side. "I'd pay for its keep. I swear I would."

The inspector shook his head. "You shelter your own babe, my girl," he said. "You give it over to them baby-minders, you've as good as murdered it, take my word. A maidservant, was you? Got a young man in the city?"

"I . . . can't find him."

"That's bad luck. But they don't want an infant at Oxslip's, you understand me? Your friend sent you fair and far wrong when she sent you there."

The girl began to breathe rapidly. Her face contorted.

The inspector held her by the hand. Leda moved closer, biting her lip. "Can I do anything?" she whispered.

The squeak of the wicket door made them both look around. Leda expected to see Sergeant MacDonald, but it was an unknown officer who burst through the door, color high in his cheeks and his collar tight from exertion. Inspector Ruby shoved himself to his feet.

"Don't leave me," the girl cried. "It hurts so!"

Leda stepped into the cell. "I'll stay with her," she said, lowering herself onto her knees on the hard floor. She took the girl's hand and patted it as the frantic fingers closed over hers.

"Thank you, miss." The inspector was already out and addressing the newcomer. "Good evening to you, Superintendent. Something amiss?"

The other man gave a bark of harsh laughter. "Amiss! Aye! Why don't we have a telegraph in this office, I ask you? I've a flock of reporters ten steps behind me and the Home Office breathing hot on my neck, if you call that bloody amiss! Bring yourself along, Ruby, and look lively."

"My reserve—"

"MacDonald? I met him in the street. Sent him ahead. The papers, man, the papers! If you think I want to be caught flat-footed in front of a bloody pack of reporters, you may think again." The man never even looked toward Leda or the woman in the cell, but kept his hand on the open door as Inspector Ruby quickly gathered his hat and coat. "It's some sort of swindle, I'll be bound, but this fellow's advertised his work from Whitehall to the *Times* and back again, and we've got to look as if we're on top of it. I judge we've got a quarter hour before the press is on the scene." He wiped at his forehead with his handkerchief. "There's been a robbery at the Alexandra Hotel, from some damned Oriental prince or other, Siamese I think it is, but that's not our job—what we've got is a bloody note from the bloody fellow what pinched it, says this bloody stolen irreplaceable prick of a Siamese jeweled crown—to be presented to the Queen herself, mind you—this thief comes right out and says it can bloody well be recovered from Oxslip's in Jacob's Island!"

"*Oxslip's!*" Inspector Ruby ejaculated.

"Well you may gape! You've only got the half of it. Do you know what the bloody devil this maniac left in place of the crown at the hotel? Some filthy little statuette right out of a nasty house, Ruby! A *truly* nasty house—and I'm not talking of some Haymarket pub full of dollymops, either. Can you fathom it? Home Office is hysterical; Foreign Office gone mad—monstrous insult to these Orientals' bloody sensibilities—international incident—trade treaties—diplomats—I'll tell you, Ruby, I'm not going to be caught looking the fool in front of a parcel of damned diplomats—"

His words were lost as the door closed behind them. Leda stared after them in bewilderment, and then down into the terrified eyes of the girl.

"It's quite all right," she said, trying to sound stout. "The midwife's coming."

"Something's happening," the girl exclaimed, with a wild motion of her head. "I'm all wet—I'm bleeding!"

Leda looked down, and indeed, there was a dark stain creeping up the girl's skirt. It seemed a massive amount of fluid, spreading out over the floor. "No—it isn't blood, dear," she said. "It's quite transparent. Your water." Leda had heard of that—that a woman's waters broke, whatever that meant. She was very much afraid it indicated that birth was imminent. "Just be calm. The midwife is on her way."

The girl cried out, her body straining. Her fingernails dug into Leda's palm.

Leda stroked her forehead. Her skin was soft and moist, with a healthy color unlike the pallor of poverty that had begun to seem familiar to Leda. She must have had decent food and lodging, at least. Her body seemed sturdy and well-formed, not delicate, but that was little comfort while Leda had to listen to the terrible sounds of effort and pain the girl was making.

"It's a-comin'," she panted. "Oh, no—it's going to come!"

"That's all right," Leda said, wanting only to soothe

the panic in the girl. "Everything is all right. What is your name, dear?"

"Pammy—Hodgkins. Oh, ma'am—is you the mid-wife?"

"No. But I will stay right here with you."

"Is the midwife a-comin'?"

"Yes. Sergeant MacDonald went for help."

"But he said—t'other man said—he sent 'im off some-wheres else."

"The midwife is coming," Leda said firmly, refusing to believe anything else. "Only think of how nice it will be to hold your baby in your arms."

Pammy's throat arched. She lifted her knees and rolled from side to side. "It hurts, it hurts so!" She took a deep breath and exploded it through her lips. "Oh, I'd kill that Jamie could I lay hands on 'im. I want to die!"

The wicker door clanged open. Leda looked up and murmured, "Thank heaven."

Two women descended upon them. "I am Mrs. Layton, the maternity nurse. This is Mrs. Fullerton-Smith of the Ladies' Sanitary Association. How frequent are the pains?"

This question was addressed with piercing abruptness at Leda. She opened her mouth, closed it, and then said helplessly, "I really don't know. A considerable amount of water has come."

"See to the kettle," the nurse said to Leda. "Mrs. Fullerton-Smith, would you be so kind as to spread the hygienic sheet here on the floor for me?"

The two women set to work with an alacrity and com-petence that relieved Leda enormously. The nurse, brisk and zealous, had no patience with Pammy's whimpers, but began to insist that she "Bear down—and no nonsense, my girl," while Mrs. Fullerton-Smith thrust a sheaf of pamphlets into Leda's hand. "Familiarize yourself with those, if you please. She must not return to any employ-ment for four weeks at the earliest. We implore you to encourage her to feed the baby at the breast. You may refer to the tract entitled *The Evils of Bottle-Feeding*. Also, opi-ates such as Godfrey's Cordial, poppy tea, or quieteners are to be eschewed. Cleanliness is paramount—all food should be covered, cow's milk boiled, hands washed after any visit to the privy, bodily waste removed promptly. Where do you live?''

"I live at Mrs. Dawkins', ma'am, but Pammy—''

"We will arrange for post-parturation visits. What is her name?''

"Pammy Hodgkins, but—''

"Just allow me to make a note. The Ladies' Sanitary Association is here to help and educate.''

Pammy screamed, and Mrs. Fullerton-Smith turned, moving into the cell. Leda sat down on the bench outside, the tracts on *How to Manage a Baby, Health of Mothers, Measles,* and *How to Rear Healthy Children* clutched in her hands.

It must have taken several hours, but it seemed to be forever that Pammy cried and groaned and made animal noises of effort. The gaslight poured down in a circle over the empty podium, while the cell lay in shadows, the source of echoing pants and firm instructions. Pammy gave a harsh shriek and subsided. For a minute the silence seemed to grow and grow as Leda peered at the huddle of figures, and then suddenly the nurse sat up and said, "Boy," in a matter-of-fact tone as she lifted a pale shape and dangled it.

A thin sound, like the long-drawn squeal of a rat, reverberated from the cell.

"Direct a light here, if you please," the nurse demanded.

Leda jumped up and lit the policeman's coal-oil lantern, opening the door and shining it into the cell. The nurse was mopping at a terrible tiny limp rag of a shape, her white apron covered with blood. Pammy muttered and heaved again. Mrs. Fullerton-Smith said, "That's done it," and attended to Pammy, clearing away the soiled sheet and placing clean padding beneath the feeble girl.

The squealing began to rise to a series of infantile wails, bouncing off the walls. Outside, men's voices echoed in the street, and the wicket door flew open. The inspector held it for his supervisor, who marched in followed by

Sergeant MacDonald bearing some teapot-sized object wrapped in a paisley shawl, and then the others poured in after; suddenly the police office was full of men, all talking, all trying to shout questions above the sound of the baby's screaming. Leda was herded back against the wall until Sergeant MacDonald squeezed next to her and gave her his hand, boosting her up to stand on the bench.

"Gentlemen!" the inspector's voice roared. "Order, if you please!"

The crowd fell silent, leaving only the howls of the baby. Inspector Ruby ignored the infant, conferring briefly with his superior and then stepping up to his podium.

"We'll make a statement," he said, speaking in a loud singsong above the baby's cries. "At quarter past eight P.M., officers of this division proceeded to the house known as Oxslip's in Jacob's Island. We found there what we expected to find, that is, a crown of foreign manufacture, believed to be Siamese and stolen from the premises of the Alexandra Hotel. The crown is secure and undamaged and will be returned to the party what owns it directly. That is all, gentlemen."

"Any arrests?" someone demanded.

"Mr. Ellis Oxslip and a woman known as Frying Pan Sally have been taken for questioning."

"Where to?"

"Headquarters at Scotland Yard, sir."

A general groaning broke out. "Why there? Why'nt you bring 'em here?"

"As you may have observed, gentlemen, we have a certain amount of disturbance in this office tonight."

"The note!" someone yelled above the grumbling and wails. "Read us the note, Inspector! What did the note say?"

"I am not authorized to read any note."

"Did it say Oxslip's is a house of resort for perverts?"

"I am not authorized to give any information in that regard."

Another man pushed forward. "Is it true the statue came from Oxslip's—the statue left in place of the crown at the hotel?"

Inspector Ruby glanced at his superintendent. The other officer nodded slightly. "We believe that to be the case, yes."

The pads and pencils rustled madly. "So it *is* a flagellation parlor! Is that right, Inspector Ruby?"

"I am not authorized—"

"Cut line, Inspector!" A man in the back, just in front of Leda, raised his voice in disgust. "This is your territory, isn't it? Don't you know what goes on here?"

"What of the young boys we saw?" someone else yelled. "Did you take 'em in as suspects?"

"The minor inhabitants of the house are not suspected in the robbery. They will be questioned as to what they may know that relates to it."

"Then what'll you do with 'em? Give 'em back to Oxslip and Sal?"

The inspector's jaw worked. He frowned fiercely and did not answer the question.

"What's the point of it all?" the man in front of Leda demanded. "Is it blackmail, or an attempt to shut down Oxslip's? Did the police arrange it?"

Inspector Ruby hesitated, and then said, "I cannot speculate on that point."

"Good job if they did fix it," the man said, and got a round of approval while the baby howled. "If you can't catch 'em in the act, root 'em out as you can, I say! Those boys— it's foul, by God!"

The inspector seemed to recall Leda for the first time. He looked up at her directly, and then raised his hands, brushing away the flood of questions. "That will be all, gentlemen! There are ladies present. Take yourselves to the Yard and ask what you will. We've police business to attend to here."

"Don't you, though!" a young man cried, cocking a thumb toward the cell where the baby still wailed and sobbed, muffled now as the maternity nurse swaddled it in linen. But the inspector and Sergeant MacDonald began shoving reporters out the door. Some left, followed by more evidently eager to keep up with their rivals, but others lingered, still trying to ask questions.

Mrs. Fullerton-Smith brought the infant out of the cell.

As Leda climbed down from her perch on the wooden bench, she found the tiny bundle pushed into her arms. "The cloth is donated by the Ladies' Committee of Marylebone Park," Mrs. Fullerton-Smith informed her. "You may keep it, but we ask that you sterilize it and pass it to another needy applicant when it is no longer of use to the infant. The mother is resting quietly, as you see. In an hour or two, when she feels up to it, she may hold him. Mrs. Layton and I must return to the medical officer, as there are several other patients who need attention this evening. If any excessive bleeding occurs, send to us immediately."

Leda was about to correct Mrs. Fullerton-Smith's obvious impression that Leda had some personal connection to Pammy, when she overheard the nurse giving particulars to Sergeant MacDonald, who wrote them laboriously in the record book. "Mrs. Dawkins' in Jacob's Island," the nurse said, for Pammy's place of residence.

"Oh, no—" Leda tried to dodge round Mrs. Fullerton-Smith and her monologue of instructions. "Sergeant MacDonald—she doesn't live there!"

Her protest was lost amid the insistent questions of two reporters, who kept asking Sergeant MacDonald if he would unwrap the crown. Meanwhile, Mrs. Fullerton-Smith and the nurse were packing their grip. The nurse pulled her bloody apron over her head and stuffed it away. The baby began to wail again, and Leda looked down into the screwed-up eyes and open mouth.

"Hush, hush," she murmured ineffectually, patting the back of the bundle. The baby only screwed tighter and wailed more piercingly, making a frightful face, all mottled red and white. Leda caught at the nurse's arm as she sailed past after Mrs. Fullerton-Smith, but both ladies were gone before she could utter more than an incoherent objection.

Inspector Ruby and his chief walked out, fending off reporters. While Sergeant MacDonald was occupied with a particularly insistent journalist, one of the others sidled up next to Leda, where the wrapped shawl lay on the bench. He tugged at the edge of the paisley, rolling it free.

The Eastern crown of gold and enamel overturned onto the bench, a peaked helmet like a small, round temple, thickly studded with diamonds that culminated in one huge ruby set into a white shell.

The reporter began making quick sketches in his notebook, until Sergeant MacDonald gave an indignant shout and shoved him away. "What're you about, now? Get on with you; out of here, all of you!" He pushed the reporter through the door, dragging another along with him. They went protesting loudly. Leda could hear their voices ringing in the street as they detained Sergeant MacDonald on the steps.

Not knowing what else to do, she went into the cell and knelt beside Pammy. "How are you feeling?" she asked. "Would you like to see him?"

The girl squeezed her eyes shut as hard as the baby did. "I don't want it!" she muttered. "Take it off somewheres."

"The nurse said you might hold him in a hour or so."

"I won't."

Leda looked down at the girl's sullen face. Pammy opened her eyes and lifted her hand, pushing weakly at Leda's arms.

"I won't take it," she said. "I hate it. Go away!"

Leda got up and went back to the bench. The tiny newborn wail just kept on and on. She sat down next to the crown and peered into the infant face. It was ugly, it truly was, all wet mouth and wrinkled skin, and its mother didn't want it.

Leda gave the unattractive bundle a hug, which only made it cry louder. She stared at the beautiful gold and rubied crown—and began, for no reason at all, to weep.

Six

~~~~~~~~~

The Song

🏵

Hawaii, 1871

Little Kai loved to swim. She squealed at the long break-
ers that rolled across the reef at Waikiki, and beat her baby
hands against Samuel's shoulders.

"Far! Far go!" she demanded. "Big!"

So he kept his arm around her and plowed into the mild
surf, a little farther out than most of the crowd of Hawaiian children. The long skirts of her bathing costume floated
and swept against his bare chest with each wave as he
bounced her up above the foam. She laughed and shrieked
and sometimes he ducked her instead of rising over, so
that they both came up with water streaming off their faces
and their mouths full of salty bitterness.

"Down go!" she cried. "Down go!"

They took huge breaths, Kai blowing out her cheeks and
pursing up her mouth comically. Samuel sank beneath the
clear water with her firmly in his arms. The force of a
wave rolled over them, carrying them a few feet back toward the shore, and the sand beneath his feet shifted. He
squeezed Kai's chubby body to signal "up," and she
kicked madly. He pushed off the sand, exploding out of
the water, carrying Kai high in the air in his arms.

She screeched with pleasure. Another wave went past,
catching them in a rush of noise and white foam. Samuel
shook water off his hair. As his ears cleared, he heard
other shrieks beyond Kai's. He looked toward the beach
and saw figures splashing out of the water.

56

"*He manō!*" The cry came to him amid the surge of another wave. "*He manō! He manō nui loa!*"

He saw it, a dark slice of fin breaking out of the surf, a murky shape, fast-moving, as long as one of the great boards that the Hawaiians rode on the surf. The shark cut between him and Kai and the beach. Samuel was distantly aware of the crowd gathering, of screaming, people running along the sand.

Afterward, he remembered mostly the great calm that descended over him as the shark turned and moved swiftly toward them.

He lifted Kai out of the water onto his shoulders. She gripped his hair painfully, still laughing, beating her feet against his chest. He clamped his hands on her ankles and held them still. She was squealing something, but he wasn't listening. Above the waves, above the thin wail of panic from the beach and the shouts of the men as they launched the canoe, he heard something more.

He heard his song, the dark song of his brother the shark.

He stood still and listened.

The surf hid the fin for an instant, lifted his feet from the sand and brought him down gently. He watched the huge shape move past a yard away. The high-pitched sound of Kai calling for her mother rang in his ears, remote, like a distant train whistle, but his mind was full of the song.

It held him silent, soundless; a fixed rock of coral, a lifeless piece of driftwood—a passive thing, unafraid. The shark glided past, turned and came again, nightmare huge. He listened to the song. He felt the shark's slow curiosity—the deep and mindless hunger in it, but he was peaceful and part of the surf, nothing that it wanted.

Kai had stopped calling. She sat still, too, perched on his shoulders, her fingers pinched hard in his hair. Through the air he heard shouts and percussions—the men in the canoe beat the water with their paddles, coming fast and hard.

The shark made a sliding turn, passing within touching distance. Samuel watched it slip by, saw the somber gray hide, the fin, the tail, and then suddenly it veered sharply back out to sea, away from the oncoming outrigger.

The canoe seemed huge, rolling down upon them on the back of a swell. The paddles slapped the water violently. Samuel felt the first shot of fear—not from the shark, but from the threat of the wooden weapons and the savagery of the shouts. The outrigger seemed ready to crash against his side, but with startling skill the Hawaiian in the stern turned the canoe against the waves and it passed behind him. Someone plucked a screaming Kai off his shoulders.

Brutally strong arms grabbed at him. He turned and jumped, blundering up against the hard polished wood, banging his thighs and knees. For a wild moment the outrigger on the opposite side lifted from the water and the whole canoe threatened to come over, but then he was hauled aboard, collapsing against a white-shirted chest, aware of English words yelled in his ear.

The words thanked God, and thanked him; Lord Gryphon gripped Samuel back against himself as if he could not let go. Facing them in the canoe, Kai squirmed in the brown arms of a Hawaiian, squealing, "Dad*dy*, dad*dy!*" and trying to break free.

The voice swore close to his ear, the arms around him so tight they hurt. "Samuel, thank you, thank the Lord for you, God love you, boy, you're a bloody damned natural-born God-given hero—" The voice kept talking, kept muttering fiercely on and on, and finally Kai got away and floundered against Samuel's lap, and her father gathered them both up together, and when the canoe ran onto the beach he lifted them both out and still wouldn't let go.

Lady Tess was waiting, standing in the water with the hem of her skirt trailing out, dragging in the slide of surf onto the beach. Her face was streaked with tears, her dark hair flying free of its pins. She jerked Kai up into her arms, knelt and buried her face against Samuel's wet shoulder and hair. The swash rolled away beneath them, draining sand from under his toes as it retreated. He stumbled a little to keep his feet.

"Steady there, son." The firm hand still gripped his

shoulder. Samuel looked up at Lord Gryphon's face. The sun blazed off the man's blond hair; he was tall and pleasant and exalted and he'd never called Samuel "son" before. He was grinning. Samuel felt his own face change, felt the shaky, uncertain smile. People crowded around, half-naked Hawaiians still dripping from the surf, respectable *haoles,* white-skinned and dressed up to their chins in dark clothes and hats, even Lady Tess' Oriental butler who had come with them in the carriage to serve Sunday picnic at Waikiki.

Someone started a cheer. Lord Gryphon swept Samuel up as easily as Samuel had lifted Kai. A multitude of hands caught his arms and legs and tossed him high in rhythm. *Hip-hip-hooray! Hip-hip-hooray!*

They tossed him three times, then pushed him upright and lifted him onto Lord Gryphon's shoulders, in spite of his wet bathing britches. Kai wriggled and screamed in Lady Tess' hold, wanting up, too, which sent Master Robert off into wails until Dojun the butler swung him up and started toward the coconut grove that overhung the beach.

Half the crowd began to move in that direction; the other half stayed on the beach and cheered on the Hawaiians who took the canoe again to search out the shark. From somewhere word came that the Hawaiian king was resting in his house at Waikiki. By the time they reached the tall palms, girls waited with garlands of flowers and maile leaves. Lord Gryphon swung Samuel down. As everyone stood back and grew silent, the girls came forward and placed the garlands around Samuel's neck, enveloping him in sweet scents and cool leaves.

"His Majesty honors your courage." The first girl kissed him on both cheeks, and as the second one began to do the same, he squirmed back, which made her and the crowd all laugh, and she grabbed his shoulders and kissed him anyway.

He backed up and collided with Lord Gryphon, who leaned over and murmured, "Tell 'em something to say to His Majesty."

Samuel wet his lips. He took a breath. "Please tell

him—His Majesty—that it was—really, it wasn't anything. Please tell him—the flowers smell good.''

That seemed to make everyone laugh, too, but Lord Gryphon put his arm around Samuel and pulled him hard and close, so it was all right. It was wonderful. Samuel was shaking a little. He looked back out at the brilliant turquoise band of water inside the reef, and beyond that to the rolling lines of surf, where the great shark had slipped like a shadow back to the dark and blue depths of the sea.

Seven

⊕

"He's made off with the goods again!" Mrs. Dawkins was pink with gusto, accosting Leda on the dark stairs with the latest news of the outlandish robberies that had begun the week before. "Third time in a sennight. Here's the paper, miss! Read all about it. A Japanee prince this time. Oh, he's a downy cracksman, this one is. Hoisted a sacred sword right out from under this Japanee's nose, with the peelers standing guard all over the place." She was almost squealing with glee over the discomfiture of the police. "There's a jolly for you, miss. And he'll have left something filthy again, but the paper don't say what, o' course. They never do come out and say, but a body can guess, can't she now? It'll be somethin' out of whatever indecent house where he sends the police to find that sword."

Leda was well aware of this third robbery, and the bizarre pattern of them, in which a priceless piece was stolen from one of the diplomatic envoys come for the Jubilee, and something indescribably lurid left in its place. That was strange enough, but even more peculiar was that this thief seemed to have no interest in the stolen property itself; he sent a note to the police telling them where to recover every treasure—each time in a "house of iniquitous accommodation," as the papers politely phrased it.

"How very interesting," she said discouragingly to Mrs. Dawkins, turning away to mount the black well of the stairs. Actually, Leda knew considerably more about the unorthodox thefts than her landlady, having taken up the habit of making tea for Inspector Ruby and lingering in the police office until after midnight, thereby giving the impression that she was still employed at the dressmaker's. "Good night, ma'am."

A quick hand tugged at her dress, holding her back. "Friday, miss. Fourteen shillings the week."

"It has been Friday only for half an hour, Mrs. Dawkins," Leda said. "I hope you didn't feel you must wait up for me. I will be happy to pay you in the morning."

Mrs. Dawkins grinned, unembarrassed. "Wanted to remind you, miss. Wanted to remind you. Those Hogginses the floor beneath you, had to run them out today. Plenty of people wants me rooms to let who'll pay proper, miss, just as you do. Them as don't pay, can't expect me to support 'em, can they? I'm no ladies' charity society, I tell you I'm not. Fourteen shillings the week, and no meals included. We're connected to the drains, miss—that's worth half a crown right there, and so I tells 'em."

So she had told Leda, frequently. Finally detaching herself from her landlady, Leda proceeded upstairs. In her room, she washed her face and watered her geranium on the open windowsill by candlelight. The night heat intensified the smells of the neighborhood, but one of the leaves on the geranium was broken, mingling a fresh, sharp scent with the heavier odors. She trimmed the leaf off with her fingernail and crushed it in her hand, pressing it to her nose to drive away the stench of the breweries.

She stared out the window into the humid darkness. The great slum that began in the street behind hers—a place she didn't wish to look, refused to look, could not bear to look—she felt it pulling at her, trying to drag her down into it like a gaping maw. She thought of Pammy, who had refused to accept or nurse her baby until Inspector Ruby informed her sharply that he'd have her up on infant murder charges if she didn't show some sense. Leda had a joyless feeling that her own life had probably begun in much the same way, unwanted and ugly, and not at all in the quietly respectable manner that she would have wished.

How long this charade could continue, Leda dared not think. Of her four dresses, she had determined that only the calico skirt and black silk showroom dress were completely necessary, one for everyday wear and the other for calling. With some regret she had taken the superfluous dresses to the bazaar and sold them. It had seemed agonizingly coarse to argue with a clothes-stall woman over pecuniary matters, and Leda was painfully aware that she had not gotten the full value of her gabardine and silvergray stockinette. She retained her good bonnet and left the boardinghouse at her usual early hour every morning, dressed in her calico, spending her days walking and scanning the papers and office windows for positions, always seeming to arrive after some employment office had just sent over an ideal candidate, or joining twenty other hopefuls queued up in a hallway, or finding that the vacancy was not suitable for a female; resting in tea shops or parks when her feet grew so tired she could not stand.

She had to pay the rent on her sewing machine and return it by Saturday, and think of some excuse for Mrs. Dawkins about why she was no longer bringing work home. But she'd money to see her another week if she was careful, and tomorrow—today, now, as Mrs. Dawkins had pointed out—was Friday, the appointed time for Leda to visit South Street again. She intended to spend thruppence in the morning on two hours in the warm side of the public bath, and wear her black silk showroom dress after she repaired the fraying at the neckline.

Amid the uncertainty and unpleasantness, only the police station seemed a sure haven, even if it was a rather more masculine atmosphere than that to which she was accustomed. Inspector Ruby seemed to tolerate Leda's unwarranted lingering cheerfully enough, and Sergeant MacDonald in particular was most pleasant and attentive, but Leda was a little afraid that it might appear as if she were trying to fix his affections.

He did seem taken with her. Miss Myrtle would have been dismayed. A policeman, after all. It was hardly what might be called an eligible connection, but he was a very amiable man. Really, Leda thought he might do perfectly well. He shared a house with his sister in Lambeth, and Leda was quite willing to conform herself to such a situation, if he thought he might have sufficient means to support a wife and sister both. And his sister, Leda understood, was still in her twenties—not beyond hope, she thought judiciously.

Perhaps Inspector Ruby and Sergeant MacDonald would be the ones to catch this infamous thief, and be suitably rewarded for their efforts. Perhaps even promoted. She wondered what position was next above sergeant.

According to the *Times,* not a single step had been made in identifying the perpetrator, or even the motive, and Mrs. Dawkins found great joy in calling the police a set of prime fools. It was brewing into a diplomatic disaster of major proportions, the *Times* went on in an editorial, straining relations with important nations. The foreign delegations must observe that the British authorities were impotent against crime in their own domain, or even worse, must believe that their nations were being made into fools deliberately.

That was all newspaper bluster. Leda knew the motive, of course. So did the police. And the *Times,* too, probably. She had not spent her hours in the police station with her ears stopped closed. Inspector Ruby and Sergeant MacDonald had done their best not to speak of it in front of her, but poor gentlemen, evidently they had no inkling of how their male notion of soft speech carried across a room. Leda knew all about the crimes. These were houses of low resort, every one of them, where the precious items were conveyed. And although Leda was not entirely clear on this point, they were evidently houses of a particularly dreadful sort, patronized by men of the upper classes with exceedingly violent and corrupt tastes.

The police theorized that it was a convoluted case of blackmail, in which some wealthy, extremely highly placed patron of these establishments was being shown the public humiliation that would happen to him if he did not pay up to his extortioner's demands. A very dirty racket, was what Inspector Ruby called it, and Leda agreed. This thief seemed to walk through walls, right past the best police and army guard they had to offer.

She rolled the geranium leaf between her fingers. It worried at her, to think that such horrible houses—whatever went on in them—had operated not one door down in her own street; that where she had seen only shiny-faced, subdued children, there had been something wicked and terrible underneath. She wondered what was happening to the children now, after the police closed the houses. She thought often of how she'd considered going to the authorities with her lesser suspicions, and had been afraid to do even that. She was no better than Mrs. Dawkins, really. Merely not as honest in admitting her selfish interests.

Tired as she was, she could not sleep. Before she went to bed, she rearranged things a little, panting as she shoved the heavy sewing machine and table to the center of the room and then pushed her washstand over by the door, trying to decide how to fit things up to take advantage of the fact that she would no longer need the best light for sewing. She wasn't sure, but a typist didn't take work home, she believed.

The rearrangement required her to move the bed, and she decided that she might just as well scrub the floor at the same time, so she pushed the bedstead over under the window, took off her skirt and blouse and corset, and set to work in her drawers. When everything in the hot little attic was as clean and polished as she could make it with a damp rag and Hudson's Extract of Soap—"Sweet as Roses, Fresh as Sea Breezes, for All Domestic Washing, Cleaning, and Scouring; Hudson's Leaves NO Smell"— she left the bed by the window, as it seemed cooler there, blew out the candle to save wax, and changed into her gown in the dark.

She lay awake thinking, staring into nothing, her mind going round and round with policemen and money and letters of character. It all fell inward into light sleep and restless dreams. When something hit her leg, she jolted instantly wide awake with her heart right up in her throat.

She started up in bed, her blood pounding so that she couldn't hear a thing. Her room was utterly black; not even moonlight or cloud reflections gave shadow or substance to anything. From somewhere outside, a cat howled and spat. Leda took a deep breath, holding her throat. A cat. Of course, a cat had got in through the window. It had been quite a heavy touch—too forceful for vermin, she thought, while an old story about rats the size of big striped toms shivered through her head.

"Scat!" she hissed, plumping the covers. "Are you still in here, you awful beast? Scat, now, kitty!" She stood up and collided with the sewing machine table where she'd moved it, clutched her stubbed toe with a vexed cry, and fell backward onto her bed—

And onto a large, living, moving shape.

She was too stunned to scream, and suddenly it was not there—it—*he*—it was a man—in her room—she whirled around and lurched off the bed in her terror. She couldn't see anything—the poker—a man—in her room—God help her—she tried to scream, but found her throat closed tight and the panic beating through her veins. She skittered backward toward the door, lunged into the sewing machine table again, and knocked it over. It fell with a crack, and another sound, a strange soft grunt.

She stood frozen, listening.

Faintly, something scraped the floor, a noise that suddenly seemed to make everything real and even more terrible. He was truly there; this was no dream; she'd knocked the machine onto him and he was pushing it off. The sound of scraped wood came again, soft and undeniable. Tears of fright started in her eyes.

"Don't touch me!" she cried in a voice that came out all quavery. "I've a poker in my hand!"

He made no response. A horrible stillness seemed to thicken in the room. If he moved, it was in utter silence. She thought he was between her and the door, blocking escape; she stood paralyzed, with little half-mad sounds of weeping stopped in her throat.

"Go away," she said in the same impossibly shaky voice. "I won't make a fuss."

The silence lengthened. Leda swallowed, and then she thought she heard him—very, very faintly—she heard a whisper, like an intake of his breath. She was sure he was still there, near the door—if he was going to leave without hurting her, he could have done it already. She would have heard him turn the lock, open the door. He was still there; he wasn't finished—what did he want, *what did he want?*

Very slowly, she bent down, her hand searching for the poker by the bed. Her fingers encountered smooth, curved metal—she jerked back, and then felt again, shaping a long blade. It was hard, and heavy; heavy enough to swing in self-defense. She gripped it by both hands and began to straighten up.

An instant later she was on the floor. It was as if her knees had just collapsed beneath her; her stomach wrenched; she felt fuzzy in her mind, uncertain of what she had been doing. She thought in confusion that she had been hit, that it was morning, that thunder echoed in the street outside.

Her fingers closed on the weapon. She heard the thump of a footstep, and could not even scramble back from the sound, her limbs shaking so that they wouldn't obey her.

"Give it to me."

The low voice made her jerk like a helpless puppet. It came from closer than she expected; he was standing up; he was not two feet from her.

"I don't mean you any harm," he said in the darkness.

Something seemed to have happened to her brain in that strange moment of collapse. In the midst of shuddering befuddlement, her mind focused on one thing only: she fixed with preternatural intensity on *him,* on his words, on his voice, on his heat. He was not British. Even in his faint murmur she could hear the accent; the different stress, strange and yet familiar, the distinctive mix of vowels.

Her heart began to pound in hazy recognition. Her body still shivered as if she were freezing. She put her arms around herself, reeling with sickness.

"Mr. Gerard!" she whispered.

For the first time in her life, she took the name of the Lord in vain, and fainted.

She recovered her senses in darkness, still wobbly and bewildered. A moment after she opened her eyes, the sharp, sour smell of a match stung her nose. Light flared, sending crazy shadows across the walls.

She could not think straight. Something dark moved above her: she looked up and saw the black figure holding

a sword, masked and hooded like an evil dream; he—it—
touched the flame to the candle and turned to glance down
at her.

She made a suffocated sound, unable to form words.
The malevolent figure moved, as if to bend over her, and
she began to cry, curling up in terror. The other paused,
then reached up and jerked at the nape of his neck. The
mask came free and drifted to the bed. He pushed the
hood back off his head.

His golden hair glittered in the candlelight. He stood
still, watching her with metal-cold eyes.

"Mr. Gerard," she whispered numbly. She tried to sit
up and only managed a feeble spasm of muscles.

"Lie still," he said. "Rest."

She laid her head back on the hard floor, unable to do
anything but obey. Wordlessly, she watched him lay the
sword on the floor and bend over her, kneeling on one
knee, supporting himself with one hand pressed heavily
into the pallet. He laid his palm against the side of her
face, his fingertips resting on her temple.

"Breathe with me," he said.

She made a sound, half of a hysterical giggle. Her stomach heaved unpleasantly and the laugh turned into a moan.

He shook his head. "It's important. Watch. Breathe in."

She gulped a breath.

"Let go," he said. "Slowly." His eyes held hers, infinitely gray. "Think of a waterfall. Follow the water as it
comes down."

She felt as if she were floating, sliding down a long
slope. Her breath flowed out of her, endless, going and
going until she lost herself in his eyes, in his silent command, and drew air in again.

The strength began to come back into her limbs. But
still he held her with his steady gaze, and the breath oozed
out of her again like that infinite waterfall, tumbling down
and down until she was empty of it, drifting free of earth.
And then it flooded into her once more, bringing strength
and heart. She used his energy to find her own, growing
easier with each breath, until finally she was rational
enough to realize how outlandish it all was.

"What are you doing?" she demanded weakly, putting her hand up to push his away. "What has happened?"

He used his arm on the bed to shove himself upright, and then slowly sat on the edge of it, one leg outstretched, looking down at her. "I nearly killed you," he said curtly. His mouth had a queer tautness, almost a grimace. "I apologize for it."

He didn't sound in the least contrite. In fact, he sounded brusque, as if he had more important things on his mind.

"But—*why?*" she asked plaintively.

For a long moment, he surveyed her. Then he said, "It was a misjudgment. I thought I needed to defend myself."

Leda sat up, still bewildered. "You struck me?"

"No, ma'am." His mouth curved grimly. "Perhaps better if I had."

Her brain ached. She let herself droop, resting her forehead in her hands. "This is impossible. Why are you in my room? You're a gentleman. I don't—"

Her eyes fell on the sword. She gazed at the gorgeous curved scabbard of reddish-gold lacquer inlaid with flying cranes in mother-of-pearl; the golden hilt, too, shaped like the head of a crested bird. Two tassels of braided bronze hung from fittings on the scabbard. The lower length of the sheath was banded by golden openwork of tiny flowers and leaves, embellished with colored enamels gleaming richly in the candlelight. Slowly her hand slid downward, covering her mouth.

"Oh, goodness," she whispered. "Oh, good God."

She lifted her head. He sat watching her without expression.

Leda's heart began to pound with greater terror than before. That he could kill her if he pleased she had not the slightest doubt; there was not one trace of humanity or compassion in his perfect face, not a shadow of mercy. She began to feel ill again.

"Think of the water falling," he commanded softly.

She swallowed and let the air flow from her lungs, still staring at him.

"Try to calm yourself," he said. "I'm not going to

murder you. Tonight my—composure—seems to elude me. I didn't intend you any hurt.''

"This is utterly insane," she said weakly. "Why are you in my room?"

"I'm presently in your room because you have broken my leg, Miss Etoile."

"Broken your . . . but I . . . oh, mercy!"

"It's something of an inconvenience, yes."

"Broken your leg," she repeated in despair. "But surely not! You were standing a moment ago!"

"With some concentration," he said. "The agent of my undoing would seem to be a sewing machine." He looked at the fallen contraption and added enigmatically, "Perhaps I should find some enlightenment in that."

She curled her fingers in her nightgown, frowning at his outstretched leg. Somber-colored fabric contoured it loosely, except where the cloth was bound tight around his calf by dark string ties on his strange, soft, split-toed footwear. Everything he wore was shadow-obscured, clothing cut in simple, flowing lines like none she'd ever seen before.

"I could walk, with focus enough," he said in a dispassionate tone. "But I think that would be foolish. It would compound the injury. I don't believe it's necessary or desirable. And I don't wish to leave until you've regained your spirit, Miss Etoile, and can remember to breathe without me." He met her nonplussed look, and smiled suddenly, a quiet smile, absurdly charming. "And no," he said, "I'm not mad, you know."

"I must be," she said. "I just can't—I never would have thought—Mr. Gerard! You're a gentleman. You—and Lady Catherine—why, this is perfectly fantastic! That it would be you. The—" She stopped on the very verge of saying, *The police will never dream of such a thing.*

His smile vanished. In a still, soft voice, he said, "Lady Catherine, of course, has nothing to do with this."

Leda dropped her eyes. "No, no! Of course not," she said quickly.

A long silence passed. Leda felt queasy and faint with

uncertainty. Her hip ached where she had crashed against the sewing table. The room began closing in on her.

"You really ought to breathe, Miss Etoile." His calm voice found her in the gathering darkness. "I'd rather you didn't expire on me."

She imagined the waterfall, followed a single drop cascading down, found the murkiness receding from the edges of her eyes. "Oh, yes," she said shakily. "Thank you." She kept her eyes on the floor, her mind racing madly.

"You should lie down again."

"That hardly—seems appropriate," she said. She could not believe that she was sitting on the floor in her own room with a notorious and dangerous criminal, a gentleman with a broken leg who calmly recommended that she lie down. She thought she should sound an alarm, but she wasn't certain she could reach the door, much less the police. Whatever he had done to her, it had sapped her strength down to the bone. If he repeated it—she thought perhaps it really would kill her.

But she should do something; scream or pound the wall or *something*. Why had no one heard the crash of the table? Why didn't she take up the poker and attack him? How fast could he move with a broken leg?

But she didn't. She looked at him sitting on the edge of her bed with no sign of discomfort, just that one leg resting straight, and was afraid of him.

"You know who I am," he said. "If you intend to turn me in, you can do it at your leisure. For the moment, rest until you recover completely."

She closed her eyes. "This is preposterous."

"I won't leave you."

She opened them. "You won't leave me," she repeated giddily, and laid her head down on the floor, cradled in her arms. "How very reassuring!"

Eight

〰〰〰〰〰

Silent Tiger

▣

Hawaii, 1871

It was in the garden, a few days after the shark, that
Dojun came to him. Kai had been climbing in the monkeypod tree while Samuel stood watchfully by until a rain
shower had brought the nanny running to whisk her
squealing inside. Samuel leaned against the tree trunk with
the big raindrops plopping down between the branches
onto his head and shoulders. He was torn between following, which he wanted to do, and staying out of the nanny's
domain where Kai was no longer his charge.

The rain brought a steamy, pleasant smell of soil. He
listened to it rattle on the broad leaves of the white ginger,
closed his eyes, and thought again of the shark and the
song and the way they'd tossed him in the air.

Hip-hip-hooray!

He smiled with his eyes closed, and opened them to
find Dojun in front of him.

The Oriental butler had come silently; stood silently.
He was only a little taller than Samuel himself, a familiar
figure with a long, square face and gloomy mouth, dressed
in a white uniform, his black hair partially shaved and tied
in an odd knot at the top. He watched Samuel for a moment, and then bowed slightly. "Samua-san. Good day."

The polite greeting surprised Samuel. He hesitated, and
then said, "Hello."

"Got question. You shark see, no move. How, ask."

Samuel just looked back at him. Dojun had never spoken to him before, outside of giving him a message from

Lady Tess or Lord Gryphon once or twice, or telling him that dinner was served.

Dojun put his finger to his temple. "Samua-san think how, ask. Shark come, no move. How, ask."

Samuel pressed back against the tree, not knowing what to answer. The butler's black eyes watched him intently. For the first time, Samuel realized that Dojun had thoughts about the people around him; that he was more than his duties and position in the household. The rain came pattering down and Dojun stood there just as Samuel did, feeling it, but choosing not to go inside for reasons of his own.

The discovery was alarming, as if the ginger bush had suddenly sprouted a mouth and eyes and begun to talk.

"You 'fraid?" Dojun asked softly. "I scare?"

Samuel turned his head, wiping a trickle of water from his cheek, avoiding Dojun's eyes. He shrugged.

Dojun tapped his chest. "Secret thing say," he murmured. "Maybe you savvy. When danger come—I tiger. Si-rent tiger." His dour mouth turned up a little, half of a smile. "You savvy, Samua-san?"

"No, sir," Samuel whispered.

"I Japan, come here before. Come down here Hawaii. No wish, choice no got. Japan stay, Dojun die. Four year come. Here Dojun find for boy. Boy, boy, boy, all boy see. Japan boy. Chinese boy. Hawaii boy. *Haole* white boy. Find for, find for. I tiger need." He jerked his head sharply and made a sound of disgust. "No boy good. No tiger. All stupid, soft, scare boy. Boy make suckling pig, no more better. I angry. I shame. What I can do? I tiger need." Dojun's eyes were intense, dark and foreign. "See Samua-san, big shark danger, no move, no scare. No stupid boy. Dojun ask—Samua-san see this shark—Samua-san think how?"

Samuel dug his fingernail into the soft bark of the tree.

"You scare? Shark see, you no can move? Just stupid, stand stop stupid?"

"No," Samuel said indignantly. "I wasn't scared."

"Ah. Big brave boy. Stand stop, shark come, shark near, show everybody brave! Number-one man then!"

He looked at Dojun uneasily. "Not really. I didn't think about being brave."

"OK. No scare. No brave. Now talk-talk, Samua-san." Dojun's voice became gentler, not so demanding. "Shark come—how think, ask you."

"Well . . . I thought of the song."

The butler's half-smile came again. He lifted his head slightly. "Shark-song?"

Samuel stirred. "Do you know it?"

Dojun's smile deepened. "Tiger-song know. Know good."

Samuel gazed at him, feeling a flicker of excitement. "There's a tiger song, too?"

"Tiger-song. Fire-song. Dragon, earth, air, shark. All song if hear."

Samuel leaned a fraction away from the tree trunk toward Dojun. "Where can I hear them?"

A grin grew across the man's worn and sour face, transforming it. He nodded slowly. "You hear."

"I want to hear them all. Can you sing them?"

Dojun laughed and shook him by the shoulders. "Long time, long time find for boy know tiger-song; find boy know shark-song. OK." He lifted his hand and rested it against Samuel's jaw, a light and cradling embrace, as if he were touching something precious. "Is OK, Samua-chan. Good fortune, yeah. OK."

Nine

❖

Just at dawn the train came through, rumbling the walls and rattling the pitcher. Leda turned over, stiff, her hip and shoulder pressed painfully against hard wood. She opened her eyes, saw the floor beneath her bed, and jerked herself upright.

He was still there.

He sat motionless above her in his dark, supple clothing, his lashes lowered, his fingers locked lightly together in a twined steeple like a child's shadow game.

She remembered his hands from the showroom: he'd picked up the silver scissors; rolled the bolts of fabric; held out the sealed envelope she'd dropped. A gentleman's hands, strong and well-formed.

She put her palms over her eyes. When she took them away, he was really still there.

Merciful heavens.

It wasn't a dream. Here was this man, in her room, on her bed, while she had been sleeping away on the floor next to a stolen sword as if she hadn't a care to her name.

His hands relaxed from their intertwining. He tilted his head and slanted a look toward her beneath his dark lashes, silent and beautiful with the dawn light behind his head.

"Good morning, Miss Etoile."

She would not say "Good morning" to a thief in her room. She simply would not; it was just too much. One had to keep one's sense of sanity about one.

On the other hand, she wasn't certain what one did say upon waking up in the awkward situation of finding a criminal and his loot still hanging about.

"Do you feel stronger?" he asked.

Her bare feet were poking out from beneath her gown. Leda scrambled up, grabbed her cloak from the peg, and pulled it around herself. As she did it, she realized that what she ought to do was burst out the door that very moment and go running downstairs to rouse the house. She was amazed that she had slept; how possibly could she have slept? With him right there, able to do what he willed, she had slipped into a dreamless sleep on the wooden floor as if she'd been drugged.

She felt herself beginning to panic again. The image of the waterfall formed in her head, unbidden, and she let out a long breath.

"Well done," he said.

"I beg your pardon?"

"You remembered to breathe, Miss Etoile."

"You stay right there!" she said in a quaking voice. "I'm going to—to fetch some water!" Without pausing, she flung the bar off the door, unlocked it, and slammed it shut behind her. She locked it from the outside and stood there, panting. It took another image of the waterfall to get her hysteria under control.

All right. She was safe now. She was out of his power. She was in the attic hall. What next? The police. She pulled the cloak around her, realized she'd forgotten shoes—forgotten even to dress—a perfect picture she would make, running along the mucky street barefoot in her night rail.

Leda stood uncertainly in the dim hall. She curled her toes against the threadbare weave of the carpet.

If she went to the police now, it wouldn't be Sergeant MacDonald and Inspector Ruby who would make the arrest. They wouldn't come on until evening. By then everything would all be done up and some other officers would have the credit.

She put her hands over her mouth, calculating wildly. His leg was broken. He couldn't leave. If she could keep him in her room until evening . . .

She didn't think she had the nerve for it.

But his leg was broken. He was harmless. Where was he going with a broken leg?

Before reason could catch up with her, she turned back and unlocked the door. She opened it carefully, preparing an excuse about being so scatterbrained she'd forgotten the bucket and pitcher.

Her room was empty.

She grabbed the door and peered behind it. The sword was gone. He was gone. She looked at the open window and ran across to it, scrambling onto the bed and leaning out so far that she almost knocked her geranium over.

From her garret window she had a clear view up and down the roofs over the canal, and no figure lurked on the shingles or disappeared over a peak. Balancing precariously, she sat on the windowsill and pulled herself up, craning her neck until she could see if he was hiding overtop her own window, but the mossy slates were unmarked and empty there, too.

"Broken leg indeed," she muttered, lowering herself carefully back inside. "Prevaricator! Horrid man!" She sat down on her bed and put her hands on her breast, letting out a deep sigh. "Oh, thank the good Lord he's gone."

She rested on the bed for a few moments, thinking of the waterfall, remembering to breathe. The sensation of relief that he'd gotten away and it was no longer her duty to rush to the police was out of all proportion to her sense of reprieve from danger. She hadn't *really* been afraid of him.

But she got up and pulled the casement window closed, latching it securely, and then locked the door.

She had a moment's uncomfortable thought that she truly ought to dress and go down to the station, to alert the officers that their thief had been in the neighborhood, at least. Even as she considered it, she realized how preposterous everything would sound as she made her report. Mr. Gerard! A thief! Friend of Lady Ashland and the queen of the Hawaiian Islands! Oh, yes, the police were quite likely to accept her word for that. She would be fortunate if she weren't committed to a lunatic asylum on the spot.

She would tell Inspector Ruby and Sergeant MacDonald about it this evening. They would believe her, she thought. At least they might listen to her.

Normally she left the house at this hour, but this morning hurrying away just to deceive Mrs. Dawkins was beyond her. If the landlady questioned her, Leda resolved, she would say that she wasn't feeling well and had overslept. And truly, every muscle in her body seemed wobbly. Her teeth actually chattered as she righted the fallen table and hefted the sewing machine back onto it, examining the device anxiously. It had a scratch in the enamel, but beyond that it seemed unharmed. The baths would not open for some time yet, so she lit her grate and made tea, pulling her gown up to her knees and settling on the bed cross-legged to eat the stale scones she'd saved from yesterday.

Her mind went round and round with Mr. Gerard. It was incredible. She must have dreamed it. She stretched out her bare legs, turning her toes this way and that. She thought she had rather pleasing ankles, trim and snow-white and refined. He would have seen them. She put her fingers over her mouth, flushing, and tucked her feet up under her gown with a bit more maidenly reserve.

Her hands were still all shaky with reaction, and the saucer rattled immoderately. She drew the curtains before she pulled the pins from her hair. The room took on colors as light filtered through the gay patchwork of scraps she'd brought home from the cutting room.

With jittery moves, she reached for her chemise and drawers, and found them still damp from her scrubbing the night before. After examining the grime at the knees, she bundled them up to launder at the bath and shrugged halfway out of the nightgown, too flustered to do things in proper order and put her petticoat on underneath first. She sat down with the gown rumpled around her waist. Her hair fell over her bare shoulders as she brushed it out with Miss Myrtle's silver brush, one hundred strokes on each side, trying to find some calm in the routine.

But her mind skipped around in a distractingly foolish way, not concentrating on the problems at hand at all. She absentmindedly coiled up her hair and pinned it before she put on anything, stepped into her calico skirt, and buttoned her blouse, trying to use Miss Myrtle's hand mirror to see if anyone could tell she hadn't a stitch on beneath it.

She put up her hair, after dropping the pins four separate times, and when she was ready, it was still over two hours before the bath would open. So she sat back down on her bed and pulled out her money box to refigure her accounts, although she knew perfectly plainly what her situation was.

She set the note and coins in piles, arranged in order of value, until the whole of her hoard lay on the bed: a single pound note, three shillings, and twenty pence, before subtracting this week's rent on the room and the sewing machine. Precisely eight shillings and tuppence with which to eat, bathe, and launder. Even if she found a position, she wouldn't have enough to carry her through until she was paid, especially if the employment agency arranged to have the premium taken out of her first month's wage.

There were still Miss Myrtle's silver-handled brush and mirror. But not yet. She was not going to part with them yet. She picked up the mirror lovingly, turning it over and over in her hand.

She stopped, and rotated it back half a turn, gazing down into the reflection.

With a stifled shriek, she dropped the mirror and sprang back on the bed against the wall, staring upward. In the early morning shadow of the peaked ceiling, he lay along the attic beam like a panther, utterly still, watching her.

Leda began to breathe in choking gasps. He moved, pivoting down from the beam like smoke materializing into substance. With controlled grace, he lowered himself by his arms, dropping lightly to the floor on one leg.

"Waterfall," he reminded her incisively—and Leda closed her eyes and regulated her breath.

For a bare instant.

"You *villain!*" she screeched, when she'd got her

breathing in hand. "You—you *voyeur!* What were you doing up there? In my *room!* You were *watching* me! And I was—oh, my *God,* I was—"

The horrible realization of what he must have seen put her out of wind again; she had to pause and discipline her inhalation, which showed an alarming tendency to outpace the capacity of her lungs. She grabbed up the brush and threw it at him. He barely shifted, avoiding it, and Leda scrambled for the poker on the floor.

"Brute!" she cried. "You contemptible *wretch!* Get out of here!" She swung the poker at him wildly; it whizzed past his nose and she swung again, but he only altered his stance, not giving up ground. "Get out!" she screamed. "Get out, get out, get out!" She was close enough now that the poker would demolish him; she lifted it over her head and brought it down with all her might.

He didn't even flinch; he only raised his hands with a motion that seemed whimsically slow and clapped them together on the descending rod, stopping it dead over his head. For a moment he looked at her between his upraised arms, as if asking if she were finished.

"Get out of here!" Recklessly Leda yanked at the poker to wrestle it away from him, throwing her weight into his resistance. He gripped it. She gave a squeal of fury, trying to regain control, winning an inch and redoubling her effort.

Abruptly, he let go. She tumbled backward with the force of her own pull, landing with a painful jolt on her bruised hip. Somehow the poker had ended up in his hand instead of hers. She looked up at him standing quietly over her and curled herself into a ball sitting on the floor, weeping with mortification and fury.

"How could you? Oh, how *could* you? You're a beast—you don't deserve to be called a gentleman! You're a low, evil, wretched blackguard, and I'll have the police on you if you kill me for it! I shall! Don't you think I won't! Monster!" She put her face against her knees. "Go *away!* Go—"

In the midst of her tirade, she became aware of Mrs.

Dawkins' voice outside. The door rattled. Leda lifted her head and froze.

"What is it?" the landlady barked through the barrier. "Who's in there with you?"

Mr. Gerard braced his hand on the sewing machine table and shifted. He lowered himself onto Leda's bed, pulling off his dark, loose coat to reveal a normal gentleman's white shirt. The coat fell over his feet in a casual tumble, hiding the strange footwear.

"Open up!" The lock shook. "You're not to have men visitors, Miss Etoile! Not on fourteen shillings the week! Open this door!" Before Leda could gather her wits, she heard a key in the lock. The door burst open.

In her nightcap and a garish red dressing gown, Mrs. Dawkins stopped and glared at Mr. Gerard, who had a hand at his shirt collar, as if he were just hastily buttoning the last button. Then she swung on Leda, her bulging baby-doll eyes blinking rapidly.

"Well, I *never,*" she exclaimed. "You little slut; butter wouldn't melt in your mouth, would it? Respectable, you said. A lady, you said. No followers, you said. I thought something smelt about the way you've taken to coming and going so sly-like, w' no basket! Been slippin' 'em up here secret-like, has you? I won't have it!" She grabbed the chemise that lay bundled on the washstand and dangled it, leaning toward Leda. "I won't be bilked of the takings by no artful little tramp—if you pick up men and bring them here, you give me my share. A fine piece of work, Lady Miss Trollop—" She tossed the underwear toward Leda and bustled over, scraping Leda's money off the bed into her palm. "We'll see about whether I put you out in the street or not for chousing me!"

"Oh, no! Please!" Leda gathered her underwear into a ball and held it to her chest. "Mrs. Dawkins, it isn't—"

But the landlady was no longer looking at her, nor counting the small pile of money in her palm. Her gaze was pinned to Mr. Gerard's hand as he turned it over and slid a folded note beneath his thumb.

Mrs. Dawkins bobbed forward, snatching the money from between his closed fingers. She glanced down, and her bulbous cheeks grew pink. "Indeed, sir!" Her whole manner became servile. "That's very kind of you, sir. Very kind, I'm sure. Would you like a refreshment brought up, sir? Something to break your fast? I can send down to the corner for bacon in a moment—"

"No," he said.

"Tea? Nor toast?" She tucked the note into the bosom of her dressing gown. "Very good, then! I'll be right away downstairs should you need anything." She sidled toward the door. "Miss has only to ask."

"Just give Miss Etoile back the money that is hers," he said coldly.

"Oh, to be sure." Mrs. Dawkins laid the coins on the washstand. "But her rent is twenty shillings, you know; twenty shillings for a lady what entertains followers in her room, due prompt on Friday. That's today, sir. Today it is, you see." She folded the pound note into her hand, gave a meek duck of her head, and opened the door.

Leda didn't speak, knowing it was hopeless; she didn't even mention anything about going for the police. Mrs. Dawkins would believe nothing that she said now. As the door closed, Leda pressed her face to her knees.

"Look what you've done," she moaned. "Oh, look what you've done!"

"I might have done worse," he said. "What a remarkably unpleasant woman."

Leda looked up. He moved one hand across the other in a flicking motion, and at the same instant a loud thump came from the door. She looked around, expecting Mrs. Dawkins again, but instead there was a silvery disc stuck in the wood. Another appeared with a biting thud, and a third and a fourth. They were shaped like stars, many-pointed, two sharp rays of each disc buried in the door.

It took a moment before she realized that he had propelled them into the wood with that swift flick of his hand. He held up a fifth one between his fingers, turned it so that the multicolored light through the curtains sent a rainbow across it, and then closed his fist. When he opened it, the disc was gone: not buried in the door like the others—simply vanished.

They would take a person's eye out, those pointed stars. Leda pushed herself to her feet, leaning back against the wall with one arm behind her and her chemise clutched against her chest. "What is it you want?" she cried. "Why won't you go?"

"How much money do you have?" he asked, as calmly as if she hadn't spoken at all.

"Oh, do you plan to steal that, too? Here!" She swept the coins from the washstand and hurled them at him in a shower. "Take it all—it's worth my last pence to have you gone!"

He caught one of the shillings in the air; the rest fell on the bed and floor and one circled around on its edge before it went down with a spinning plop. He dropped the shilling he'd caught onto the bedclothes.

"You didn't go to the police," he said. "Thank you."

Leda watched him, suddenly wary. She didn't answer.

"I wasn't certain what you intended when you left," he added. "It seemed best to conceal myself." He picked up the mirror, turning it, holding it the way Leda had held it when she saw him. A faint smile touched his mouth as he watched the reflection of the ceiling beam.

She hugged the chemise, pulling up one of the folds that had fallen free.

"I'm not a thief," he said, still looking in the mirror. Then he put it down and reached for his coat. "A trespasser, perhaps. A changer of things that resist change." He looked at her directly. "That's why the police really want me, is it not? Not because I've hurt anyone, or taken for myself what isn't mine. They want me because I've disordered the pattern that they know, and it alarms everyone."

"It alarms *me*," she exclaimed.

He shrugged into the dark coat and belted it. "I would like you to trust me."

"Trust you!" she echoed. "You must be mad."

"Miss Etoile, I have been in this room every night for the past week and more. Have I hurt you? Have I touched one of your possessions?"

"What?" Her voice went up to an unladylike squeal. "You've been coming in my room for a week?"

"And you've known nothing of it, have you? Until you moved everything and bathed yourself and the whole room in that exceptionally odorous soap."

"You *are* mad! What has soap to do with anything?"

"It reeks. That hampered me."

"It does not reek," she said indignantly. "Hudson's has no smell."

"It reeks," he said. "But it's my responsibility—my mistake—I was too impatient; I allowed my perceptions to become disordered."

"Certainly it's your responsibility. It isn't mine! I've every right to clean my floor and move my furnishings if I please, without some housebreaker complaining of it! And—and then hanging up in the eaves like a horrid vampire bat!" She felt herself flushing. "I will never forgive you for that, sir! Never! You could have spoken, when you saw I hadn't called the police! You could have revealed yourself!"

His eyes shifted away from her. For the first time, he looked somewhat guilty.

"You have forever forfeited the right to be called a gentleman," she concluded haughtily. "Why didn't you just go the way you came?"

"Because my leg is broken."

"I don't believe you. You can't go out the window, but you can climb onto ceiling beams?"

He reached down and pulled the string ties free on his leg. The dark cloth came loose, falling full like a skirt.

"That's quite all right," Leda said hastily. "You needn't feel you must prove it."

He bent over, moving his fingers up and down his calf beneath the fabric. "If you'll help me, I can set it. Then find me a splint and I'll be gone."

"But—" She put her fingers over her mouth and stared at his veiled leg. "—wouldn't you rather have a doctor?"

"No," he said simply. "You can help me."

"I really don't think I can," she said.

"Can you hold my foot?"

"Really, I think you should have a doctor," she said, backing up a step.

He looked up at her. "Keep breathing, Miss Etoile. We haven't even started yet."

Leda realized she was inhaling in unsteady gulps. She took a deep breath and let it out again.

"What of those newspapers?" he asked, nodding toward the pile on the stool which Leda had been saving all week, reading up on every detail of the robberies. "I think I could use them for a splint, if you've something to tie them with."

She looked at the thick sheaf of paper dubiously. "Would that work?"

"If we tore up your petticoat to secure it. I'll buy you a new one."

"Certainly not! I won't have strange men buying me petti—" She cleared her throat, refusing to discuss something so unseemly. "The towel, perhaps."

"Fine." He leaned over and pulled the pile of papers toward him, folding and arranging them in an even stack an inch thick. Hesitantly, Leda took her towel and clipped the edges, tearing it into long strips. Then she stood clutching the pieces, backed up against the wall.

"This is absurd," she said. "You can't possibly set your own leg. You'll pass out."

"I don't think I will."

"Yes, you'll pass out," she insisted, her voice rising. "Or you'll make some horrid loud noise. And then what am I to do? What will Mrs. Dawkins think?"

His mouth thinned in a quizzical tilt. "Why don't you move out of here, if you care so much what Mrs. Dawkins thinks?"

"I haven't the money, nor hope of employment, not that it's any of your concern, Mr. Gerard."

He turned his head, and then slanted a look back at her beneath his lashes. "There's a reward for information about who's committing the robberies," he said.

"Is there?" she asked, too brightly.

"Two hundred and fifty pounds."

"Yes, I . . . I suppose I read that."

"You might relocate and live pretty handsomely on that."

Leda straightened her shoulders and gave him a chilly stare. "I'm sure a citizen does not require a reward to know when to do her duty. I would disdain to improve myself on—on *blood* money."

"And you don't think it's your duty to turn me in?"

"I'm very sure it is my duty, sir." She took a deep breath. "I also daresay that if I should leave this room— if you should allow it without flinging one of those monstrous stars at me and taking my eye out—that you wouldn't be here when I returned. Neither could I depend upon Mrs. Dawkins to believe me, nor to fetch the police, not after you've thoroughly convinced her with your twenty-pound note that I'm entertaining gentlemen in my room. And you've got rid of the Japanese sword very neatly; I suppose you threw it in the canal, which is a great shame, and a wicked, thoughtless, barbarous waste of something that no doubt cost some accomplished craftsman a great deal of time and effort, but it is the only evidence I might have had for my assertions, and without it I should only look a fool to go to the police, shouldn't I?"

"I'm afraid that might be true."

Leda sank against the wall. "And it really is too bad," she added glumly. "I had hoped that Sergeant MacDonald might get a promotion on the strength of it."

"A particular friend of yours?"

She gave him Miss Myrtle's most elevated scowl. "My friends, particular or not, are none of your affair, Mr. Gerard."

He smiled. "Sergeant MacDonald is not on duty this morning, I take it?"

"I've no idea," she said stoutly.

"What of the fellow with the fancy seal on his letters?"

"I've no notion what you're speaking about." Leda felt herself turning crimson.

To her relief, he didn't pursue the topic, but only looked at her for a few moments, and then down at his leg. "Bring the toweling over here, please."

Leda twisted the cloth between her fingers, brought

abruptly back to the task at hand. Her stomach felt a little queasy.

"Come here," he said gently. "Just hold my foot."

She swallowed down a great lump in her throat and went forward. She knelt in front of him. "I'll hurt you," she said plaintively.

"I assure you that I already hurt. Intensely. Only hold my ankle—and when I ask, pull on it. Not a tug, just a slow, strong pull. It will probably require putting your whole weight against it." He looked at her beneath his lashes. "And whatever you do, Miss Etoile—don't let go."

"It will hurt."

"Only if you let go."

"Oh, dear," she said. "I don't think I can do this."

"Put your hands on my ankle, Miss Etoile."

She bit her lip, took another deep breath, and put her hands over the black cloth footwear he wore. Very gingerly, she moved her palms upward, under the loose leggings of dark cotton. The covering helped; made what she was doing seem more decorous. She imagined herself a nurse, accustomed to touching men to whom she'd not been introduced. Men to whom she *had* been introduced. Men of any sort, for that matter. The footwear ended just above his ankle, and she could feel his skin beneath her fingertips, hot and swollen. She glanced up at him, for the first time comprehending the extent of the injury and the pain he'd been enduring.

He was no longer looking at her. His lashes were lowered, his face as silent and withdrawn as carved marble. Gradually his breathing changed, grew deeper, slower, something she could feel but not hear. As it altered, he altered: he still seemed powerful and solid, and yet the aesthetic purity of his features gave him an unreal aspect, like something from an artist's dream of absolute and flawless force. In the colored light, his hair was gold and red and a thousand subtler tints; his body in the dark clothing distilled midnight into life.

"Now," he murmured, lifting his lashes. "Pull."

Leda clasped his ankle and slowly began to exert a light tension.

"Harder than that." He met her eyes, and she bit her lip, gripping more firmly. His face never changed, and yet she felt his intensity, his active acceptance of the agony that this must cause. She felt him begin to oppose her strength with his, and had to set herself back against him, harder and harder, until her whole weight hung entirely on her hands. She heard a grating sound.

"Don't let go," he said softly, catching her in the instant of revolted surprise before the nerve fled her fingers.

She nodded, feeling faintly sick, puffing her lower lip free, still holding steady and hard as he leaned over. She closed her eyes quickly, before she saw his leg, and kept them squeezed shut.

"All right," he said in a calm voice. "Very slowly, ease your hold. That's enough—keep some traction on it." She heard the sound of the newspaper. She couldn't help herself; she opened her eyes. He moved with methodical assurance, wrapping the stiff splint of newspaper, an inch thick, around his leg, tying it fast with the strips of towel above his knee and twice down his calf. He held the last strip toward her. "Can you tie it at my ankle?"

His peaceful manner gave her confidence. Carefully, without allowing his foot to touch the floor, she bound the splint closed. It took some effort, for the paper stuck out an inch beyond his heel, requiring her binding to hold against the pressure of the thick casing bent over the top of his foot. But she was surprised at the strength and rigidity of the makeshift dressing.

"Are you a doctor?" she asked.

"No."

Something in his voice made her look up. Now, after his leg was immobilized and the punishment over, he sat very still; for a frightening moment his eyes seemed to lose focus and drift, sliding halfway closed. She lunged up and seized his wrist, thinking to catch him before he toppled forward in a faint, but he did not move or slump down onto her push—he seemed to yield and yet check her at the same time, so that she stopped halfway through the motion with the sensation of pressing against a wall, though it was only his forearm beneath her fingers.

She groped for equilibrium and found that instead of steadying him, it was he who braced and balanced her against collapsing over on his shoulder. "Forgive me," she gasped, finding her feet. She let go and stepped back. "Did I hurt you?"

He looked up at her. His subtle smile, so improbably beguiling, seemed to focus all the controlled energy of him into a ray of light on her heart. "You didn't hurt me. You did well. I want to ask you something important."

"What?" she asked warily, recalled to the reality of conversing casually with a commonplace thief.

"Can you write?" he asked.

"Certainly I can write."

"Type?"

She almost hesitated. She almost took an instant too long to answer. He was alert and observant, but her sudden lie came out with the smoothness of utter reckless desperation. "Forty words a minute," she said, repeating what she'd read in an advertisement for expert typists. "With accuracy."

He appeared to accept this lavish exaggeration with complete confidence. "I have a great need of someone like yourself. Will you come to work for me, Miss Etoile?"

"As a robber?" she squeaked.

He gave her a weak grin and shook his head. "I'm finished with stealing. Just being in your public-spirited presence has reformed me of burglary."

Leda gave a little snort of disbelief.

"I find myself in need of a secretary. A man Friday, you might call it. It may be a little surprising to you, but I have rather extensive—and legitimate—business interests." He bent down and began to retie the full black cloth over his calf and the makeshift splint. "It looks as if this leg will be somewhat confining to me for the rest of the time I'm in England. I'm going to want someone to assist me with my concerns. In Hawaii I'd pay a hundred and fifty American dollars a month. With the exchange rate—" He straightened up. "Say—ten pounds a week?"

"Ten . . . pounds . . . a week?" Leda repeated.

"Does that sound fair?"

She sank backward against the table. "Fair," she said, weak with astonishment. "Fair!"

"For forty words a minute."

She stood up, her spine stiffening. "I cannot. I couldn't possibly. You're a criminal."

"Am I?" He looked at her steadily. "Truth is something you have to know for yourself. I don't have the words to persuade you."

She put both hands on the sides of her face. He *was* a criminal. How could he not be a criminal, sneaking about with stolen goods and a mask in the middle of the night? Ten pounds a week! Only an outlaw could pay such absurdly high wages for a secretary. He might have killed her in the dark—he almost had; he'd admitted it himself. And stayed with her, and helped her breathe. Hidden up in the ceiling beam, no gentleman, the wretched beast; and then looked guilty for it.

She lowered her hands. "If you're not a criminal, then what are you doing stealing all these swords and things?"

For a moment he was silent. Then he rubbed his chin and said, "There's no name for it in English."

"Oh, is there not? 'Burglary' seems descriptive enough."

"*Kyojitsu.*" He looked levelly into her eyes, not wavering. "False-true."

" 'False-true'?" she repeated with heavy skepticism.

He made his hand into a fist and spread it open, as if a better definition would unfold out of it. "Deceit and honesty. Tact. Subterfuge. Weak and strong. Bad and good. A ruse. It means all of those things."

"I don't know what you're talking about."

He looked at her patiently, as if she were a backward child. "My intent. You asked me why I removed things from their conventional place."

No wonder Miss Myrtle had always warned her against men. Provoking creatures.

"Well, I'm afraid I've no talent for Oriental riddles," she said testily. "Perhaps you will tell me what are these 'legitimate' businesses of yours?"

"Shipping, for the most part. I manage the Arcturus Company for Lord and Lady Ashland, and I have my own—Kaiea Shipbuilding and Transport. I have a timber mill on the North American coast. Some holdings in cotton and sugar markets. Several banks. Marine insurance." He smiled. "Do you believe me?"

"I don't know."

"I might be making this up. *Kai ea* means 'rising sea' in Hawaiian. *Arcturus* was the name of the tea clipper Lord Ashland's uncle built in 1849. Lord Ashland rechristened her *Arcanum*. But perhaps none of that is true. I might be a quick thinker and a good liar."

"I believe there are such," she said majestically.

"Then I could answer your questions for a thousand years, and you wouldn't be any nearer judging what I truly am."

"What I know, Mr. Gerard, is that you're the most singular person I've ever had the ordeal of encountering!"

He watched her, his eyes dark silver, like the moon on a wild and cloudy night. Slowly, he shook his head. "What you know here," he said softly, holding his fist against the center of his body, "that is the truth."

Ten

Breakfall

Hawaii, 1872

Dojun never taught him the songs. Dojun never taught
him anything except Japanese, never sang him anything
except orders to work, errands to run, heavy wood to chop,
and buckets of carp to carry from the fish pond to a distant
neighbor who hadn't even asked for them. Often Dojun
wanted strange things: a flower from a tree limb far out
of Samuel's reach, a stone from the highest cliff at Diamond Head, a feather from a live bird that nested in the
eaves of the lanai.

The flowers and stones were not impossible: Samuel
learned to climb and jump; he walked with Dojun to Diamond Head on Saturdays, ten miles there and back, no
stopping, and Dojun merely accepted the hard-won prizes
with a nod and floated them in water in a black bowl above
Samuel's place at the dinner table. When dinner was over,
Samuel carried the bowl to his room and lay on his bed,
staring down into the bowl on the floor, studying it, wondering what it was about the object that made Dojun
choose it.

The feather eluded him. He studied the bird and the nest
for hours, watched what it ate and where it landed. He
talked to some Hawaiians and learned to build a trap with
a net and sticky sap spread on the branches. He trapped
the sparrow, and took a feather from its tail before he let
it go.

Dojun accepted the feather silently. In halting Japanese,
Samuel explained the trap, pointed out the clever sticky

snare and how he'd chosen where to hide it. Dojun listened without speaking.

At dinner, there was no black bowl and feather.

Samuel felt ashamed, not knowing how or why he'd failed. He spent long afternoons on the lanai, staring at the sparrow as it hopped along the eave. He climbed the nearest tree and sat still, unblinking, watching the tiny bird flit among the thin branches far out of his reach.

One day Master Robert came into Samuel's room and caught Samuel practicing with a pincushion, trying to move with the flash of speed it would take to capture the unhampered bird in his hand. Robert thought it was play; he was six years old and rather foolish to Samuel's mind— even little Kai, at three, could be quiet and thoughtful sometimes, but Robert never stopped wriggling or talking or crying except when he was asleep.

Samuel made it into a game for him, tying a string to the cushion, but Robert was so impatient and clumsy that he could never once jerk the target away before Samuel could capture it with his hand. Even if Samuel closed his eyes, he could outstrip Robert, over and over, until the younger boy began to cry, his wails of frustration rising to greater frenzy with each defeat.

Lady Tess came, standing in the doorway with a vexed look. Robert ran to her, burying his face in her skirts, crying so that he couldn't even speak over his hiccuping sobs.

Samuel stood up as she hugged her son. "I'm sorry!" he said quickly. "I was teasing him. I'm sorry."

He waited while she comforted Robert, a sick uncertainty curling in his stomach, making his breath seem thick and achy in his chest. She patted the boy's back and let him cry out his baby frustration against her neck. When she stood up, Samuel took a step backward, watching her face, dreading to see a disapproving frown. His secret fear was that she wouldn't want him anymore, that she would discover that she didn't like him after all, and his room and his place and his anchor would disappear. He didn't know where he would go or what he would do if she made him leave, but he only cared that she wanted him to stay.

"What a very silly pair of boys," she said, and held
out her hand to Samuel. "Come here and tell me what
monstrous torment you've caused this little wretch."

A huge relief swept him at her smile. He went forward,
and when she put her hand on his shoulder he suddenly
did what he hadn't done in three years—he gripped her
skirt in his fist and leaned into her embrace, holding tight
to the single steadfast kinship he'd had in his life. "I'm
sorry," he whispered again. "I'm sorry."

She stroked his hair. Suddenly Robert wriggled from
her arm, already out of sniffles and on to another topic of
interest. Lady Tess let him go and stood with her hold
tight around Samuel. The sound of Robert's bare feet on
the floor receded as he trotted off down the hall.

Silence fell around them. Samuel kept his fierce grip.
She rubbed his hair between her fingers and squeezed him
hard. "I love you, Sammy," she said softly. "You're safe
here with me."

She was the only one who could call him by that old
and hated name; the only one who knew it. No one, not
Dojun, not even Lord Gryphon, understood what Samuel's
life had been the way that she understood. She had been
there. She had seen it. And still she said she loved him,
and he wished that he could stand here in this secure and
protected place and hold on to her for the rest of time.

When he looked at her face, she was wiping her fingers
across her eyes. "There now," she said, in a muffled
voice. "You see that Robert is not entirely heartbroken.
But I shouldn't think you'd find it very rewarding to tease
him anymore, unless you have a fondness for passionate
scenes."

"No, ma'am," he said obediently, not letting go.

She took out her handkerchief and blew her nose.
"Smile for me, Samuel. You almost never smile."

"Yes, ma'am," he said, and made a curve with his
mouth.

She held the handkerchief and shook her head. "Good!"
she said cheerfully.

He broke away from her and went to his koa-wood chest
of drawers. He dug down beneath his clean shirts and

found the sharp, pockmarked brown stone with the tiny sparkling shards of green in it that he'd brought from the cliff at Diamond Head. "This is for you," he said, and held it out in his cupped hand.

She took the stone, and looked at it, and rolled it over with her fingers, touching it gently, as if it were something precious. "Thank you," she said. "It's beautiful."

He did smile, then. It wasn't beautiful, not really, but he felt embarrassed and pleased anyway, and sat down on the floor, toying with the string on the pincushion, tugging it in little jerks across the slick wood. He heard her blow her nose again.

"You're still helping Dojun," she said. "You remember what Gryf told you, Samuel—you don't have to do that. You mustn't think you have to work."

"Yes, ma'am." He flicked the pincushion back and forth. "I remember."

"As long as your schoolwork is as good as it's been, all you have to do is play."

"I like to work," he said to the floor between his crossed legs. "I want to do it."

She stood silently behind him. He felt her looking at him, felt all hot and agitated, but he only sat still, as still as if he were in the tree with the bird, and stared down at the floor.

"All right," Lady Tess said finally, in a reluctant voice. "If you truly like it."

"Yes, ma'am," he said. "I do."

She stood there for another moment more, and then he heard her soft sigh, and the sound of her skirts rustle as she went away.

That afternoon, he tried to catch the bird. He waited in the tree, dived to grab the sparrow when it came, and fell out of the branches. Dojun found him woozy and helpless at the root of the tree. Samuel vaguely remembered that the butler put his bare foot on Samuel's armpit and pulled on his arm, and it hurt awfully for an instant before he went blank. He woke up in bed, and stayed there for a week recovering from a dislocated shoulder and concussion.

He was afraid Dojun was disgusted with him. For a long time after that, he could not find the courage to speak to the Japanese butler. When Dojun came near, Samuel faded away, making himself unnoticeable: quiet and still and humble the way a mouse would hide in shadows. Until one day Dojun came upon him unexpectedly, passing through the empty dining room. Samuel heard his step; he had time only to move behind the door and freeze into invisibility. The butler laid the table setting, moving around the room with small chinks and clinks of silverware.

"Good at that, aren't you?" he said in Japanese as he leaned over to place a fork. "*Kyojitsu* is difficult to learn, and already you know how to do it."

Samuel knew Dojun must be speaking to him: no one else had any Japanese at all. Samuel didn't know the word *kyojitsu*, and he was pretty sure Dojun knew he didn't.

"Foolish people use only one kind of disguise." Dojun went on setting the table. "*Shin* is what you are in your mind. What you are in your heart. *Itsuwaru* is pretending to be what you're not. Together, they can be *kyojitsu*. It's too easy to be a tiger all the time. If you're a tiger, you do things the way a tiger does, you move the way a tiger moves, you use only set form, the *kata*, of the tiger. You meet a bigger tiger, and then what? You're in trouble. Better to know the *kata* of a mouse, too. Better to know how to be small and silent. Maybe then the big tiger won't see you, and you live to be a tiger again."

Samuel listened, startled to hear Dojun speak of a mouse as if he'd seen into Samuel's head. But he didn't sound angry or scornful about it; he sounded as if it were a good thing. Slowly, Samuel took a breath and stepped out from behind the door.

Dojun just went on laying out the silver.

After a moment, Samuel bowed respectfully the way Dojun had taught him. "I can't get the feather," he said in Japanese. "I'm ashamed, Dojun-san."

Dojun straightened up from the table and looked at him. The very foreignness of his features was reassuring. Samuel had never known anyone like Dojun: he never looked mad or hungry or eager. The enigmatic Oriental eyes made Samuel feel safe and curious at the same time.

"Why ashamed?" Dojun said blandly. "Got the feather, first time you tried, with the trap." .

Samuel hesitated. "I thought—it was wrong. You didn't put it in the bowl."

"You think too much. How do you know what's right or wrong? You're too young to know. You want too much. You want a feather in a bowl. So what do you do? You fall on your head to get it. Tonight I'll put a feather in a bowl for you. Will that make you happy?"

Samuel frowned down at his feet. "No, Dojun-san."

"You're hard to please."

He looked up. "I think *you're* hard to please," he said in English, and then backed up a step and hung on to the doorknob, daunted by his own effrontery.

Dojun made a careless motion with his hand. "No can please all anybody," he grunted, dropping into pidgin, as if disdaining Samuel's clumsy Japanese. "Gotta savvy when use tiger-*kata,* when use mouse-*kata,* Samua-kun. Gotta savvy here." He struck his fist just below his navel. "What Dojun want ain't no big thing when Samua-kun fall out from tree. Big thing how hard ground, *nē?*"

Samuel leaned against the door, rubbing his hand up and down the wood.

"How hard been, Samua-chan?" Dojun asked.

"Pretty hard," Samuel said, keeping his head down.

Dojun began setting out plates. He spoke in Japanese again. "What if I teach you how to roll and break your fall?" he asked. "This is called *taihenjutsu ukemi.* I could teach you that. But I ask myself, what good will it do this boy who wants so much? I can't put a fall into a bowl of water. I can't give him what he seems to want. If he learns to fall, that's all he gets. He only learns how to turn hard ground into soft. What is that to a boy who wants feathers in bowls of water?"

"It wasn't just the feather in a bowl," Samuel objected plaintively in English. "You don't understand."

"Stupid fellow, me. Real stupid."

"I don't think that!"

''More smart you then, eh?''

Samuel twisted the doorknob, frustrated and confused. ''I don't know what you want!''

Dojun stopped and looked at him. He smiled.

Samuel's shoulders sank. He watched Dojun go back to the plates, waited until they were all in place and the butler was almost ready to leave the room.

''Dojun-san,'' he said in a whisper of Japanese. ''Will you teach me how to fall?''

''This Saturday,'' Dojun said, ''come with me again to the diamond mountain.''

Eleven

⊕

Leda found herself glancing suspiciously at every scruffy loiterer among the throngs of people in the street, half-expecting to find Mr. Gerard's clear gray eyes beneath the battered hat of some stoop-shouldered day laborer with coal dust smearing his hands and hair. After she had declined his offer of employment—taking a position as secretary to a thief; impossible!—the manner in which he'd transformed himself had been rather disconcerting: shrugging his coat into shapelessness and using a swipe of coal smut from her grate to rub into his hands and face. That alone hadn't seemed to make such a difference while she stood in her room watching him do it, but after she returned from a brief, furtive journey downstairs to abduct a walking stick from Mrs. Dawkins' hall tree, she mounted the last landing and gave a little gasp of fright upon meeting a strange man in the stair, a ragged and boneless figure leaning like a drunkard on the rail.

It had truly taken her a suspended moment to realize who it was, so convincingly had his frame seemed to slump into the listless hunch of a tramp straight out of the Casual Ward. A soft hat, slung low over his face, showed only the grimy edge of his jaw; his jacket hung open, disclosing his shirt, which had lost two buttons and acquired a tear at the collar seam; he'd ripped the toes out of the strange footwear and stuffed newspaper into the holes—all of a piece with the curious poor-man's splint they'd fashioned for his leg, which was the only recognizable thing about him.

He looked at her from beneath the hat. Amid the gloom

99

of the hall and shadows of coal dust on his face, his eyes reflected translucent gray, a shocking light of intelligence in the sullen and wretched picture.

She held out the walking stick. "You had best keep your eyes down," she advised, "if you wish to avoid scrutiny."

He grunted, touching his hat in a gesture of morose assent. "Ma'am."

If Leda hadn't known perfectly well that his hands were flawless, she would have succumbed to the very effective illusion that his thumb and middle finger were missing. She stood back on the landing, leaning against the wall, pursing her lips. "Are you certain you can walk?"

He lifted his eyes to hers again. Leda thought suddenly that this was the last moment—she would never see him again, likely enough.

"Do you have my card?" he asked softly.

His card was burning quite a hole in her skirt pocket, in fact. She nodded.

"Perhaps you will reconsider," he said.

There was no threat in his tone. No emotion at all. Perhaps when he was gone she would go to the police, but while he stood before her, watching her so intently . . .

She remembered suddenly that Miss Myrtle had never allowed her to sit on the public benches in the park when she was a child, because a strange gentleman might have sat there lately. And patent leather shoes were indecent, because a gentleman could see the reflection of one's petticoat in the shine.

He leaned on the walking stick, shifting his weight, and she saw a dark hollow form at the edge of his mouth.

"You should not walk," she said. "I'll find a cab."

He came down the last three stairs to the landing in slow and easy moves, graceful even with the crutch, as if awkwardness were so alien to him that even in disability it was impossible. "Is your landlady at hand?"

"She was in the parlor when I came up."

"Her door's shut?"

Leda nodded. "But she'll come out at the slightest disturbance. I almost didn't manage to . . . ah . . . borrow her stick. Do you wish to go in secret?"

"I'm afraid that particular hope is long past. But I'd prefer she didn't see me again. You'll save yourself trouble if you let her think the stick stolen."

"I believe it *will* be stolen, by my definition of the word," Leda said tartly.

He smiled from the corner of his mouth. "I paid her enough for it. Remind her of that, if she hits upon me as the culprit. Good day to you, Miss Etoile." He leaned on the stick and held out his free hand.

Leda took it automatically, and then stood there with her bare fingers against his palm, the first time in her life she had ever taken leave of a man without her gloves. A gentleman always removed his, of course, before he offered his hand—it was a natural mistake for Mr. Gerard to forget that she herself wasn't properly dressed.

"I hope I haven't inconvenienced you beyond forgiveness," he murmured, holding her hand firmly in his, as if he were in no hurry to correct his impropriety.

"Oh, not at all," Leda said in a faint voice.

His hold was warm and extraordinarily pleasant. He gave her another of those looks—the way he'd looked at her the first moment she'd set eyes upon him, as if she held some answer to a question that he needed resolved.

Which she did. The question of police or no police.

His eyes dropped away from hers. He let go of her hand and bowed slightly.

He'd left her there on the landing, moving down the stairs with slow fluidity, avoiding the squeaky spot on the fifth step as if he knew it well.

Now, a whole day and night after he'd left Jacob's Island, she kept looking for him, absurdly, as she allowed herself to be carried along with the roaring flow of traffic in Whitehall. The Queen was expected to enter London on Monday, and the congestion seemed tripled already; boisterous; surging and stalling in the streets. Yet Leda looked for him—as if he would be loitering about still, in the midst of this of all places, on a broken leg in his tramp's guise. It was nonsense. He would be comfortably in bed. In bed and under proper care at Morrow House. In Park Lane.

He'd scribbled the direction on the back of his card—as if she were actually in some danger of forgetting it.

Decorating crews making last-minute preparations for the Queen's arrival in London added to the chaos with their scaffolding and thousands of yards of red and white bunting. It all had a festive air—the bright sky, the vivid banners, the endless pushing crowds. Leda walked along in tumultuous gloom, caught between the spirit of the Jubilee and the knowledge that she had two shillings left to her name.

Yesterday she'd spent part of her hoard on her bath and then called on the South Street ladies, finding them at last willing to write a letter of character, but perfectly obstinate that it must be copied word for word from a particular book, published privately by Mrs. Wrotham's late husband, in which the proper locution for every sort of letter might be found—which book, Mrs. Wrotham knew with perfect confidence, had last been used as a prop behind the breakfast-room door. It was no longer to be found there, but she was quite positive she could eventually locate it among her belongings, given enough time. Writing Leda's character from scratch was not to be thought of. Mrs. Wrotham was very sure that Leda would find any letter made up out of whole cloth to be painfully inferior to the brilliant expression and excellent style of the late Mr. Wrotham. Anything less must be such a poor hubble-bubble affair that it would absolutely lose her any position that she had the slightest hope of obtaining.

In her anxiety, Leda had actually contemplated forging a letter herself as she left South Street. Not that it would have made any difference in the end, for upon making an early check at Miss Gernsheim's Employment Agency, she'd found a large card tacked to the door.

Closed in Honor of the Jubilee Celebration Commemorating the Fiftieth Year of the Reign of Her Majesty Queen Victoria, Queen of England and Empress of India. Business will be recommenced on Monday, 27 June.

As if everyone was not perfectly well aware of what the Jubilee was meant to observe, Leda thought darkly.

Monday. It was Saturday today—the Queen wouldn't even arrive until the day after tomorrow, and the great climax of the celebration would be Tuesday, followed by a week of festivities. Eight more days at the very best before Leda might even find out her prospects. Eight wretched days, and two shillings.

She thought of the police, and a reward of two hundred fifty pounds. She felt her face go to an agitated flush amid the crowd.

They wouldn't believe her anyway. She was certain they wouldn't.

She was walking without a goal, allowing the traffic to carry her. The day's papers held no new advertisements for employment; everything was the Jubilee, the Jubilee. And yet it was all so lively and spectacular—everyone seemed ready to burst with excitement, talking of how one would have to arrive Sunday evening and stand all night in order to catch a glimpse of the Queen as her carriage rolled into town on Monday. The whole world was there to greet and cheer her, and dear England, and Leda's heart grew so full of it all that in a fit of rebellion against her fate she went right ahead and spent her last two shillings on a commemorative rosette with a miniature of Her Majesty nestled above a long tail of scarlet and blue and gold ribbons, along with a Jubilee Memorial Mug, a precise copy of the ones that the Prince had commissioned of the Doulton Company, the vendor assured her, to be given one each to the thirty thousand British schoolchildren who would greet the Queen on Wednesday in Hyde Park.

It was very foolish. It was so foolish of her that as she walked away her eyes filled up with frustrated tears and she had to pretend a very earnest interest in a shop window.

She would have to sell the black silk showroom dress she wore now, and the gloves, too, likely, to have enough to eat for the week. And then what would she wear to interview for positions? She always looked a quiz in that calico skirt. She looked a shopgirl . . . and that was what it appeared that she was going to be.

There was still Miss Myrtle's silver brush and mirror. Perhaps the time had come at last to sell them. Or . . . a less melancholy thought: perhaps Sergeant MacDonald might really be taken with her, and overcome his shyness. He'd never seen her in the black silk and hat she wore now; she'd always changed out of the dress before she left Madame Elise's. Mirrored in the shop window, the colorful rosette of ribbons looked very pretty pinned against the elegant black background of her bodice. She turned from the window. Her wandering steps took on a more purposeful direction.

On Saturdays, Sergeant MacDonald and Inspector Ruby came on duty in the early afternoons instead of evening. When Leda reached Bermondsey they were already there, sipping at cups of tea just poured by a young lady laced into an hourglass gabardine with a large bustle, who looked up and set the kettle aside as Leda entered.

"This will be her," the young woman said in an unfriendly tone, as the two policemen jumped to their feet.

Sergeant MacDonald's face was shining red; he popped his belt and made a stiff bow, smiling unhappily at Leda. "Yes, this is Miss Etoile," he said. "Miss—this is my sister." He looked at the other woman and moved his hand awkwardly. "Miss Mary MacDonald."

Leda instantly saw how it was. Miss MacDonald eyed her with an air of middle-class condescension. "Miss Etoile," she said, pronouncing "Etoile" with an affected, overly French accent. She did not offer her hand. "My brother has spoken of you so often that I felt I must come and see you for myself."

The wording of this comment was so obviously rude that Leda simply ignored it and pasted a social smile on her face. "I'm very pleased to make your acquaintance, Miss MacDonald. It's a lovely day for you to come out and into this neighborhood." She spoke as if Bermondsey were as appealing a prospect as Mayfair. "Will you be watching for Her Majesty to arrive with all the rest of us tomorrow?''

"My brother says it will be a vile crush. All the lower orders and hoi polloi will be on the street. I believe I must stay at home in those circumstances. But I assume you don't mind such, Miss Etoile. I daresay you must be quite accustomed to it.''

"Would you like some tea, miss?'' Sergeant MacDonald asked hurriedly, while Inspector Ruby gave her a dry smile.

"Thank you,'' Leda said, and held out her mug. "As you see, I have just the proper thing to drink it in. I shall propose a toast to Her Majesty.''

The mug gave Sergeant MacDonald and Inspector Ruby something to pore and exclaim over cordially, and the inspector declared that he would buy one for his wife.

"Oh,'' said Miss MacDonald, "you won't wish to carry home such brummagem ware. I saw a sterling cup engraved with the proper sentiments, if your wife would like something to remember the occasion.''

"Now then, I couldn't afford sterling, Miss MacDonald,'' he protested. As Leda finished pouring tea into her mug, he held up his cup. "To Her Majesty!'' he offered.

"Her glorious and beloved reign,'' Leda added, lifting her mug.

"How very silly, to make a toast with tea,'' Miss MacDonald said, and Sergeant MacDonald lowered his cup and shut his mouth on the verge of joining in.

Leda and the inspector tapped their ceramic vessels together. He gave her a faint wink.

Leda smiled back, but her spirits had sunk to her toes. It was perfectly clear that Miss MacDonald had no intention of allowing a nobody from Bermondsey to snatch up her brother.

After a moment of silence while they sipped, Sergeant MacDonald said in a reckless way, "That's a bang-up outfit, miss.''

"Thank you,'' Leda said. She took another sip of tea and asked with an air of incidental curiosity, "Have the police made any progress with our infamous thief?''

"Nay, not a mite." Inspector Ruby helped himself to a heaping spoonful of extra sugar. Leda would have known how to prepare his tea just the way he liked it, but evidently Miss MacDonald had not thought to ask. "Bit of a facer that this Japanese sword disappeared, same way as the others, with a note and—ah—something unusual left in its place . . . and when they went to where he sent 'em, sword weren't there as the other loot had been. Still haven't found it. There's some think it might be an imitation crime—not the same fellow a'tall."

"Or perhaps—something happened that prevented him from completing his plan," Leda ventured.

The inspector shrugged. "Might be. That's what the chief thinks—that the extra men stationed at all the—" He cleared his throat and glanced at Miss MacDonald. "Well . . . the places we thought it likely he'd take the sword—the extra men made him sheer off."

"You've still no idea who it might be?" Leda asked. She thought the words came out quite normally, considering how her heart was working so hard.

"None that anyone's told me, and that's the truth. Never know what they're keeping to themselves at the Yard, though."

"He should be hung," Miss MacDonald announced. "He should be drawn and quartered when they find him. It is disgusting."

"Well, I don't know," Inspector Ruby said. "I'm not sure it's been such a bad thing after all. You can't be expected to know it, Miss MacDonald, but in a manner of speaking, these thefts have done some decent good in the city."

"It is vile and abhorrent. It should not be in the papers. The very thought of it makes me ill."

"Perhaps you shouldn't think of it, then, Miss Mac-Donald," the inspector said.

"I don't. I wonder that Miss Etoile can take an interest in such foulness."

Sergeant MacDonald just sat there, looking at his feet. A flush of anger flowed through Leda. There was no chance she was going to meet with Miss MacDonald's approval. Some devil that she'd never known she had inside her made her say, "Oh, I'm avidly interested in it! It's my hobby. That's why I've enjoyed my acquaintance with your brother so thoroughly—he can tell me all the awful details of every *sort* of vile crime!"

Sergeant MacDonald looked up at her in astonishment.

"That doesn't surprise me in the least, Miss Etoile," his sister said. "I've told him you're no better than you should be; coming in every day with your sly ways; hoping to fool a decent man into believing you're a lady."

Sergeant MacDonald pushed to his feet, mumbling a faint, embarrassed protest to his sister, but she pulled her elbow from his grasp.

"I will not have you hoodwinked, Michael. I was sure this woman must be a cunning little slut—but I see that it is worse even than I suspected."

"Indeed," Leda said, standing up. "I'm sure it must be far worse." She glanced once at Sergeant MacDonald, but he avoided her eyes, which told her all that she could have been told. "Good day, Inspector. Good day, Sergeant. Miss MacDonald." She took her mug and turned in a stiff rustle of silk, not even giving the briefest of nods to the sergeant as he stumbled over himself to hold the wicket door open.

"Miss—" he said as she passed, but she ignored him, marching down the steps, gripping her mug and holding back tears of mortification and fury by main force.

She was in no mood for Mrs. Dawkins when she reached her own street, but she hadn't been in her room for ten minutes, hadn't even gotten control of her frenzied breathing enough to think, when the landlady knocked loudly on her door.

"Gentleman to see you, miss," Mrs. Dawkins called.

Leda looked around the squalid little room, her throat full of rage. Come after her to plead and grovel, would he? After not a *word* to stand up to his sister, not a coherent murmur in Leda's behalf . . .

She threw open the door and walked right past Mrs. Dawkins.

"In my parlor," the landlady said, hurrying after her.

At the bottom of the stairs she pushed past Leda and opened the door. "Here she is, sir, fine as fivepence, as y'can see. A fine gel, sir, old enough to know how to please you, young enough to be fresh as daisies."

Leda stopped in the hall. She had expected Sergeant MacDonald. Instead it was a strange man, fifty if he was a day, crushing out a cigar in a teacup on Mrs. Dawkins' table. He looked up at Leda, and then nodded and grinned. "Very nice," he said politely.

For an instant, that politeness distracted her. Her anger faded into bewilderment—and then dawning realization.

He moved toward her, out into the hall. Leda caught a whiff of the cigar and felt sick: sick and humiliated and frantic and terrified. Her room had been her last haven, wretched as it was; paid up for the week, with a lock on the door to bolt out all the reality.

The man reached for her hand. She flung his arm away and made for the door, darting into the street with Mrs. Dawkins squealing indignation and apologies behind her.

Leda walked. She marched and marched, until the crowds began to thin at suppertime, and the public houses and tea shops grew teeming and jovial. She thought of battening herself upon Mrs. Wrotham, who had an extra bedroom: it was the only thing left to do, really. She must confess the whole awful situation—only how did one explain to Mrs. Wrotham, with her trembly hands and gently bobbing silver curls, that one couldn't go home because one's landlady wished one to . . . to entertain an unfamiliar man?

Leda actually walked to South Street, and paused in the lengthening shadows of early dusk, and looked at Mrs. Wrotham's aging house with no gas lit and no lamp or even a candle in the window, because Mrs. Wrotham's jointure no longer allowed her such small luxuries, although one never spoke of it, but went on as if it were only a sample of the personal idiosyncrasies of any aristocratic nature that required Mrs. Wrotham and Miss Lovatt and Lady Cove to pinch their pennies so desperately, even sharing the woman who acted as maidservant and

cook between their two houses. Leda had a fair idea of
how each of their accounts stood, though it was not dis-
cussed aloud. She knew that the feeding and clothing of a
guest would cause Mrs. Wrotham to feel very uneasy about
keeping her third share of the maidservant-cook; Leda also
knew that once she revealed her circumstances to the ladies, nothing would prevent them from insisting upon
stretching their meager resources to support a fourth person whom they could ill-afford to keep, nor feeling most
miserable and tormented if they did not.

Her feet were tired. She was fatigued and hungry, trying
hard to think of what was right and proper to do: what
Miss Myrtle would have done, had she ever been so careless as to come to such a pass, which Leda doubted. She
walked on to the corner—it was only a few steps—so se-
ductively close for her weary feet, to turn down Park Lane
toward Hyde Park Corner . . .

In the dimming evening, Morrow House was aglow with
gaslight. A row of lamps tinted pink and yellow gleamed
from behind the plate glass of the long, narrow conservatory that fronted the house above the ground floor, hiding most of the simple Georgian facade behind a
framework of wrought-iron and greenery. From the bal-
ustrade along the roof hung colorful bunting for the Jubilee, and at every swag a flag was suspended down between
the upper windows, the Union Jack alternating with a different banner, one striped in red, white, and blue with a
small replica of the Union Jack in the upper quarter.

Leda had known Morrow House all her life. She'd
passed it a thousand times, another mansion in a street of
mansions overlooking the traffic and the park. She and
Miss Myrtle had even called there once, when the late
Lady Wynthrop had still been alive and in the habit of
moving into it for the season in lieu of her own smaller
and less fashionable address in King Street.

It wasn't as if the house appeared any differently than
Leda had expected. It was just that she could not find the
least possibility of connection between the scribbled direction in her pocket and the solid reality before her.

She could not walk up the steps to the porticoed door, lift the knocker, and ask if Mr. Gerard were home.

Not only did it seem improbable—impossible—that anything that had happened to her in the last forty-eight hours was even real, but the lateness of the hour and her position as lone female calling on a bachelor gentleman seemed inexcusably forward—not to say shockingly outré.

But she could not go home, and she dreaded going back to Mrs. Wrotham's, so she stood hesitating at the foot of the stairs, her gloved hand resting on the iron railing along the walk. A muffled drift of voices and laughter came to her, and just as she hastily lifted her hand to turn away, the door opened and golden light streamed out. Lady Catherine, dressed in what Leda instantly recognized as one of the tulle-trimmed rose silks she had suggested at Madame Elise's, stepped down onto the terrace.

She wore a white, knitted wool shawl over her shoulders, which quite damaged the effect of her tulle, but carried a nicely complementary fan of creamy plumes which she kept brushing back and forth beneath her chin, as if she enjoyed the sensation. In the midst of turning back toward the door, she saw Leda.

"Why, here you are at last, Miss Etoile!" she cried, to Leda's complete astonishment. "And high time—we were all about to fall into fits of worry. Mama—oh, pray do pay me some mind, dear Mum!" She leaned back into the door frame, laughing. "Leave off poking at your orchids— Miss Etoile has finally come to us."

There was an exclamation from inside. Lady Ashland appeared in the doorway. When she saw Leda, her face lit with pleasure. "Miss Etoile! Do come in. We are so grateful to you." She bounced down the steps, twitching the elegant scarlet silk of her skirt out of the way, and took Leda's hand. "Aloha. Come in. Aloha *nui!*"

"That means 'Welcome' in Hawaiian." Lady Catherine met Leda with a hug as Lady Ashland drew her up the stairs. "And 'We love you.' Thank you so much!"

Leda stood back from the embrace, bewildered. "Oh— but—I'm sure you've nothing to thank me for!"

Lady Catherine squeezed her hand. "Perhaps it seems

trifling to you, but Samuel means the world to us. We were frantic about him when he went missing at breakfast—we knew it must be something badly amiss, because no one could recall having seen him come in the night before, and he was to drive us to breakfast at the Roseberrys', and he is never, *ever* unpunctual.''

A footman was still holding the door, and Leda found herself drawn inside amid a small party that was obviously just on the point of leaving for an evening engagement. She was suddenly being presented directly to Lord Ashland himself, a distinguished gentleman whose black formal dress, white tie, and white gloves handsomely complemented his golden hair and severely aristocratic features, and to the son of the house, Lord Robert, a few years older than Lady Catherine, perhaps just into his twenties, with a grin very much like his sister's, charming and open. When Leda glanced again at Lord Ashland, she knew where they both had inherited it.

He held his wife around the waist while she reached out and caught Leda's hand again. ''The doctor has been in this afternoon,'' she said. ''He told us that now that the swelling was down, he could see that it had been set properly. Tomorrow he'll put it in a dressed splint. He said to compliment you upon your resourcefulness, for he'd never realized himself that rolled newspapers could be so stiff as to provide the proper support.''

''Well, it wasn't really my—'

''He's asleep now,'' Lady Catherine said. ''I could tell that he was in pain, though he won't admit it, and I told Cook to sneak the laudanum into his dinner somehow.''

''Kai!'' Lady Ashland said in exasperation. ''You didn't!''

''He won't mind,'' her daughter said. ''Not if I did it.''

Lady Ashland looked vexed. ''Perhaps not,'' she said. ''But if he doesn't wish to take laudanum, it's not your place to trick him into it.''

Lady Catherine bit her lip. ''Well—I've done it now, and he's asleep, and perhaps he'll thank me in the morning.''

This did not seem to quite satisfy her mother, who

turned away with a little frown. Leda saw Lord Ashland watching his wife, but he said nothing more than, "Perhaps Miss Etoile would like to settle in to her room."

"My room?" Leda echoed faintly.

"Oh, yes—I'll show her up!" Lady Catherine said. "We're only walking half a block—we won't be very late to dinner."

"To dinner!" Leda disengaged her arm from Lady Catherine's impetuous grasp. "Then you must not be a minute late, my lady. Not for a dinner invitation."

"Oh. But someone told me just the other day that here in town it was the worst blunder to arrive on time."

"Oh, no—not for dinner. Perhaps they were speaking of a ball. For a dinner engagement, you must be there within a quarter hour of what was specified on the card, Lady Catherine, and ideally you should be much earlier than that." Leda heard a strong ring of Miss Myrtle in her own voice, but really, this lamentable, sunny girl was in dire need of some social instruction.

"I didn't realize," Lady Catherine said, taking the advice with perfect amiability. "I suppose we should hurry along, then."

Lord Ashland shook Leda's hand without removing his white kid glove. "Sheppard will show you up, Miss Etoile. Make yourself at home."

"See you later, ma'am," his son said, offering his cheerful grin and gloved hand in the same way.

As they moved toward the door, Lady Ashland herself turned to Leda, took her hand, and said, "Thank you. Again. I'm so glad you've decided to come."

Leda smiled, still quite uncertain of it all, and watched as they went out the door. Lord Ashland stood back, waiting for the others to precede him. As his son stepped out the door, Leda suddenly found herself tiptoeing quickly forward and leaning up to Lord Ashland's ear.

"Excuse me. Do forgive me, sir—but—perhaps you aren't quite aware . . . a gentleman removes his glove when offering his hand to a lady."

He gave her a startled glance, and then actually blushed beneath his tan as he grinned at her sideways. "My God, where do they think up these details?'' He lifted his top hat in salute. "Thank you. I'll tip Robert, too."

She hesitated, and then offered, ''For a dinner, you may take them off in the hall and give them over with your hat and stick.''

''To the butler.''

''The butler, yes. He will hand them to a footman.''

He shook his head, chuckling, and stepped out the door, as elegant a picture of a formally dressed gentleman as Leda had ever seen. At the threshold, he paused to look back. "Anything else I should know?''

''No, sir,'' Leda said, responding to his wink with a shy smile. ''You look wonderfully fine.''

Leda stood in the middle of the exquisite bedroom, willing herself not to gaze up at the gilt plasterwork or stare around at the furnishings, all done in blue on white, with a pink-and-blue carpet on the floor and a chintz of trailing morning-glory designs to cover the delicately stuffed chairs. And everywhere there were flowers, not in vases, but sprays of potted white orchids, pink-tinged, that sprang out of wide, leathery fans of living leaves.

''No,'' she said in answer to the housekeeper's question. ''I have no valise.''

She was painfully aware of how bizarre the circumstance must seem to the woman, but the housekeeper only said, ''Very good, miss. The house has just been electrified—you'll find that if you push this button, you will have all the light you require. I'll have a supper tray sent up, if you like?''

''Yes, that would be most welcome.''

Leda eyed the electrical button with distrust and decided she was not brave enough to attempt it. She removed her hat and gloves, walked to the open window, and gazed down at the side street onto which her room opened. Evening traffic was brisk: the polished carriages clattered up and down around the corner in Park Lane; gentlemen strolled in pairs, their silk hats catching the gleam of the street lamps; early music drifted from some party nearby.

The orchids had no perfume, but as she stood in the

window, the soft petals of one spray brushed her cheek gently, clean and fresh. The incredible awkwardness of her position seemed easy to forget. Clearly Mr. Gerard had proclaimed her some sort of heroine to his friends, or family, or however he stood in relation to Lord and Lady Ashland. And they seemed more than willing to take him at his word. This room had been waiting ready for her, as if he'd known she would need it. And him.

Her only regret was when she realized that she had abandoned Miss Myrtle's silver brush and comb in Bermondsey. There was no way to retrieve them now, and no doubt Mrs. Dawkins would sell them the moment she found the chance.

The housekeeper herself, not a maidservant, came with the tray. She arranged it for Leda and then said as she was leaving, "I'll bring a gown and dressing robe for you with the warm water, miss, after your supper."

"Oh, yes," Leda said, as if gowns and dressing robes were commonplace furnishings for the odd houseguest. She saw a folded note on the tray, and bit her lip. "I won't require anything else presently."

The housekeeper bobbed her head and left. Leda picked up the note.

I would like to see you this evening. Anytime is convenient for me, as you may guess, since I'm not going anywhere.
Your servant,

Samuel Gerard

Hungry though she was, Leda could barely swallow the excellent smoked salmon and cold lobster. When the housekeeper returned for the tray, Leda was obliged to ask where she might find Mr. Gerard, and waved the note in a casual way, to show that she was not herself responsible for the irregularity of the proceedings.

"If you'll follow me, miss," the housekeeper said, still giving nothing away of her sentiments. She led Leda down the main stairs to the first floor, along a well-lit hall lined with Turkish carpets, and knocked at a door. A male voice answered, and Leda felt her stomach turn over.

Somehow, she had expected it would be a study, or a drawing room, or some neutral territory. The fact that it was a bedroom, with a bed, and Mr. Gerard ensconced very plainly in it, made her halt frozen on the threshold.

"Come in, Miss Etoile," he said from his pillows, his hair all tousled gold against the bedclothes.

The housekeeper started to pull the door closed behind her. Leda caught it by the edge.

"That's all right," he said. "Close the door, Mrs. Martin. Thank you."

"Oh, I don't think—that's quite—the thing," Leda protested, holding it open. "In the morning—when you're feeling better, and the family is home—perhaps we might rather talk then!"

"I'm feeling as well now as I will tomorrow, I assure you."

"Lady Catherine said you must be asleep," Leda said desperately.

"Ah. Well, I'm not, am I?" He gave the housekeeper a significant glance.

That lady turned pink and bobbed her head. "It won't happen again, Mr. Gerard. I can promise you that. I had a word with Cook."

"Thank you. Lady Catherine doesn't have to know."

"No, sir," the housekeeper said.

"And close the door, if you will."

"Yes, sir." With a firm tug, the wood slid from Leda's hand and the door clicked shut.

She backed up against it, curling her fingers around the knob. It was almost embarrassing, how strikingly beautiful his face was, how difficult she found it not to stare in fascination at him. "This is most uncomfortable. I should not be here."

"I asked you to come."

"That only makes it worse!"

He shifted his leg beneath the bedclothes, cocking his uninjured knee and pushing up straighter. "Haven't we made you welcome?" he asked.

Leda gave a little wild laugh. "Very welcome. I'm overwhelmed!"

"Good." He smiled, passing his hand idly across the sheet that lay over his leg, and then more intently, as if smoothing the wrinkles were an interesting and absorbing occupation. "I hope your coming here means that you're willing to accept the position?"

"I . . . suppose that it does."

He was silent for a moment, still smoothing the sheet, not looking at her. "I told them that a barrel fell off a dray and hit me. I passed out from the pain, and when I woke up, you had happened along and taken charge. Quite a coincidence. I made a lot of your spirit and sluffed over the details. It went down very well." He looked up beneath his lashes. "They took quite a liking to you at the dressmaker's, you know."

Leda stood uneasily at the door. "I wonder why I didn't see you safely home, if I was such a jewel."

"You refused to take anything for your trouble. You arranged for a hurdle and saw me to a doctor, and left. Vanished like a good angel. But I'd given you my card, and offered a position with my firm."

She gave an unbelieving huff. "Amazing that your head was so clear as to think of it, being in such pain."

"Oh, by that time you'd set my leg nicely. I wasn't in much pain."

Leda took a breath. "I fear you must live with sadly credulous people, Mr. Gerard."

"They're the finest friends on earth." He looked at her with a straight, cool challenge, as if inviting her to contradict him.

She dropped her eyes. "You're very fortunate, then. I really must go now."

"As your new employer, Miss Etoile, I really must ask you to stay."

Her back stiffened. "Mr. Gerard, this is a highly inappropriate time and place to conduct business. I must ask you to excuse me."

"I can see why you were dismissed from your position,

Miss Etoile, if arguing with your first instruction is any indication of the way you mean to go on."

"I was not dismissed. I resigned."

"Why?"

"That's none of your affair."

"I've just hired you. It seems to me to be emphatically my affair."

"Very well. Madame Elise wished me to assume duties which were—impossible for me to perform."

"What duties were those?"

Leda simply stared at him in silence.

He held her stubborn gaze, but after a moment a certain consciousness came into his face; he looked down and ran his palm over the sheet again. Leda felt herself turning scarlet.

"May I now be dismissed, Mr. Gerard?"

He rubbed a fold of sheet between his thumb and forefinger. "Are you afraid of me?" he asked in a low voice.

Leda hardly knew what she was. Her fingers seemed to have no capacity in them but to hold onto the doorknob. "Do I have reason to be?" she asked shakily.

"You're extremely eager to leave." There was a note of dryness in his words, but still he didn't look up.

"This is a highly improper situation. I don't know what manners may be in your part of the world, but here—for a lady to be in a gentleman's . . . bedroom . . ." She moistened her lips. "It is not decent. The servants will talk."

He gave a moody chuckle. "Surely the servants won't think I'm capable of violating your virtue in my present case."

"Then they clearly don't know you very well, do they?" she said stiffly. "I am better informed."

Her hand tightened on the knob in expectation of a mocking reply, but instead she was startled to see a dark flush of blood rise in his face as he stared down at his fist. "I beg your pardon for that," he said. "And for detaining you in a compromising situation, if that's what this is. You can go."

He looked up at her directly, and for an instant it hung

between them, the image of him watching her in her own room while she dressed. Leda felt all her skin grow hot with mortification. His mouth seemed tense with some unspoken emotion, and she suddenly felt that she was precariously too close to him.

"Good night," she said, pulling open the door.

"Good night. I'll see you in the library at nine o'clock tomorrow, Miss Etoile, if that meets with your standards for proper conduct."

"Tomorrow is Sunday," Leda pointed out.

His mouth twisted. "Of course. And I suppose you demand the week free for the festivities?"

"Certainly not," she said. "Nine o'clock Monday will be perfectly appropriate. Good night, sir." Without waiting for an answer, she closed the door firmly.

Twelve
〰〰〰〰〰
Chikai

◉

Hawaii, 1874

Samuel dreamed about women. He dreamed about them
almost every night, something that seemed so shameful to
him that he never said anything about it to anyone.

He tried to stop doing it, but he couldn't. In the daytime
he could bend his mind to study, or train in Dojun's demanding games: drive himself to the limits of his strength
and balance until he was good enough to tumble headfirst
off the upper ledges at the top of Diamond Head and land
on his feet amid dry brush and talus fifteen feet below.
But at night he could fall asleep reciting Bible verses to
himself, or practicing Dojun's ways of breathing, or reading *Around the World in Eighty Days,* and still he dreamed
of things that made his face burn when he thought of them;
made him hot and miserable and horrified at what was
inside of him.

He didn't have any friends at school. He didn't want
any friends; he much preferred going home to watch over
Kai, amusing her until supper was over, when Dojun came
to him in their private place and they began the rough
exercises, the stretches, the bruising falls and rolls and
leaps that gradually grew better; grew quicker and softer
and easier; grew into something as natural as answering a
question when one knew the solution well.

After a year, when Samuel could fall twenty times from
the monkeypod tree in the garden and come up ready to
climb it again, Dojun left his place as butler for Lady Tess
and Lord Gryphon. He went to live in a small house far

up on a knee of Mount Tantalus, where the ferns were like trees and the moths were as big as Samuel's hand. From Dojun's lanai, Samuel could see all the way from Diamond Head to Pearl Harbor. The gray-green sweep of the kukui-nut forest hid the city below; Tantalus was like an earth-scented heaven where the mists drifted in and out and triple rainbows formed above the shoreline and the constant horizon of the sea.

Dojun became a carpenter. He built furniture of koa, running his hands over the smooth wood, the light and dark, the infinite grading from golden blond to chocolate brown, from straight grain to figured—the best was the deep reddish-brown fiddleback grain: the prized "curly" koa—and after school each day Samuel carried endless board feet of it up the mountain on his shoulder for Dojun to work.

Dojun taught him how to use his hands, delicately, shaping the splayed curve of a table's legs in the same way Samuel was learning *shūji*, to draw the bewildering system of Japanese and Chinese characters, using his spirit and his body—making a simple, beautiful line that fit together into a koa-wood stand that looked to Samuel like calligraphy itself. Dojun snorted and said that with writing, Samuel had no art—that was *shodō*, a mastery far beyond Samuel's clumsy efforts, something that a man might devote his whole life to. But when Dojun looked at the woodwork, he criticized and made curt suggestions for improvement, so Samuel thought he was doing very well, and loved the smell of sawed wood and oiled metal.

Samuel made his wood scraps into blocks, carving them into fanciful shapes of birds and flowers, and took them home for Kai. At five—almost six, as she insisted—she found them moderately amusing for a quarter hour, and then wanted him to ride her on her pony and watch her dive in the fish pond.

When he finished the koa stand, he wrapped it carefully in burlap, carried it down the mountain, and gave it to Lady Tess. She put it in her bedroom, right beside her bed, with the rock on it he'd brought from Diamond Head, which looked very silly and homely to him now that he was older.

At school, he was on the blue team. Both the teams wanted him, because he was one of the bigger boys in his class, stronger and more nimble than most, and had more wind than any of them. In one skirmish a boy from blue tripped and fell across Samuel's legs. He sent himself into an easy roll and came up in a crowd of reds, who fell onto him from all sides. He lay face-down at the bottom of the pile, catching his breath as they got off of him one by one.

The bell rang, and everyone ran except the last boy, who didn't get up off Samuel's back, but lay there heavily, breathing in his ear.

Samuel froze.

He felt for a moment as if the real world had vanished; it all went to black; all he heard was an awful sound and then he was sitting on his knees in the long grass, shaking, staring at the other boy and panting viciously.

"Damn—what's the matter with you?" the red boy yelled, picking himself up clumsily. "You knocked me galley-west, you loonie! I oughta make you eat spit."

Samuel just stared at him. He was afraid he was going to be sick, so he only swallowed and didn't say anything.

"Apologize!" the other boy demanded, standing over him.

Samuel's hand trembled beneath him as he shoved himself to his feet. He was taller than the red boy, heavier, but there was something close to a sob stuck in the back of his throat. "I'm sorry," he mumbled.

"What?" The boy stood with his hands on his hips.

"I'm sorry!" Samuel shouted.

The boy grinned. "All right." He reached out to shake hands. Samuel didn't move, and the boy took him around the shoulders, heading toward the school building. Samuel endured the sweaty embrace for half a step, and then pushed him away, sitting down and putting his face in his crossed arms.

One of the teachers was shouting at them. Samuel heard the other boy hesitate, and then run toward the building.

When he came back, the teacher came too, and asked if Samuel was feeling well.

He took a deep breath, stood up, and said, "Yes, sir."

The teacher put his hand on Samuel's forehead. "You're a little clammy. Sit outside in the shade for a few minutes—Wilson, go bring us a dipper of water."

Samuel moved back, not wanting to be touched. "I'm all right," he said. "I want to go in." He forgot to say "sir." He walked past them both and inside the building, sitting down at his desk. Everyone was looking at him curiously, all their white shirts like pale moths in the dark fern-forest shadiness of the classroom.

When he went up Tantalus that afternoon, he was still shaking. He couldn't hold his hands steady with the wood.

"Sick, you?" Dojun demanded in pidgin.

Samuel retrieved the *nomi* chisel that he'd dropped. He wanted to tell Dojun, but he was so ashamed. He never wanted Dojun to know what his old life had been, and there were no words to explain what had happened to him on the school field.

"No, Dojun-san," he said. "I feel fine."

Dojun took the *nomi* from his hand. "You lie me, Samua-chan," he said. "All sick not body."

The way he said it; the word he used with Samuel's name—it was like so many Japanese words, a thousand meanings in one sound—I love you; I'm stronger, wiser, older; I'll take care of you, Samua-chan.

"I'm afraid," Samuel said, staring down at the workbench. "I don't want to go back to school."

Dojun turned the *nomi* and sat down, starting to work on the joining of a chair leg. "For why 'fraid?"

Samuel clenched his empty hands and took a deep breath. "I don't like the other boys," he said, more strongly.

"Fight you?"

He wished they had fought him. He'd like to kill them all, especially the red boy who'd lain on top of him and didn't get up, blowing hot breath against his ear. He thought, for the first time in a long, long time, of the shark and the song, of dark water full of blood. Dojun had never

mentioned the songs again, and Samuel had given up waiting to hear, and then forgotten them, but now when he
thought of it he knew that Dojun had been teaching him
anyway, showing him how to sing songs without words;
with his body and his hands and his head.

"No, Dojun-san," he muttered. "I didn't fight."

"Come here."

Samuel lifted his head and went to stand by the stool
where Dojun worked. Dojun laid the *nomi* aside, carefully
swept some tiny curls of wood into the shavings box. He
stood up—and smashed his open palm across Samuel's
face.

Samuel reeled back under the force of it. He hit the
workbench, grabbed it with his hands and then twisted
away as Dojun moved again. Samuel shied behind the
bench, staring at Dojun, his body pushing back against
the corner between a half-finished *tansu* chest and the wall.

Through the blaze of tears he couldn't even see Dojun
as more than a glimmering shadow among shadows. His
face stung. It didn't hurt so badly; there were a hundred
of Dojun's exercises that had hurt more, but still his body
trembled and he flinched uncontrollably when the smeared
shape in his vision moved.

Dojun. Dojun had hit him. The betrayal of it seemed so
huge that Samuel couldn't think; could only hold himself
up against the wall like a fractured doll, clinging to a
wooden prop.

Dojun took a step toward him, and Samuel winced
again. It felt as if something crucial had collapsed inside
him, crumpled in on itself and liquefied and went sliding
away, taking what he had of himself with it, leaving a
hollow shell that stood there backed in a corner, trembling.

He saw it all as if he were standing outside, looking in,
watching it happen. He saw the tears begin to slide down
his own face, splash down from his chin to his shirt and
make dark spots of moisture.

Dojun stood still. He didn't come any closer. The Samuel who watched had a feeling that Dojun was surprised,

though nothing on his face showed it. The empty shell Samuel just stood there, weeping.

"Samua-san," Dojun said, and Samuel flinched.

Dojun watched him another moment, then went back and sat down on his stool. He adjusted a board in the vise, picked up the *azebiki-noko*, and began to saw a crosscut.

"I'll tell you a story," he said in Japanese. "This is a story all Japanese boys know, but maybe foreign boys don't know it. You should hear it now. It's about the pupil who wants to learn to fight with the sword, so he goes looking for the greatest master who is alive. He follows rumors, and travels into the wild mountains, until he finds a shrine, and beyond that, the hut of a ramshackle hermit. This hermit is the master, a fighter of unequaled skill."

Dojun finished the cut and took the board from the vise, laying it out and measuring it. His hand moved up and down the wood once, caressing it, as a man would touch the neck of a favorite horse.

He spoke again. " 'I'm here to study the sword!' " He imitated the grand way the pupil announced his plans to the hermit with a sweep of his arms. " 'How long will it take me to master it?' The hermit went on with sweeping the floor of his hut. 'Ten years,' the hermit said. The pupil was dismayed. "But what if I study hard and work twice as much?' 'Twenty years,' the master said."

Dojun spread a cloth across his lap. With the *nomi*, he began working to shape another chair joint. He didn't look up from his hands as he spoke.

"The pupil decided not to argue, but asked to be taken on as a student. When the master put his new pupil to work, it was only to chop wood and clean and cook, so many chores that lasted all day and half the night. There was no time for any training with the sword. The pupil never touched a sword, and after a year he grew impatient. 'Master,' he demanded, 'when do we start training? Am I nothing but a slave for you?'

"But the master just ignored him, and the pupil went on with his chores, though he grew more frustrated every day. He was washing clothes one afternoon, thinking about leaving this crazy old man, when a blow from a huge stick sent him staggering. He lay on the ground in a daze, looking up at the master above him. 'Sir,' he cried. 'I was only washing your clothes! I do a good job. Why'd you hit me?' But the master only walked away. The pupil couldn't figure out what he'd done wrong, but he determined to do better.

"The next day he was chopping wood diligently, when the master struck again, sending him flat on the ground with the blow. 'What's wrong?' the student yelled. 'Why are you punishing me?' The master only looked at him in silence, with no sign of anger. The student thought again about leaving. This old man was nuts. The student began to watch out for him, and the next time, when the blow came, the student managed to scramble out of the way. He fell down into a ravine doing it, but he managed to escape.

"After that the attacks began to be more frequent, and the student got better at avoiding them, and finally he began to understand what was going on. But it didn't get any easier. The better the pupil got at avoiding his master's *bokken,* the more often and unexpectedly the master attacked. He came after the student when he was sleeping, and when he was bathing, and when he used the toilet. The pupil thought he would go mad, but slowly his senses grew so sharp that it was almost impossible for the master to catch him. Still the blows came, ten thousand blows, from any place, at any time. Until one day, after the pupil had been at the hut for four years, he was crouched over the fire, preparing vegetables to put into the cooking pot, when the master attacked him from behind. The pupil merely seized a pot lid, warded off the blow, and went back to peeling vegetables without even moving from his position."

The little curls of hard koa fell from Dojun's tool onto the white cloth across his legs. The familiar sound of the *nomi* chiseling into wood made a small, rhythmic scrape in the room.

"From that time," Dojun said, "the pupil became a master, without ever having touched a sword."

Samuel understood what Dojun was telling him. He

wanted to be that tenacious, dedicated, humble student who became a master without ever touching a sword; he wanted it like breathing, like his heart beating, like life. And he huddled there in the corner, knowing that if Dojun hit him again he would not learn to dodge, but would have to go and take up the sharp blade of the Japanese saw and kill himself.

Dojun looked up from the chair leg and into Samuel's eyes. Samuel felt his face go beyond his control. The tears kept squeezing out, as if the liquid despair inside him wouldn't stay trapped, but just leaked and slid out of cracks.

"Please." The word barely came out a whisper. "Dojun-san . . ."

Dojun would send him away. Dojun's training was inflexible, that Samuel knew; nothing given away for a special weakness, a personal limitation, a particular fear of any part of the routine. Dojun offered what he taught as it was; take it or leave it.

Dojun was watching him, his hands motionless in his lap, his eyes intent and unreadable.

He broke the silence abruptly. "I make promise you," he said. "Never hit. Maybe other fella make hit. Me, never."

For a moment Samuel wasn't certain that he understood. He swallowed at the thickness in his throat. "What?" he said hoarsely.

Dojun flicked his hand from his chest toward Samuel. "Me. You. No hit. No time never. Promise. Savvy, yeah?" He never smiled, never took his eyes off Samuel. "You make body believe Dojun, yeah? Head believe. Arm believe. Toe believe."

Samuel only stared at Dojun warily. He knew it when he heard something that was too good to be true.

The Japanese man got up and walked to Samuel, stood in front of him with his legs spread in the *shizen no kamae,* the relaxed stance of readiness that would allow him to move easily in any direction. When he suddenly lifted his hand, Samuel flinched.

Dojun stopped the move with his hand at the level of

Samuel's shoulder, a foot away. "No buy it, eh?" He smiled dryly. "OK. Me you, no buy already either. No stupid, eh?"

He started to turn away. Samuel caught a small movement in the corner of his eye. Before he could recoil, Dojun's hand swung with a lethal flash of white. Samuel stood braced against the wall, his soul dissolving, his eyes wrenched shut to take the blow.

It never came. He felt something like wind on his cheek, and when he managed finally to blink open his watering eyes, Dojun's hand was still there, palm open and frozen in suspension, a bare breath from Samuel's face.

Dojun's fingers came against his skin, feather-soft. "Samua-chan. You believe Dojun. I promise. I no lie. No hit never."

Samuel bit his lower lip, the only way he could keep it from trembling like a baby's. He set his mouth hard against the weakness. "Tell me the word for 'promise,' " he said hoarsely.

"Chikai."

"Promise me in Japanese," Samuel said.

Dojun stepped back, pressed his hands together and made a formal bow. "I pledge to you, Samua-san," he said in his own language, "I will never strike you by intent for any reason."

Slowly, Samuel gathered himself from his position mashed against the corner and stood straight. He put his palms against one another and copied Dojun's obeisance, only he made his twice as deep, to say he was ashamed of himself, and sorry, and would do better, and believed Dojun's promise with every fiber of his being.

Not quite every fiber believed, because when Dojun's knee came up into Samuel's face in the midst of the bow, his eyes squeezed shut automatically and his body started back in self-protection. But he caught the move halfway, just as Dojun stopped the motion of his leg precisely short of impact. Samuel straightened up and stood waiting, trying to pretend the tears of relief and reprieve that were coursing down his face didn't exist.

Dojun ignored them also. He seated himself again and

went back to work on his chair leg. "No like boys down school, *sō,*" he said, as if all the intervening crisis had never occurred.

Samuel picked up a piece of sandpaper and fiddled with it, testing the rough edge against his finger. "It's not so bad, I guess," he said—and it truly didn't seem so terrible, compared to how close he'd just come to utter annihilation.

"School-time, lotta fight boy. Fight bad thing, Samua-san. Dojun no like fight. OK, yeah, but boy don't fight, only know two thing make for why. Boy scare. One thing. Boy too damn good never lose, two thing. You scare?"

"I'm not scared."

"You say scare, no wanna go back down school."

Samuel busied himself with sanding the planed side of the *tansu* chest. His cheek still ached from Dojun's slap.

"You no scare. You good fight, eh?"

The sandpaper swished in a faster rhythm. Samuel bent over his work. "I've never had a fight."

"Hey, I gonna teach fight, OK? Dojun damn good fight. Tiger-song, Samua-san. Remember tiger-song?"

"I remember."

The strike flashed out of nowhere; Samuel saw it as Dojun's fist rushed up under his chin. He jerked, freezing with Dojun's hand just touching his jaw. He hadn't even heard the Japanese man come up behind him.

Dojun moved back slowly. "Time here now. Listen good." He held up his hand, and Samuel saw that it was closed in a fist, with only the little finger extended. Dojun opened his hand and made a fanning motion, as if scaring away a fly.

"Only one thing bad, Samua-san. You fight, somebody gonna hit. Me no hit, make *chikai,* got honor, no hit you. Dojun teach all day good fight, work, work, work. Samua-san learn how number-one fight, *sō.* Then you go out, one time get hit—*kotsun!*" He slapped the heels of his hands together with a sharp sound. "You hurt, you stop fight, you one dead duck."

Samuel didn't have an answer to that. He put his head down and went back to sanding the *tansu,* and thought of taking the air all the way down into his body when he breathed, to calm himself.

"OK," Dojun said. "OK. Sometime me, you, go down Chinatown, find somebody hit you."

Thirteen

◈

The maid who arrived in the morning with tea and fruit informed Leda that m'lady wished Miss Etoile to know the family would be attending the second service, and if it was convenient for miss to join them, the victoria would be ready at half-past nine, but if she wished to rest herself this morning, she was most welcome to do so.

The maid with hot tea and the simple, thoughtful message added to the dreamlike sensation Leda had felt upon awakening beneath a gold-and-blue canopy to fresh sunlight and creamy flowers. If she had thought about it at all, she would have assumed she would attend church quietly, slipping out of the house alone—or perhaps, just this once, neglect going in order to lie in bed and imbibe the amazing luxury of her surroundings. But declining Lady Ashland's invitation was unthinkable: she hastily assured the maid that she would be honored to accompany the family to service.

Leda had never eaten pineapple, bananas, and oranges for breakfast before. Miss Myrtle had sometimes peeled an orange for dessert after dinner, but she had not much cared for any item which was not readily subdued with knife and fork. Pineapple was not something that heretofore had formed part of Leda's experience. After the maid showed her how to remove the presliced crown and extract the sections that had already been cut inside the tough, prickly shell, Leda wasn't entirely certain that the fruit was worth the trouble. It had a tangy, sourish taste that did not appeal. However, there was excellent toast, still warm and soaked in butter, and the tea tasted divine as she sat next the open window and sipped it just as she had been used to do in her own bedroom at Miss Myrtle's.

Her black silk appeared, pressed and freshened. Leda was well-used to dressing herself and made certain that she was prompt to meet the family in the front hall. They were just as friendly and indulgent as they had been the night before, and by the time the carriage reached Hanover Square, Lady Catherine had managed to give a full account of last night's dinner party. She particularly wished Leda to tell her if she had done the proper thing by declining the decanter of wine which the host had passed to her at dessert, because he had looked a little perplexed when she had done so.

After a more detailed inquiry, Leda made the conjecture that the host had meant to pass the wine decanter to the gentleman just beyond Lady Catherine, since a second glass of wine at dessert was something a lady was not supposed to require, and even if she did, by no means should she help herself to it, but the gentleman seated next to her would fill her glass.

"So you did very well to decline," she assured Lady Catherine, "but perhaps he was concerned that the decanter didn't go round the table then. Next time you may decline, and indicate to the gentleman next to you that he should fill his glass if he likes, and then things will proceed the way the gentlemen prefer. But I daresay they won't be any the worse for not having had a second glass with dessert for one night."

Lord Ashland and his son denounced that sentiment with good-humored jeers. "We need all the brain anesthetic we can get at these flings," Lord Ashland said.

"Why, whatever do you *mean*, sir?" his wife inquired archly, sitting up straight and fanning herself. "I'm sure it's the very *best* society, and the conversation is *most* uplifting, and the sooner one finds oneself falling asleep, the more select one may assume the company to be."

"Well, I like it," Lady Catherine said cheerfully. "Some people are a little dull, it's true, but they try so hard to make us welcome, and get so fluttery and anxious about something going wrong, that I can't help but feel a little sorry for them.''

"When you ruined their party by not passing the wine, you silly cluck!'' Her brother reached over and patted her knee. "Wait'll Mother brings one of her pet jaguars to a ball because the poor thing's too sick to be left alone. They'll forget all about the wine.''

"I never brought Vicky to a *ball*, Robert. It was a charity luncheon. And I could not cancel because I was to speak.'' Lady Ashland looked at Leda with a self-conscious dip of her chin, for all the world like a green girl caught with a spot of jam on her nose. "No one minded in the least, I assure you. She was never off the leash.''

Leda found herself nodding in spite of her bemusement; she couldn't have helped herself from it, even if she hadn't caught Lord Ashland's teasing wink.

"This is Victoria the Fifth who attended the luncheon,'' he said soberly to Leda. "She's presently returned to hold court in her country seat. We find we've supported quite an ancient lineage of jaguars in Sussex from afar.''

"Taken over Westpark, the artful devils,'' Lord Robert complained. "Fine thing, when a fellow finally gets a first look at his ancestral acres and can't walk around the garden without some jaguar leaping through the bushes and scaring the wits out of him.''

"And we won't even *discuss* the boa constrictor,'' Lady Catherine added.

"Keeps the riffraff out,'' their father said blandly.

Their mother cleared her throat, plied her fan, and maintained a dignified silence until they reached the church.

In the late-afternoon light, the drawing room of Morrow House seemed very airy, in spite of the massively carved marble hearth and majestic plasterwork ceiling. Against a background of faded gold damask walls, the furnishings were a strangely pleasant mixture of gilt-and-needlepoint love seats, bamboo chairs of the japonaiserie style, a plump sofa covered in multi-flowered chintz, and several lovely, simple tables of shining wood and alien design.

As Leda looked about her, she finally realized that the effect of lightness arose from the fact that, instead of the endless collections of picture frames and figurines and albums and antimacassars that made most drawing rooms she knew into cozy, cluttered nests, the tables and mantelpiece of Morrow House were bare of anything but more living orchids. Out in the conservatory that opened off the drawing room over Park Lane, the exotic blooms made spots of rich pink and purple color among the more mundane potted kentia palms and aspidistras.

Lady Ashland would not allow gas to be lit in the house, for it killed her flowers. The family were very particular in their requirements, the housekeeper had advised Leda in that manner that a good servant had: communicating with deferential loftiness that they were as strange as Chinamen. In order to safeguard the orchids and yet avoid a return to tallow and torches, Mr. Gerard himself had caused the house to be electrified on an earlier trip to London last year, among other prearrangements for the whole family's first return to England in two decades—including having a closed cooking range, refrigerator, and ice cream freezer installed in the kitchen, the conservatory added along the entire front of the house overlooking Park Lane, filling the whole place with the rare tropical plants, and hiring a greenhouseman to care for them full time until the family arrived.

Her hosts really were quite endearingly outlandish, Leda thought. Lady Catherine, having returned with her mother from a Sunday garden tea, had knocked on Leda's door in person, given her a piece of seedcake the girl had brought home in a lace "hanky," as she called it, and begged Leda to come down and join everyone for cold supper in the drawing room. The girl was now busily plumping pillows around Mr. Gerard in his place by the front windows. Leda wasn't quite certain what his feelings were about the attention; she thought Lady Catherine was perhaps not aware of how much it must hurt his leg to be padded and adjusted in that enthusiastic way, but he bore it with heroic calm. No doubt the new plaster dressing helped to protect him, but Leda saw the strain in his smile.

Lady Ashland must have seen it, too, for she lifted her head from the notebook in which she'd been writing and said, "For goodness sakes, Kai, you're all but killing him."

Her daughter straightened up, looking stricken. "Oh, no! Have I been hurting you, Manō? You should have told me!"

"It doesn't hurt," he said.

Leda wondered if the man ever admitted that he felt any sort of bodily distress at all.

Lady Catherine, however, just gave a sigh of relief. "Good. I'll only slip this pillow—"

"Kai!" her mother said warningly.

Leda saw Mr. Gerard and Lady Catherine exchange a look, the brief communication of two people who knew one another very well. "Perhaps you might bring me a book," he said.

"There isn't a book worth reading in this house," Lady Catherine declared, settling herself in a chair next to Leda. "Let's talk story."

"You humbug *wahine,* talk-talk story all time plenty," her brother said, strolling into the room and brushing her hair as he passed her. "Bumbye no got tongue left."

"Close you ear, you no like, you," she responded promptly.

"Mo' bettah mahke-die-dead you mout', blala."

"It isn't nice to speak pidgin when Miss Etoile won't understand it," Lady Catherine said righteously, and turned to Leda. "Did you know that Samuel once saved my life, Miss Etoile?"

"No, I didn't," Leda said politely.

"From a *shark,*" Lady Catherine said, with a theatrical lowering of her voice. "A great white shark, as long as from here to . . . that table."

"Talk-talk," her brother said, from the chair where he'd settled in with the newspaper.

"That's why we call him Manō," she continued, without a pause. " 'Manō' is 'shark,' and 'kane' is the word

for 'man.' '' She pronounced it "kah-nay." "Manō Kane.
Shark-man. The princess herself named him that. It was
a very great honor—because he was only ten or eleven
years old, and he held me up out of the water on his shoulders while the shark went right past, like this—" She
leaned over and made a graceful, sinister curving motion
with her hand, passing within an inch of Leda's arm, and
then turned with a snap of her fingers all together that
made Leda jump. "It was that close. It could have eaten
us both. Chop-chop."

"Would that it had," Lord Robert's voice floated from
behind his paper.

"Honestly, Robert!" Lady Catherine flounced back in
her seat.

"Well, I've only heard you tell this story about a hundred thousand times. You'd think you'd fought the dratted
fish off with your own bare hands."

"It's a good story!"

He bent a corner of his paper down and looked at them
over the top of it. "Why not let Samuel tell it himself for
once? Might get a whole new angle on the thing."

"Oh, yes!" Lady Catherine sat up and leaned over the
arm of her chair toward Mr. Gerard. "Do tell it, Manō!
Were you afraid? I was too little to even know what was
happening, Miss Etoile, so I wasn't really afraid. But I do
recollect the shark. It was huge, wasn't it?"

Mr. Gerard seemed to be more interested in his fist
resting on the arm of his chair than in the size of the shark.
"I don't remember," he said mildly.

Leda could see why it was Lady Catherine who usually
did the story-telling honors.

"Well, it was huge. Wasn't it, Mother?"

Lady Ashland took a deep breath. "Hideous," she said
briefly. "And huge."

"They never caught it," Mr. Gerard said.

It seemed a casual comment, but some undertone in his
voice made Leda glance at him. He was still looking at
his hand—until he slanted a glance of cool gray toward
her. She had almost said, "What a shame," but she held
her tongue when she met his eyes. He did not think it was

a shame that the shark had never been caught. He was pleased.

How she knew that, she could not have said. But she knew it.

He seemed about to speak again, and for the first time Leda allowed herself to look directly at him for longer than the briefest of instants. Though he said little, he seemed to drain her attention so effectively that she had to labor just to make civil conversation. She actually had to strive against the temptation to sit and gaze at him like some ill-bred pumpkin, for Michelangelo's mastery could not have created a more superb tribute to the human form than Mr. Gerard presented in living reality.

He was truly, forcefully beautiful, in a way Leda had never before known a man could be, outside of paintings and idealized art. One had, on occasion, seen gentlemen one might term "handsome," or possibly even "fine-looking"; one did not as a rule see Apollo and Mars and Mercury fused into human shape and crowned like a ruined angel with hair of sunlight and eyes of hoarfrost . . . not, in any event, dressed in a smoking jacket and sitting with one leg propped up on pillows, quite in the manner of a tame man about the house.

A frown drifted into his expression while she held his look. Abruptly, as if she had disturbed him, his glance traveled back to Lady Catherine. It had seemed perfectly proper that Leda give him her whole attention, because he had appeared to be about to add something to the conversation, but the way he looked away so pointedly mortified her.

No doubt she had been staring. Most probably all sorts of vulgar people stared at him. He must be weary of it, and glad to be among those who had known him long enough to be accustomed to his appearance. The Ashlands did not give his flawless countenance the least notice. Even Lady Catherine, amid her solicitous attentions as she hopped up to take his supper tray from the maid and arrange it herself on a table beside him, only gave him a fond glance and a pat of her hand when she finished—just as if he had been a favorite uncle with the gout.

Leda was not overly familiar with the conduct of lovers in general, but the conduct of this pair seemed to her to be singular. His intent gaze followed Lady Catherine all the while she prattled on about the shark, and the tea party, and interrogated Leda on what was best to see in London. He clearly worshiped her. Leda could not imagine a man more obviously in love—or a girl with less notion of his regard. She treated him with wonderful devotion, and an utter lack of real attention, running ahead into the dining room to see that he had every variety of food from the cold buffet, never noticing that it was impossible for him to reach over and eat from the tray where she'd placed it without angling his leg in what must be quite a painful position.

Lord Robert was standing by the door—waiting for Leda to precede him to the dining room, she realized. Lady Catherine had already drawn her mother impatiently ahead; the girl's voice echoed in the hall, greeting her father, who had just come in from his own afternoon engagement. Lord Robert made a pleased exclamation and stepped out of the drawing room to join them.

Leda paused at the door and looked back at Mr. Gerard. She took a breath, walked over to his table, and set the tray in his lap, turning away without daring to look up into his face. She did not wish to make a bustle about it, but really, if the gentleman was too moonstruck to give his ladylove a small hint about his common comfort, then something must be done for him.

As she made for the door, he murmured his thanks, but she took a quick step into the marble-floored hall and pretended not to hear.

The same maid brought her another message the next morning with her tea. From Mr. Gerard. He wished her to attend him at nine o'clock in the conservatory, instead of the library.

Leda was aware that the rest of the family was leaving the house shortly before that time in order to join the Hawaiian party at the Alexandria Hotel, where Queen Kapiolani and the princess awaited their summons to a private audience with Her Majesty after she arrived in London. Leda wasn't quite certain whether Mr. Gerard would have been one of this party if he'd been able-bodied—she had yet to discern precisely in what relationship he stood to the family. He distinctly resembled Lord Ashland in his coloring, although there was no other particular likeness. Indeed, Lord Ashland was an exceedingly well-looking man, with a noble profile and a fine daredevil grin, but even in his youth he could not have equaled Mr. Gerard. Leda guessed that perhaps her employer was a cousin of some sort.

Whatever his affiliation, it was clear that he would not be attending any festivities in his present circumstance. Also obvious was that no one of respectable standing was going to be left in the house. Leda would be alone with him and the servants.

Given that to be the situation, she far preferred the conservatory, with its doors opening into rooms all along the house, to the secluded library for any meeting between herself and Mr. Gerard. But if she had been asked her opinion, she personally would have desired to have no private encounter at all with a bachelor under the present circumstances. Furthermore, in order to observe the proprieties, she was perfectly willing to put on her hat and gloves and join the crowds below in Park Lane waiting to see the Queen. She was aware that her opinion had not been solicited; nevertheless, she fully intended to offer it.

She sat down and wrote a short note to Mr. Gerard, cataloging her reasons why their conference should be set back until a more appropriate time. After sending it off with the maid, she received a prompt answer.

Who do you imagine is watching us? it asked succinctly. It wasn't even signed or sealed.

Leda reseated herself at the delicate French desk and pulled another piece of notepaper from the drawer.

The servants, she wrote. She folded the paper into an envelope, sealed it with extreme care, and forwarded it by the housemaid to Mr. Gerard.

The reply came with alacrity. *I thought you a modern woman, Miss Etoile.*

Leda felt her temper begin to rise. Her handwriting suffered a little from extra emphasis at the end of each word. *I would not wish to embarrass my extremely kind hosts with indiscreet behavior.*

The answer to that was slightly longer in coming. This time it was sealed into an envelope as hers had been.

Do I understand you to mean that I must employ someone of my own sex in order to have ordinary business commerce with my secretary? Please give your answer the most earnest consideration.

I hope to see you at nine o'clock, Miss Etoile.

Leda read this under the innocently averted eyes of the maid, who stood waiting with her hands clasped. Feeling rather unnerved, Leda glanced at the little porcelain clock on the desk. It was five minutes to the appointed hour.

"Where is Mr. Gerard at present?" she asked the maid.

"In the conservatory, miss. He took his breakfast there. It's the best place to watch from. All the staff, we've been given leave to collect there from nine o'clock until the Queen herself passes, so that we may overlook the street. The crowds is gatherin' something wonderful. You can hear it if you open the window."

Leda busied herself with the drawer in the desk in order to hide the scarlet heat that she felt mounting in her face. "There is no reply," she said quickly. "Please go on, so that you may see everything."

The maid dropped a curtsy. "Thank you, miss." She turned and shut the door.

Leda pressed her palms together against her lips. He had not intended a private meeting at all, of course. What an incredible fool she had made of herself now, and nearly sacrificed her place because of it. She could put no other construction upon that last line of his note but a pointed, and deserved, reminder of her situation. She was expected to act in every capacity as a gentleman would act in the position of secretary—as he had a perfect right to demand of her, after all, if she wished to occupy the post.

It was difficult to compose herself and go downstairs.

She had only a moment; under the particular circumstances, she did not wish to be an instant late. She was sure that her face was still fierily red as she stepped through the open French doors that led to the conservatory. The temptation to hide behind a pair of tweeny maids who were giggling between themselves and hanging back from Mr. Gerard's vicinity was extremely strong. But the butler Sheppard spoke sharply to the chortling young girls, calling them to order, and Leda was left with nothing to do but present herself to her employer.

He looked considerably more at ease this morning, sprawled in the corner of a wicker sofa that faced the open glass doors overlooking the street, with his splint stretched out the length of the plump cushions, his other foot on the floor and his arm resting along the back of the couch. A pair of crutches lay propped against the plant stand beside him. On either side of the doors opening onto the terrace, flag stands held the Union Jack and the second banner that decorated Morrow House, which Leda surmised was the flag of Hawaii.

He lifted his hand and propped his cheek against it as Leda stepped into full view. "Miss Etoile," he murmured. "I'm so glad you could see your way clear to join us."

"Good morning, Mr. Gerard," she said in a brisk voice that came out a shade too loudly. "What may I do to be of service?"

He regarded her for a long moment; long enough that Leda was certain the gathering staff must be taking notice of the way he seemed to assess her from the inside out.

"Sheppard," he said at last, and nodded at a chair placed at a sociable angle to his sofa. "Bring Miss Etoile the *Illustrated News,* and she can read to us about the occasion."

The butler bowed and vanished for a moment, returning with an ironed copy of *The Illustrated London News.* Leda felt painfully self-conscious, but she folded the paper, selected an article describing the observances to be expected, and began to read. By the time she had reached the third paragraph, she was aware of a slow migration of the gathering nearer to her vicinity.

She went on reading, moving down the page to the next story, a preview of the gown to be worn by the Princess of Wales. At the end of that, she looked up, and found everyone in the conservatory watching her expectantly.

"Pardon me, miss," one of the tweenies said diffidently. "If you please, miss, might you read again the part about the dress?"

Leda complied. She found herself relaxing into her chair. This was not so very difficult; she had often read to the South Street ladies; she knew just what would be of interest. She skipped the political columns and searched for every item of news about the Jubilee, of which there were many.

A cup of tea appeared on the table next to her. She looked up with a glance of thanks at the parlor maid in her crisp white cap and flounced apron. While Leda had been reading, at the far end of the conservatory the kitchen staff had set a table with a festive array of light luncheon food, but everyone else was still gathered around her with intent faces. She grew daring, and concluded her reading with a droll advertisement for the Patented Patriotic Bustle, which was guaranteed to play "God Save the Queen" whenever the wearer sat down.

The scullery maids found that impossibly funny, especially after Sheppard solemnly pointed out what an exhausting device it must be, since every good Englishman must immediately stand up upon hearing the tune. Even the French chef laughed.

The crowds in the street had been a low roar all morning, but now a different, more excited note rose from below. It was half past eleven—the great moment was approaching. Sheppard asked if Mr. Gerard wished to move to the terrace for a better view, but it was evident the butler's offer of help was merely nominal; Mr. Gerard showed himself perfectly capable of standing up and retrieving his crutches himself. Leda was fairly sure that his main wish was to be left untouched, instead of being pushed and pulled and otherwise mauled by overeager helpers. Sheppard appeared to have divined this, too, merely standing back and directing a footman to place chairs outside for sir and miss.

From the small terrace over the front door, they had a fabulous view up and down Park Lane. As Leda and Mr. Gerard emerged, the spectators just below Morrow House gave a cheer, as if they were notables in their own right. With an ironic smile, Mr. Gerard discarded a crutch, reached back, and lifted first the Union Jack and then the Hawaiian flag from their holders. He thrust the British banner into Leda's hand and limped forward on one crutch, pushing her along with his other arm. The crowd flowed and rumbled. He looked at her with his eyebrows raised expectantly.

Feeling exceedingly audacious, Leda lifted her heavy pole in a tentative wave. He raised his; his arm took it higher than hers, and suddenly he reached out and locked his hand over her fingers, lifting the weight of both banners to full height. The light breeze unfurled their full expanse, spreading royal color. The crowd's cheers grew to a roar of appreciation. The sound rolled away as all the spectators along the street took it up, a sensation like nothing Leda had ever experienced. Her heart filled to bursting with pride and loyalty for her country—and even, in a strange way, for the faraway, unimaginable islands that Mr. Gerard's flag represented.

She stood with a wide smile, her arm raised alongside his, the flags draping and fluttering against her shoulder and then streaming out under a puff of wind, the sunlight of a perfect day pouring down over the park and the mass of people. The sound of distant music beat over the noise; from the corner of her eyes she could see the bunting and flags that decorated Morrow House as they, too, lifted and swung in the soft air.

He lowered the banners, resting the shafts on the terrace without removing his hand from overtop hers. She glanced toward him, unable to hide her enthusiasm, and found him watching her past the folds of the flags. He grinned.

Leda felt something happen in the vicinity of her stomach; something breathless and sensational—oh, really, she thought in sudden alarm, if she didn't watch what she was about, she would find herself in the suds, rather.

She looked quickly away, and tried to withdraw her hand. For an instant he didn't let go, and then he did, leaving her with the staff of the Union Jack. The flags blew between them so that she couldn't see his face.

For Leda, the rest of the event seemed anticlimactic, though the crowd cheered themselves silly for the Life Guards and the Queen herself when they came, passing in brilliant formation, and Leda and Mr. Gerard held their flags in salute to Her Majesty's carriage—separately, this time—and the dear, stout, frog-faced Queen even glanced up at Morrow House and gave them a gracious nod as she passed . . . and Leda made an appalling discovery about herself: that she would be quite happy to trade the personal recognition of Her Majesty the Queen of England, Scotland, Wales, Ireland, and Empress of India for one casual, intimate smile from Mr. Gerard on any day.

Fourteen
~~~~~~~~~~
Kai

⊛

Hawaii, 1876

They didn't go to Chinatown for a long time. Dojun
taught Samuel fighting strikes, how to use his thumbs and
his fingers and toes as weapons. He learned strangleholds,
and toughened his hands and feet by using them against
the rough bark of a koa tree. Dojun hung a big, smooth
stone from a rafter, and Samuel butted his forehead against
it until hot stinging tears ran down his face.

He learned to evade, too. He learned to watch for Dojun's secret strikes—and when he was too slow to elude
the hit, which was often, Dojun stopped it a hairsbreadth
from completion. There were still the other exercises, too,
the breathing and *taihenjutsu* rolls and breakfalls, and new
things: how to care for a sword, how to judge one, the
history and names of the greatest blades; practicing to walk
in silence, to watch for hiding places in every destination;
learning to inhale the steam from a cup of tea and identify
it out of twenty-two varieties on Dojun's shelf, to sit motionless for hours and absorb the world, noting things
he'd never noticed before—because any tiny thing might
matter.

His time with Dojun came to seem farther and farther
from the rest of his life. No one at home ever appeared to
think anything of it; they knew he went to Tantalus to
practice carpentry, and the rest of it was, by unspoken
consent, a secret between him and his teacher. Samuel
went to school, keeping his distance from the other boys,
and went to Dojun, and then came home and played with

Kai. At dinner he talked about what he was studying in mathematics with Lord Gryphon, and watched Lady Tess when she smiled, and felt safe again and lucky.

When Kai was seven, she crept downstairs and saw a waltz at a ball that Lady Tess gave in honor of Mr. and Mrs. Dominis' wedding anniversary. It was a particularly grand occasion because Mrs. Dominis was no longer simply Lydia, she was the new king's sister, and now called the Princess Lili'uokalani. Upon discovering the dresses and lights and music, Kai decided she must have dancing lessons and be known as Lady Catherine.

Of course Robert would have none of it, and Kai refused to accept the notion of a female partner, so Samuel became her beau for practice. At fifteen, or possibly sixteen—he had never known his birthday—he was so much taller than she that she only came up to his waist, but he didn't mind the task—he teased her to see her giggle and preen and pretend she was a grown-up lady.

He loved Kai. He always had. He'd forgone Lord Gryphon's offer to legally adopt him years ago, when he was no more than eleven, because he'd been sure that he was going to marry her, although he never said so out loud. He was still certain now, long after he'd realized that it was an intention considerably more weighty than he'd understood at the time.

But he could wait for Kai. He was determined to. He kept himself decent, he thrust away the dreams and thoughts that shamed him, he governed his body with Dojun's work. It was a relief to be with Kai; he never felt with her the way he felt when he saw one of the Hawaiian women canter along the street astride a raw-boned mount, with her feet bare and her hair unwound, falling down her back in waves that haunted his days and nights.

The visions seemed to come out of the walls and the sky and the air; fantasies of women spreading arms and legs, flashes of things he remembered, female curves and female skin. Once he was standing in a hardware store in Honolulu while Lord Gryphon placed an order for glass jars for Lady Tess, when one of the American wives walked in. She stopped a moment to speak to Lord

Gryphon, a cheerful figure in a modest dress, and Samuel caught the scent of her: an intimate, secret, explicit scent that blossomed in his brain.

He stood paralyzed. He knew that scent; he saw her head thrown back on a pillow, her face flushed and her breasts arched. His body suffused with heat and hunger and loathing. He could not bear the sight of her. He turned away and imagined pressing his face to her belly and breathing that salty, strong aroma, craving the taste until she filled him up to exploding.

The things he invented shocked him. He wanted to shout at her to go home and bathe herself; to leave him alone.

He left the store and stood in the street, breathing deeply. Without waiting for Lord Gryphon, he began to walk, then run. He found Kai in the front parlor at home, practicing at her scales on the piano, a gloomy scowl on her face as the teacher corrected her frequent flat notes. Samuel sat down in a chair in the corner of the cool room, facing a window where the sweet, clean breeze blew across his face, listening to the notes go up and down, and up and down, over and over.

Kai was his. He protected her. He was going to make sure her life was always exactly as it should be. Nothing was ever going to hurt her or frighten her or make her really cry. He loved her, and when she was old enough, she was going to love him.

When summer vacation came, Lord Gryphon asked Samuel if any position at the Arcturus Company held an interest as a future career. Samuel went to work in the harbor office, profoundly pleased with the suggestion that Lord Gryphon thought of him as a protegé. Sitting among the logs, poring over shipping manifests and warehouse inventories, he learned the accounts of the enterprise, and slowly, with astonishment, came to realize that the shipping company was really just an avocation for his foster father; that the reason there weren't enough steamships and too much profit was poured into maintaining the sailing fleet was simply because Lord Gryphon loved his sailing ships and had the money to waste lavishly on them.

Lord Gryphon was rich. Astronomically rich. Samuel had never had the faintest notion of what his foster family must be worth until he saw the money that flowed through the company books. They lived well, but nowhere nearly as grandly as half the American businessmen in Honolulu. The Arcturus fleet was better manned and better maintained than any other, and it barely broke even with the competition. It was a wealthy man's form of amusement, with one ship always moored in Honolulu harbor for Lord Gryphon to command if the mood took him to do it.

The office agents were happy to educate Samuel as to the real source of the money: Lord Gryphon's ancestral holdings in England, and the huge trust he managed for his wife. As Samuel listened to the details, his heart grew cold with dismay.

Kai's parents were unthinkably wealthy. He could not offer himself with nothing.

He trained with Dojun and worked all summer at the shipping office. When September came, he told Lord Gryphon that he'd rather continue his position there than return to school. Lady Tess seemed distressed, and said his schoolwork was so excellent that she'd hoped perhaps he would think of college—but that meant the United States or England. It meant leaving. He tried to convince her that he knew some of the boys who'd gone to Harvard, and the young men who'd returned. They were elegant and sophisticated, and liked to show it, but they were stupid. She talked of Oxford and education. He said that he enjoyed the shipping work, and promised to read all the same books they read at Oxford. She said that he deserved better instruction than Honolulu could provide. Finally, he locked his hands together behind his back and stood facing away from her, staring out into the sparkling shade of the lanai, and asked her not to send him away.

Not yet.

Please God, not yet.

And she didn't.

Samuel decided that it was not his place to tell Lord Gryphon how to conduct his business. He worked, and learned. When the books showed that a certain Ling Hoo was skimming ten percent off the warehouse stocks each time they passed through his hands, Samuel didn't mention it to anyone else. He simply walked up Tantalus one day and asked Dojun if it was time to go to Chinatown.

Fifteen

❖

Somehow, Leda had thought the second day of the Ju-
bilee would go much the same as the first. The family was
again to be away, of course—their part of the procession
to Westminster Abbey for the Thanksgiving service was to
leave Buckingham Palace at 10.45, and they were to present themselves at the Pimlico entrance to Buckingham at
quarter past the hour. Leda had spent the evening listening
to a detailed account of their private audience with the
Queen, which had taken place just after Queen Kapiolani
and the princess had left Her Majesty.

It seemed to have gone off well—there hadn't been much
time for any peculiarities to manifest themselves in the ten
minutes they were with the Queen, but Lady Ashland kept
saying, "Thank goodness *that's* over! I'm so relieved
nothing happened!"—which led to the conjecture that she
was not entirely unaware of her family's potential for social calamity, and made Leda want to hug her reassuringly.

Instead, she tried to help in whatever way she could in
the preparations for the next ordeal, or adventure, or fusty
old nuisance, depending on which member of the Ashlands happened to be speaking about it at the time. Leda
made certain by a personal visit that Lady Catherine was
up at five A.M., and consulted with her on her hair, which
would not take a crimp and had to be pressed out with the
iron and wound in a heavy, dark coil on top by the maid,
while Leda concentrated on the placement of the head-
piece for the most fashionable effect. By luck, both Lady
Catherine and Lord Robert had inherited their mother's

aquamarine eyes and thick, charcoal eyelashes—a most handsome combination that was flattered by any color range from black to pastel, so although Leda would have chosen blue for her, Lady Catherine's daffodil satin trimmed with ribbon of jade-green was very becoming.

The girl rather balked at having her corset laced tightly enough, but Leda was firm, pointing out the unattractive wrinkles which the proper lacing smoothed out. Lady Catherine then took it upon herself to seek out her mother and harass her into a similar hourglass shape. At some moment in their hasty traverses from bedroom to bedroom, Leda received her message from Mr. Gerard, again appointing the conservatory for a meeting, but she barely glanced at it before moving to check a badly wrinkled fold in Lady Ashland's train.

By half past nine, they were all assembled in the hall, while Leda performed a last-minute inspection, making certain that Lord Ashland had the Lord Chamberlain's ticket of admission, instructing Lord Robert to keep his cocked hat under his arm and by no means to forget that he was wearing a sword with his dark blue velvet court dress, since he seemed inclined to turn about and stab the ladies without realizing it. Lady Ashland looked so pale and uneasy in her simple, elegant, lilac watered-silk that Leda gave in to her impulse to hug, whispering, "Everything's quite perfect, m'lady. Don't worry a moment!"

Her Ladyship smiled suddenly, and squeezed Leda's hand. "If only one of us doesn't do something too very conspicuous!"

Leda stood back. "I must tell you, ma'am, that at Madame Elise's I've dressed half the ladies who will be present, and there is not one of them so beautiful, nor with such handsome escorts. Not even the Princess of Wales. So if you find people staring at you, you must remember that it's in admiration."

"Manō!" Lady Catherine cried. "Come down and look at us! Miss Etoile says we will be the most beautiful ladies and gentlemen there! And she knows what she's talking about."

Leda glanced up to see Mr. Gerard on the stairway. He

came down on his crutches and stopped on the bottom step, leaning on the newel post. "Obviously she does. Your magnificence is blinding."

"Oh, I do so wish you could go," Lady Catherine said. "And you, too, Miss Etoile. It's not fair!"

Before either of them could answer, Sheppard stepped inside from the portico and announced that the carriage was at their service. Lord Ashland took his wife's arm. "Let's not ruin Miss Etoile's good efforts by being late. Kai—can you manage to let Robert escort you out the door?"

With all the exaggerated style of a princess, Lady Catherine offered her gloved hand to her brother, who made a little bow and tucked it under his arm, turning with a careful move that kept his sword free of her train. Leda applauded.

Their parents followed, looking every inch the Marquess and Marchioness of Ashland, Leda thought proudly. She did wish it were possible to see how they shone among the noble assembly that would grace Westminster.

"It really is too bad about your injury," she said, turning to Mr. Gerard as the butler and a footman followed the party outside, closing the door behind them. "What a shame that you can't go with them."

"I wouldn't have gone in any case." He stood with his splint resting against the lip of the stair, his trousers inset with extra material along the outside seam to cover the dressing, his foot encased in a dark sock. "Not invited."

"Oh." Leda gave her skirt an embarrassed twitch. "I thought—I didn't realize—that is . . . I thought it was your indisposition," she finished lamely.

"No," he said, with a faint smile, "it's that no one knows who the devil I am."

She looked at him standing easily, his arm around the ornate newel post. *I know who you are,* she thought with a sudden tingle at the base of her spine. *A thief.*

An amazing, mystifying thief, who could walk the night like a jungle cat. Who moved about gracefully in cast and crutches not four days after breaking a bone.

She cleared her throat. "I see," she said, trying to sound as if that were a commonplace revelation.

He let go of the post and put his crutch tips on the marble floor of the hall, easing himself down the last step. "I'm adopted, more or less. Fostered. In Hawaii, they call it *hānai*. In England, they don't seem to know what to term it."

"Oh," she said again. She thought of saying more, but couldn't quite bring herself to admit that she too was—rather adopted, more or less. She glanced instead at the clock that hung over a side table. "It's approaching ten o'clock. I believe you wished to join everyone in the conservatory again, Mr. Gerard?"

"That will be quite satisfactory, Miss Etoile," he said.

She ignored the mocking tone and proceeded to the appointed place, fully expecting to see the same gathering of servants. It was when she reached the empty gallery, overlooking a street nearly as crowded as it had been the day before, but this morning full of pedestrians and carriages all headed south, that it dawned upon her today was not at all the same as yesterday—the procession would not pass Morrow House, of course; not on the way to Westminster. There was nothing to watch from the conservatory, and no staff gathered there.

She took this circumstance in the nature of a gross betrayal, and tried very hard to recollect how Mr. Gerard had led her into believing that the servants were to assemble today, too, in the conservatory. The fact that she could not actually determine on any specific evidence that he had said so only made her feel further misused; when he arrived on his crutches a few moments after her, she refused to be seated, but lifted her eyebrows and said freezingly, "I believe you would be more comfortable with Sheppard in attendance."

"Sheppard has the day off," he said, lowering himself with his arm braced against the back of the overstuffed wicker settee. He lifted his lashes. "All the staff does. There's meat for sandwiches in the refrigerator. I hope you don't mind fixing them?"

Leda's mouth fell open, and then shut with a snap. "Yes,

I do mind! I mind very much! I have an idea of your station, and the distinction of this house, if you do not. *Who* gave them all the day free, if I may be so bold as to inquire?''

He seemed a little taken aback at her vehemence. ''I did.''

''And Lord and Lady Ashland agreed?''

''The staff here is my responsibility, Miss Etoile. No one else will be home until after five; there's the Thanksgiving service and then some tremendous luncheon and review at Buckingham Palace—I doubt they'll be back here before dark. Why keep the servants sitting, when they might be off watching the great day?''

Leda was unwilling to admit to any soundness in such a flimsy defense as that. ''They need not have sat.'' She began to pace up and down the conservatory in her agitation. ''There is dinner to think of, when the family arrive home. The ladies' toilettes will have to be attended to; Lady Ashland's maid hasn't given proper attention to cleaning the settings of her jewels—I had to redo the amethyst myself this morning. Lord Robert's shoes could stand a far better polish than his valet has provided them to date. You yourself require attention—and I was employed to be your secretary, Mr. Gerard, not your cook.''

''Precious little you've done in either capacity,'' he murmured.

Leda felt it best not to acknowledge such an ignoble jab. She assumed a militant pose. ''I'm shocked that Sheppard agreed to this. It does not do my opinion of him any good. He should have insisted upon a skeleton staff, at the least.''

Mr. Gerard tilted his head. His mouth flexed faintly.

''He did!'' Leda said triumphantly.

''He was a little obstinate, yes.''

''I imagine you see now that I am justified in my opinion.''

''I see that I seem to have an eye for engaging pigheaded employees.''

''That is just what a man would say. Gentleman cannot be depended upon to deal sensibly with servants. They insist upon taking charge, and then blame the troubles upon the staff when it is their own lack of judgment which brought about the situation. Allow me to know better than you in this circumstance, Mr. Gerard. Sheppard is an excellent butler. You should give him rein to do his job as he sees fit.'' A sudden thought struck her. She turned abruptly and walked into the drawing room to pull the bell. It was a few moments, just about the time she judged it would take to proceed in an unhurried fashion from the kitchen to the hall, before Sheppard appeared at the door.

''Miss?'' he inquired, with a very nice sense of sedate respect, just as if she were one of the family.

''Sheppard. I wished to know if you would be going out this morning?''

''No, miss.'' He gave her an astute look. ''I've seen Her Majesty's carriage several times. I've no notion to get myself into that Jubilee crush. You must just ring for me if you need anything. Do you know what time would Mr. Gerard prefer his luncheon?''

''No, I'm afraid that I don't.'' Leda maintained a grave demeanor. ''You may interrupt us at any time to ask him. Any time at all. The door will be open.''

''Certainly, miss.'' Sheppard made a nod of acknowledgment and withdrew. Leda returned to the conservatory, satisfied that Sheppard understood the matter as his master evidently did not.

She sat down in the same chair where she had been told to sit yesterday, keeping her back straight. ''Now, Mr. Gerard. Sheppard assures me that he will be here at your service, so we shall make do with that, considering this is a day of many unusual aspects. It is unlikely there will be any callers, so we won't worry over that difficulty.''

He leaned his cheek on his hand, as he had done the day before. ''Thank you, Miss Etoile,'' he said, with a strange little smile.

''You're quite welcome,'' she said, a little flustered from being rather afraid that he would be angry at her, and somehow more embarrassed by his smile. ''It's only what I owe to you as my employer. I wish for you to be taken care of properly.''

"You seem to be a great caretaker."

Leda blushed, and glanced at him suspiciously for any sign of mockery. He didn't appear to be ironic in his tone, and the way he looked at her made her feel rather silly and weak inside, full of giddy pleasure at the compliment. She turned up the corners of her mouth in a skittish smile and then looked down at her hands.

"Kai likes you very much," he said.

Leda felt the delight of his prior compliment drain abruptly away. "Lady Catherine?" She put a polite smile back on her face. "I'm honored that you think so."

"They all do."

"That is most gratifying," she said. "The Ashlands are very fine people."

He nodded slowly, as if his thoughts were not really on her answer. After a moment, he said, "She's eighteen."

"Is she?" Leda said, as he seemed to be leaving a pause for a response of some sort. "She is certainly a lovely girl. Very fresh and innocent."

He lost the thoughtful look; his eyes met Leda's with a suddenly troubled expression.

She added quickly, "I'm sure that she'll take very well. She's a little naive, but I understand that society is quite welcoming to American girls these days. That is, Lady Catherine isn't American, of course, but girls with, ah—" She cleared her throat delicately. "—American ways of going on. It isn't expected that they will know every tiny nuance of etiquette. Her family clearly has the *entrée;* I'm sure the Queen held very few audiences yesterday—it's the greatest possible compliment to be commanded to attend her so soon."

This view of the matter didn't appear to reassure him. He scowled more deeply and rubbed one eyebrow. "Miss Etoile," he said abruptly. "You are a woman."

Leda bridled up a little. She put her hands together in her lap, trying to think of how Miss Myrtle would have responded to such a barefaced statement, unsure of whether to preen or to be alarmed.

"You have experience of the world," he went on, before she could say anything. "You will . . . know things

. . . understand things—that aren't self-evident to a man. To someone like me.''

With a peculiar mixture of relief, disappointment, and pleasure in the idea that she appeared to him to be sophisticated and self-possessed, she said, ''Well, yes, perhaps that is true.'' Miss Myrtle had always said so. She hadn't ascribed to this modern notion of equality between the sexes. Women were patently superior.

''Do you have a pen and notebook?'' he asked.

''Oh!'' She started up. ''How silly of me. I'm very sorry.''

Leda quickly went to the library, returning with a fountain pen and unused notebook from the stock. She reseated herself, trying not to appear too breathless, and looked up at him expectantly.

''I wish to begin courting her,'' he said, as if he were announcing a business arrangement. ''I'd like your help in planning the best way to go about it.''

Leda blinked. She closed the notebook that she'd opened in her lap. ''Excuse me, sir. I don't think I could have understood you correctly.''

He looked straight into her eyes. ''You understood.''

''But surely . . . your courtship . . . that is an exceedingly private matter. You would not wish me to make it my affair.''

''I'd appreciate it deeply if you would make it your affair. I'm not well-versed in how it is that ladies wish to be courted. I don't want to make any blunders.'' He smiled on one side of his mouth.

Leda's spine was poker-stiff. ''I think you must be mocking me, sir.''

The smile disappeared. He turned his head, looking out past the bank of plants and flowers to the tops of the trees across the street. When he turned back again, his eyes were cool and intense. ''I am not mocking you, I assure you.''

His somber concentration was unnerving. It was like being watched by some silver-eyed Grecian statue, come alive in the shadows of a marble hall. She pressed back against her chair. ''Really, Mr. Gerard,'' she said helplessly. "I cannot imagine that a gentleman such as your-self is not perfectly conversant with—the courting of ladies."

He made a scornful sound, raking his hand across the plump, cushioned back of the sofa. He thrust against it, as if to stand up, and then abandoned the effort with a grimace. "Well, I'm not," he said fiercely. "What makes you think I would be?"

Leda shrank deeper yet in her chair. "You must not imag-ine—I did not mean it as an insult. It's only that—you really are an exceptionally well-looking gentleman . . ."

He looked at her with such violence in his eyes that her voice trailed off.

"She cares nothing for how I look, thank God," he muttered, as if he were the hunchback of Notre Dame.

Leda doubted that many other ladies had been of quite the same blindness as Lady Catherine. He was magnifi-cent even as he sat in moody silence, contemplating his splint, a brooding Gabriel brushed by dark, invisible wings.

"This matter is of the utmost importance to me," he said suddenly, without looking at her.

She fingered the notebook.

"I don't know how to begin," he said through his teeth.

She opened the book, uncapping the pen with a faint snap, blotting it against the square of absorbent paper tucked inside. Watching ink spread from the tip, she ven-tured, "She does not know of your—intentions?"

"Of course not. She's been too young—I wouldn't im-pose myself on her. She thinks of me as a brother."

Leda allowed herself a wry smile, directed downward. "Perhaps more as an uncle, I should judge."

"Do you think I'm too old for her?" he asked harshly.

Leda's pen made an extra blot as her hand started at the sharp question. "No, sir," she said. "Certainly not."

"I'm not over thirty. I don't know precisely. Twenty-seven or twenty-eight, I think."

She bit her lip, her head still carefully lowered over the book. "I don't think that is a concern," she said.

"I'd wait until she was older, but I'm afraid—" He broke off suddenly and drummed his fingers across the sofa's wicker arm. "She might be old enough to interest one of these damned English lords of the manor, anyway."

Leda pursed her lips. "I'm sure that you wouldn't like to fall into the habit of using rough language in her hearing," she said quietly.

"I beg your pardon!" He met her eyes and immediately looked elsewhere, leaving an instant's burn of barely suppressed emotion.

She ducked her head again. To Leda, it almost seemed as if he were aggravated by *her*, instead of any nebulous threat of English lords. It wasn't a normal sort of conversation in the least—he only looked at her in flashes; he seemed to prefer not looking at her at all, for each time he did, his face grew taut with some strong feeling that Leda could not begin to fathom. Embarrassment, certainly—the whole topic was decidedly awkward enough—but there was more to his expression, something subtle and unsettling. She felt painfully self-conscious, her fingers fluttery. The blot beneath her pen grew larger as she watched it with her head lowered shyly.

A potent silence stretched between them, a bright mystery, full of uneasy fancies.

"She'll be considered an heiress," he said in a vague tone, the way someone would take up the thread of a topic that had been lost to contemplation.

Lady Catherine. They were speaking of Lady Catherine, of course. Leda cleared her throat and said, "I'm afraid that's true."

She gathered the courage to glance up. He was watching her hands, but just as she lifted her head he looked away, grabbing the newspaper that lay on the floor beside him, drawing it into his lap as he sat back. "I want you to take some notes," he said, folding the paper and resting it against his thigh, scowling down at it as if what he wanted to know might be written there.

Leda sat with her pen poised over the book. She hoped that he would not speak too quickly in dictation.

"What do you recommend first?" he asked.

"With respect to Lady Catherine?" she asked dubiously.

"Certainly." He rattled the paper. "What else would I mean?"

"Well, I . . . find myself at something of a loss, Mr. Gerard."

"I suppose you haven't known her long," he said, with a touch of moodiness about his fine mouth. "You can't be expected to be aware of her tastes yet." He folded the paper, smoothed it, and then rolled it between his hands. "I've known her since she was a baby, and I can't seem to figure them out myself."

Leda had no ready answer to that. The whole topic disturbed her profoundly.

He held the rolled newspaper between his fists, frowning down at it. "How would you wish to be courted, Miss Etoile?"

Leda felt a sudden, wrenching weakness at the back of her throat. In dismay she stared down at the blurry book, desperate to hide herself and her silliness. "I'm not sure," she said, very quickly, so that perhaps he wouldn't notice anything wrong with her voice.

"You don't have a single suggestion?" He slapped the paper against his open palm and gave a short, humorless laugh. "Take it backward, then. How *wouldn't* you wish to be courted?"

She blinked rapidly. Sergeant MacDonald's embarrassed face, all red and unhappy and helpless, crystallized against the blue-lined blank page. "I would not wish to be abandoned to contempt," she said. "I would wish . . . to be stood up for."

She felt Mr. Gerard looking at her. She felt it, because she could not lift her head—not after saying something so ludicrous.

She thought he would laugh at her, or think she was mad.

"I see," he said slowly.

"Excuse me. That's hardly to the point, is it?" She straightened her spine, trying very hard to be brisk. She clutched the pen and wrote the date and time and place at the top of the page. "I think—I believe that propriety demands you begin by asking Lady Catherine's father for permission to pay your addresses, if you have not already done so. Shall I make a note of that?"

He reached for his crutches and pulled himself to his feet, swinging forward a step until he stood facing out the great window. "I'd never abandon her to anything— contempt or anything else. Never. I would have thought she would know it. Do you think I should tell her so?"

Leda looked at his back, at the athletic width of his shoulders and the strength in his hands. She remembered his face as she had set his leg: concentrated and severe and beautiful in its intensity.

No, this man would not fade in the face of anything. Whatever else he might be, he was not impotent.

"I'm sure that she knows," Leda said. *How could she not?* she thought.

He looked at her sideways. She could not hold his glance, even for an instant. Something inside of her would not manage it.

She evaded his eyes, seeking an orchid hanging near his shoulder as a focus. "She told me about the shark, you recall. She seems very fond of the story, and your part in it."

"Yes," he said. "I've always watched over her."

"You're very good," Leda said mechanically. "I'm certain Lady Catherine is much obliged to you."

He was silent for a long while, staring out the window. "So," he said at last, "I'm to tell Lord Gryphon? I suppose that's sensible." He didn't sound as if he looked forward to the prospect.

"I believe most young men find it rather dire, speaking to fathers." She attempted to put a note of sympathy into her voice. "In this case, as Lord Ashland is well acquainted with your background, it would seem to be merely a polite formality."

He gripped the crutch again. "How sanguine you are."

"I shouldn't think he would have any objections—" She stopped.

"Unless he knows me as well as you do?"

Leda moistened her lips, fiddling with the pen.

"I hope I haven't been mistaken in you, Miss Etoile. I've given you the power to ruin me. Are you a turncoat?"

"No," she whispered, not knowing why, or why not, but sure that, God forgive her, she would not go to Lord Ashland and tell him that the man who wished to marry his daughter was a nightwalker and a thief.

Mr. Gerard looked into her eyes then, with an intimacy and connection that Leda felt all down through her in a bloom of painful pleasure.

If only, she thought, a foible she had been careful not to indulge in all of her life.

Oh, if only . . .

Sixteen
~~~~~~~~~~
Heart Blade

⊕

Hawaii, 1879

"*The warrior who walks in disguise will avoid salty things, seasoned things, food pungent with oils, garlics, and other such stuff,*" Dojun said. "He does not reveal himself to the enemy by what he has touched, or where he has been—his passions do not betray him. *Shinobi* is to be one hidden. Another way to express this is *nin*, which is patience, endurance, perseverance."

Samuel listened to the words, to ten thousand repetitions. His intrigues had been as easy as sweetening an Arcturus deal by making a large donation toward the purchase of the first steam fire engine in Honolulu, and as hazardous as tangling with a secret Chinese Hoong Moon society over protection payments, then bending to light the gas cookstove in the harbor office one morning . . . and smelling gunpowder an instant before he struck the match.

"Consider," Dojun said, "the character for *nin* is created by writing the character for 'blade' above the character for 'heart.' *Shinobideru* is to go out in secret; *shinobikomu* is to steal inside; *shinobiwarai* is silent laughter; the *jihi no kokoru* is the merciful heart. All of these things are yours. Do not strive. Do not want. Be as the bamboo leaf bent by the dew—the leaf does not shake off the drop, and yet the moment comes when the dew falls and the leaf rebounds, releasing strength."

Samuel considered the leaf. He did not think of it in a conscious manner, but without boundaries between himself and the bamboo and the dewdrop. Something shifted at the edge of sight. The drop fell. Samuel's body drifted backward with Dojun's strike, riding the force and slipping outside it.

He resumed his kneeling position. There was not a man in Chinatown now, Oriental *pākē* or native *kanaka,* who would move on him.

Samuel knew it. He could stand in a Chinatown street and sense it, as he could sense the spicy, sickly odor of opium that floated on the back of mango and fish and mud-smell. No one would give him any particular notice; no one would skirt him as if he were worthy of exaggerated respect; but some burly Hawaiian who guarded the door of the nearest gambling den would watch him with a lazy smile of brotherhood.

With his blond hair and height, Samuel was not the only *fan kwai* who dealt in Chinatown, but he was foremost of the foreign devils, as Arcturus was the preeminent non-Chinese business in the quarter now, because Samuel contracted with anyone fair and to his word, and fought fire with fire if the need arose.

Dojun still demanded the limit of Samuel's reserves. It had long ago become a strange contest between them, nothing so profitless as sauntering into a saloon and picking a fight with drunken sailors for practice. Samuel had encountered aggressive drunks once or twice, and it was too pathetically easy to turn and give way and let them defeat themselves by crashing face-down on the floor. No, it was Dojun who challenged him, who pulled invisible strings and found the subtle discords and weaknesses in Arcturus affairs where there should not have been snags. It was Dojun who matched Samuel and Arcturus against every faction and clan in Chinatown, one after the other, and then let him find his way out of it, by strength or by guile.

He knew what it felt like to fight for real now. They break you head *kotsun,* you no get out the way.

So he got out of the way, and then came back—to pivot, strike hard, and slide into silence.

Wind. Fire. Water.

And always there was Dojun, speaking of peace and

instructing in violence, telling him that he must take the ruthless center he'd discovered within himself and make stillness and serenity of it.

Dojun could have hit him a thousand times. And a thousand times, Dojun froze the attack one breath from completion, never touching Samuel; never breaking his vow.

"The *shinobi* warrior must carry the truth within him." Dojun's voice was calm, inexorable. "He does not fight for money or a love of destruction. Strength and power are nothing. He maintains intention. He is an illusion within a real world; he has given himself a disguise, as the mantis imitates the twig. It does not become the twig. It does not forget that it is a mantis. You must be careful of this."

Samuel bowed low over his lap in acknowledgment, his hands resting palm-downward on his thighs.

"What do you do about women, Samua-san?"

The question came gently, a bombshell, as unexpected as one of Dojun's ambush strikes. Samuel felt his face go hot; his body flooded with shame.

"Ah." Dojun's voice was interested. "They give you disharmony."

Samuel didn't know what to say. Awkwardness had taken over his arms and legs; he just sat there like a dumb beast, waiting for Dojun to reach inside and shred that part of him into scraps.

"You do not go with women?" It was phrased as a question, but Dojun spoke as if he knew with certainty.

"No," Samuel whispered, staring straight ahead.

For a few moments, Dojun didn't speak. Then he said in a thoughtful voice, "Women congest the senses. In general, it is best to avoid them. It is best to live in the mountains and eat mild foods—then the senses are sharpened; a warrior can perceive a woman at a distance, knowing even what work she is about without ever seeing or hearing her. But women are desirable, are they not? A warrior must know his own weakness. The bodies of women are beautiful, they move gracefully, their breasts are round, the skin is sweet and soft to touch. Do you think of that?"

Samuel was silent. He didn't have the words for what

he tried not to think of. He had only the images that beleaguered him to fierce desperation, and suddenly—appallingly—no way to hide what they did to him from Dojun. Samuel was horrified. Scalding humiliation covered him while he betrayed himself as he had not done since he'd been a schoolboy.

"Your body answers to this appetite even while I speak of it, Samua-san."

Samuel felt the blood heavy in his veins. He kept his eyes open, gazing into space. Breathe in. Breathe out. He felt as if he were drowning.

Dojun's voice wove softly in the silence. "This is *shikijō*, to lust, to flush color for a woman. Women distract you. But by a man's passion for a woman the universal force of life, the *ki*, becomes concrete, and new life is created. It is a delicate question. It is not wrong for a warrior to lie down with a woman, but it is better in many ways if you do not. You must not yield to personal weakness. You must have the essential principles within you: rectitude, courage, compassion, courtesy, utter truthfulness, honor, loyalty. By these things you will know."

Like everything Dojun taught him, it was simple, and yet agonizingly complex. But in this one thing Samuel hid himself, kept the terrifying strength of his hunger concealed even from his teacher. He had no rectitude that would control it, no courtesy, no honor, no compassion. Only the bone-deep fear of losing himself, of falling, falling, falling, down a well to nowhere.

"Instead, take this energy of *shikijō* and use it in the art I teach you," Dojun advised. "It is a young man's vigor. Focus your *ki.*"

Samuel bowed to show his gratitude for the lesson, as if it were like the others.

"Do not scatter your life force on women."

"No, Dojun-san," Samuel said.

"Remember this as a particular weakness within you. Exercise discipline in all things."

"Yes, Dojun-san."

"You are a warrior. Your heart is a blade."

Samuel bowed again, and closed his eyes.

Seventeen

❖

Miss Myrtle had never had any quarrel with the spirit
of benign curiosity; indeed, she had often said that it added
a much-needed dollop of piquancy to the conversation of
ladies who knew one another well, and had no evil habits
such as a tendency to gossip or meddle marring their characters, which the South Street ladies agreed that they did
not.

Miss Lovatt seemed taken aback for a moment after
Leda had announced her new position. "Amanuensis!"
she exclaimed.

"What a very long word," Lady Cove murmured. "I
shouldn't like to be asked to spell it, though I daresay that
our dear papa would have spelt it in a moment, and just
exactly, too."

"It will be Latin, won't it?" Mrs. Wrotham looked ap-
prehensive. "I never was comfortable with Latin. It seems
a very manly language, and dead at that. Why ever should
one wish to put words that are no longer living into one's
mouth?"

Lady Cove shuddered. "Like swallowing fish."

"Fish!" Miss Lovatt gave her sister an exasperated
frown. "The word has nothing to do with fish. It is a
person who takes dictation."

"Yes," Leda said quickly, "and I have my own bedroom in the house, and whatever provisions that I require
for correspondence, fresh paper and pens and so forth,
and in place of a common desk, Mr. Gerard has provided
me with a very fine secretary commissioned by Lady Ashland's father, the late Earl of Morrow, designed by His

166

Lordship himself and built to specifications out of precious wood brought from the South Seas. Lord Morrow was a great traveler and explorer, Mr. Gerard said, and his house is full of exotic things.''

"Did His Lordship speak Latin?" Mrs. Wrotham asked, still anxious.

Miss Lovatt took issue with the question as being nothing to the point. After fiercely snubbing Mrs. Wrotham with a sharp suggestion that Mr. Wrotham himself, not to mention Lord Cove, had certainly spoken Latin, or read it at least, as any gentleman must who had attended Eton, she swept an arch glance around the little gathering and said, "You realize, of course, what this family must be?"

Leda and the other ladies humbly confessed ignorance.

"You will be too young to remember," Miss Lovatt assured Leda. "But Lady Cove and Mrs. Wrotham must recall it. The Ashland tragedy—oh, it will be all of forty years ago now. All the family, the little children too, perished in a fire aboard ship on their return from India. A terrible, terrible thing—the poor old marquess was left here at home with nothing—I believe his heir was unmarried, and the younger son's family was all on board, too. They were burnt up, every one of them.''

"Yes, I do remember!" Lady Cove said, with a sad shake of her head. "It was such a ghastly misfortune. I remember it perfectly; that was the year Lord Cove took his business trip to Paris, and even the St. James' *Chronicle* wrote of the disaster, because the family were of such very high lineage, about the poor little children and how the pirates had killed them. And then not long after there was the India mutiny, and oh—the dreadful, shocking stories! I could not bear it; I couldn't read of it, but people would go on speaking of it until it made one's heart break.''

"Yes, indeed—dreadful," Miss Lovatt said, quickly disposing of the mutiny. "But you recall what came of the Ashland matter in the end—the grandson didn't perish after all, and sailed all about the world until he was a man, in the same ship that was supposed to have burned, and then he came back and avenged himself upon his cousin—''

She stopped suddenly and frowned, looking rather vexed. "I believe it was the cousin; the name escapes me at the moment—Ellison—Elmore—"

"Eliot!" Lady Cove said, sitting up with her hands fluttering in excitement. "Oh, yes, I remember it as if it were yesterday! That great trial!"

"The last trial of a peer before the Lords," Miss Lovatt intoned, keeping her voice conformed to the solemnity of the topic. "At Her Majesty's request. So there! You see what it must be."

Leda and Mrs. Wrotham only blinked in bewilderment at the triumphant conclusion to this confused-sounding tale. "I'm sure I don't see what burning up little children in the House of Lords has to do with Leda, any more than does Latin," Mrs. Wrotham said in an injured voice.

"Of course it has nothing to do with Latin," Miss Lovatt stated with certainty. "Leda's position will be with the same man. Lord Ashland. The marquess."

"No, no," Leda said. "He's not the marquess at all. His name is Mr. Gerard."

Miss Lovatt gave her a pitying look. "You're a very good girl, Leda, but not very clever. I'm sure I don't know what sort of an amanuensis you will make to anyone if you are so easily perplexed. I'm not speaking of Mr. Gerard, dear. I'm speaking of his connections. Lord and Lady Ashland. It will be the same man, do you not see? The lost marquess himself."

"Oh," Leda said humbly.

"And whom did he marry?" Miss Lovatt asked herself. "There was some further scandal attached to it . . . I cannot put my finger—Morrow, do you say?"

Leda was dispatched to retrieve Mrs. Wrotham's Peerage from the boudoir. When she returned, the ladies pounced upon the book as if it had been the tablets brought down from the mountain, disputing delicately over who should make the investigation. Lady Cove was quickly dismissed for her inability to spell, and Mrs. Wrotham, though sole proprietor of the copy, could not turn the pages quite promptly enough for Miss Lovatt, who finally took the volume into her own hands and made the identification.

"Meridon," she announced, poring over the page with her lorgnette. "Gryphon, Arthur. G-R-Y-P-H-O-N. What a heathenish spelling of Griffon! Lord Ashland, sixth Marquess, tenth Earl of Orford and fourteenth Viscount Lyndley; born 1838; son Lord Arthur Meridon of Ashland Court and Calcutta and Lady Mary Caroline Ardline; married Lady Terese Elizabeth Collier, daughter Lord Morrow; one son, one daughter of the union; traveled extensively in scientific and botanical expeditions; naval advisor to H.M. King Ka—Kala—I don't believe I am able to pronounce that—His Majesty of the Hawaiian Islands; Chairman, Arcturus Limited; a director of—some other outlandish name—K-A-I-E-A—"

"Oh, yes," Leda said eagerly. "That is Mr. Gerard's own company."

"Pray do not interrupt your elders, Leda," Miss Lovatt said. "Lord Ashland is a director of this company, president of a number of what appear to be charitable organizations having to do with sailors, a member of several clubs, and prefers yachting as his recreation. His seat is Ashland Court, Hampshire. Other addresses, Westpark, Sussex, and Ho-no-lu-lu, Hawaii."

"They came with the Hawaiian party for the Jubilee," Leda offered, "but Mr. Gerard said that no definite date has been set to conclude the visit. He believes they may remove to Lady Ashland's home at Westpark and stay into autumn."

"Ashland," Mrs. Wrotham murmured, fretting her fingers. "Dear me, I believe I saw that name—do bring me the Court circular, Leda my love. I'm certain it is on my dressing table."

Leda, knowing Mrs. Wrotham, took her certainty with some mistrust, and finally located the requested paper on the sideboard in the breakfast room. After another deep perusal, the names of Lord and Lady Ashland were duly noted as having attended several exclusive functions of the Jubilee, just as Leda had said, and it was verified that their daughter Lady Catherine Meridon had already had the honor of being presented to the Queen. When Mr. Gerard's name was located, quite by accident, in tiny print on the long list of those invited to attend the Queen's garden party, Leda's situation was assured. If the office of the Lord Chamberlain considered Mr. Samuel Gerard of Honolulu suitable to appear at court festivities—informal ones, at any rate—then the ladies of South Street must naturally do the same.

Ancient and dimly recalled scandals were forgotten. From being somewhat suspicious of Lèda's new employment, the ladies began to be rather in awe of her and her noble connections, and Mrs. Wrotham felt that she should have put on her Parisian cap instead of the second-best lace, and begged Leda's pardon for overlooking this mark of respect. Leda beseeched her not to give it a moment's thought, but the old lady really was distressed, and wished several times that Leda might not think her exceedingly dowdy, and hoped Leda would call again next week so that everything could be done just in the proper manner, and Mrs. Wrotham would have time to bid Cook to make her special lemon cakes in honor of the occasion.

Leda departed in a warm cloud of congratulations that burst into a regular blaze of glory when it was realized that the victoria waiting in the street outside had been provided by Mr. Gerard. For just a moment, Miss Lovatt frowned a little and wasn't quite certain that it was perfectly proper for Leda to be seen in an unmarried gentleman's carriage, but a little further thought convinced her that as it was an open victoria, very modestly trimmed with only one thin and discreet band of gold paint around the wheels, and a footman up beside the driver, both in their burnished top hats and white gloves, really, no one could find anything lax about the arrangement. A very pretty mark of regard it was, she believed, to put a proper vehicle at his secretary's convenience. She was sure that Mr. Gerard was an excellent gentleman.

Even though Leda, being an intimate in South Street, had stretched her call a little longer than the correct quarter hour, she still arrived back at Morrow House very early in the afternoon. Sheppard informed her that Mr. Gerard

was still occupied with business in his own chamber. Over
the past few days, Leda had found that her employer spent
a deal of time at business in his own chamber, the nature
of which seemed to be obscure, although she was evidently the only one who found that circumstance intriguing. But then, she found altogether too much about Mr.
Gerard intriguing, she reminded herself sternly.

He had left a request with Sheppard that he wished for
her to await him in the library. Leda obediently repaired
there, after accepting Sheppard's suggestion for tea. She
knew from experience that the tray would arrive piled high
with macaroons, sandwiches, scones, and cream in a most
ungenteel manner, but having spent the luncheon hour
amid elegant scarcity in South Street, Leda was willing to
be vulgar.

She thought that with her first compensation, due on
Monday she believed, she might send a crassly heavy basket of excellent comestibles from Harrods grocery shop to
South Street—perhaps even give a small dinner in a private
parlor at Claridges, if the ladies could be persuaded to
enter a hotel.

Before the tea arrived, Leda considered the situation of
meeting with Mr. Gerard in the library, and opened all
three doors in the room. He would not like it; no doubt
he would insist on closing them, but Leda was determined
at least to make an effort. She stood for a moment looking
through into the empty ballroom, admiring the exquisite
plasterwork and huge chandeliers. It was famous as the
most gorgeously decorated such room in Mayfair. To add
to the superlative embellishments of gilt and crystal, between each window stood tall stands full of living orchids,
their blooms all in shades of yellow and gold against the
crimson damask walls. Leda imagined a waltz, the gowns
drifting out in whirls of color as the ladies held up their
trains over gloved arms; the gentlemen dark and splendid.
She did not happen to know how to waltz, but she had
seen one once, and imagined it must be the most delightful sensation to spin about the floor to the lilting music.

Inevitably, she thought of dancing with Mr. Gerard, and
turned away vexed with herself. Her tea came, carried by

one of the footmen, and Leda took herself back to sit down in a straight-backed chair of *faux* bamboo. She had brought home a copy of the *Illustrated News*. If she'd had the leisure, and the nerve, she would have called at the offices of the *Times* and asked to see the preserved newspapers from forty years ago, but her audacity was not quite up to her inquisitiveness. And after all, it was an agreeably irreproachable pleasure to sip her tea and chew thoughtfully at a macaroon as she read the latest intelligence of the Jubilee. The eventful week was half over—there were several reviews scheduled for tomorrow, and Her Majesty's garden party remained for Friday. Leda read the anticipated details with particular interest, knowing now that Mr. Gerard had been invited, even if he could not attend.

Her heart gave a heavy pump when she saw the second-page headline. JAPANESE SWORD FOUND. Beneath it, a subheading informed her Thief Still At Large. As she read in frowning concentration, it became clear that no progress at identifying the criminal had been made—or at least, no information about progress had been given to reporters. The sword itself had been located by an estate agent during a routine audit of an unfurnished house to let in Richmond—miles away from Bermondsey. Now that all of the stolen property had been recovered, a private source at Scotland Yard had been overheard to admit, the investigation might temporarily slacken, as the police were heavily employed with other duties during the Jubilee. The sum of the bizarre case appeared to be nothing more than the closing of a number of houses whose sordid business would not bear any such notoriety as that of being identified in the newspapers. Diplomats were busy soothing ruffled feathers, and it appeared that the series of strange thefts was on its way to being forgotten by the press.

She was so intent on this topic that she only became consciously aware of the voices in the ballroom when Lady Ashland's drifted clearly through the door, raised in consternation.

"He has what?" Her Ladyship exclaimed, as if she could not have heard her informer correctly.

Some trick of the big, echoing ballroom brought the

sound of Lord Ashland's footsteps and his lower voice into the library as plainly as his wife's. "He's asked permission to court Kai. That's actually how he put it. Charmingly old-fashioned, I thought. You know Samuel."

Leda froze with the cup of tea lifted halfway to her lips. She thought wildly that she should reveal herself, or sneak away, or simply stand up and shut the door—but she did none of that. She sat still and quiet, listening . . . in the interest of benign curiosity.

"Oh, God—I've known this would happen," Lady Ashland said. "I've seen it coming for years."

"You don't like it?" Her husband's voice was softer, a little surprised.

"What did you tell him?" she demanded.

"I told him he was welcome to do as he wished, of course, what else—" He broke off at Lady Ashland's smothered exclamation. "I had no idea you'd object."

Leda turned her head. Through the open fretwork edge of a japonaiserie screen, she could see a reflection of Lady Ashland in the big mirror above the mantel. She held her fingers over her mouth, as if holding back a torrent of objection. When her husband reached out and laid his hand on her shoulder, she shook her head and went into his arms. Leda realized with a shock that Her Ladyship was weeping.

Leda knew she should leave. This was not meant for her ears.

But she stayed silent.

"I didn't know you'd feel this way," Lord Ashland murmured, stroking his wife's hair, putting his fingers into the dark mass, not seeming to care when it came tumbling down in his hands. "Tess—is it what he came from?"

Lady Ashland broke away, still shaking her head. "No!" She shook her head more vehemently. "*No!* Do you think I would ever, *ever* hold that against him? It's not Kai I'm worried for. She'll hurt him. She won't mean to do it, but she'll destroy him. She'll tear him into pieces. She's too young; she'd never understand what she was doing—she never *can* understand what it's like!"

There was an edge of panic in her voice, but her husband did not argue with these wild accusations against their own daughter. He held her again, rocking her against him, murmuring, "Tess, Tess . . . my beautiful Tess. I love you more than life."

"I wanted him to be happy," she said brokenly, resting her head against his shoulder, holding tight.

"I know." He brushed his hand up and down her back. "I know."

"If you could have seen him." Her face crumpled, and she began to cry again. "Oh, if you could have seen him . . ."

"My brave Tess—how often do you think of that?"

"Sometimes," she said in a small voice.

"Listen to me." He held her a little away, and skimmed the hair back off her temple. "Whenever you think of it, come to me. Wherever I am. Whatever I'm doing—it's not important. Come and hold on to me."

She made a deep sniff and nodded.

"Promise?"

She looked up at him. She put both hands on either side of his face and stared up at him as if he were something unutterably precious. "I always come to you."

" 'Aye-aye, sir,' " he said sternly.

She smiled through her tears. "Aye-aye, Captain."

He took her hands and lowered them, holding them in his own. "We can't force Samuel to be happy, love. We've done our best for him. It's his life."

She bent her head. "I wish you hadn't given him your permission."

"Tess . . . how could I not? Even if I'd known how you'd feel—there's no way I could have told him I wouldn't allow him to think of marrying Kai. It wouldn't matter how I said it, or what reasons I gave—you know what he'd be bound to believe."

"That we don't think he's good enough," she said, her voice so muffled that Leda barely understood it.

"Worse than that. God, far worse than that. We're the only ones who know. We're the ones who can wound him with a word wrong—especially you. Most especially you, Tess."

She nodded, with a little gulping sob.

"You tell him not to think of your daughter, and you'll decimate him in a way Kai never could."

"Yes . . . that's why I never . . ." She made a small, helpless sound. "I've seen this for the longest time; I've known it; but I never had the courage to do anything. I just wished it away. I wished for something to happen; someone else to love him—he deserves someone who can understand, and still love him, and Kai . . ." She gripped her hands together. "I would not change a hair of her head, but she is so young and careless; she treats him as if—she doesn't even see the way he looks at her."

"She'll grow older. Wiser, one hopes."

"Too fast. Oh, too fast! And not fast enough." She turned away from her husband. "Not for Samuel."

"He's a man grown," Lord Ashland said gently. "If she tells him no, do you think he won't get over it? At least Kai's plainly ignorant of his background. He wouldn't have to wonder if she'd rejected him for that."

"Do you think he wouldn't?" His wife sounded sad. "Do you think he doesn't believe in his heart that anyone can look at him and see it?"

"Tess . . ."

"He's never forgotten it. I didn't find him soon enough. I wanted him to forget."

He caught her hand again and stood looking down at it, folding it between his. "You haven't forgotten."

"No. And what happened to me—with Stephen—a few months in a cold room—it was nothing to what Samuel lived through for years. Just a little boy . . ." Her voice cracked. "Such a little boy . . ."

"He's not a boy any longer, my love. He's become a hell of a man."

She turned to the window and was silent. He moved behind her, enfolding her in his arms. They stood together with the late-afternoon light drifting down over them, a woman with the sheen of tears on her face, a man quiet and constant, not offering anything of hopes or solutions, but just standing solid at her back, holding her close.

"Have you said anything to Kai?" she asked him.

"No. I haven't seen her."

"Don't tell her."

"It won't change anything, love."

"Please," she said.

He reached up and pulled her loose hair together, letting it drift through his fingers. "I won't tell her. He didn't ask me to."

Lady Ashland leaned back against him, still gazing out the window.

"Leave your plants to the greenhouseman—he can water them." Lord Ashland turned her back to face him. "Come take a walk with me."

She wiped at her eyes. "Looking like this? In London?"

He produced a handkerchief. "Let's lock ourselves in our room, then. We'll skip dinner and create a scandal. I think the staff's getting too nonchalant about our eccentricity."

Lady Ashland made a peculiar sound; Leda suddenly realized it was a watery, smothered giggle.

"I feel a strong urge to be bizarre coming upon me," her husband said. "I'd like to see you skin something disgusting. A lizard, maybe. A snake."

She pushed at him. "You."

He caught her waist and put his face down in the curve of her shoulder. Leda's eyes widened as she saw what he was doing with his hands.

Lady Ashland didn't seem properly shocked at all. She tilted her head back a little, the misery in her face beginning to relax into something else entirely.

"Forget the bed," Lord Ashland muttered. "Let's be barbaric in the ballroom."

He was certainly applying himself to that. Leda squeezed her eyes shut and opened them again, to find that it was perfectly true, he was verifiably unbuttoning his wife's bodice.

"Gryf," Lady Ashland protested, not very convincingly. "The doors . . ."

Leda sank instantly down to the level of her chair behind the solid part of the screen as she heard his purposeful footsteps come toward the library door. It boomed shut, and a moment later she heard a key in the lock. She put her fingers over her mouth. From the open door to the hall came the sound of another slam—the other portal into the ballroom locked.

Leda sat still, utterly shocked and burning with benign curiosity.

She was still sitting there, slumped down in her chair with her hand over her mouth, when Mr. Gerard came. She shot upright, springing out of the seat guiltily.

He leaned on his crutches and gave her a peculiar look. "Did I startle you?"

"Oh, no! I was just reading the paper."

He lifted an eyebrow.

"Well, I was," she said, rustling the sheets in her hand. "You hadn't left me any other instructions."

There was a sound from the door to the library. Her glance flew to it in dismay. The lock clicked, but the door remained closed, to Leda's vast relief, and in a few moments there was a distant sound of soft voices and footsteps in the hall.

She knew she was bright crimson. She simply could not help herself.

"Concealing secret admirers?" he asked.

Leda took the high ground. "I believe you wished me to attend you here at your convenience, Mr. Gerard?"

He reached around with one crutch and knocked the door behind him shut. "Close the other one, would you?"

She pursed her lips in disapproval, but he only stood watching her expectantly. With a sigh, Leda stood up and obeyed.

"I spoke to Lord Gryphon," he said, as she turned back to him.

She resisted the impulse to blurt, *I know.* Instead, she walked to the secretary and took up her notebook. "We can cross that off the list, then." She opened it and sat down. "I've been considering recommendations for the next step, but I'm afraid that your injury is something of a hindrance. You cannot conveniently invite Lady Catherine to view the paintings at the Royal Academy, or ride with you in the park.''

He leaned back against the door. "I'm not an invalid.''

"I'm quite sure you think you could jog-trot all over the gallery on one foot," Leda said tartly. "But you are not, perhaps, an entirely heroic figure on crutches. At least as the escort of a young lady going into society for her first season.''

"It's no longer a question. I'm going to have to leave.''

Leda looked up sharply.

"I've had some news from Hawaii. It's necessary that I return. Immediately.''

The shock closed her throat. She sat staring at him in dismay.

"I'll need a stateroom on the first steamer available. Use the telephone to make arrangements. It doesn't matter what port—New York or Washington are the same. And a private coach to Liverpool.'' His mouth curled upward. "Keep breathing, Miss Etoile.''

Leda took a gulp of air and swallowed. She looked down at the notebook and wrote with a shaking hand. *Stateroom. First steamer. Private coach.*

The she stood up jerkily. "Have the police discovered something? Is that why you must leave the country?''

"It's nothing to do with that." His tone was easy and unremarkable. "There's a political crisis in Honolulu. The king's been made to sign away his dominion by the reform party. By Friday, Kapiolani and Princess Lydia will be informed of it. They'll go back, too, I imagine, and lucky if they find their thrones intact.''

"You know of it before they do?''

"Yes.''

She did not ask him how that came to be: something in his steady gaze forbade it.

"I can't conduct affairs at this distance with the government shaky,'' he added.

Leda looked down. She had known it could not last. It had been too wonderful to last. "Well," she said in a subdued voice, "it has been an honor and a pleasure to assist you as your secretary, Mr. Gerard.''

"I hope you'll find it as enjoyable in the future."

Her heart made a bound. "You wish me to accompany you?"

"No, that won't be necessary. You can stay here."

In a welter of disappointment and relief, all she could think of to say was, "Here? In this house?"

He shrugged. "Wherever the family is. I told you, they may go down to Westpark."

"They won't go back to Hawaii also?"

"I can take care of what has to be done. I've already talked to Lord Gryphon about it."

Leda remembered the voices from the ballroom, which hadn't drawn her attention until they concerned him. "But—they truly don't mind? They wish me to stay with them?"

He smiled a little. "I believe they view you as something in the nature of a lifeline amid the social tempest."

"Oh," she said.

"You've only to continue as you've been doing—excepting that you may feel free to leave every door in the house open, once I'm gone."

"I don't believe it will be necessary once you've gone," she said quellingly, fortified by the idea that she was a lifeline in a social tempest.

He looked rather self-conscious at that, she thought. Perhaps she was having some refining influence upon him after all. She desisted from mentioning that Lord and Lady Ashland liked one another rather more than was decorous, and appeared to prefer their doors closed, too. With a pattern such as that before him, no wonder he had no notion of setting an example for the servants.

He gave her one of those silver stares. "What would be your opinion, Miss Etoile, of my speaking to Lady Catherine before I leave?"

"Oh, you must not." Leda grabbed at the book as it slipped down her lap. "It would be—it would be entirely too precipitate."

She managed to catch the notebook before it fell. Without thinking, she quickly brushed it off, as if it had actually hit the floor.

"She'd refuse." He said it coolly, with no trace of emotion, but Leda suddenly saw what Lady Ashland saw—the way his hands gripped the crutches, the vast uncertainty behind his impersonal facade.

"As to that, I'm sure I can't say." Leda took on Miss Myrtle's most academic tone, as if it were a mere question of etiquette. "But in consideration of a lady's natural delicacy, a gentleman will not embarrass her by dismissing convention and becoming too previous in his overtures."

His hands relaxed a little on the crutches. The faint trace of a smile returned. "Not even in an emergency?"

"You are not going off to war, Mr. Gerard," Leda informed him. "There is every expectation that you will be restored to us alive and intact. I do not think attending to unexpected business affairs can justly be ruled an emergency."

He inclined his head. "No doubt you're right. As always."

"I feel that I am in this case," she said modestly. "With all respect."

"There is one other thing," he said, "if you'll agree to help me."

"I will be happy to be of service in any way that I can."

"Good." He leaned his head back against the door and looked down at her, his eyes half-closed in an ice-man glitter that made Leda suddenly begin to regret her ready compliance. "There's a certain item that needs to be retrieved from your former room before I leave," he murmured. "This evening, Miss Etoile, you and I are going to go and get it."

Eighteen

~~~~~~~~~

The House of the Sun

◈

Hawaii, 1882

They said that Haleakala was ten thousand feet above the sea.

Ten thousand rivers collect in the ocean.

One true intention will defeat ten thousand men.

Only the wind came here; the wind and the clouds rolling up through a giant, empty gap in the cliffs that rimmed the crater wall. The mists slid silently into the House of the Sun, dimming the vast red sweeps of gravel and cinder, the charred hills and stark distance. The clouds tumbled and boiled and vanished. Samuel and Dojun had walked for half a day within its fantastic expanse, and still the far cliffs were clear and remote—like many things: no closer and no farther than they had seemed at the beginning of the effort.

Count the last ten miles of a hundred-mile journey as but half the way.

Samuel asked no questions. He'd never come here before. Nor had Dojun, that he knew of. It was two days' travel from Honolulu: one day on the inter-island steamer to Maui, another to walk up the mountainside through the cane fields and cloud forest and then above the tree line to the rim of the monumental crater. The air was thin, a dry ache in the lungs. An alien silence held all life frozen—even the scattered plants were strange icy silver starbursts, glowing from their centers with a faint illumination, as if the inner blades caught daylight and reflected it back upon themselves, intensifying it to a metallic radiance.

181

Here where there was no one to see, Dojun openly carried a sword in a long scabbard. By his own custom, Samuel favored a less conspicuous knife, though he'd trained with the sword as a weapon and as a tool for prying and cutting, even as a convenient prop for an extra boost in climbing. He knew the secret chambers in the deceptive scabbard—his knife's sheath had the same, filled with blinding powder and poison.

"Rest," Dojun said, halting at the foot of a long slope that led up to the round mouth of a cinder cone. They had been following a bridle trail that wound across the desolation, but Dojun suddenly left it, walking out over the unbroken stretches of gravel toward the hill.

Samuel stood still, watching. As the minutes passed, Dojun's figure seemed to become tiny; the cinder cone grew bigger in perspective until it was huge and Dojun nothing but a dark speck moving up the slope. He disappeared over the concave lip.

The silence was a physical presence, a humming in Samuel's ears. If he shifted his feet, the magnified grate of stone made a loud crackle. This place played tricks on the senses, causing small things to seem large and huge things to seem insignificantly sized.

He savored the nothingness of it. The empty space, the fearsome isolation—he felt it as a respite in his heart from things he had not known troubled him. He was even glad that Dojun had left him. He was thoroughly safe; there was no weapon that could reach him, no shame that could touch him here.

He knelt, waiting. When the clouds came down it was glacially cold. For years he hadn't felt this kind of cold. He remembered, for the first time in a long time, wintry rooms and frigid water, his hands swollen from it and his wrists bands of freezing fire where he'd jerked against the cords that held him. He hadn't jerked to escape; he'd never even thought of flight; he'd only flinched each time he was hit or touched, because he couldn't help it, and that was what rubbed his wrists raw.

There were some he could remember who had not survived; who grew ill and faded, who cried until someone tired of hearing it. He'd been stronger, but not strong enough or smart enough to know life could be different.

Lady Tess had done that, freed him, and now he was here, breathing clean, high, sterile air—so clean and empty and unsoiled; even the cinder beneath him was pure. He swept up a handful of it and rolled the chinkery black angles between his palms. The ebony facets glittered, ugly and beautiful at once, like the volcanic crater that had spawned them.

He opened a length of drab cloth and scooped a small pile of the sparkling gravel into the center to take as a gift for her. As he tied it, a sensation of darkness swept over him.

The world seemed to collapse in on itself; he came out of a sideways roll with the whoosh of steel passing, the high-pitched whine singing close to his ear. The sword flashed down even as he escaped it, unleashed power that sliced without hesitation in a full killing arc, the point biting into the ground in a three-inch gash that buried the tip in black cinders.

Dojun let go of the hilt with both hands, and the sword stood alone in the earth.

Samuel stood balanced, washed in menace; when Dojun walked toward him a shadow seemed to drift past—Samuel leaped to the outside of the driving hand that came at his neck, brought up his crossed wrists and ducked the following kick that would have struck with an impact meant to smash bone. The strikes pounded one after another; Samuel floated in the shadow, evading, arresting, his conscious mind blank, amazed at the situation—Dojun was assaulting him, all-out, the quality of each motion full and deadly with that black intent casting a shade before it came.

Samuel didn't attack in return; in the end he only twisted and bowed to the shadow, lowering his shoulder to invite it in as Dojun kicked through his guard, hit the ground on one leg, and followed the invitation, his body fully committed to a driving lunge that took him where Samuel had been, over Samuel's ducked shoulder as if he'd been thrown, though Samuel never touched him.

Dojun struck the ground with his hands and rolled, springing up in a patch of dusty sunlight, the shadow fading with the mist as if it had never been.

Samuel stood panting, staring at him, trying to believe the earth had crumbled, the sun gone to ashes and the sea to dry rock: that Dojun had broken his vow.

"*Sō,*" Dojun grunted, resting his hands on his hips. "Make promise you. No hit Samua-san, eh?"

Samuel's lip curled. He could see the sword from the corner of his eye, buried point-deep in the ground where he'd sat. *You bastard,* he wanted to shout. *I trusted you!*

Dojun shrugged as if he'd spoken. "Been try hard. Damn hard. No can do."

Samuel sucked the thin purity of the air into his lungs, looking down at the sword. He remembered Dojun's vow as if it were engraved upon a wall in his mind.

I pledge to you, I will never strike you by intent for any reason.

Dojun had tried to hit him.

Tried. *Been try hard. Damn hard.*

And had not succeeded.

Samuel lifted his eyes, with shock and the truth dawning. "You couldn't do it," he said slowly. "You knew you couldn't do it."

"You more young, eh?" Dojun, too, was breathing heavily. "Got small-little edge."

Samuel clenched his teeth together, pulling cold air through them. He found himself laughing. He tilted his head back and laughed without sound at the sky.

" 'Assa madda you?" Dojun asked grumpily. "Think you number-one man now?"

But he was smiling as he said it. He went and jerked the sword free of the ground. He looked up sideways at Samuel.

"Good song you got, Samua-san. Lucky me, yeah? This sword kill you, what I gonna do?"

It could have killed. There had been no safety catch in that lethal sweeping downswing.

Dojun spoke in his own language. "In the training halls, there are tests. There are forms and patterns they teach you. There is *kyujutsu*, the art of the bow and arrow. There is *jiujutsu*, the art of yielding. There is *kenjutsu*, the art of the sword. There is first *dan*, second *dan*, third *dan*, up the ladder.'' He sheathed the blade. ''The art I teach has no ladder. There is no training hall. You live. Or you die. That is the only test.''

Nineteen

⊕

Mr. Gerard had a true talent for contriving to have his own way. Before Leda's eyes, he suddenly became a most recalcitrant invalid, snapping peevishly at Sheppard when the butler arrived at his summons, complaining that his leg hurt him, refusing the medication that the doctor had left, and insisting that he needed some fresh air and exercise.

A small crisis ensued, in which an open window, a chair on the terrace overlooking Park Lane, a bench in the back garden, and finally a sedate ride round the park in the victoria were pettishly refused. He wanted exercise. He wasn't accustomed to confinement and inactivity. In short, he wanted to walk.

Since he'd been up and walking about the house for three days, no one could seem to convince him that he could not perfectly well walk outside. He wished to ask Lady Catherine to accompany him. Sheppard murmured that Her Ladyship and her brother were out bicycling with a party of young ladies and gentlemen. A note was sent to find Lady Ashland wherever she might be in the house—the reply came back that she would lend herself to no such nonsense as Samuel walking in the park. Mr. Gerard then scowled at Leda and said that the two of them would go; and no, he did not wish for a footman or a maid or a damned bath chair—it was only across the street, for God's sake.

The descent of his language into the gutter seemed to shock Sheppard into compliance. Leda did not feel it appropriate to correct her employer in the presence of servants, but she gave him a thin, eyebrows-raised, Miss Myrtle look.

Beyond the fact of his injury, she could not feel that it was perfectly appropriate for her to be walking out with a bachelor in the park, unaccompanied. However, when she ventured to mention this, she received such an expression of palpable menace from him that even Sheppard agreed that perhaps Miss Etoile could look out for him well enough on a short jaunt.

So Leda and Mr. Gerard went for a walk in the park. They walked in one gate, Mr. Gerard moving briskly on his crutches, and out the very next, where he hailed a four-wheeled growler from the cab stand on the corner.

It took her that long to realize it had been a performance the entire time—that he cared nothing for a walk at all. With a sense of impending doom, she heard him give directions to the cabbie. The old clarence rumbled and rattled along Piccadilly, avoiding the crowds at Buckingham Palace, rocking amid the traffic in the Strand. As they crossed the bridge, the familiar smells of river and vinegar crept into Leda's nose, stronger even than the stale smoke and perspiration scent of the cab.

Mr. Gerard was watching her. She could see his face as he sat across from her, profiled by the faint, steady light from the grubby window that intensified to a rush of golden color over his features as the cab crossed an intersection where the afternoon sun shone down between buildings.

"You don't like coming back here," he said, breaking the silence that had held them.

Leda pressed her gloved fingertips together. "Not really."

He turned to look out the window. Light fell fully on his face, burning ethereal icy fire. "I need you," he said. "I'm sorry."

She didn't want him to apologize. She rather wanted to be needed by him.

He pulled the check strap. As the growler slowed to a halt, there seemed to be a challenge and a question in his expression; Leda glanced aside and realized that they were stopping in front of the police station. She caught the edge of the seat as the vehicle swayed to a standstill.

"Ready?" he asked.

Her fingers curled hard into the cushion. "What must I do?"

"Keep breathing," he said with a half-smile, "and do what seems best."

"You've no plan?"

"How could I?" The question was soft. "I don't know what's going to happen."

"But surely—" She spread her hands and clenched them again nervously.

"Think of us as two cats," he said. "Maybe we'll be tigers. Maybe we'll just be house cats. It doesn't matter. When the time comes, we'll know."

"Mr. Gerard," she whispered, "you are as mad as a hatter."

She wished he had chosen some other location to leave the cab. But it was obvious that in this neighborhood, the safest place to let it stand was directly opposite the station. Mr. Gerard made no explanations or excuses as the cabbie held the door open, only giving directions to wait with the simple certainty of the ruling class—if he chose to linger in such a locale, it was of no interest to him what the driver thought.

She was horrified, however, when he slipped the cab man a bill and sent him into the station with instructions to bring back an officer. She'd cherished some small hope that she might slip out the opposite side of the clarence cab without being seen—but Mr. Gerard was leaning forward, holding open the door and motioning her out. She stepped down to the street just in time to look up into Sergeant MacDonald's astonished face.

"Miss!" He reached to help her onto the curb. "Oh, miss, I'm that glad to see you! We were afraid you—" He broke off, the surprised relief transforming to an instant of blankness. He let go of her arm as if it scalded him.

"Good afternoon, Sergeant," Mr. Gerard said, using his good leg on the step and swinging himself neatly down on crutches. The cab man stepped forward as if to steady him, but it was a pointless gesture; he already stood firm on the pavement and held out his hand to the policeman.

"This is my new employer," Leda said quickly.

"Samuel Gerard," he said, ignoring the dark flush on Sergeant MacDonald's face. He gave the reluctant officer's hand a firm shake. "Of Honolulu. Sandwich Islands. I'm settled in Park Lane for now."

"I am Mr. Gerard's secretary," Leda added, anxious that the sergeant might not misunderstand.

He appeared to misunderstand anyway. She could see him change color, his freckles growing more prominent against his skin. "Secretary," he repeated in a chilly tone, never looking away from Mr. Gerard. "That's doing well for yourself."

The words might have been pleasant—the manner in which he said them was unpleasant in the extreme. Leda drew a breath of distress, but before she could speak, Mr. Gerard laid a firm hand on her elbow.

"Miss Etoile must retrieve some of her belongings from her boardinghouse. She anticipates that there might be a little dispute with the landlady and her bully over some of the valuables. I'd not trouble you, but as you can see—I'm not in a condition to safeguard her as I'd like. I wonder if you might spare a moment and go with us?"

Leda felt his touch like a brand. The proprietary manner obviously confirmed Sergeant MacDonald in his assumptions. She almost thought he might be so indignant as to physically assault Mr. Gerard.

But the policeman's big hands only moved up and gripped his belt. "I don't know, sir. I'll have to speak to the inspector."

"Thank you," Mr. Gerard said, as if the matter were settled.

The sergeant didn't look at Leda as he turned away. He didn't even speak to her.

"He thinks I'm lying!" she said in mortified despair.

"He doesn't know you very well, does he?" Mr. Gerard didn't let go of her.

"But he thinks—"

"It's better this way. Let him think it."

"Oh!" Leda said in horror, as she saw Inspector Ruby coming out the station gate. "Oh, *please—*"

Mr. Gerard instantly released her arm. He shifted back, putting a decent distance between them.

"Miss Etoile!" The inspector's welcome was much warmer; he shook hands with Mr. Gerard and congratulated her on her new position, just as if it were all the most commonplace visit, clucking his tongue over Mr. Gerard's injury and assuring them that he'd be pleased to send MacDonald along to avoid any trouble with Mrs. Dawkins; it was on his regular beat. The inspector couldn't leave the station himself—but he held Leda back a moment and squeezed her hand as the other two started off.

"Miss, you know this don't look very respectable," he said in her her ear. "Are you certain what you're doing?"

"I am acting as secretary to Mr. Gerard," she said defensively. "He has been all that's kind."

The inspector looked after them. "Surely is a pretty fellow." He shook his head. "Poor old MacDonald—daresay he deserves it, the way he sat there like a lump and let his witch of a sister ride roughshod over you, and so I told him. He's been beside himself since you disappeared."

"I'm sure that Sergeant MacDonald need not concern himself with my welfare," she said, goaded into stiffness by the mention of Miss MacDonald.

"Well, you made him sorry that he didn't. Just take care now, miss. I know you're Quality. Don't do nothing foolish. What sort of man hires a lady for a secretary and rides around alone with her in a closed cab?"

"A very good sort of man." She was becoming rather vexed with these suspicions. "A hansom cab would have been impossible for him to get in and out of, that's why it's a clarence. Mr. Gerard might have just let me come here and try to get my things from Mrs. Dawkins by myself, mightn't he? I doubt that many employers would trouble themselves so!"

"Aye," he said, as if that proved his point. "Aye, not many. Pardon my plain speech, miss, I wouldn't never speak so but I didn't think it was important—but don't be surprised if he tries to make up sweet to you. If he hasn't done it already, I can't think of anything more likely.''

Leda was incensed. ''Well, I can think of nothing more *un*likely!'' she hissed. ''Indeed, Inspector—I don't know how you can say such a vile thing! I may tell you that he is a most superior person, devoted to an heiress of excellent breeding who has known him all his life. He is on the point of offering for her. I very much doubt he has any such low thoughts as everyone in this neighborhood seems to be obsessed with!'' She started to walk away, and then turned and snapped, ''Besides, his limb is broken!''

''Small bother to a determined man,'' Inspector Ruby said knowingly.

''Good after*noon,*'' she said firmly, and turned to cross the street, lifting her skirts to run after her employer.

Two cats. Leda had no idea what she was expected to do. She could not believe that Mr. Gerard was so brazen as to ask the police to accompany them to the scene of his crimes. She really thought perhaps he was not quite right in his head, which made her even more frightened, because she was hopelessly entangled in his schemes now. She would be fortunate indeed not to end upon a gallows.

This was what came, she supposed, of having to do with gentlemen. They were entirely too adventurous, and taken to imagining themselves as tigers, or alley cats or such, when they would be far better off sitting at home with their broken limbs propped upon ottomans, resting quietly while being read to. Leda had a very fine reading voice and would have been happy to lend it to this endeavor.

Instead, she heard it quavering a little as she said good afternoon to Mrs. Dawkins.

''Come back, have you?'' The landlady wobbled out of her parlor at the sound of the front door. ''I thought you might, Miss Hoity-Toity . . . and brought your gentleman back with you. Afternoon, good sir—'' Her amiability came to an abrupt halt as she saw Sergeant MacDonald pushing open the door. ''Now, now—what's this, then?''

The policeman looked more sullen yet, glancing from the side of his eye at Leda in an accusatory manner. She ignored him. He was no better than his sister, ready to leap to any despicable conclusion on the smallest evidence. Leda told herself that she was fortunate to see him in his true light.

It was humiliating, nonetheless. Mrs. Dawkins didn't precisely say that Mr. Gerard had visited Leda in her room, but Leda feared that it must be glaringly obvious.

"Miss Etoile has come to collect her things." Mr. Gerard made the landlady's familiarity seem an unwarranted encroachment. To be perfectly candid, as he handed her his hat, he looked as if she were something offensive he'd found on the sidewalk, which put Leda in a slightly better humor.

"Her things!" Mrs. Dawkins laid her hand on her bosom. "Why, I'm very sorry, but Miss Etoile left here lock, stock, and barrel, without a word to me about her things. She took them all with her."

"I did not!" Leda exclaimed. "I haven't removed anything!"

"Then why's the room as bare as a widow's cupboard, and me without my rent? I'm sure *I* didn't remove them."

"I paid the rent," Leda cried. "I was paid up to Friday."

"Do you have a receipt?" Mrs. Dawkins asked.

"You never gave me one!"

"Of course not. Because you never did pay, Miss Fancy Pants. I should have known you as a bunter from the start. If there was something left, I guess I have the right to recover my losses by selling any little trash you might have forgotten when you slunk away offhand. Ain't that the law, Sergeant?"

The policeman shrugged. "Depends."

"But have you sold the mirror and brush?" Leda asked anxiously. "Just Miss Myrtle's dressing set—if I could have that . . ."

"I told Jem Smollett to take it all away and get what he could for it, and nothing in the lot worth two bob," Mrs. Dawkins grumbled. "I don't know anything about no silver dressing set."

"You know it was silver," Mr. Gerard said.

"A dressing set—what else would it be?" the landlady demanded in a huffy tone.

"Tortoiseshell. Ivory. Wood. Any number of substances," he said reasonably. "When did he steal it?"

Mrs. Dawkins waved her hand. "Steal it! Let's have no talk of that! All I know is the gel left me no rent."

"Did it cover what she owed you?" He leaned on one crutch and pulled a money wallet from beneath his coat. "I'll pay you whatever's in arrears. How much?"

Mrs. Dawkins bobbed closer. "Twenty shillings the week, for a lady what entertains followers."

"I have never entertained followers!"

"Why, miss, with my own eyes—"

Mr. Gerard interrupted the landlady. "Since you've already sold the dressing set, how much should I subtract?"

Mrs. Dawkins' double chin bounced as she started to speak and then hesitated. Anyone could see that she wanted the whole twenty, with nothing at all deducted. She seemed to lose a little of her boldness as she met his look.

"Can't you remember?" he asked, with a soft, controlled edge in his voice.

"N'more than two bob, like I said," she mumbled.

"Are you very poor at numbers, Mrs. Dawkins?" His tone was indeed like a tiger's, a large and sleepy one, still purring politely, but switching its tail.

"Tinsel stuff, it was," she said, watching him slip the money wallet away as if she were mesmerized. "Not real silver."

He looked at Leda. "I doubt that anything's been moved yet. Go up and see."

"Oh, no, you don't." The landlady roused herself abruptly. "You've not paid; you've no right to set one foot on me stairs, miss."

"I did pay! You had the money off my washstand yourself!"

Mr. Gerard took no part in this dispute; he simply lifted his crutches onto the first step and started up. Mrs. Dawkins grabbed at his arm, but somehow as he faltered under her hold, she stumbled and fell back, bending over with a yelp.

"Oh, me knee! Me knee's gone out!"

Mr. Gerard looked back. "Pardon me. Did I hurt you?"

"Oh, law! Help me sit down!" She clutched at Leda and Sergeant MacDonald. Between them, they supported her to a chair in the parlor. She collapsed into it with a moan and wobble of her rouged cheeks.

Mr. Gerard followed them to the door on his crutches. "Perhaps some hot water," he suggested. "That's what the doctor recommended to me."

"Never mind hot water," Sergeant MacDonald said roughly. "She'll come out of it. Come along, miss—I can't hang about here all the day long. No use for you to go up, with your splint 'n all, mister."

Leda looked at Mr. Gerard helplessly, but he only stood back, allowing the policeman past. He didn't say thank you, but then, Sergeant MacDonald's offer had not been particularly politely phrased.

"Miss," Sergeant MacDonald said curtly, holding back for her at the staircase, while Leda picked up her skirt and climbed.

She looked back down once, through the rails at the first landing. Mr. Gerard appeared to be mostly interested in a piece of lint on his trousers, while the sergeant clumped up the stairs behind her.

She reached the attic floor. Sergeant MacDonald stood very close to her shoulder as she fumbled in the dim light to find her key in her purse and fit it to the latch, close enough that she could feel his breath on her nape.

With a creak and rattle, the door came open. Leda stepped into the room, which was just as bare as Mrs. Dawkins had claimed, only the bed and table and chair remaining.

Now what? Her cloak gone, her washbasin, her sewing basket—not that any of that mattered, but to lose Miss Myrtle's mirror and brush . . .

And what on earth did Mr. Gerard expect her to do? What was she doing here? She'd assumed that he had some reason to want to get into her room himself, but he hadn't made much effort to do it. Perhaps, having so neatly in-capacitated Mrs. Dawkins, he wanted Leda to occupy the sergeant while he pursued his mysterious objective from some other location.

"I can't believe this, miss," Sergeant MacDonald said in a strained sort of way.

She swung around to face him. "I can't either. All my things!"

"I don't give a da—" He grabbed her arm. "I don't give a fiddle for your things! I can't believe m'sister was right about you."

"Your sister," Leda echoed, stepping back in his hold.

"I thought you were fine; I thought you were an honest girl." His face was flushed, his voice passionate. "I waited. I treated you respectable. I wanted to *marry* you!"

She wrenched her arm free. "I am perfectly honest, Sergeant. And I wish you will not speak of this to me!"

He took her by both arms; his hands were so tight that it hurt. "Is this the first time? Have you gone off with men before?"

"Unhand me!" Blood throbbed in her fingertips from the hold. She tried to twist free and could not.

"Mary warned me. She warned me that you were no better than you should be. But till I saw it with my own two eyes—!" He made a bitter sound and pulled her right up against his chest.

"You forget yourself!" Leda cried. She pushed at him, but he only seemed to grip harder. He put his face close to hers, and Leda strained back, panicking. She might have screamed; she felt she must, but mostly she pushed and pushed and tried to free herself, while he just pulled her tighter and closer.

"Sergeant!" She was panting, straining back as far as possible from him. "Let me go!"

"Let you go! So's you can go off with him because he's handsome as sin, and just as wicked. I know his kind. And yours! A plain man's feelings don't matter to your sort, do they?" He shook her hard. "Nothing but what you can get for yourself—just the way Mary said."

"Sergeant MacDonald!" Leda twisted, breaking free.

She saw Mr. Gerard in the doorway and gave a low cry of relief and mortification.

He didn't say anything—he merely looked at the policeman with a level gaze. He paired his crutches and rested them against the wall, bracing his hand on the door frame.

"Oh, is it a fight you want?" Sergeant MacDonald demanded wildly. He took a step toward Mr. Gerard, his fists closing. "I'll give you that, Fancy Man, limping or no. Is that what you want?"

"Not really," Mr. Gerard murmured. Leda saw the tiger very clearly in his easy, ready stance, crippled but still with lethal claws.

She had a spurt of apprehension for Sergeant MacDonald, who didn't know—who puffed and swung and never saw the danger. She drew in a sharp breath as he threw himself into the punch.

Mr. Gerard just seemed to move past him. For an instant they were together in the doorway, and then Sergeant MacDonald was lurching past onto the landing, grabbing at the stair rail to save himself from falling, while Mr. Gerard turned in front of Leda and stood there, planted between her and the policeman.

She heard Sergeant MacDonald come back, a clump of boots and furious breathing. She rubbed her palms up and down her aching arms and peered around Mr. Gerard. The sergeant stood in the doorway. "I'd have married you," he muttered. "Against Mary and everything! Ask him what he's offering!"

Leda felt her mouth pucker, chagrin and tears and nerves all tangled up together. "You wouldn't have," she said in a small voice. "You wouldn't even speak for me to your sister. I wish you would go away!"

"He's scum! Miss—look at him! You can tell his sort a mile distant. *Look at him.* Everything that's low and shameful, that's his kind. You think he's so handsome, but he's trash. You'll find out what he wants from you." He gripped the doorway and shoved off of it. "Ah, miss— damn you! Both of you!" He turned away and started down the stairs.

His boots echoed in the silence that he left. Mr. Gerard

stood motionless, still facing out the open door as the sound of the policeman's footsteps receded. When the distant sound of the front door shook the air with a faint vibration, he turned. He had a strange look, lost, as if he didn't recognize her for an instant.

It was gone in a blink. He leaned on the table and hefted himself up, balancing on one bent knee and foot on the wooden surface. He rose, swinging his splinted leg clear of the edge, reaching for the attic beam. With both hands, he hauled upward, straddled the joist, and came down off the other side, all in one swift flow of motion. Then he was back on the floor, holding a felt drawstring bag of a terribly familiar, long and narrow shape.

She stared at the bag, but he gave her no time to think about it. "Under your skirt," he said quietly, holding the thing toward her.

"What?"

He didn't answer, but pulled her toward him and started to bend down on one knee, lifting her dress below the bustle. Leda squeaked, but managed to clap her hand over her mouth. She grabbed the bag, twitching her skirts away. "I can do it," she hissed. "If you please, Mr. Gerard!"

He rose, with a look that she could not interpret. She glared at him. He turned away, using the table edge to support himself for one stride back within reach of his crutches. Mrs. Dawkins shouted something from below. Leda pulled up her skirts with shaky hands, trying to hide the sword and check to make sure Mr. Gerard wasn't looking at the same time.

He wasn't. He just took his crutches and started at a leisurely pace down the stairs.

Unable to contain her anxiety, Leda dragged open the neck of the bag. Inside, the golden handle of the sword caught a gleam of light.

She gave a little gasp of consternation. How could it be *here,* when it had been located by the police?

A madman. He was an utter madman.

Hurriedly, she slid the bag through the wire cage of her *tournure* and tied the drawstring to her waistband, not without some effort. She finally had to take off one glove to handle the cord. The weight of the burden was awkward, and she knotted the string three times, in desperate fear that it might work loose. As she took a step, the sword banged against her legs—she had to slip it further to the side and brush down her silk skirts while Mrs. Dawkins yelled up the stairwell that she wouldn't have any lovemaking going on right under her nose.

Leda clutched her skirt and hastened to the stairs. Mr. Gerard was already at the bottom, in conversation with the landlady where she'd limped into the hall. When Leda reached the first landing, he was leaning over Mrs. Dawkins in a way that seemed most intimidating; the landlady was sinking down into a convenient chair with her eyes glued to his face. He didn't stop speaking as Leda passed him, but she was in no mood to linger and listen to whatever he was saying in that low and formidable voice.

She went right out the door, pulling on her glove, stepping briskly up the street. "Sir will be along in a moment," she informed the waiting cabbie, and pulled open the door of the cab herself, entering from the side away from the police station. She settled into the musty seat with the hard press of metal against her leg, and switched frantically at her skirts, trying to make them fall naturally over it, but the curved point of the weapon insisted upon sticking upward in a manner that she feared made a painfully obvious bump at the level of her knees.

Mr. Gerard arrived. The cabbie handed the crutches inside after Mr. Gerard had hefted himself within the carriage. He sank back into the seat across from her as the door closed.

The cab moved forward with a rocking motion. Leda rested her face in one hand, suddenly feeling as limp as a wet petticoat. She took a few deep, rhythmical breaths, and then lifted her face. "Oh, my." She drank in another gulp of ancient cab air and pushed it out of her lungs in a rush. "Oh, my."

Mr. Gerard was looking at the lump in her skirts. Leda brushed at the telltale point, trying to make it disappear.

"I believe you have it on backward," he said gently.

"How was I supposed to know?" She tugged again at

her skirt. "Whatever are we doing with it? I thought the police had found it!"

"Obviously, they haven't."

"But—in the paper—"

"It's intriguing. I think there must have been a copy. Why, I don't know. But someone has decided to save some diplomatic embarrassment, and serve up the fake to Her Majesty." He shrugged. "It makes no difference. I've done what I wished."

"Well, this is too Oriental for me. Whatever are we to do with it now?"

"Take it up to your room. Is there somewhere you can put it that the maid won't be into before tonight?"

"*My* room!"

"Unless you prefer to give it to me now. I could try to conceal it alongside the splint, but I don't think that would work overly well."

Leda could see that it would not, nor did she care to lift her skirts and struggle to untie the thing right here in the cab, with him watching from the forward seat. She frowned at the passing buildings outside the besmudged window. "I suppose—it would go under the skirt of the dressing table. But that will be swept in the morning."

"I'll remove it before then."

She looked at him swiftly. "How?"

He just made that faint curl of his mouth, not quite a smile. He seemed remote, somewhere far beyond her in his thoughts, even though he was speaking to her from two feet away.

Leda made a little moan, pressing her fingertips together at the bridge of her nose. He was a singularly uncomfortable sort of man, and a thief, and now he would be slinking into her bedroom in the middle of the night to retrieve his ill-gotten goods.

"Are you with me?" he asked.

She pressed her fingertips harder and nodded.

"Miss Etoile," he said softly, "you are a remarkable lady."

* * *

The family were dining at home that night, and Leda found that she was to have a place at the table. Mr. Gerard ate in his room, stating that his walk in the park had worn him out, which seemed quite plausible to Leda.

She was seated by the foot of the table, next to Lady Ashland. To the right of Her Ladyship's cover, a shiny black bowl sat amid the crystal and delicate china plate. It held a handful of fragrant wood shavings, upon which rested a square of black silk. An unadorned silver ring lay in the middle of the square.

Lady Ashland made no move to touch or examine it, but Leda saw her eyes rest on it several times when the talk was of the troubles in their islands and Mr. Gerard's leaving. When the ladies rose from the table, Lady Ashland lifted the bowl and carried it with her, pausing in the hall to tell her daughter and Leda that she would be back down to the drawing room in a moment.

"That's one of Samuel's gifts," Lady Catherine confided. "He's the most provoking thing—they always mean something very deep, and I can never puzzle out what it is. But it's sweet of him. It means a lot to poor old Mum, you know, even if it is only feathers and bits of cloth and such. I like to give her practical things. She always needs new notebooks, and last Christmas I saved my pin money and had a carpenter make a glass cabinet for her specimens. It turned out very well. I have to think of what I'm going to do this year, since we might be spending it at Westpark. Maybe you can help me."

Leda was happy to lend herself to such an agreeable task until coffee arrived, and Lady Ashland came, and later the men, when the conversation turned political again, full of unpronounceable names and untold complexities of sugar and treaties and labor shortages. Leda sat listening quietly. She would have been willing to sit up quite late, hoping that if Mr. Gerard was going to slip into her room, he would do it while she was downstairs, but in the end she had no reason to stay longer than Lady Ashland and her daughter, who rose to go to bed at ten.

The sword bag was still under Leda's dressing table when she returned to her room. She didn't change, fully intending to sit up wide awake until he came, which some-how seemed more respectable than just drifting off to sleep when expecting a bachelor in one's bedroom.

She sat in a cushioned chair and took up the only book in the room, smoothing her hand over the pages of a pe-culiar, pleasantly soft and pliable paper decorated by an Oriental chrysanthemum motif. The book was written in both English and the quaint bird tracks of Chinese-looking characters, with pictures of little temples and ships and people, and called *Descriptions and Oddities of Japanese Culture Identified for the Englishman.*

It was interesting, but not interesting enough to keep her eyes from drooping as the night wore on and the elec-tric light glared steadily from overhead, much brighter and harder upon the eyes than gas or candlelight. Finally, as the sound of Big Ben drifted in three slow tones on the night, she finished the entry on the meaning of *maru,* which was a circle, and perfect completeness, and some-times an affectionate suffix for things like good sword blades.

She rolled her eyes at that, and thought, *Men,* as she closed her lids to rest them for a moment. She mused about the word for circle, and the silver ring, and thought drowsily, *I know what the circle means. Completeness. It means he's coming back.*

She sat up with a start, finding that the room was dark. It was confusing for a few moments, until she realized she had fallen asleep in the chair, and her back was stiff. She squinted her eyes against the sleepy scratch in them.

He must have come and gone already, and extinguished the light as he left.

She could see quite well in the lamplight that filtered into the windows from the street, reflecting back all the pale creams and light blues of the room. She rose, think-ing to slip out of her dress and into her borrowed gown, so that she would get some little sleep for the night.

"You're awake."

His voice was soft; it came from the darkness and should have made her jump, but instead it was calming, instantly familiar to her.

"Oh," she whispered, putting her hand to her throat. "You're still here." She located him as he moved; he had been standing quite near her chair, but he crossed silently to the window where she could see his face in the cold light. He had only one crutch with him, and carried the felt bag with the sword in the other hand.

As she watched, he slipped open the bag and drew the sword from inside, holding it up so that the golden hilt and lacquered sheath gleamed, and the bronze tassels fell down over his fist.

"Come here and look at it," he bid her.

Leda walked to the window, caught by the night and the silence, and the pearly shimmer of the sword. The round guard below the hilt reflected inlaid gold: swirling clouds with the face of a lion or a Chinese dog amid them.

"It's beautiful, isn't it?" he asked quietly. "The mount is probably at least five hundred years old."

It was beautiful.

He touched the hilt. "This should have a blade forged by a master, with a dragon carved down the length of it, or a war god, for the spirit of the sword."

She looked up at him. He grasped the hilt and the scabbard and drew them apart.

There was only a piece of rough iron, a foot long, loosely set in the hilt like the cut-off stump of an arm.

"What happened to it?" she gasped.

"It was made this way. It's a *kazaritachi*—a ceremonial sword. A gift to be dedicated to the honor of some temple, I'd guess. Never meant to be used." He slid the hilt home and looked down into the lamplit street. Shadow and silver lined his face in spartan planes. "All this gold outside. Hammered-out iron inside." He rubbed his thumb against the lacquered sheath. "Do you think your sergeant is right?"

"Right . . . concerning what?"

He only gazed down into the street.

"Sergeant MacDonald is ill-mannered and impertinent," Leda said. "And I shall certainly cut him the next time I see him. He is entirely mistaken in his conjectures about me."

His lashes lowered. "And what of his conjectures about me?"

"I take leave to doubt he is right about anything whatsoever," she said tartly. "He is evidently a rather stupid man."

"He frightened you. I'm sorry for that."

"Oh, well—I suppose it made an excellent diversion. He was so busy accusing me of nonsense, I don't think he had any suspicions about anything else at all."

He looked up into her eyes. "Miss Etoile, is there anything I can do for you before I leave?"

The sudden depth of his look made her shy. "I'm sure that it should be the other way round. I'm your secretary."

"Would you like me to make it right with Sergeant MacDonald? There are ways I could correct his mistake about our—association."

"No!" She gave her head a fierce shake. "No, I don't believe you should have to do with the police any more than you've done already. Sergeant MacDonald is a great disappointment to me. If he wishes to believe disagreeable rubbish, that is his business."

"If not entirely his fault."

Leda sniffed. She had no mind to become sentimental or forgiving over Sergeant MacDonald. "What are you going to do with the sword?" she asked instead.

He rubbed the felt bag along the scabbard. "I'm not certain yet. I didn't intend to have it this long. And now that they think they've found it . . ."

His frown alarmed her. "Please do be careful."

The corner of his mouth tilted. He shifted his crutch and leaned on it. "As careful as an aged house cat."

"A *lame,* aged house cat. I feel that it would behoove you to stay off of ceiling beams in your condition."

He turned his face to the window again, making no promises. Below, some late party-goer whistled along the empty street. Leda remembered suddenly that she was in her bedroom in the depth of the night, with a caller of very questionable credentials.

"I'll say good-bye now," he murmured. "You can sleep late in the morning."

His train was to leave at eight A.M., a fact which Leda had ascertained by the rather terrifying and wonderful instrument of the telephone, which, after she had overcome her fear of electrocution, and in spite of the earpiece sounding like a hive of buzzing bees, had made a half-day's worth of travel arrangements into a quarter-hour task, with the tickets delivered to the door by a runner before dinner. The world was really extraordinary for a secretary in this modern age.

"Oh, yes, well—good-bye, then. *Bon voyage.*" She felt a little maudlin, suddenly. It was beyond reason difficult to say farewell to a gentleman she barely knew, and a man at that. She reached out impulsively and put her hand over his on the sword. "Thank you! Dear sir—thank you for everything."

The air seemed to grow hushed. She realized that it was her bare palm against his skin; he looked at her with a severity and focus that went through her like the shimmer of moonlight on water and steel. His hand moved beneath hers, tightening on the sword. No more than that.

No more than that, and yet she felt that everything changed, took on a form and substance that made her heart sound loud in her own ears.

You'll find out what he wants from you.

She did not know; she could not tell—but there was such frozen force in him, in his eyes as he traced her face, in his motionless hand, in his very stillness . . .

She dropped her eyes. He caught her hand in the same instant, pressing a small roll of cloth into it.

"Good night, Miss Etoile." He pushed back from the window, and from her, and moved into the shadows of the room. She heard nothing, not even the click of the door latch, but she knew when he was gone.

She sank down into the window seat. The cloth in her hand unrolled into a ribbon of dark silk. She could not tell the true color in the lamplight from outside, but a small foreign coin gleamed in the middle.

A single coin.

A single coin, like bits of feathers and a silver ring. She found her way to her chair and then back to the window, bending over to try to read in the book by the outside lamplight.

It was there, among the simple line drawings of Japanese money. Five yen. She flipped forward to a section of festivals and gift-giving. *A roll of silk is a mark of respect, which still survives in ceremonial rites,* the book said. And a few pages on: *By the peculiarity of a pun on* goen, *meaning both the coin and a sense of relation, the five-yen coin is considered a symbol of friendship.*

She wrapped the coin and silk between her fingers, holding the bundle up to her lips until it grew as warm as her own hands.

Twenty
〰〰〰〰〰
Rising Sea

🔯

1887

He wanted her. He wanted to touch her. Aboard the Atlantic steamer he woke up wanting, on the train west he went to sleep to the sound of the rails and to lust, and dreamed of touching her—in dreams, where there was no shame in it, and he would hurt no one. Out of San Francisco, in the state cabin aboard a ship of his own line he stayed isolated, welcoming dreams, not wishing to wake each dawn and look into the mirror at his own face.

Honolulu was green and sun and windblown flowers—and empty. He lived in his small spare room at the harbor office, instead of at home, where the tall shutters were closed and the rooms dim and echoing.

Seeing him on his crutches, Dojun recommended a Chinese bone-setter. The Western splint was taken off, an Oriental support put on. Through a course of ill-smelling herbs and hot-cupping, and a few clandestine visits to an American surgeon, the leg healed slowly; painful, but hurting less each time he tested it.

While Samuel had been away, Dojun had acquired a houseboy, a son of one of the new flood of Japanese immigrants. The boy swept wood shavings and didn't say much, even in Japanese. He addressed Dojun *Oyakata-sama* with a deep bow, giving him a high title and the most courteous of honorifics. Toward Samuel the boy was almost equally respectful, designating him a *meijin,* a notable person, for no reason Samuel could fathom beyond excruciating Japanese manners.

206

In the last two years, since Japan had agreed to allow plantation workers to emigrate to Hawaii, Dojun was no longer so solitary and remote in his house halfway up the mountain. As often as not when Samuel came there was some Japanese visitor drinking tea or *sake,* a game of *go* in progress. The guests were reticent with Samuel, polite but wary, finding him a strange beast that fit no pattern: a rich *haole* who owned ships, who spoke their language and read *kanji* ideographs and Japanese script.

As Dojun became more sociable with the world, he seemed to become more brusque with Samuel. They had seldom trained together in the last years. Samuel did the physical work on his own, the constant conditioning and practice, but he still went up the mountain nearly every day. Dojun sometimes wished to speak of his art, sometimes only greeted him and went back to his conversation and game of *go,* more often just sat in silent concentration, offering nothing. Or attacked with the random frequency that never quite let Samuel rest.

There was no indulgence given for injury, as Samuel had known there would not be. The path did not end because he'd broken something; nothing stopped and waited for his limitation. *Let go,* Dojun would say, *let go of limitations. Give yourself wholly to the day. Every day. Live as if a sword hangs over your head—because it does.*

Not only in a metaphorical sense. The ceremonial sword he'd stolen was hidden where Samuel hoped to God Dojun would not stumble on it. About that, he never intended his teacher to know. There were days he did not even go to visit—avoiding danger altogether—and then had to double his watchfulness on his own ground, because Dojun would not hesitate to strike him there.

It would not have been so difficult, except for the distraction, the fate that had taken all the floating, chaotic energy of *shikijō* and fused it on *her.* Samuel thought of her with her white shift pulled up over her bare legs, drinking tea and arching her feet in a delicate motion like a dancer; he thought of her head bowed, all that shining hair, her hand poised over her notebook and the soft skin of her nape above the demure turned-down collar. He could not keep his center; he kept falling from the way, losing *zanshin*, the vigilant unattached mind, and with it years of exercise and discipline.

To combat it, he spent long night hours sitting silently, trying not to want, attempting to shed all conscious desire, and still she crept into his mind like a slow heat. He sat peacefully, facing a wall, thinking of nothing . . . and out of nothing the essence of her formed, the image of her brushing out her hair over naked shoulders, the curve of her back, the white roundness of her hips as she bent to step into her skirt.

He could not go to Dojun with this. The political currents, his contracts, his strategies and plans—those things they could discuss. Even when he was never quite certain whether Dojun was for him or against him in a particular goal, it was good to talk and listen, to expand into possibilities and consider outcomes and intent—like a game of *go*, an infinite potential of combinations in the white and black stones on the board.

Rumors of counterrevolution rose and faded and rose again. Samuel had his sources on both sides; he watched the reformers and sugar planters press to cede Pearl Harbor to the United States, while the king fought to keep the harbor sovereign. He watched the September elections ratify the reformed constitution and bind the king hand and foot. He watched men posture and shout and indulge in petty vindictiveness, but the current ran inexorably in favor of money and power—there was no doubt in Samuel's mind that it was the reformers and their American connections who would prevail in the end.

It seemed an ugly thing, but he understood power and the battle to maintain it. He understood fear. He understood the frustrations of an intelligent, cordial, all too jovial and extravagant monarch. For all of his adult life he'd dealt with the ambitions of businessmen, Western and Oriental, and seen the bewildered islanders slowly stripped of land and potential, shoved into a game with rules made by more cold-blooded men. He understood all of this—whether he approved or objected was immaterial; the important thing was to understand, and predict, and know when and how to move.

He'd built his enterprise for Kai, not for money or influence, not to dance at the palace or topple governments. He'd lent himself to neither side, but kept his intention pure. One future. One task. To be whole and untouched. To make himself more than the sword mounting, more than coarseness inside a fine facade. To forge away what he had been from what he was now, as the anvil forged impurity from iron to create fine steel.

To be worthy of the things he wanted.

To be what she would love.

His heart was a blade . . . and flawed . . . flawed . . .

This weakness dragged him back to the dark, had floated within him for years, never purged. It crystallized now, falling in on itself. It made an opposite pole—on one side Kai and honor and everything he would be; on the other, this warm beckoning darkness that he despised and craved to drown in.

Two years ago, he had bought a four-acre lot high up beside the Nuuanu Valley. In his present restlessness he had plans drawn for the house to be built there. He envisioned Kai in every room: one for her piano, one for the dining table he would build her, a wide lanai because she liked the breeze, a stable for her horses. He interviewed builders and ordered teak and monkeypod and paulownia wood. Just after the September election, the ground was cleared and construction commenced.

When he stood in the mud amid the new foundations, he only leaned lightly on a cane. Where there had been a mass of brushy vegetation, he could see out over the ocean now. He thought of names, of christening the place in Hawaiian *Hale Kai*—Sea House—and decided that was too obvious.

She had advised him not to be precipitate, and he trusted her in that.

He thought of her face, her throat, her supple hands and the curve of her breasts.

He stared at the horizon.

Put it aside, he thought. Put it aside.

Far below him, beyond the slope of the island, beyond the city, beyond the church spires and roofs glistening amid deep greenery, the tide was coming in, flooding the reefs and the sands.

He'd done this naming once before, thinking himself ingenious when he'd registered his own company as Kaiea—running together the Hawaiian words that meant water washing high on the land—thinking now that Dojun had made him inclined to be entirely too subtle. Kai had never caught the implication; never, for all he knew, even noticed her name in his endeavor.

He would be more straightforward with her. She was all honesty and candidness; it was his own tendency to conceal himself that hindered him. Perhaps he should name the house Hale Kai after all. Perhaps he should just go to Kai and ask her outright what she'd like.

What should I name this home I'm building for you, Kai? And by the way, will you be my wife?

He did neither. He watched the sun go down over the ocean in a glory of orange and gold. He couldn't even hold the question of Kai clearly in his mind; he kept seeing *her*, the drifting softness of her hair in the clouds, the scent of her body in the rain-washed earth—damn her, damn himself, blind and deaf in his visions. Dojun could have killed him ten times over if he'd been there. A child with a grudge and a green coconut could have.

The tide came in, a slow and steady force, unstoppable. *Kai ea,* the water drowning the land.

He named the house in English. Rising Sea.

And did not understand himself, knowing that for the deepest folly of all.

Twenty-one

Leda was town-bred. The closest she had ever come to the Sussex countryside had been an excursion to Kew Gardens once, when she was eleven. Westpark seemed infinitely amazing to her: the fine old Georgian house, huge and yet somehow friendly, full of trees planted and flourishing in the very middle of the house, strange collections of all sorts of impossible objects, stuffed anteaters, dried leaves, glass cases displaying thousands of shells and insects and stones, photographs, jars of things she had no wish to identify. And the park! In spite of the jaguars, which really weren't allowed to roam free as Lord Robert had claimed, it was pure joy for Leda to walk in it, breathing clean country air, or simply to look out her window each morning and see nothing but lawn and trees as far as the distant hills.

There was a quaint lavender house at the end of the pleasure gardens, a little octagonal building of plaster, decorated by vines of autumn scarlet and half-hidden behind the boxwood hedge. Chased out of the stillroom off the kitchens, Leda and Lady Kai had taken it over as their own, pushing the dusty old funnels and vases for lavender oil aside, scrubbing up and commandeering the long benches and the table beneath the leaded glass window for their task.

The task was Miss Myrtle's special cherry brandy. In August, when they'd first come to Westpark, the orchards had been loaded with the small cherries called brandyblacks. Leda's memory of the beverage, and her fond descriptions of the ceremonial filling of jars and pouring off of brandy for Christmas, excited Lady Kai into action. Nothing would do but they must pick their own cherries and make cherry brandy for the holiday with their own hands.

The first stage had been Leda's and Lady Kai's exclusive occupation for all of a week. Everything was done according to Miss Myrtle's receipt, as recalled by Leda: the cherries picked and sorted, carefully cleaned, then pitted, the proper wide-mouthed jars washed, the fruit packed in and the sifted sugar with Miss Myrtle's particular combination of spices layered on top—half the jar cherries, the other half sugar.

Lord Ashland was presented with an appeal concerning the required fine French brandy. After exacting a promise that he would be the first, not counting Leda and Lady Kai who reserved to themselves the critical tastings during the process, to sample this ambrosia, he agreed to provide spirits of the necessary caliber. Upon casting up the number of their jars, Leda and Lady Kai discovered that they had been most enthusiastic in their efforts, and fifteen gallons of brandy might just cover their output.

Lord Ashland had lifted his eyebrows and cleared his throat, rather as Miss Myrtle had been used to do when she took the first sip. But the brandy appeared as promised and the labor went forward, until the lavender house was finally locked up and left alone in early September with every horizontal surface lined by jars of deep reddish-black color steeping in rich gold.

Leda was pleased at the way the summer and autumn had gone. The Ashlands—her Ashlands, she was rather fond of thinking of them—had taken quite well in London. They weren't precisely in the Marlborough House set, but Leda felt that level of society was entirely too fast for respectability in any case.

H.R.H. the Prince of Wales had, in fact, several times recognized Lady Tess by dancing with her at a ball, much to her consternation and puzzlement, for she seemed to have no notion of the Prince's much-publicized predilection for beautiful married ladies. Leda did not enlighten her. Reportedly, the Prince had spoken very kindly to Lady Kai, and asked Lord Ashland if he was interested in horse racing. Since Lord Ashland was not, and had not been coached ahead of time in polite pretense, he'd simply said no.

Leda thought that *faux pas* was probably the reason they hadn't been inundated with invitations from the most glittering of the fashionable set, but there were invitations enough—more than enough—of a more suitable nature, and gracious acceptances to the house parties at Westpark which proved no one was about to cut her Ashlands cold. Even in early December, in addition to the new guests—which included Lord Scarsdale and his son the Honorable George Curzon, who were expected to arrive on the noon train—Lord and Lady Whitberry were staying on, and the Goldboroughs with their three daughters, and of course, Lord Haye.

Leda paused in her dusting of jars, glancing covertly at Lady Kai. Beneath the heavy shawl she wore against the sunny chill of the room, the other girl was dressed in a simple navy-blue wool with a white apron borrowed from the kitchen, humming and cleansing the funnels and strainers, laying them out over the table beneath the window.

Lord Haye made Leda feel guilty.

Lady Kai liked him. She liked him very much. Even now no doubt they would have been having tea in the drawing room, conversing about fox hunting, if he and Lord Robert had not joined a party of guns intent upon pheasant at a nearby estate this morning.

Lady Kai had become a great enthusiast of riding to hounds, as long as the fox got away. In September, the first time Lord Haye had been invited to Westpark, he'd been present at Lady Kai's maiden run with the local pack. Having pronounced her a bruising rider, he'd made it his particular business to explain to her all the etiquette of the field, advice which she took with good grace and cheerful common sense. He'd promptly accepted a second invitation to Westpark, and been present for a week.

The gentlemen weren't expected back until late afternoon, so when Leda had announced that the time had come to pour off the cherry brandy, Lady Kai jumped up merrily. The Goldborough girls, though game to pour, were set by their mother to write letters to a great-aunt instead. Amid woeful protests, they dragged themselves to their rooms. Leda and Lady Kai had set to work alone in the lavender house.

"That's ready," Lady Kai announced, giving an earthenware colander a final pat with the towel. "What next?"

"Now we pour off one jar, and sample it. First we put it through the colander into that bowl."

It took both of them to conveniently accomplish the job without bruising the fruit unduly. The familiar aroma of the brandy, spirit-sweet, filled Leda's nose. "I do believe this will be an excellent batch," she said confidently, just the way Miss Myrtle had always said it. "One cherry apiece from this jar."

Solemnly, they each selected a cherry from the colander, holding them on the tips of their spoons. Before Leda could warn her, Lady Kai popped hers directly into her mouth whole.

She broke into a fit of coughing.

Leda patted her back, still holding her own cherry on the spoon.

"Oh, my!" Lady Catherine straightened up, spreading her hand across her breast. "It's very strong."

Their eyes met, and they both began to giggle. Leda put out her tongue and licked at the cherry on her spoon, allowing her mouth to become accustomed to the hot, spicy richness. "Eat it like this."

She took the cherry between her teeth and bit down delicately, halving it. Then she allowed the liqueur from the fruit to slide down her tongue, swallowing the sample in stages.

Lady Kai took a second cherry and followed her example. This time, she only had to clear her throat and blow air across her tongue. "Well," she said. "It's turned out quite well, I think."

"This jar is acceptable. We must sample every one, to make certain it's ready. Sometimes the sugar hasn't quite mixed."

They looked at one another again, and at the ranks of jars arrayed across the tables. Leda put her hand over her mouth, patting her lips gently.

"I suppose we had better get started," Lady Kai said.

By the time they were halfway through pouring off the jars, Leda's hands and lips were sticky. The white cloth over the table was sprinkled with red drops. Lady Kai had put off her shawl, and everything seemed perfectly hilarious.

"Look at this cherry," Lady Kai said, holding out a particularly shriveled sample. "I believe it resembles Lady Whitberry."

Leda was determined not to laugh at anything so absurd as that. She accepted the cherry in a sedate manner. "A Lady Whitberry Cherry."

They both dissolved into giggles.

"Do you know," Leda said, opening another lid, "I really don't believe Miss Myrtle ever made more than twelve jars at a time."

"We've made twelve *dozen*," Lady Kai said grandly, sweeping her spoon round the room. "Christmas will be legendary."

Leda thumped the next jar down beside the colander. "There had to be enough for everyone."

"Of course. It's a big house."

"A huge house."

"A positively *tremendous* house."

They spluttered. They fell back against the tables, laughing.

Lady Kai put her arm around Leda's waist, brandishing the spoon with her other hand. "You're so much fun," she said. "I'm so glad you came to us."

"Thank you," Leda said. "So am I. I think—I think—" She paused, trying to gather her spinning thoughts. "I believe we should begin to strain the liqueur into the bottles." She frowned, concentrating hard. "Double this cheesecloth."

Lady Kai obeyed her with the dignity of a clergyman preparing mass. They lined a funnel and put it into a bottleneck. The deep reddish-gold liquid poured inside, sparkling in the sunlight through the window.

"Look at that." Lady Kai sighed in rapture. "That's magnificent."

"Exquisite," Leda said reverently.

"Breathtaking," said another voice, masculine and familiar.

Lady Kai turned around and squealed. *"Manō!"*

Mr. Gerard took off his hat, just in time to catch her as she flung herself at him. He stepped back and lifted her as if she were a child, giving her a boost in the air and a welcoming grin. Cold sunlight through the doorway sparkled on his hair.

Leda had forgot; in five months she had forgotten the impact of him, forgotten how potently, improbably beautiful he was. In the mixture of sun and deep shadow from the boxwood hedge, he shone with his own austere radiance.

She felt light-headed, looking at him. She felt giddy. There was a poem . . .

Tyger, tyger, burning bright . . . in the forests of the night . . .

Blake, that was—savage and stunning in two simple lines. Like him. She couldn't recall the rest of it. Her mind did not seem very nimble at the moment.

It seemed strange to see him standing so freely. She'd forgot that, too—that he would heal, of course. Not a crutch, not a walking stick, not even a limp as he came into the room.

"Oh, Manō!" Lady Kai hung on to his shoulders, resting her head on his chest and swaying from side to side. "I've missed you. We're having a smashing time."

Leda picked up her skirts in a curtsy, wobbling a little as she straightened. "Welcome back."

He looked up at her over Lady Kai. Leda pushed back the lock of hair that had fallen loose from her chignon. The whole coiffure seemed in danger of coming down, but she could not seem to think what to do about it.

He smiled. Leda felt such a flood of warmth and pleasure that she almost wanted to weep. She blinked her eyes closed, and the room seemed to spin around her.

"We're making Miss Myrtle's cherry brandy," Lady Kai announced. "You must have a—cherry."

She let go of him and scooped one into her spoon. He caught her wrist and steadied it before she dropped the fruit. With a kind of fascination, Leda watched as he looked down at the spoon—she found it amazing that he could focus on it so easily, when everything seemed so wayward to her.

He brought the spoon within a few inches of his mouth, took a breath, and said, "My God."

"Please do not swear, Mr. Gerard," Leda intoned reprovingly. And began to giggle.

He looked up at her. She clapped her hands over her unruly mouth. Then she gathered her pride and her scattered wits and said earnestly, "Do try one. There's only a drop of brandy in it. I think it will quite animate you, after your journey."

"I don't doubt that," he said.

He swallowed the cherry. They could not, however, coax him to take more than one. He did not wish to ruin his dinner, he explained gravely.

"Dinner! What time is it?" Lady Kai blurted. "Is it after three?"

"Four-ten," he said.

"I must go." She dropped her spoon on the table. "Oh, Miss Leda—look at this! How will we ever . . . Manō, *will* you help Miss Leda to finish? She can't possibly do it all alone, and I promised—"

She did not say what she had promised, but only grabbed her shawl around her and ran out the door, banging against the jamb and bouncing off as she went.

Leda was not really sorry to see her go. Vaguely, she knew that she ought to be; that she should not be here alone with Mr. Gerard—but she was rather happy to be alone with him. She was so glad he'd come back. She could not keep herself from smiling when she looked at him.

But as he stood by the door, she remembered why he

would have come at all. Not to greet herself, of course.
And Lady Kai had run away to find Lord Haye after less
than five minutes of welcome.

She felt a little angry with Lady Kai. Mr. Gerard had
come so far; he was in love with her; he wished to marry
her—how could she be so thoughtless as to go away just
now?

Leda did not want him to be hurt. She thought of sending him after Lady Kai . . . but then he would only find
her mooning about Lord Haye, who was a perfectly acceptable gentleman, if one had a preference for foxhounds,
but nothing and no one next to Mr. Gerard.

Leda could not understand it. She did not believe she
was thinking clearly. But she did know that she wanted
Mr. Gerard to smile at her again.

Toward that endeavor, another cherry seemed like an
excellent notion. She took up her spoon and licked daintily
at the single fruit balanced on the tip. Mr. Gerard turned
from the door. She tilted her head and looked up at him
beneath her lashes. With her tongue tasting the hot sweetness of the cherry, she gave him a tentative smile of her
own as encouragement.

The preoccupied expression left his face. He looked
back at her as if he'd just then seen her standing there.

Leda took the cherry into her mouth and let it slip down
her throat. She licked her sticky fingers. "You don't need
to help, if you don't like to," she said shyly. "But it's
great fun."

He didn't say anything. He just stood there, gazing at
her lips as she sucked at a tacky spot on the tip of her
little finger. When he met her eyes, there was the most
peculiar tautness about his face: not a smile at all.

"It's more diverting when there are two to pour," she
offered. She transferred the funnel to an empty bottle,
grasping it by the neck when it did not want to stand in
an orderly manner on the table. With both hands, she lifted
the bowl of liqueur, but without someone else to hold the
bottle, she couldn't rest her burden against the edge of the
funnel. "Not so difficult, either," she said, looking around

at him hopefully. "Would you mind just steadying the bottle?"

He came up behind her and lifted the bowl away from her with one hand. "Hold the thing," he said, nodding at the bottle in an abrupt way.

Leda curled her palms around the neck of the glass in front of her. He was standing quite close as he raised the heavy earthenware bowl full of liquid. He leaned nearer to her, regulating the flow as the liqueur cascaded in an even stream over the edge of the vessel. Leda watched the level rise in the bottle, and said, "There. That's enough."

She set the filled bottle aside and put the funnel into another. It was very nice to have him standing so close by. She drank in a draught of brandy-filled air and sighed deeply. He poured again. As the liquid ran into the funnel he cocked his thumb over the rim of the bowl, letting go with his other hand and leaning more over her shoulder to watch the brandy as he tipped the bowl high.

It filled the bottle just exactly. Leda closed her eyes with a sense of satisfaction. She rested back against him. He was so comfortably solid, when everything else had such a tendency to revolve around its proper place.

She remembered Lady Tess standing with Lord Ashland in precisely this way. It was agreeable; it truly was, though Mr. Gerard didn't put his arms around her. He stood still. She could feel his breath in her hair, uneven, deeper than normal, as if he had just run a distance.

"Thank you," she murmured. She turned her head, so that her cheek brushed the front of his jacket. Her hair came tumbling loose at last as it had been threatening to do.

She didn't even care. She did not think she had ever been quite this content with the world before.

Samuel thought desperately of inner balance. Of discipline. *Rectitude*, he thought. *Courage, honor, loyalty.*

He felt none of those things in him. He felt only her hair beneath his jaw, a braid turned inside out and loosened. It fascinated him, because it was so soft; because he had seen her brush it out and coil it up and pin it. He could not move. If he moved he would plunge his hands into it, spread it and bury his face in it. He would pull her against him, into him; he would die on his knees, engulfed by that hot dark flood.

She tilted her head back, nestling closer to him.

Don't, he thought. *For the love of God—*

He lifted his hands, not quite touching her. Her body seemed velvety, pressing his along secret curves and paths. His own was hard in answer. His blood pulsed with arousal.

Remember this. Remember this as a particular weakness within you.

He gripped her elbows and firmly pushed her forward, away from him.

She turned. He expected . . . something—pique or indignation, that he would not give in to her enticement. But she leaned against the edge of the table and smiled radiantly at him, tilted her head like a kitten stretching in the sun, her throat exposed, her hair falling down behind her shoulders, lit by the window so that red and gold played amid the mahogany—a sight that exploded inside him, sent force and weakness to his fingertips.

While he stood paralyzed in black lust she pushed back her hair and stoppered the last two bottles. "I suppose we might . . . finish tomorrow," she said, with a cheerful, tipsy break in her voice. She gazed at the ranks of bottles and jars for a moment, then burbled laughter. "Really, I fear perhaps we made too much, don't you?"

He heard the faint, slurred innocence in her voice, but he did not want her to be innocent. He wished her like himself, wanted to pull her down onto the bare floor with him—beneath him, her smiling mouth on his mouth, her laughter and her body like warmth and satin smothering him. He wanted it and loathed it, and himself, not wishing pain, not wishing brutality, wanting only her smile and her laughter and afraid of what he would do if he let it have him.

He took up a cloth and wiped it hard over his hand, trying to clean away the stickiness. "If you'll excuse me," he said stiffly, making a bow without looking at her. He threw the rag onto the table, seized his hat, and strode out the door, breathing in clean, cold air and the musty odor of boxwood. He filled his lungs with it, and still was unable to escape the lingering scent of cherry brandy on his hands.

He did not even follow Kai. He could not, not now. He wanted no one to see him; not Kai, not her parents—no one who mattered to him to see.

Twenty-two

※

Leda's head had rather a trick of pounding unpleasantly when she woke. Her insides felt none too agreeable, either, and there was a recollection tugging at the edge of consciousness that did not seem as if it would be something she wished to remember at all.

She turned over, digging deeper into her pillow at the soft scratch on her door. But the maid entered anyway, whispering, "Miss! I'm so sorry, miss; it's that early, I know, but we don't know what to do and Mr. Gerard says you must come down, miss."

Mr. Gerard. The memory that she did not wish to admit sprang full-blown into her head.

She moaned and buried herself deeper, feeling utterly ghastly. "I can't." The words came out a mumble. "I'm afraid I'm—ill."

"Oh, miss—I do be sorry—but Mr. Gerard said; he said ye might not be just the thing, but you must come down anyway. He said to tell you that there would be tea a-waitin' for you."

Tea sounded . . . acceptable. But to face Mr. Gerard, to gather her muzzled perceptions and swallow down the roil inside her and actually, voluntarily, without being dragged by chains and strong beasts, put herself into his presence—she did not think that was possible.

The maid, however, seemed to believe it was not only possible, but imperative. With whispered badgerings and manual efforts, she got Leda up and dressed. A whiff of cherry brandy from the discarded apron Leda had worn the day before almost overset her, but the maid rummaged

222

up a fresh skirt and a blouse embroidered in crisp white at the high collar.

With her hair done up into a tight French braid, Leda descended one wing of the curving double staircase from the balcony that overlooked Westpark's domed central hall. Trees quite the size of forest giants grew right inside the house, spreading tropical fronds to the early-morning light filtering through the rain-soaked skylights, the legacy of Lady Tess's naturalist father. For all the years the family had been away, the house and greenhouses and gardens and jaguars at Westpark had been kept by a Mr. Sydney, a spry and ancient gentleman who could reel off the scientific name of any plant at a moment's notice, and often did, without being asked.

Of necessity, she kept her hand firmly on the banister for support. No one else, family or guests, seemed to be stirring yet, but a footman awaited her at the bottom of the stairs and directed her to the small parlor. At the threshold, she felt a very uneasy moment of rebellion in her middle, but the footman was already holding open the tall, varnished door with its giltwork and brass trim.

At Westpark there was no gas or electricity either. Everything was lit by candles and oil. In the dim, watery illumination of the day, a glass-shaded lamp near the window threw scarlet warmth across the carpet, one colorful corner amid the early gloom. At the edge of the glow, Mr. Gerard stood with his arm resting on the end of the mantelpiece. A small fire, newly lit, sent white smoke up the flue.

Leda pulled her heavy shawl closer. She looked in bewilderment toward a sober-faced woman who rose from a chair in the half-light, dressed in a naval-blue cape with a red uniform jacket beneath. A gold badge and single red ribbon trimmed her matching poke bonnet. "Miss Etoile?" She held out her hand, speaking in a voice that was mercifully soft. "I am Captain Peterson, of the Salvation Army."

"Good morning." Leda kept hers equally soft. She shook hands, swallowing a faint wave of illness. Even breathing seemed distressful in her present case.

"I am on my way to a meeting at the hall in Portsmouth. As I would be passing this way, I felt it would be best if I conveyed the child directly to you."

Leda blinked at her. Captain Peterson lifted her hand, indicating the darkest part of the room. Leda noticed for the first time a large basket set upon a table. She looked back at the Salvation Army officer, her lips forming a faint "Child?"

"The girl Pammy Hodgkins, with whom you left him, was not equal to the task." There was a note of steel in the quiet voice. "Although she did well enough; by God's grace he's healthy for a babe that's been put out to a minder."

"Pammy?" Leda looked at the basket, and the officer, and Mr. Gerard, who looked back at her with frost-gray eyes. "But he's not *mine!*" she gasped. "The baby isn't *mine!*"

"Miss Etoile, I appeal to your higher instincts as a mother." The basket rustled. Captain Peterson glanced at it, and lowered her voice to an intense whisper. "We were informed by Miss Hodgkins that she had accepted money from you to care for the child. She was present at the birth, I understand? We requested that a copy of the police record be forwarded to us with the particulars." She extracted a folded paper from beneath her cape and handed it to Leda. Inside, stamped and initialed by some clerk, was a short copy of the record concerning the birth at the station house of a boy to Miss Leda Etoile, resident of Mrs. Dawkins' boardinghouse in Jacob's Island, witnessed by Mrs. Fullerton-Smith of the Ladies' Sanitary Association, and Mrs. Layton, midwife-nurse; Sgt. MacDonald and Ins. Ruby being called out upon the investigation previously noted.

"This is mistaken!" Leda protested in a forceful undertone. "I was a witness, certainly—but it was Pammy's baby. Sergeant MacDonald must have noted it wrong. Everything was very confused—but Captain Peterson, you may believe that this child is *not* mine."

The officer did not argue, but merely gazed steadily at her, as if she could compel the truth in that way.

Leda put her hand to her aching head. "The date alone." She had difficulty keeping her voice from wavering. "You need not take my word. Mr. Gerard—look at the date of this record. This is the very day after the Queen of Hawaii and the Japanese party visited Madame Elise's showroom, is it not? You must see that it is impossible."

She held out the paper toward him, but he made no move to take it.

"I believe Miss Etoile is correct." His even tone was a welcome deliverance back to rationality. "A mistake has been made in the record. What has become of the girl Pammy?"

The officer lowered her eyes. "I am sorry to say that Miss Hodgkins succumbed to typhoid fever four days ago. That is what led us here. With her last words, she asked our officer to bring the baby to its mother." She pursed her lips. "I suppose—it is possible that in her extremity, she might have hoped to prevent the child's being thrown on the parish." She included Mr. Gerard in her searching look. "It is possible, but it does not seem to me likely."

"It is not mine!" Leda whispered vehemently. "I'm very sorry that you've come out of your way, but it is *not.*"

Without moving perceptibly, Captain Peterson seemed to slump a little. She frowned at the basket, and then held out her palm toward Leda. "I should like the record, please. It must be corrected." She arched her eyebrows, and the medal on her bonnet glittered. "Or if it is correct, then there is the recourse of legal action to be considered, to compel parental support."

Leda handed her the paper with a stiff, offended motion. "Most certainly. Further inquiry will provide you with the true case. Please trouble yourself to speak to Inspector Ruby, who was present at the station that night."

"Well." The woman looked at each of them in turn, as if she felt she had been deceived, but could not prove it. "Very well! I shall take him back to the parish, then." She walked to the table and hefted the big basket, peering down among the plain blankets. "We must put you among the orphans I'm afraid, Samuel Thomas."

The fire hissed in the silence. Mr. Gerard did not move; he gazed down into the grate with his mouth expressionless.

"Samuel Thomas?" Leda repeated faintly.

Captain Peterson looked up, as if catching the irresolution in Leda's voice. "Perhaps you would like to see the little soul that you are sending away." She carried the basket to Leda.

In spite of herself, Leda looked. Samuel Thomas lay on his back, profoundly asleep in his homely cradle, with fat pink cheeks and a snub nose, a faint dusting of light brown hair. His face screwed up on one side as she watched, like a funny half-smile, and then he released the squint with a baby sigh.

"He's a dear little boy." Captain Peterson lifted the head of the basket slightly, as if to better display its occupant.

The baby squirmed as she spoke, half-waking. Then he squeezed up both his eyes, gave another faint sigh, and subsided.

"We shall pray to God to take care of him. Do you know what an orphans' barracks is like, dear?"

Leda's head ached. She felt miserable. She covered her mouth with both hands and looked up at Mr. Gerard.

His impassive eyes met hers. She read nothing there, no encouragement, no accusation, no denial. The rain gutters echoed a rhythmic plunk of water, over and over.

"Do you think . . ." She could not quite get it out. "Mr. Gerard . . ."

The lamplight played on the side of his face and his hair, kindling the bright, inhuman beauty in the shadows. "Keep him, if you like." He inclined his head toward Captain Peterson and walked out of the room.

Samuel Thomas Hodgkins made himself known to those still lying abed immediately after the Salvation Army officer had left in a hurry to catch her train. Filling the small parlor first with minor snufflings and small sobs, and then, as Leda attempted to comfort him by trying to pick him up, with wild shrieks, he brought Sheppard, two maids,

Lady Tess, and finally a very white and wretched-looking Lady Kai to the room.

Before Lady Kai arrived, her mother had already got things partly in hand, pacing up and down with Samuel Thomas' red and unhappy face peeping above the shoulder of her dressing gown each time she passed. His sobs had subsided enough for Leda to stammer out a tumbled explanation of the circumstances, which Lady Tess seemed to accept with only a little perplexity, patting the baby's back and crooning in between Leda's tangled sentences and pauses.

If Mr. Gerard appeared to accept a baby with no more consideration than he would adopt a stray pup, and Leda herself could not say she was much better, the rest of the Ashland household was not quite so innocently sanguine. Lady Tess sent the maids off for something that would do for baby napkins, and a little rice gruel and warmed milk. When the towels arrived, it was Lady Kai, smiling gallantly through her pallor, who took the wailing child and deftly cleaned and changed him, while Leda thought that the sudden odor would finally overcome her willpower and make her gag.

She looked at the young and frivolous Lady Kai with a new respect. Everyone else seemed to know exactly what was to be done, while Leda stood aside, feeling stupid and useless in her ignorance. While she kept trying to explain to Lady Kai where the baby had come from, Lady Tess worried aloud about more practical things: that he might not have taken any solid food yet, if cow's milk might make him break into hives, if there was a wet nurse to be found on such short notice, and numerous other concerns that Leda would not have had the vaguest notion to consider.

But Samuel Thomas seemed to take to his rice cereal with enthusiasm. When the spoon clinked in the dish, he stretched his eyes wide and opened his mouth like an anxious baby bird. A single tooth could be observed in his lower jaw as he gaped.

"There." Lady Kai wiped his face when he had finished the bowl and sucked water from a clean cloth dipped in a glass. "How are you now, poor little muffin? Do you feel better now? What's your name?"

"Thomas." Lady Tess answered before Leda could speak.

"Tommy, Tommy!" Lady Kai made his name a sing-song, sitting him up on her knees and swaying him back and forth. "Little Tommy Tittletumps!"

The baby stared at her, and then his mouth curved up in that one-sided grin. He reached out toward her nose with his plump hands, laughing.

"You silly muffin." She pressed her face into his tummy, shaking her head. "Silly little muffin!"

He shrieked with laughter, grabbing at her loose hair.

"Sweet muffin!" She gathered him up and gave him a hug. "Have you come to visit? Have you come to visit Auntie Kai, mmmh? Did you lose your mummy and dad, poor, *poor* little Tommy Tittletumps? What is to become of you?"

"Mr. Gerard said he might stay," Leda offered tentatively.

"Samuel is a brick!" was Lady Kai's comprehensive endorsement of this news.

Leda looked up at her mother with considerably more diffidence. "If it is quite all right with you and Lord Ashland, ma'am? Perhaps I could find a woman in the village who might like to take him in."

"What?" Lady Tess lifted her head from a frowning contemplation of the carpet. "No—certainly not. I have just been thinking of what we shall require to refurbish the nursery."

To strengthen his leg, Samuel walked. He used it against tree trunks in lethal kicks, pushing off sometimes into a backward roll and then immobility, a suspended space of time, breathing the long, silent breath of the woods around him. The rain slid down his face when he was still. The scent of leaf mold clung to his hands and clothes.

He recognized fear in himself. He recognized the gaping hole that had appeared in his intentions. He stood in the rain and thought of elemental things. Fire. Water. Wind. Faith. Will flowing into action without pause.

There was a time to hide himself, and a time to walk into the open.

Leda felt that her recent encounters with Mr. Gerard had not been entirely satisfactory. She had a great urge to meet with him in a situation of which she was the mistress, in order to show how very collected and temperate she was, not at all inclined, as a rule, to overindulge in brandied cherries and lean back for support against bachelor gentlemen.

He managed, however, to startle her out of her sobriety by appearing—damp, and with part of a dead leaf in his glittering hair—just as she exited the library on her way to convey the new week's place settings for dinner to Sheppard.

"Where is Lady Kai?"

No greeting, just that brusque demand, as if she were a footman. His gray eyes held hers only an instant.

Leda pressed her notebook against her breast. "In the nursery."

"The nursery!" His mouth tightened. "Why?"

"She and Lady Tess are taking stock of the furnishings, to see what will do for the baby."

He looked at her with a slight, chill narrowing of his eyes. "Miss Etoile, will you be so kind as to step into the library a moment?"

She clutched the notebook much harder and ducked her head, obeying him with a sense of apprehension very far from the dignified composure which she had hoped to produce. As he closed the door behind them, she turned and reopened it. He waited until she had moved to a chair and seated herself before he reached around without looking and swung the door shut again with a resounding boom.

"Miss Etoile, I would like to make it inflexibly clear to you that this infant is your responsibility. Not Lady Ashland's. Not Kai's. Yours, if you wish to keep it here."

"Certainly." She swallowed down her distress. "But—"

He turned away and addressed the bookcases. "You will locate a wet nurse, and arrange for whatever else it happens that a baby requires. If the nursery wants refurbishing, and Lady Tess consents to it, you will see to the work. Bring me a list of what you believe it will cost, and whatever bills you incur. Is that clear to you?"

She lifted her head, indignant that he seemed to think she had neglected her duties. "It is quite clear, Mr. Gerard."

Her offended gravity appeared to be lost on him. He gazed at a row of leather-and-gilt bindings with their Latin titles, as if that were preferable to looking Leda in the face. "If they wish to amuse themselves with the infant, that is their privilege."

"His name is Samuel Thomas."

"The name is a matter of indifference with regard to what I'm saying to you, Miss Etoile.

"Lady Kai calls him Tommy."

He looked around at last, one eyebrow lifted. He might be angry, but he was not at all a stupid man.

"She's taken to the child?" There was a faint surprise in his question.

"Mr. Gerard, if you wish to win Lady Kai's admiration, you will find that you went a very great way toward it with your decision this morning. You are presently wearing shining armor."

"Only for saying you might keep it?"

" 'He,' Mr. Gerard. I would not advise referring to Tommy as an 'it' in Lady Kai's presence."

He walked off toward the window, gazing out into the rain. It seemed to be a piece of news that confounded more than pleased him. After a moment, his mouth curled in slight humor. "And what of it? I don't see how I can provide babies to her on any regular basis."

Leda had a flash of Miss Myrtle's incisive irony. "I should think that would be the primary purpose of your marriage, would it not?"

Mr. Gerard went still. A rigid shadow carved his cheek. He closed his eyes and slowly tilted back his head. The smile on his face was of sable etched in stone, bitter cold.

"Of course. You're right, of course. As always, Miss Etoile."

She was already blushing furiously before he spoke. Miss Myrtle, in her age and eccentricity, and allowing for her daunting reputation as a conversationalist—a point of community pride in South Street—Miss Myrtle might have been excused a very forward remark, among ladies, and behind her hand. For Leda openly to mention such a thing was inexcusable. She bent her head. "I am unforgivably impertinent."

"Are you?" He spoke to the ceiling with a low, ferocious coolness. "It's nothing but the truth." He lowered his face and stared into the window glass. Against the gloom outside, the faint reflection of his features made a half-portrait in the pane. "Am I in competition, Miss Etoile?" he asked suddenly. "What of this Haye?"

Leda tucked her chin. She found the corner of her notebook most interesting. "Lord Haye, do you mean?"

He began to prowl the room, touching a chair back, a marble-topped table. "I've told myself that I must be more forthright with her." He stopped, looking slantwise at Leda. "In New York, I went to Tiffany's. I bought a necklace. What do you think?"

Leda did not know what to think. The coal fire in the grate seemed exceptionally warm: the Ashlands expended fuel as if it were seawater, keeping a good fire in every room and the full-time attention of a hall-boy to attend them.

"Should I give it to her?" A note of impatience edged his voice. "For Christmas, I thought."

"Oh." She cleared her throat, realizing she was expected to address the problem.

Leda had a fair notion of Lady Kai's jewelry. She favored modest and elegant pieces, highly appropriate to her age. A gift so personal was not precisely proper, perhaps, but if it was something simple—a pearl drop, or a cameo—then Leda supposed it would not be unseemly, since Lady Kai and Mr. Gerard were so well-known to one another already.

She made a constrained nod. "I believe that it must

depend on the necklace. What style it is in, and the expense of it."

"I'll show it to you. I wasn't certain—" He shrugged. "I'm no judge of feminine taste."

"I think I will know what Lady Kai would like." She kept her voice prim, trying to make up for her earlier indelicacy.

"Then come here before dinner." He put his hand on the doorknob. "I'll bring it then."

He felt absurdly restless, waiting in the library for her to keep the appointment. The velvet box from Tiffany's lay on the broad expanse of a well-polished partners' desk, lit by a candle that flickered with each little hail of raindrops against the darkening windows. The wood paneling and rows of books ate up the candlelight: only the mirrored front of a closed secretary against the far wall returned illumination.

Shut inside the box, his choice rested on blue satin. To care for her opinion of it was a kind of weakness, but he did not fight the notion. Better to use the force of his free impulse, direct and distill it, and thereby make it unexpected strength. There were things he wished to understand; she was a source of a certain level of truth, of baffling, cloudy, ever-changing female truth that eluded even what Dojun had taught him.

She had comprehended what Samuel had not. His blindness had been monumental, so huge that he was hung between shame and grim laughter that he had so far shunned reality. Of course Kai loved children, of course she wanted her own; all afternoon she'd done nothing but cuddle Tommy, and talk of him when the infant could not be pried away from Lady Tess. And it was no momentary enthusiasm: he could look back over the years and see endless evidence of it. All of her friendships, her volunteer work, her hobbies; they all involved children.

He had known it all along. And he had never, until today, come face-to-face with what it would mean.

Kai herself didn't know what it meant, he was certain. She could not know. She would be different if she knew, she would not be so easy and merry, she would not turn to him or to anyone so openly, with hugs and kisses that were like children's hugs and kisses, guileless and clean.

The children like she had been, anyway. He did not wish for those others, the kind he had been, to exist. He wished in a way that he did not exist. He wanted always, and only, to protect Kai from what he knew.

From what he was. From the difference between his love for her and what had coursed through him yesterday as Miss Etoile pressed her body against his. Of all his certainties, the most certain one was that he never wished to injure Kai. She was completely safe with him. He wanted no more from her than those naive hugs and kisses; needed nothing but to be the shield and defense of her open innocence. The sum of his life and intention came down to that: he would marry her, and they would both be safe. They would be protected. He would be whole.

And she wanted children.

He turned it over in his mind, searching for a path around that pit. To even attempt to think of Kai and the other hidden part of him in the same moment gave him a physical uneasiness, like the scent of poison in Dojun's tea. All of his instinct, every fiber of him reacted *no*.

Kai understood nothing of that, nothing of what he concealed, but it was possible that Miss Etoile did. Kai threw herself into his arms: the same Kai, the same free trust, drunk or sober. Miss Etoile wore her propriety like thorns—except when she was drunk on cherry brandy. She held herself aloof . . . perhaps she understood . . . perhaps she felt what he felt and struggled too for mastery.

It would be a relief, he thought. Dark welcome relief, to lie down with her and assuage this hunger.

He knew the moment she paused outside the closed door. She was always clear to him, a distinct sense of life. A scent, a step, a certain soft breath, a swish of fabric—those characteristics he knew, of course, but there were things beyond the threshold of his common perceptions, so clear, so very clear to the deeper awareness inside him. Since the night he had begun using her room as a place to conceal his stolen goods, he had known her; had recognized her instantly in the dressmaker's, though he'd never seen her face in daylight.

The essence of her was female. She seemed more feminine, more opposite to him, more hidden in mist than Kai or Lady Tess had ever seemed. The weakness inside him yearned toward her.

You must be ingenious, Dojun had often said. *To see weakness only as a flaw is to limit intention. Face the truth, then turn it to your own use.*

But this was a weakness that he did not dare to use. To empower weakness he had to know the dimensions of it, and that he did not know, or wish to.

There were others in the hall with her, no one familiar to him. He heard them speak, and her reply in tones of hasty excuse, a promise that she would not be long. She didn't knock, nor crack the door until the other footsteps had continued down the hall.

A scent of foliage swept in with her, cool air in the dry warmth of the room. She shut it out quickly, with no attempt at all to leave the door open.

She wore a green gown cut low, the draped skirt washed in emerald shadows, her skin and unadorned throat like the pale white blush of night-blooming flowers.

He felt weightless, as if he had just voluntarily stepped off a cliff. For months he'd been associating with Dojun and businessmen, Chinese shopboys, architects and carpenters, railroad conductors, ship captains, sailors. He might as well have been a *yamabushi* warrior monk on a mountaintop, as far as women were concerned. If avoidance had sharpened his senses to what he had shunned, then every perception and faculty was flooded by her now.

She was merely dressed for dinner. He knew that. Kai had worn more revealing necklines to the opera. Still it unnerved him. He had never seen Miss Etoile dressed in anything but the most modest of high collars, except for the memory that rushed in on him of her breasts and back and shoulders as she had brushed out her hair in her room.

All of that mahogany hair, that hair that had fanned his jaw yesterday in feathery softness; she had swept it up into a loose mass of some intricate, impossible-to-decipher coiling and braiding. She was not as classically featured as Kai; Miss Etoile's face might be called pretty at best, her eyes not quite pure green, her chin heart-shaped. Her mouth had a pleasant curve even when she wasn't smiling. How well he knew it, from stolen moments of observation. Next to Kai, it hardly seemed that she should even be noticeable, and yet he noticed.

She did not look at him now. She stood with her hands behind her on the knob, Joan of Arc at the stake.

"I won't make you miss the dinner bell," he said, taking refuge in a mocking tone, irritated at her unease and his. "I wish only a moment of your time."

"Of course." She looked up at him and made a vague motion behind her. "That was the Misses Goldborough and their mother."

She seemed to think that he would make something of that. He did not.

"They wouldn't understand." She spread her hands and moved them in a flutter. "That I am *your* secretary, you see. I'm afraid Mrs. Goldborough wouldn't like it. They believe I am Lady Kai's companion and Lady Ashland's social assistant."

"You told them that?"

"Certainly not!" She went into her posture of brisk and offended propriety, which usually made him want to smile. Tonight it made him notice the lift of her bare shoulders and the curve of her waist. "It was not necessary to prevaricate. I have merely gone about the duties which have fallen to me, and allowed the houseguests to draw their own conclusions."

"And does this mean you can no longer function in my personal employ?"

She bit her lips. Clearly, she would have preferred it that way, but she walked past him and turned, shifting her skirt behind her. "I'm completely at your service, of course. But—I would so dislike to have anything reflect badly on the family."

"As would I." The faint annoyance in him grew stronger. He put his hand on the velvet box. "Will you look at the necklace?"

"Yes. Certainly. I've had a peek at Lady Kai's jewelry box this afternoon. She does not have a pearl—if that was your choice, perchance."

"It isn't pearls." He pulled back the lid and tilted the box in her direction.

The candlelight caught the stones with full intensity. He looked up at Miss Etoile.

He watched her breathing catch, an intake and a long pause while her skin grew pink. She closed her eyes and then opened them again, very wide.

"My gracious me." She let out the air in a rush.

The necklace was a fitted collar, designed like a wide, filigree ribbon completely done in diamonds, with diamond flowers and leaves twining along the middle of it. At the front it widened, simulating a bow, the center represented by a large marquis-cut stone, the two filigreed tails of the bow curving downward to tassels of tiny glittering blossoms strung like flowers on a lei. On each tail, the tassels were finished with three pear-shaped diamond drops.

He waited. He was reduced, finally, to asking outright. "Do you like it?"

She put her fist to her mouth and shook her head.

Samuel lowered the box. He set it on the desk, fingering one of the diamond tassels. In an obscure way he felt personally rebuffed. It was only a necklace, for God's sake; he had thought it pretty, but if it was not, it wasn't. "I'll send it back." He kept his voice stolid, fearing that she would hear the disappointment in it.

"No!" She lowered her hand. "No. It's magnificent. I'm sorry, I was—overcome, for a moment."

He looked up at her.

She tilted her head, and gave a small laugh. "How fortunate Lady Kai is." She blinked twice. "And how silly I am. You have brought tears to my eyes, Mr. Gerard." She made a stilted gesture with the handkerchief that had been tucked in her sleeve.

"You approve?"

She made another small and peculiar laugh. "I assure you, your taste is most laudable. However—" She lifted her head and took a deep breath as she pushed the lacy piece of fabric back into her cuff and smoothed it. "I think it is perhaps better saved as an engagement gift, unless your suit has been accepted before Christmas."

Though her voice was steady, there was still something of candlelight swimming in her eyes, and a faint fluttery wistfulness to her mouth; that sweet and curving mouth.

"Would you try it on?"

He heard himself ask it. Again the weightless feeling had come on him; he felt carried by tides, blown before a rising storm.

"Oh, no. I could not."

"I'd like to see it." He attempted nonchalance. His artificial shrug rustled the formal collar of his shirt. He, too, was dressed for dinner, in black swallowtails and white tie. "There were only men at the jeweler's."

"We should go to the drawing room. They will be assembling."

He lifted the necklace from its bed of satin and moved near the mirrored secretary. "Come here, Miss Etoile. I haven't worked you overly hard in my employ."

Her lips pursed. She put her head down and walked to where he waited. He pulled out the chair at the secretary and she sat with her hands clasped before her, her back to him.

He slipped the jeweled collar around her neck without touching her. But the necklace was made to fit close to her throat, and the tiny, hidden catch required him to work with his fingers against the nape of her neck.

A light fan of hair at the base of her coiffure brushed his finger. It felt warm, her skin cool. He looked up into the mirror.

She was gazing at the reflection, at the diamonds, at him.

He meant to take his hands away. He let go of the diamond catch, raised his fingers too abruptly. A lock of her hair fell free of the loose pinning. The necklace sparkled on her breast. She and the stones were like light, with darkness all around: himself darkness . . . and falling . . . falling . . .

He should not have done this. The necklace should have stayed safely shut in its box; he'd never needed to know her opinion of it, hadn't turned his weakness into strength, had done nothing but allow it to consume him.

The candle found deep highlights in the lock of hair. She lifted her hand as if to tuck the curl back into place, but before she could, he touched it. He gazed down at his hand, fanning the curl between his fingers, resting his fist against the slope of her bare shoulder. It was as if his actions did not belong to him—and yet they did: he felt every texture, every delicate strand of hair, every light breath she took.

He slid his knuckles in a feathery brush up her throat, past the necklace, to a place beneath her ear that was soft with a sensation he had never in his life known before.

He stood silent, touching her. It was beyond him; beyond him; he could not turn back of his own will.

Stop me, he thought. *Don't let me.* He could not remove his hand; could not speak. No sound at all came out of his mouth when he moved his lips.

She only looked at him in the mirror, her eyes wide and dusky green. In the months he'd been gone, she'd lost the fine-drawn hollows below her cheeks; her face was fuller, gentler. He knew that she had been hungry, lived on the thin edge of destitution; he'd used the desperation in her to bind her to him, one coil after another to hold her, make it impossible for her to betray him.

But she had never betrayed him. Not from the first, when he had come within an instant of killing her. Her vulnerability seemed enormous, her stillness beneath his hand an act of infinite trust.

With his fingers, he could lay open bark on the trunks of trees . . . and he could feel her heart in the fragile pulse at her throat, so light and quick. He lifted his other hand and cradled her face.

Small. Delicate. Like the life of a small bird within his palms. Lust flooded him. What he wanted . . . God, what he wanted . . .

He thought of Kai, his plans, of the house he'd built. It

all seemed another universe: fantasy and mist, and he had never been alive until this instant.

He spread his hands, his thumbs brushing the skin beneath her earlobes, his fingertips resting on her temples, just tasting her cheeks. Still she only stared at him in the mirror. Such fine eyes she had, the subtle green of a foggy meadow, of her English woods, the lashes so long that he felt the sweep of them against his fingers.

He stood there touching her, imagined her hair all around in waves, her body: the voluptuous scent, the sounds. His own throat tightened with a suppressed moan. He wanted only to hold her, to gather her up and cradle her against him—and he wanted to overpower her. There was a terrible violence inside him. All he knew, all he had experienced and mastered in his life was destruction. Will and shame kept it in check, but will had failed him.

Remember this, Dojun had warned. *Your overflowing passion, your heart that holds so fiercely to the tumult of the body and so rejoices in it, will become a forest of swords to hack your soul to bits.*

Remember this.

It was only shame, vast shame, that finally impelled him to open his hands and let her go, and walk blind and mute from the room.

Twenty-three

Leda sat paralyzed in front of the mirror. From what seemed a long way away, the bell chimed for dinner.

She was aware of the door standing open behind her. The necklace sparkled on her neck in a blaze of diamonds. The image began to swim in her eyes.

She fumbled for the catch, could not find it, and began to weep in earnest.

It is because my mother was French, she thought. *I am frivolous. I am wanton. I am happy.*

I cannot be happy.

She stared at herself through the blur. Mortification and miserable joy muddled together inside her breast.

She could not be happy. It was indecent to be happy. She had been deeply and dreadfully insulted. He had behaved with gross impropriety. It was an affront to Lady Kai, to the family, to the very roof over their heads. It was unforgivable.

She was unforgivable. For the tears were not tears of remorse.

The necklace would not come free. She struggled with it, heard a step and voices from the domed hall outside, and in panic forced open the clasp. She grabbed the box from the desk, darting into the shadows of the room. In a few moments the houseguests would all be leaving the great drawing room through the open double doors at the head of the staircase, the gentlemen taking the ladies down to dinner in the order of precedence that Leda herself, after careful consultation with Burke's Peerage, had outlined for Lord and Lady Ashland.

Now, after months of dining happily with the family, the very notion filled her with panic. She had the order of the evening's dinner partners by heart. As an employee and female of common rank, she would go down last, just before the hostess, on the arm of the gentleman whose lack of social precedence matched her own.

Mr. Gerard.

And she would sit on his right hand through the meal, while Lady Kai sat directly across the table from him.

Leda was horrified to realize that she had planned it that way. Within the boundaries of precedency, she might have instead paired a daughter of the house with Mr. Gerard, and herself with elderly Mr. Sydney, who had no more business than she to eat in the dining room, if one were stricter in one's conventions than the Ashlands ever cared to be.

But in writing out her place settings, she had indulged herself, just a trifle, just for this one week, taken just a tiny advantage of the circumstances that she and Mr. Gerard had in common: the fact of being nonentities in society, if one disregarded his steamship company and directorships and the timber mills and the banks and marine insurance and ten pounds a week to a secretary who did precisely nothing.

The sound of conversation grew louder, Lady Whitberry's voice a distinctive quaver echoing in the domed spaciousness of the hall. Leda daubed hastily at her eyes with her handkerchief, praying that they were not reddened and swollen. Unable to think of anything better, she pulled down the first book within reach and stuck the necklace behind it. With a clearing of her throat, a smoothing of her skirt, and a deep, steadying breath that did nothing whatsoever to steady her, she walked out into the hall and along the arcaded balcony toward the murmur of conversation.

Lord Ashland and Lady Whitberry had already started down the stairs. The rest of the couples, fifteen in all, formed up in the drawing room and followed. Just as Leda arrived outside the double doorway, she saw Lady Tess lean across her escort, Lord Whitberry, and speak to Mr. Gerard, who stood alone.

Leda knew perfectly well that Lady Tess was informing him of whom he was to take down, just as Leda had coached her to do for all the guests. She thought the intensity of her blush must warm the air around her. Worse, when he looked up and met her eyes, he too changed: the shadow in his jaw grew taut and he seemed too rigid even to nod. Lord Whitberry waggled white brows at him and said loudly, ''Deuced lucky chaps, ain't we, Gerard? Got all the best gals well in our sights.''

Leda saw the dark flush that rose at Mr. Gerard's collar. Whatever he answered, it was spoken so briefly that she could not hear it. Lady Kai, three inches taller than Mr. Sydney, blew Leda a kiss as the brisk little man sailed her past—and then there was no choice left for either of them: Mr. Gerard stopped before her and offered his arm.

He said nothing. He did not even look at her. She heard the conversations in front and behind them, Lady Tess and her daughter well-versed in Leda's dictum that guests must not proceed to the dining room without speaking, but should at once begin a pleasant interchange with their partner.

Leda and Mr. Gerard, however, descended in stifling silence.

She kept her fingers not quite touching his arm, looking down at her other hand, pretending a great concentration upon keeping her skirt lifted on the stairs. At the foot of the staircase the pose betrayed her; she expected the level floor one step too soon and swayed forward out of balance.

She was never in the least danger of falling. Yet her hand tightened instinctively. He took her weight without a waver, his balance flowing into hers. And for a moment the remembered sensations of his fingers on her shoulder, his hands cupping her face, seemed truly real, as they had not seemed when she had experienced them. Every detail came to vibrant life: the way the necklace had lain warming against her skin, the pads of his fingertips spread over her cheek, the brush of his satin-lined lapel against her spine. She walked into the dining room washed in the ghastly truth that the man beside her, perfect and cold in profile, full of subtle strength and cast like a black-and-golden icon in his evening clothes, had touched her intimately, with intent; had all but embraced her.

He *had* embraced her. It would be splitting hairs to say that he had not, to pretend that he had merely brushed her hand in passing. To stroke the bared curve of her throat was nothing less than a shocking iniquity. To caress her face!

She withdrew her arm from his before it was quite polite. He held her chair, and she wondered if the look that Mr. Curzon gave them was as arch as it seemed, or just a twinge of his bad back. The wicked poem that one of the Miss Goldboroughs had recited last week ran absurdly through Leda's head. *My name is George Nathaniel Curzon; I am a most superior person. My cheek is pink, my hair is sleek, I dine at Blenheim once a week.*

Mr. Curzon certainly held himself very much up, and his father was worse. Neither had spoken to Leda or Mr. Sydney since they had been introduced this afternoon, and Lord Scarsdale had positively cut them, looking away when Lady Tess had made the presentations. Leda could understand particularities and niceness, but she had become so accustomed to the easy atmosphere of the Ashland household that it was difficult not to feel the Curzons unpleasantly stiff.

But she could not bring her mind to dwell on it. Mr. Gerard had touched her. Mr. Gerard, who was in love with Lady Kai. Who was sitting at her left hand. Who said not a word, either to Leda or to the Miss Goldborough on his other side.

Leda really felt too distraught to eat. She toyed with her soup while Lord Whitberry boomed some lengthy story at her from her right.

"Manō!" Lady Kai addressed Mr. Gerard's silence with a tap of her spoon against her glass. She never had any patience with the axiom that she should not speak across the table at a large dinner party. "We have decided that Tommy will be a botanist when he grows up. He has already tried to eat two of Mum's orchids. If you are to pay his support, as Miss Leda says, then you must arrange for him to enter Oxford.''

"Cambridge, my dear!" Mr. Sydney announced his correction with authority. "Cambridge is the place for a scientific young man.''

"Cambridge, then. I'm sure they consume orchids with consummate flair at Cambridge.'' She turned a laughing face toward Mr. Gerard. "What do you think?''

"I'll provide whatever Miss Etoile deems appropriate for the child.'' He did not look at Leda.

"Miss Etoile is a mere amateur in the field, I greatly fear.'' Lady Kai shook her head. "She looks at Tommy as if he is a contraption that she can't quite puzzle out.''

Leda managed a smile. "I'm afraid I've no experience with children.''

"You may give him to me, then. He's such a darling, I could just eat him up! Did you know that he can pull himself up to stand in the crib? And a tooth already! He's very precocious for barely six months. I'm so glad you didn't let them take him to the orphans' home; I can't endure the thought of it.'' She abruptly grew more sober than Leda had ever seen her. "Manō Kane, you must promise that you will never, *never* send him there.''

She looked to Mr. Gerard rather than Leda for this vow, as if somehow his was the primary obligation to the child. He did not deny it. He only said in his even manner, "No, I won't.''

With most people, it might have sounded casual, merely placating. But Mr. Gerard had a way of speaking that made one believe.

The soup was cleared away. As the second course began, he looked across at Lady Kai again. "Would you like me to adopt him formally?''

"*Would* you?'' Her gasp mingled with her mother's shocked murmur of his name and Lord Whitberry's harrumph of disbelief.

"I'm considering it. I don't yet know what the process would entail.''

Leda glanced at him beneath her lashes. The idea shocked her, too; the more because she was certain, utterly, that he mentioned it—and indeed would actually do it—only to please Lady Kai. At Kai's enthusiastic response, there was a certain relaxation in the tautness of his face.

"But would you not have to be married to adopt a child?" Lady Kai frowned.

He took a sip of his wine and looked across at her. "Perhaps."

Lady Tess glanced from him to her daughter, and then lowered her troubled gaze to her plate.

"And how are the jaguar kittens faring?" Leda inquired of Mr. Sydney, her voice emerging only a small degree too high-pitched. "Is the biggest one still a terrible bully?"

The little man calmly cut a bite of fish. "I fear that is the case. And we have another tyrant on our hands in his mother. She's become quite protective—I'm afraid I've had to confine her away from the others in a smaller run."

Mr. Curzon surprised Leda by so far unbending as to mention that he intended to travel out to Samarkand and central Asia soon, and wondered if Mr. Sydney knew what exotic animals he might expect to see there. The dinner-table conversation went back to more suitable topics, and Leda went back to reality.

Mr. Gerard wished to marry Lady Kai. Leda's mother had been French, and gentlemen found it difficult to govern their animal spirits when it came to French ladies. Miss Myrtle had always said so, citing *that unspeakable man* as an excellent case in point.

That was all there was to be made of it. Mr. Gerard's masculine humors had overcome his manners for a moment. He was plainly embarrassed by the lapse, and would certainly apologize the moment opportunity presented itself.

She could just hear what Miss Myrtle would say about it. She could suddenly understand why Miss Myrtle had been so careful to instruct her in proper conduct, and had so often spoken of the foolishness of young ladies, and young half-French ladies in particular—because Leda had the most lowering feeling that she was quite absurdly in love with Mr. Gerard.

And love, Miss Myrtle had always said, was a strong stimulant to unwise minds, only to be indulged in with exceeding circumspection, in small and refined sips, like her special cherry brandy.

Samuel tried to court Kai. He tried. He watched Haye tease her the way he had used to do himself, when she was seven and he years and worlds older. He did not feel so much older now as alien, unable to find common ground in bullfinches and in-and-outs and the proper way to ride an ox-fence and ditch. Even with Tommy, Haye cut him out. As the uncle and cousin of a number of promising young relatives, he turned out to be the kind of man who got down on the floor and hiked squealing babies over his head every day before breakfast.

Not that she ignored Samuel. Their relationship was as warm as it had always been. The same as it had always been. He could talk to her, dance with her, give her advice that she would take. He described the house he'd called Rising Sea and she listened with animation, offering suggestions for decorating it, approving his choice of names. But he could not break through the familiar, well-worn comfort of their friendship; could not bring himself to say he loved her, could not force himself to touch her in any way that might frighten or upset her.

And yet he saw that Haye had intentions. The threat that she might accept another man before he had ever spoken made him uneasy and angry. He fought the feeling, because anger had no place in his intentions, it could only blind and hinder him. But if he could empty himself of hostility, he could not banish the disquiet, the sense of certainties fragmenting, pushing him farther and farther from the people he loved more than his life.

Even Lady Tess seemed to be more distant. He was aware sometimes of her silent attention on him, but when he turned to her, she always found some excuse to withdraw, or speak to someone else. And that, of anything, crystallized his uneasiness into the thin edge of alarm.

He had to act. Things were changing. In politics and

business he could keep his balance, but in this—he felt his own clumsiness, his capacity for error.

You care too much, Dojun said. *You want too much. What I gonna do with you, huh?*

For a week he had avoided Miss Etoile—though "Miss Etoile" was not how he thought of her anymore, even when she appeared in the demure lace collars that she wore. *Her,* was what he thought: heat and softness and desire.

She and Kai went about the house full of secrets, heads bent together, giggling and hushing one another when he came upon them unexpectedly—one more sensation of exclusion, though he knew it was only Christmas, and gifts, and Kai's delight in holiday intrigue. The house smelled sharp and fresh of evergreen garlands: English things, English cold, when at home it would have been the scent of roast pig and flowers, and sand in the coconut pie at the Christmas luau.

He wished they were there instead of here.

Want too much, you.

Mistletoe hung in convenient spots, tacked to chandeliers and a few doorways, under the direction of whom, no one would ever admit, but Robert labored beneath heavy suspicion, particularly since he and the oldest Miss Goldborough were the first to be caught in the drawing-room door.

Miss Goldborough blushed and held her hands behind her back, presenting her cheek—but her mother was at her afternoon nap, and Robert took her arms and kissed her full on the lips. Her sisters shrieked and danced in horrified laughter. Curzon lifted his eyebrows. Samuel saw Kai glance beneath her lashes at Lord Haye.

Haye, standing with a book half-open in his hands and looking on at Robert's gambit, did not appear to notice. As Samuel watched her, she lifted her eyes and met his own. She smiled a little. Her cheeks turned faintly pink.

He froze inside. It was a look he did not know how to answer. He became a sudden coward, finding a Chinese dog in porcelain blue-and-white on the table next to him to be of striking interest. As he picked it up and turned it over in his hands to examine the mark, Kai gathered her skirts about her and chasséd to the door, turning and presenting herself there with a little curtsy and a mischievous smile.

In his inaction, staring blinding at the porcelain mark, Samuel felt rather than saw the subtle shift of Haye's stance. Tension surged in him. And yet he sat still, unable to rise: sat there losing his chance, knowing Haye would move.

But it was Robert who grabbed his sister and whirled her in a circle in the doorway, ending with a deep bow over her hand and a kiss on the fingers.

"Oh, fiddle!" Kai snatched her hand away. "Spoilsport!"

He pushed her out of the doorway. "Only trying to keep us from being trampled by the rush. Don't you see the elephants massing to charge?"

Curzon looked down his English nose. Haye grinned and settled on a chair arm, leafing through his novel. "Every dog has his day, Orford," he said to Robert.

" 'Orford'!" Kai gave a delicate snort. "As if he were a real lord. No one calls him that at home."

Robert smirked. "As real a lord as you're a lady, m'dear."

"It is merely a courtesy title, in your case. That's what Miss Leda says. Real lords can sit in Parliament. Daddy could, if he liked."

Haye held up his novel. "I say, you two. Has anyone read this yet? It looks a corking good story." His interruption smoothly forestalled what threatened to degenerate into a sibling bicker. *"A Study in Scarlet.* Listen to this."
He cleared his throat and dropped his voice to a dramatic tone. " 'On his rigid face there stood an expression of horror, and, as it seemed to me, of hatred . . . which was increased by his writhing, unnatural posture. I have seen death in many forms, but never has it appeared to me in a more fearsome aspect than in that dark, grimy apartment, which looked out upon one of the main arteries of suburban London.' "

That caught the attention of Kai and of everyone else.

"Oh, start it from the beginning, do!" She sank back into her chair with her eyes wide and expectant.

As Haye took up the story of Dr. Watson and Mr. Sherlock Holmes, Samuel turned the Chinese figure over and over in his hands. He looked up under his lashes, listening, watching the others respond to the idea of deduction by detail and analysis. He'd read the book, and the character Holmes seemed to him a shadow of Dojun—clumsy and obvious with his magnifying glass and brute logic, too certain of his universe, arrogant in his conclusions. "There is nothing more to be learned here," the fictional Holmes said often. "My mind is entirely made up on the case."

A man could get himself killed believing that. Dojun could kill him with a thought. Samuel knew it, because he carried the potential within himself.

Concentration is intuition. Intuition is action: the way he had nearly destroyed *her* with *kiai,* a spirit shout, in that critical moment in her attic room. The intensity of his attack had been too much because he could not detach his mind from her. Even then, opposing her, he had wanted her. He had meant only to disable, to daze her for a few moments, but there was more than a casual connection between them. He was not the master that Dojun was: he did not know himself; he made mistakes. He could not remain calm. He was not at peace. He could not even stand up and offer a mere kiss beneath a mistletoe.

Sitting motionless, holding the blue-and-white dog in his hands, he knew that he was in panic flight from himself. And he knew that until he turned and faced what he feared, all his intentions were no more than smoke and daydreams.

The fire in her room had gone to coals, tiny cracks and halos of orange against black, casting no light beyond the grate. He moved past it, though he knew she was asleep and would not see his silhouette before the glow.

The room seemed full of scent and female presence. She slept softly, her breath quiet, undisturbed by dreams. The ease of her sleep gratified something deep inside him. She felt safe here; he had brought her; she was in a subtle way connected to him by peace as well as necessity.

He stood in the darkest corner of the room. He watched, although there was nothing to see. He listened, though there was nothing to hear. He waited, anticipating nothing—no action, no thought, no feeling.

And yet feeling was there. He was aware of every curve of her body. Memory rippled the calm surface of concentration; her skin beneath his fingers, the shape of her face between his hands.

Let it go. He was here to confront it and let it go. But there were contradictions, paradoxes; to try to let go was to hold more tightly. Dojun had taught him. The hunger that he wished to uproot went so deeply to the center of him that it seemed to *be* him. To separate it, to excise it— nothing would be left.

He imagined lying beside her, over her; things that he knew and yet did not know, never sure what had been real and what his contorted fantasy. He had dreamed and remembered, uncertain which was which, loath to ask questions that might reveal what he kept hidden.

He could not kiss Kai. Not even a light, teasing kiss like Robert's with Miss Goldborough. He was not Robert. There was too much pain and misery in those dreams and memories, tangled and confused with pleasure. One touch—and he did not know what would happen.

But Kai would want children. Her own. His. When he could not even bring himself to touch her.

It was not Kai he burned for.

He stared into the darkness. He gripped his hands in *kuji*, forming the complex interweaving of his fingers that should guide and focus his will, mobilize intent to action, forge his strength and mind into his goal. But there was no focus, no unity, no vanishing of restraint. His body craved what his mind despised. Beyond that, he had power for nothing.

He left her sleeping peacefully and retreated to the vast, cold night. Walking the grounds while the household slept, he felt himself remote from all their contented warmth, a stranger still after all these years, a black ghost in the silent moonlight.

"I have a card case for Manō." Lady Kai bounced Tommy on her lap while he cooed "Ah-ah-ah" with each bump, an occupation which he appeared to find exceedingly agreeable. She consulted her list with her free hand. "I bought it in London, so it's very smart—not that he will care anything for that. Last year I gave him a shaving mug and mirror, and he liked it very well."

Leda thought of the necklace he'd bought for Lady Kai, a whole brilliant cascade of diamonds.

"Will you give him something?" Lady Kai looked up at her. "Perhaps you should consider it—he's bound to have a gift for you."

"Oh, no. I shouldn't think so." Leda bent her head over the openwork mesh mittens that she was knitting for Lady Tess. "I am his secretary."

"Well, he will. I would be surprised if he hasn't brought everyone something back with him from home; perhaps even something he made himself. He does the loveliest woodwork, if you like the Japanese style. Our old butler taught him. I really prefer more intricate carving, myself. It seems more artistic. But Manō's things are very pretty, even if they're plain. He never puts birds or flowers or anything like that on them."

Leda knitted a row in silence. She had several gifts in the making, one for each of the Ashlands, for she wished very much to show her gratitude for the manner in which she had been befriended. Beyond that, Lady Tess had asked her to hide in her room the surprise packages that her ladyship was accumulating for her family. The pile of tinsel paper and boxes growing beneath her bed made Leda feel quite festive and part of the fun.

She had thought of giving something to Mr. Gerard, but had not dared. She laid down the knitting in her lap and caught a loop of the silver yarn around her forefinger, tugging at it, twisting it round and round. "What do you suppose he might like?"

"For a gift? Here, Tittletumps, down you go. No, you

must not eat Auntie Kai's skirt. Take this spoon, darling. Let me think. There really isn't time to get anything beyond the village, is there? You might have ordered a fountain pen, if we had thought of it earlier. Perhaps you could put his initials on some hankies."

Somehow, Lady Kai's suggestions made Leda feel rather melancholy. A shaving mug, a card case, a fountain pen, handkerchiefs.

Her heart ached for him.

She remembered his face in the half-light of a street lamp outside her window, the brief pressure of his hand as he pushed a small roll of cloth into her palm. She still kept the five-yen coin, the symbol of friendship, on a thin ribbon beneath her blouse.

He had not apologized for his ungoverned conduct, nor even spoken to her since. He avoided her, she was quite sure.

Perhaps, because she was half-French, he did not feel he must apologize. Perhaps she had given him a disgust of her upbringing on that day with the cherry brandy. Perhaps they were friends no longer.

The thought made her feel more dismal still.

"Yes. Of course." She allowed the silk yarn to unwind from her finger, caught up a stitch that she had dropped, and sighed. "Perhaps I'll embroider some handkerchiefs."

Twenty-four

It was the jaguar that made Samuel a hero for the sec-ond time in his life. How the animal got free of her cage and fenced run, a frantic Mr. Sydney never determined, but she and her cubs were loose when Kai bundled Tommy up, put him in a perambulator scrubbed out of the attics, and took him for a stroll alongside the reflecting pool.

All the younger set of houseguests had gone, too, dressed in fur-trimmed capes and pelisses, taking advantage of the unseasonably sunny weather. Kai was hardly alone and unprotected when the confrontation occurred, although Samuel thought it might have been better if she had been. Kai had common sense, but the Goldborough girls apparently didn't: at first sight of the animal crouched, tail switching, under the neat shadow of a box-wood at the edge of the lawn, they took screaming fright and dashed behind the men, their flaring skirts making exciting targets as they went. Samuel himself had the youngest one hanging onto his shoulders from behind while the jaguar lay yellow-eyed and tense, uneasy in her freedom, staring balefully at the startled group.

At first the cat made no move. But as the girls continued their half-laughing shrieks and peeked around their shields, the jaguar cuffed one of her tumbling cubs, pushing it behind her, never leaving the crouch, never taking her eyes from the human intruders. She laid back her ears and curled her lips, showing fangs. One claw lifted, open in razor warning. The hands on Samuel's shoulders tightened sharply. The girls grew suddenly silent. Just as Robert

253

said, "Don't move," the oldest Goldborough let go of him and broke away, bolting back toward the house.

The dash of motion broke the cat's tense spell. The jaguar rushed forward a few yards and paused, glancing back toward its cubs. But the incomplete charge sent the other girls into panic. The group splintered in all directions—one girl ran toward the steps in the garden wall, Robert shouted and sprinted after her; the other let go of Samuel, turned, and tripped, flinging herself full-length on the grass. The nervous cat reacted instantly to the confusion, racing after the running girl; then turning and propelling itself after Robert, then surging toward Kai and Tommy in a wild zigzag.

Kai lost her nerve and snatched Tommy from his perambulator. The awkwardness of the motion, the flash of skirt and trailing blanket: Samuel saw the creature rivet on that target, bounding across the lawn, a dark, powerful beauty gathering speed. He moved, cutting across the cat's line of attack. The jaguar homed in on his action, angling on its haunches to make the turn—he backed and accelerated sideways to draw it to him. In three bounds the animal was there, launching into a flying strike, pure force to be directed. Samuel went into a roll. One claw caught his coat and ripped it open as the cat somersaulted over his shoulder. He came upright to the sound of a great splash and the splatter of water across the pavement and his trousers.

The jaguar's dark head emerged from the sparkling, shattered surface of the pool. She blinked and paddled, transformed abruptly from a snarling menace to a wet and bewildered animal with ears and fur pasted down to her skull. She began frantic attempts to rejoin her cubs, thrusting her front paws up onto the edge of slick marble, unable to get a foothold in the depth of the pool to heave herself free.

"Good God." Haye was the first to find words. "I say, are you all right, Gerard?"

"He's bleeding!" Kai suddenly came to life. "Go and get Mr. Sydney, Robert, and some footmen to capture that animal! Lord Haye—" She pushed Tommy into his arms.

"Do take him back to the house quickly, in case she should manage to get out of the pool. Miss Sophie—Cecilia—do you need salts? Don't swoon, if you please—go with Lord Haye back inside—and call Mother; she will know what is to be done."

Samuel pressed his hand over his arm, feeling the stinging throb now, and wet blood from the slash. "We'll need a net, or blankets."

"Certainly they will." Kai turned on him. "*You* will not. You will come in with me and have that dressed, before it can become infected. A cat scratch always will. Mr. Curzon, you shall stay here and make sure that she doesn't climb out before they can trap her. I'm sure that you will—anyone ready to travel out to Samarkand must be wildly intrepid."

"Certainly, ma'am." Curzon slapped his walking stick in his open palm. "She won't like this across her nose, if she tries to escape."

"Well, she is only frightened, so don't be too rough. There now—here is Robert back already to the rescue. Manō, come with me, and leave them to it. Don't let them forget to gather the cubs, Mr. Curzon."

Samuel allowed her to bear him away into the house. She took him up to the empty nursery, where there were clean cloths and cotton wool and rubbing alcohol, and stripped off her gloves. Without the slightest hesitation, she demanded that he remove his bloodstained coat and shirt.

As he sat bare-chested in the low window seat, she knelt before him and dabbed at the set of deep gashes. The burn of the alcohol went through him like a rush of flame; he took air deep into his lungs, not making a sound. When she had the bleeding slowed and the wounds cleaned to her satisfaction, she bound his arm and tied it off. She didn't speak the whole time. When she finished, she sat back, closed her eyes, and let out a long, shuddery breath.

She opened her eyes and looked at him. "Manō. Thank you."

They were alone in the nursery. From far below the

closed window, the shouts and splashes of the capture broke the peace of the silent room.

He thought: *Now.*

Speak now.

"You're not hurt?" he asked absurdly.

"Of course not." She rolled her eyes and smiled. "Silly. Only you would ask that." She had not stopped to take off her cheerful red pelisse before. The white fur trim brushed his hand as she unbuttoned it now and tossed it aside.

He tried to think of some compliment, some way to begin what he had to say.

"Manō—" She put both of her hands over his suddenly. "Sometimes I forget—" She stopped. "No . . . it isn't that I *forget,* because I don't, but that I forget to say it out loud. I love you. You are the dearest and best friend anyone could ever have. You're always here when we need you."

He thought he should take her hands in his. He thought he should do a hundred things.

"I love you too, Kai," he said at last. And watched her with his heart taut in his chest.

"Not that I deserve it, I'm sure!" She leaned up and gave him a kiss on the cheek.

He ought to have turned; he could have turned; she was only a breath away. But the paralysis came on him. He felt the brief warmth of her face against his, only an instant, and the chance was gone. She squeezed his hands and pushed herself to her feet.

"Come down as soon as you've changed. I want you to be there when I puff you off to everyone as the bravest thing this side of China." She swept up her pelisse and started for the door.

"Kai—"

She looked back, with the fur-lined cape tossed over her shoulder.

He felt powerless. "You're sure you're all right?"

"Manō, you are the sweetest idiot. It's you who're hurt. Do try to remember, and look heroically pale and grim for the fawning masses."

* * *

Leda and Lady Tess had seen most of the incident from the library window, drawn there in haste by the shrieks of the Goldborough girls. Afterward, the young ladies were inclined to install Mr. Gerard as a hero. The gentlemen who had been present, although sporting with their compliments, were a bit less impressed. Leda heard Mr. Curzon confide to Lord Haye that it had been a damned lucky thing that Gerard hadn't had his throat ripped open, attempting such a trick.

Leda knew better. She knew Mr. Gerard. From her first-floor vantage point she'd seen that decoy and roll, precise to the inch, timed to steer the cat's leap inevitably into the reflecting pool.

The incident upset Lady Tess and Mr. Sydney quite miserably. Once the jaguar had been caught and returned to her cage, the two of them went about apologizing to everyone they met. Lady Tess burst into tears, and promised Mrs. Goldborough that the jaguars would be got rid of once and for all—she should have known that this might one day happen; under Mr. Sydney's care, Vicky the Fifth had always been the most tractable of creatures, but a wild animal was not to be underestimated; she should never have allowed them to be kept in the first place.

Lord Gryphon finally bore her off to a private conversation, which seemed to provide some comfort and relief. When they returned to the drawing room where everyone had gathered, she managed to smile weakly and even laugh a little over Robert's description of the jaguar's astonished expression as it had sailed over Samuel and into the pool.

Lord Gryphon announced that an extra full-time keeper would be hired immediately to guard the animals, and the little zoo would be expanded and strengthened, with an outer perimeter added to contain any escapees before they could get into the main park. Mrs. Goldborough looked as if she might like to expound at length on the wisdom of keeping vicious jungle animals anywhere within a global hemisphere of a house in which her daughters resided, but since her oldest was wildly determined to have Lord Robert, and anxious to squelch any maternal quaverings, she stifled her mother's protests with an emphatic "Pray don't think a thing of it, Mama—if I had listened to Lord Robert when he said not to move, instead of being so poor as to try to run, it shouldn't have become a difficulty. It is entirely my fault."

Everyone chorused a denial, but Leda rather felt that the girl was correct. However, it was by no means her place to mention it, and she had several duties left to perform in preparation for the informal holiday party that was planned for after dinner: a small exchange of gifts that the young people had insisted upon before the guests left for their own Christmas celebrations. She withdrew quietly to the hall.

Mr. Gerard met her as he came up the staircase. The late-afternoon sun played down through the miniature forest inside the dome. With his athletic form in a black coat, his golden hair, he carried the flavor of the jaguar itself: fluent motion and the ghost of topaz eyes in the green jungle. For the first time in a fortnight, he paused to speak to her, standing on the step below, his hand resting on the opposite banister of the wide sweep of stairs.

"Miss Etoile." He inclined his head slightly.

Leda did not wish to appear giddy. She felt that she was bound to keep order in spite of the considerable palpitations which possessed her heart at this unexpected renewal of recognition. "Good afternoon, Mr. Gerard." She nodded in a dignified manner. "May I say that you are to be commended on your courage and quick action. I saw the incident from the window. I hope you took no serious hurt?"

He moved his hand, as if dismissing that. "This party tonight—we're to exchange gifts?"

"Yes. You need bring only one. Everyone will draw lots from a bowl. I am just going to prepare them."

For a moment he gazed past her, into the sunlit green shoots and emerald shadows of the layered forest canopy rising up toward the skylights. Then, with a subtle move, he slanted a look toward her, the sort of look she imagined of lesser immortals—those nameless, unpredictable demigods of fields and lonely mountains, with both murder and grace at their fingertips. "No drawing." His voice was too soft to make echoes in the well of the dome. "Let's play blindman's bluff, Miss Etoile. Whoever we catch—that person opens our gift."

Leda's hand tightened on the banister. "Mr. Gerard—"

"If you don't care to suggest it, I will. I think they'll like the idea."

"I'm certain that they will." She rubbed her fingers on the polished wood, then frowned directly at him. "But if I comprehend what you mean to do—Mr. Gerard—I cannot but think that it is not wise."

His intent gaze held hers. "Why?"

"It is not suitable." She could not say that she didn't wish to see him hurt; that Lady Kai would not understand him; that it might be disaster to his hopes. "It is too soon to give her such a gift."

His mouth tightened into the ironic semblance of a smile. "It's by no means too soon. Of that I assure you, ma'am." With a cursory bow, he moved past her, not even crediting her advice with a word of appreciation.

The idea of blindman's bluff met with high approval, as did the tiny glasses of cherry brandy arranged with sprigs of holly on a silver tray. Leda herself did not feel quite up to cherry brandy, but everyone else, with the exception of Lady Whitberry, who thought it interfered with digestion, seemed to find that the liqueur added a certain *joie de vivre* to the proceedings. As the evening proceeded, the blind man's twirls and fumbles became more droll, the jokes more witty, the intermittent carols more melodious, the laughter—even the Curzons'—warmer. Only Leda seemed to feel a certain constraint in her smile.

Only Leda, and Mr. Gerard, who stood watching from behind Lady Kai's chair. Not that one could accuse him of gloom, certainly—he smiled at the appropriate moments, if he did not laugh aloud. When she thought of it, she did not believe she had ever seen Mr. Gerard laugh. Tonight the element of latent alertness in him, the sense of a steady and unfailing attention within his relaxed stance, seemed striking to her.

The diamond necklace lay amid the pile of gifts. She had seen him place it there, a box instantly recognizable to her by the size and shape in its tissue wrapping. She thought the awkward bow unlike him, inconsistent with the spare and subtle elegance of the gifts he'd made to her and to Lady Tess.

Having known him to scale ceiling beams with a broken limb and pass silently in the dark through locks and walls, she wholly believed that he could locate one rather talkative girl when merely blindfolded. However, why he was not afraid that some other guest would single out Lady Kai, Leda had no notion. She would have expected him to insist on taking the first turn, at least.

When she watched him surreptitiously, though, she had the most uncanny impression that he held a direction over the course of events; that amid all the giggles and conversation, the rip of paper and the admiring comments on each gift, his discreet intensity as he stood over Lady Kai radiated some invisible shield against the other players in the game. It was nonsensical, of course . . . and yet, though the participants were spun and careered in all directions, and often let go immediately facing her, no one touched Lady Kai until all the small presents had been claimed but the tissue-wrapped box.

Leda had held herself in the background for most of the game, and rather suspected that Lord Ashland had been shamming just a little when he'd caught her by the sleeve during his next-to-last turn—peeked beneath the blindfold to find her, which was very kind of him. She liked exceedingly the photograph album that she'd unwrapped, although she didn't have any photographs to put in it.

She tapped her finger nervously against the small album. Mr. Gerard did not put on the blindfold—there was no point. His was the last gift, Lady Kai the only one without a present. He merely left his place and brought it to her, and yet there was something in him that caught notice. All the chatter and rustle of paper and examining of presents paused; everyone looked at Lady Kai and Mr.

Gerard as he stood in front of her and laid the box in her outstretched hand.

"This is no fun at all!" She made a pout that broke into a sudden smile. "Although I suppose I must be the winner of this game, since the blind man never caught me. What a very silly bow, Manō." She held it up, dangling the lopsided red ribbon for all to see, and then tore at the paper with the enthusiasm of a toddler.

Leda closed her eyes for an instant when she saw the velvet box. Until that moment, she had still hoped it was something else. She opened them again, full of an anxiety out of all proportion to the situation.

Mr. Gerard stood beside Lady Kai as she raised the lid. She looked inside the box. While everyone waited to see her turn it around, an expression of amused exasperation crossed her lovely face. "Manō! What on earth!" She tilted her head back and dropped her shoulders. "Of all the absurd things! You're absolutely hopeless when it comes to choosing gifts, poor dear. Now I ask you: what if Mr. Curzon—or . . . or *Robert* had been the one to be presented with *this?*" She held up the box to display the contents to the room.

Several ladies drew in their breath with audible murmurs. Someone said, "How magnificent!"

And then a dead and collective silence reigned.

It's worse, Leda thought. *It's even worse than I'd feared.* The most of them knew, or guessed instantly, what Mr. Gerard meant by it: Leda could see it in the shocked and speculative stares.

"Darling Manō." Lady Kai gave him a hug. "You just haven't a clue, do you? You were supposed to wrap up something like a nice book. I ought to have known—Miss Leda and I might have helped you to choose something, if I'd thought."

Mr. Gerard stood without speaking, without any open sign of chagrin, but when she went to her mother, taking the necklace and holding it up to Lady Tess' throat with a comment on how prettily it would suit Mum, his silent gaze fell away from both of them.

"It would suit any of the ladies here," Lord Ashland

said gallantly. "I doubt Samuel would have let it go to the wrong sex."

"Not a chance of that." Mr. Gerard smiled. He did it well, lightly, with no outward sign of what it must have cost him. He moved behind Lady Tess, slipping the necklace out of her daughter's fingers to clasp it around Lady Tess's throat. She looked up at him and squeezed his hand, with an expression very much like the one she'd had when she'd tried to express her regrets to Mrs. Goldborough over the danger to her daughters.

"Could I serve you with a little more cherry brandy, ma'am?" Leda turned to Lady Whitberry, willing to do anything to break the spell of attention.

Like dependable clockwork, Lady Whitberry launched into her discourse on the unwholesomeness of sweetened spirits, the evils of indigestion, and the untoward effects of cherry brandy in particular. Lady Tess sat in her chair with the necklace sparkling around her neck. Lord Ashland engaged Mr. Gerard in a discussion of the recent changes in the city of New York, a topic of such painstaking neutrality that it encouraged the rest to fall back into their previous conversations.

Leda thought for a few moments that Mr. Gerard would find some reason to excuse himself, but in the end it was she who could not seem to maintain an ordinary air of unconcern. She had the most dreadful urge to burst into tears—on whose behalf, she had no notion. But when the earliest pretext to pardon herself and retire arrived, she took it with unbecoming haste.

She sat up late in her room, poring over and over the *Descriptions and Oddities of Japanese Culture*, trying again to find some special item to give him for Christmas. A simple, exquisite gift, full of shades of meaning. It did not have to be costly. None of the traditional gifts such as the five-yen coin that the book mentioned were expensive, but somehow the idea of giving him a salted strip of abalone meat did not appeal, nor a piece of dried seaweed as a symbol of joy and happiness, even wrapped in the pretty little folded fans of red and white paper that the book illustrated. She really could not imagine giving him shell-fish or seaweed, even supposing that she could obtain such items.

Much nicer would have been a pair of the beautiful long-tailed Japanese goldfish shown in the pictures, but that too was impossible. She finally gave up leafing through the book and went to bed, though she lay awake for a long time, with the pillow wrapped up close beneath her chin.

Sometime in the darkness, long after the house had gone quiet, she became aware of him. There was not a sound that proved it, not a breath of motion that she could see. She just had a fancy that he was there.

"Mr. Gerard." She sat up in bed.

No answer.

It felt a bit strange to be talking to what was most likely an empty room, but since there was no one to hear her, she spoke again. "I hope you are not very disappointed with Lady Kai."

No one answered that, either. She plumped her pillows up against the headboard, resting back against them. The room was in utter darkness.

"I wish I could give you some goldfish." It felt rather nice, to speak to the dark, imagining him to be there. To say things she would never have had the courage to say in person. "I don't believe Lady Kai would ever think to give you goldfish with long tails. They aren't very sensible, I suppose, as handkerchiefs would be. But I think they must be lovely. I should like to see one, someday."

She drew her legs up and curled her arms around them, resting her cheek on her knees, building dream-castles.

"Really, I should like to have my own garden, with a fish pond in it, full of goldfish with tails like silk. Do you ever think of things such as that, Mr. Gerard? Whatever do gentlemen think about, I wonder?" She pondered the question, and answered herself. "Political difficulties, I suppose. It must be very trying and dull to be a man."

She stared into the dimness. She knew the sex to be useful on occasion, primarily in carrying one's parcels, or in discovering the cause of leaky ceilings and smoking flues, but all the ladies in South Street had advised against allowing a man in the house. One could expect him to be forever tracking-in because he *would* forget to remove his boots in spite of all attempts to tame him.

Men were a mystery: formidable and comforting, elusive and forthright, full of strange passions and turnabouts.

"Mr. Gerard . . ." She whispered it—afraid, even alone in the darkness, to ask it aloud. "Why did you touch me? Why did you look at me so in the mirror?"

She thought of all that the ladies in South Street had forewarned. She did not think they ever could have met a gentleman quite like Mr. Gerard. She pressed her hands together and admitted to the imaginary man in the shadows what she had not even admitted to herself.

"I wish you would again."

She covered her mouth with her fingers, shocked. But the wish was real, very real, once she gave a name to the restlessness and misery inside her, to the emotion that seemed to keep tears and laughter so close to the surface that she never knew which would well up at any small crisis. Not only was she idiotically in love with Mr. Gerard, she was longing for him to touch her.

It seemed such a stupid and lowering situation to find oneself in that she hugged a pillow to her, feeling hot tears well up and slide down her cheeks right then and there. How very lonely life must turn out to be, for a female of delicacy and refinement and no background. A female who really did not belong anywhere at all.

Twenty-five

I wish you would again.

Samuel stood silent, motionless, with temptation all around him like a tangible coercion. He saw in the dark by eyesight and heart sight; he could close his eyes and feel her tears.

He did not know why she was crying. He thought, in that moment, that he did not know anything but the urge to answer her. *I wish . . .* she said, and the solid earth failed him; the ground beneath his feet disintegrated.

She sat up suddenly, startled, a quick rustle of bedclothes. "Mr. Gerard?"

He tilted back his head. How could he think that she would not feel him there? He emanated desire. He burned like a bright flare with it, an invisible torch in the midnight room.

She sniffed quickly, a muffled sound, trying to hide it. "I know you're here."

"Yes," he said.

She made a little squeak, surprised after all at his voice. He heard her breathing, quick and soft.

A long moment passed. Nothing moved.

"Why?" She barely spoke the word. It hung, whispered, on the still air.

Samuel closed his eyes. "I don't know."

But he knew.

"Oh, dear." Her voice had a small tremor in it. "I suppose you've been here for some time. I suppose you've been listening to me. How excessively mortifying."

There in the dark, she could almost make him smile.

She made him ache to reach out his hand to her, twine her hair in his fist.

Ah, no . . . but he would not. He would contain the black fire that ran in his veins, that shamed and scorched him.

From the bed came sounds of movement. Her feet touched the floor, a vibration he felt rather than heard. "I really should find my dressing robe, if you wish to hold a conversation."

She stood up, a tumble of hair and luscious sleepy scent, the warmth of a woman's body beneath the bedclothes. He could have evaded her. But his will and his action split apart from one another. He stood planted, with a lifetime of endurance fracturing, and allowed her to walk straight into him.

In spite of the hand she'd put out to feel her way in the dark, she came up against his chest as if she had struck a wall. He caught her arm, imposing balance. "I don't wish to hold a conversation."

His voice was low and rough. He had anarchy inside him.

"Oh." She stood fixed in his hold. "What, then?"

"What you wish. What you said."

She lifted her face. "Goldfish?"

"Oh, Jesus." He cupped her cheeks, bent his head to her mouth. "This. I want this."

His lips grazed hers. A heaviness weighted him, an overwhelming pressure. Kai—there was Kai; there was what he had forged of his mind and his body. He could not do this. It was destruction.

He did not know how to kiss a woman. He thought he should press his closed mouth to hers, but the contact disarmed him, the softness of her cheek sent soundless shudders of pleasure down his body. He opened his mouth, breathing in, taking the essence of her deep inside him as he tasted the corner of her lips with his tongue.

Her body fluttered. He perceived a blush in her, a warmth beyond the range of eyesight in the dark. She brought her hands up between them. "I suppose—I suppose that you must be distressed by the reception of your necklace?''

He cared nothing for the necklace. It seemed only one more step on the course that drove him.

''I daresay—that is why you are here.'' Her voice sounded breathless and thin. ''I could have wished—that you had not been so eager to present it. I advised—that is—oh, dear. Mr. Gerard.''

How could she imagine that was why he was here? He stood holding her, tasting her, feeling her agitation, knowing himself part of the shadows in his midnight-gray clothing. He doubted she could even see him—and suddenly he let go of her, brushed one hand across the other in a familiar sorcery, and made light in his open palm, heatless blue, like ocean phosphorescence illuminating the startlement on her face, the puffy sleeves and lacy tucks of her white nightgown.

He felt suspended, offering himself in the open, without the dark to hide him.

She gazed for a moment at the rounded stone in his palm, and then up at him. In the ethereal light she seemed bewildered, and more lovely than he could have imagined, the luster of her unbound hair and the velvet curve of her face, all of his forbidden fantasies materialized into life. He rued the light already; he would frighten her, a black warrior conjured out of the night: what he desired so unmistakable, without disguise or softness.

''Oh,'' she said in a hushed, plaintive voice. ''You should not be here. I'm afraid this is very foolish, Mr. Gerard. This is most dreadfully ill-advised.''

He closed his eyes, his fist going tight over the stone. ''Let me lie with you,'' he whispered.

''I don't believe . . . that does not seem . . . it really would not be—'' She sounded dazed. ''With me?''

He reached up, stroked her cheek with the back of his closed hand, the glowing light barely perceptible between his fingers. ''Here. Now.''

She hesitated, as if she could not quite comprehend him. ''I daresay you are weary, to be up so late, but—''

He took her chin and lifted it on his fist. "I'm not weary."

"Oh." She looked up into his eyes. "Oh . . . dear sir, is it that you are lonely? If it weren't such an awkward hour, I might have rung for tea."

Lonely. God. So hot and intense and alone.

He opened his hand, and the ghostly light colored her for a moment as he brushed his mouth against the side of her throat. Her fragrance was of pristine woman-things, powder and flowers, and that underlying heat of her body: deeper, provocative, a veiled flame that caught fire and blazed inside him.

"Oh—you should not." Her voice echoed what he knew; her hands held a light quiver as she nudged them ineffectually against his shoulders. "This is not—decorous."

It was not decorous. It was madness. But he did not let her go. He gripped his arm across the small of her back, pulling her to him. The lacy collar brushed across his temple. He allowed the lightstone to fall away onto the floor as her hair slid back in a heavy mass over his hands. Excitement flooded him. He had imagined it that way when first he'd seen her in daylight, at the dressmaker's; when he'd reached down and picked up a coronetted note inscribed to her and realized what it was.

He exerted a subtle pressure, compelling her backward toward the bed. She yielded, wavering and easy to control, her lack of resistance telling him that she did not even recognize the leverage that directed her.

At the edge of the bed, his expertise ended. Not his hunger, not his visions, not the sensation of her pressed between his body and the bed as his leg braced hard against the wood of the frame. He was breathing deeply, unevenly, ungoverned in his physical action, on the brink of a fierce and all-consuming void. He held himself savagely in check, resting his forehead against the curve of her throat.

"I won't hurt you," he whispered.

Utter truthfulness, Dojun said.

"No," she said. "Of course you would not."

Her simple conviction shattered him. She could not trust him; he was lying, he knew he was, and yet he would not let go. He surrendered sixteen years of bruises and sweat and dreams, sinking slowly to his knees as he pulled her to him. He pressed his open mouth to her body, meeting the soft underswell of her breast. The flannel held her scent and heat, slipped over her skin beneath his tongue, promising silk beneath.

"Oh . . . Mr. Gerard." The protest was hardly more than warmth in the night air.

"You said you wished it." He slid his hands down, tightened them on her waist. He had dreamed of this; dreamed of it for a thousand years.

Her voice held a clouded wonder. "I suppose . . . because my mother was—French . . ."

Her hand lay against his hair. He turned his head and kissed her palm. She curled it closed, and he kissed the back of her fingers.

He felt her stillness. And then: lightly . . . gently, she drew a lock of his hair between her fingers.

It took all the strength he had to restrain the force inside him. He touched her as if she might vanish in his hands, a skim of contact when what he wished was to crush her to him, a brush of his fingers outlining her shape, the curves beneath her breasts, the swell of her hips. He felt himself so hot and hard that he was afraid he would terrify her if he did not contain his moves.

He had never in his adult memory touched a woman for so long before. His life had been Kai's quick hugs and a skip away, or Lady Tess' brief, quiet welcomes. The sweetness of the embrace amazed him; he felt absurdly close to tears with the warmth of her against his face and beneath his hands.

He wanted to tell her, but he had no words for it. He wanted to say *warm, delicate, soft; your hair, your beautiful hair falling free, your hands, your waist . . . do you understand? I won't hurt you. I don't want to hurt you. I'm dying.*

Her hand rested around the back of his neck. He felt

her breathing, the rise and fall of her breasts against his cheek.

"I am afraid we're very shocking." Her hand tightened slightly. She lifted a lock of his hair, slid it through her fingers, and brushed it back. "But . . . dear sir . . . I have been a little lonely, too."

"Leda." He had only a hoarse whisper to answer her. Slowly, so very slowly, not to frighten her, he rose. A ribbon held the nightgown at her throat; he caught the loop in his forefinger and pulled the bow free. His hand slid downward—he had expected buttonholes like a man's shirt, but there were none: his finger caught light satin hooks that fell away from tiny pearls of buttons without resistance, descending almost to her waist.

Her body went stiff as he did it. The base of the slit stopped his hand; he closed his fist on the fabric.

"Don't be afraid of me," he said fiercely. His own muscles were tense; his body felt unfamiliar to him, as if he were moving within heavy armor.

She stared up at him. He could see the dismay dawn upon her, saw that—God—until this precise moment she had not really understood him—that somehow she hadn't expected it, would require him to stop; that the words to deny him were rising to her lips.

He would not let her. He covered her mouth with his, a relentless kiss to stop those words, pulling her to him with his hand spread in her hair. He broke his promise that quickly; the kiss hurt her—he knew it must, because the violence of it bruised his own mouth. He made himself a catalyst, created influence, a controlled force that overcame her equilibrium and took her down onto the bed full-length with him.

Her hair fanned across her face. She braced her hands against his shoulders. He hung above her, breathing hard, instinct and memories and desire driving him. His body was shoved against hers, exquisite sensation, so close, so close to explosion, her legs all along his with only thin layers of fabric between them.

The glowing stone frosted barely perceptible outlines in

the room. She lay wide-eyed in his shadow, holding him off.

Her strength he could have conquered in an instant, and they both knew it. But she looked up at him with a sort of desperate dignity, all tumbled and sober. "I'm sure— Mr. Gerard—you would be sorry to behave dishonorably."

He could have laughed at an appeal to his honor at this moment. But her face . . . in her face he saw doubt and faith and earnestness, a wholehearted dependence upon him . . . and a sweet, impossible bravery: the heroism of small defenseless creatures facing peril.

In her weakness, she defeated him. He could not go on, and he could not let go.

He lowered himself with his arms around her, shaking, his face buried against her ear.

Leda lay without protest in his embrace. He was solidly heavy, and held her quite tightly, but that somehow seemed comforting rather than uncomfortable. After a long time, she felt a slow easing of the tension in his arms; he shifted, moving to her side, still embracing her but not so closely. Neither of them spoke.

Finally she drifted in and out of a strange sleep, constantly startled to find him there, constantly pleased and then confused by it. It was so singular. Rather wonderful, really.

In a dreamy way, she understood it; he'd asked to lie down with her, and who would have thought it to be anything more than an odd fancy? Who would have thought it could be so gratifying? She lay at an unfamiliar angle across the bed, without a pillow—waking to find herself snuggling into warmth, flinching at the hard pressure of his arm beneath her head. Whenever she started awake in that way, he moved his hand, brushing back her hair in a soothing gesture, and the natural thing to do seemed to be to nestle closer into the cradle of his arms and body and sleep again.

The alien stone had long ago lost its glow—it seemed

like a dream by the time the faintest gray of dawn tinged
the room.

Waking then from a sounder sleep, her first drowsy impression was of a black shadow beside her, too dark to
discern a shape or detail. Then she distinguished form,
comprehended the line of his leg, the length of chest, his
arm curved over her. She blinked her eyes fully open.

He watched her. From six inches away, she could see
his dark lashes tangled at the edges. His eyes were translucent gray, colored like the outermost perimeter of the
winter dawn, the place where starlight became day.

His wakefulness, the way she was settled and sheltered
from the cold by his body—she knew, somehow, that he
had not slept for one moment.

A sudden consternation gripped her. She remembered
something that had happened long ago in her schoolroom
days—a maid and an illicit follower—something the cook
had whispered to the man who brought the coals. *She
sleeps with him,* Cook had muttered. *Don't think she
doesn't, the little strumpet.* And soon after that the maid
had been sent away in awkward circumstances that Miss
Myrtle never would explain.

Leda stared into his dawn-gray eyes.

She had slept with him.

Dear God.

In the night she had felt that she'd been saved from
something—in the daybreak she knew that she was lost far
beyond anything Miss Myrtle had ever warned her against.
He was in her room. He had touched her. Undressed her.
He had kissed her in a way no man would kiss a respectable woman. She had slept with him.

She shivered convulsively. His arm rested on her shoulder; he tightened his hand for a moment against her neck,
then opened his fingers and slid them through her hair.
The mahogany strands fell away from his hand. He pushed
himself up on one arm.

Gracious heavens. It was done already—and so little to
it! She had slept with him. And she felt no different; no
worse, no better—not even ashamed for it, not in her heart.

Belatedly, as he was moving away from her, she realized that he meant to leave. For no reason, with no sensible thought in her mind, she reached out and caught his wrist.

He looked around at her with a startling intensity, going still in the faint morning light. Again she thought of demigods, lonely deities born of the mountains and sky and sea.

She sat up, her hand on his rigid arm, not knowing what to say.

"I shouldn't have stayed." His voice was hard. "I'm sorry. You fell asleep."

The sash that held his black coat had loosened. She saw the base of his throat and the curve of his chest. Something glittered within the hidden folds of dark fabric. A weapon . . . violence and elegance; a master of both—and somehow she wished to reach out and draw him into her arms and hold him very near her heart.

"You didn't sleep," she said.

He gave a caustic chuckle and looked away. "No."

She did not want him to leave. The morning was coming; she did not want it to come. What she would do, what she would say, how life would be changed . . . it still seemed impossible. She had slept with a man. He had kissed her.

She did not feel properly guilty at all. She felt—feminine. A little shy and flustered. "Must you go?"

His eyes lifted to hers. "Why should I stay?"

The harshness in his tone perplexed her. It was as if he accused her of something. She moistened her lips and spread her hand across his forearm, sliding her fingers over the fabric, feeling the strength beneath.

His muscle flexed under her palm. "Tell me yes or no."

"Yes," she said. "Stay."

He did not move toward her, nor away. "Last night . . . you said yes. You said you wished it. And then—God." He blew out a rasping breath.

She blushed at the bald mention of last night. His hands on her, his mouth. She should be ashamed, and instead she felt . . . flattered. Excited.

Oh, was this what it was to be a strumpet? To be a

fallen woman? To be selfishly glad that when he was lonely he had come to her instead of Lady Kai?

She could not bring herself to be vulgarly bold, even cast as a strumpet. Really, she could not seem to think of herself in that way at all: as one of the blowsy shopgirls who winked at cab drivers and cried, " 'Aven't yer got a kiss for me, gov?''

It just did not seem as if it were the same thing, to wish for Mr. Gerard to kiss her again.

The chill in the room went through her gown, now that she was no longer sheltered by his nearness. She shifted, drawing the down-filled counterpane around her shoulders, and glanced at him hopefully. "It's quite cold, don't you think?''

She held the counterpane up to her mouth, peeking over it to see whether he understood the hint.

He sat unmoving, leaning on his hand. But he didn't draw away.

She grew wildly venturesome at the meager encouragement. Tentatively, she reached out and touched his hair. She drew her fingers down his cheek, fascinated by the faint prickly stubble there. Last night—had it felt so last night? How remarkable; how exotically appealing a man could turn out to be. She remembered that Mrs. Wrotham had very carefully preserved her late husband's razor and brushes in a rosewood box. Personal things, that had had no particular meaning, no very clear reality, to Leda until now.

She had always wondered a little why the gentle old lady would so cherish a razor, while at the same time using the much-respected book of sample letters that Mr. Wrotham had written for an incidental doorstop. *Because of this*, she thought now. Because in a few short hours, a man's face was different to touch.

She bit her lips together, overwhelmed suddenly by emotion: empathy for gentle, fluttery Mrs. Wrotham who treasured her husband's razor; a mysterious tenderness for the man who did not move beneath her hesitant caress, whose only response was a deep tremor, a motion within stillness.

She leaned forward, touching her lips to the corner of his, as he had done to her. Maleness: her tongue found him both smooth and bristly, with a heated tangy scent. She opened her mouth to sample more, and brought up her hands to explore his hair.

The tremor in him grew to hard stiffness. He gripped her shoulders with a rough sound. He turned his face into hers, capturing her mouth.

For an instant she felt nothing but stirring excitement in it. Then his strength took control of her; forcing her backward and down into the pillows. He sought within the disarray of bedclothes, dragging her gown up; his fist tangled in her hair, holding her fixed as he kissed her face: everywhere on her face, her throat, down the open length of her gown.

He shocked her. She had no time to protest before his full weight came over her, pushing her deep into the bed. His leg shoved between hers, his body pressed against her thighs and her tummy, his hand dragged and yanked at the fabric between them—then the heat of bare skin against bare skin in the most appallingly intimate place—and something—something else—what?

He moved as if he would overwhelm her with his body, his breathing savage and quick in her ear, his movements raising waves of a teasing, extraordinary stimulation from the mortifying spot where he pressed her. The electrifying feeling flushed through her: a rising, thickening pleasure, drawing her muscles taut, making her body arch toward him instead of away.

He lifted himself on his hands. For an instant she looked up at him, her lips parted in hot chagrin—and what he did then amazed her. The peculiar pleasure of his pushing contact began to hurt—she shrank downward with instinctive avoidance, but he seemed not to realize it; his eyes were closed; he came fully against her—*inside* her!—with a powerful move, an aggressive thrust in a place she could not even name.

And it *hurt*. It hurt them both, for as she let out a sharp gasp, he arched his head back and his whole body wrenched and shuddered. A sound like an anguished groan vibrated in his throat. He held above her, forced into her, the muscles in his shoulders and arms and chest taut with strain.

Leda realized that she was making little sounds of distress with each breath, frightened whimpers, choking back astonishment and panic. The moment of frozen violence seemed an infinity.

He let go of an explosive breath. His body eased its rigid tension. He sucked in air as if he had been sprinting hard, lowering himself onto her with shivers she could feel running through his arms, with rhythmic shudders that pressed him into her in smaller convulsions.

It hurt still. It was very uncomfortable, burning in that secret place, joined with him. He did not look into her face, nor relieve her of his weight. But he rested his head in the pillow next to her ear, stroking her hair, over and over. "Leda," he whispered. "Oh, God—Leda."

And she thought hysterically: *How stupid I have been. This was it. This.*

Now . . . *now* I am a fallen woman.

He knew she was crying. Through the pounding of his own heartbeat, he felt rather than heard the little twitch of each sobbing breath.

Shame and passion consumed him. In his mind, he rose and left her, ending the offense—ending it, at least, if he could not change it. But his body only closed around her, his arms enfolding her; already he wanted to move in her again.

Instead he kissed her and spoke to her, trying to comfort her when he didn't even know what he was saying. He kissed her eyes and the tears on her cheeks; he kissed her bared shoulder where the gown was pulled down tight against her arm. He said her name, and tried to say that he was sorry, to explain, when there was no explanation but himself. He could not control himself; he could not.

She felt . . . delicious. Lush and erotic beneath him. He knew from her tears that he'd hurt her, and it unnerved him that he felt such exquisite pleasure.

"Oh!" she murmured, as if it surprised her when he pressed into her again.

He rose onto his elbows, nuzzling her cheek with his lips, drying her salt tears with his tongue. She closed her eyes as he kissed her lashes and brows.

The sight of her with her throat bared: pale skin and her hair thrown loose all around on the pillows . . . luscious, erotic, exciting . . . renewed fire washed through his veins. He tried to console her, but the consolation became sensual, his kisses harder and deeper, in places that he longed to taste.

He put his hand beneath her breast, lifting it, bending his head down to savor the soft roundness beneath her gown. A vivid recollection of how she had felt beneath his tongue last night made him open his mouth again, licking flannel against her skin.

She made a small sound, a faint half-protest, shifting beneath him. And then—he felt some of the rigidity flow out of her, and a new, lithe tension take its place.

His tongue found the tip of her breast, circling it, dampening the flannel. She made a sharper move, a quick sob and a shiver beneath him. The gown fell fully open, exposing her nipple to him: round and gorgeous it was, deep pink against white.

The smoldering fire in him flamed. He pressed his lips against her breast as he pressed himself harder into her. His mouth opened and he drew his tongue ardently across the plump nub. He pulled it between his teeth, and she made the sweetest sound he had ever known in his life—a gasp that was not pain at all.

His hand came up to cradle her other breast, to caress and taste them both, while she kept her eyes closed and made those small, constricted noises.

He knew what caused her pain; it was his invasion of her—and in some deep and corrupt part of him, he understood that this other caressing could assuage the hurt. Old lessons, half-forgotten, from a place in himself that he hated.

But she was arching beneath him, so beautiful in her rosy warmth that the shame and anger burned away, fell into dust beside the reality of her in the silver light. He held her and pushed deep again, with that rush of pleasure and lust surging through him, drawing him upward to the flash point.

He began to move more forcefully, closing his eyes, caught in the intensifying sensation. It took longer this time, grew stronger; each thrust added height and exquisite heat, until he forgot to breathe . . . forgot to see or hear or think . . . forgot anything but the passion that engulfed him and burst into her like the shock of black powder set alight.

When it was over, the scents and sensations seemed to settle on him in a strange lethargy. He found her looking up at him with those lovely, dusky-green eyes, as if words failed her.

A confusion of emotion rotated inside him, relief and pleasure and kinship and things beyond describing. Clear thought eluded him. He wanted nothing more than to sleep in her arms.

Not long. He could not stay long. A brief thought of Kai swam through his head, but he could not even hold on to that. He felt drugged with happiness, with completion.

"Are you all right?" The words seemed to come out sluggishly as he bent his head over her, his lips almost brushing hers.

"I don't know." She sounded plaintive, like a child.

He tried to think of what he could do to console her, and knew he should surrender this enchantment. He lifted himself free. She made a little grimace as his still firm body slipped from hers.

He kissed her, gently, tilting from joy to remorse and back again. He felt the most pressing need for sleep, and to hold her close to him. The counterpane she'd cuddled to herself earlier had tangled around their legs; as he moved aside, he pulled it over her and half over himself against the crisp dawn chill.

He turned on his side, hugging her, one arm around her waist, his hand between her breasts, the other arm beneath her pillow. She was quiet in his embrace for a moment, and then she caught his hand. "Dear sir," she said, and paused.

That was all. The drugged feeling slowly overcame him. He sank into the velvet darkness without answering, without knowing if it was an endearment or an accusation.

He dreamed that there was someone knocking on the door.

His eyes came open.

Full daylight flooded the room, illuminating everything: the bed, Miss Etoile, her mass of rich, ruddy brown hair and the dark slash of his sleeve across the cream-colored counterpane, like a strip of the night left behind.

Beyond her tumbled hair, he saw the door. He saw Lady Tess standing in it. She held a present wrapped in white-and-green striped paper, tied with a red bow.

And he knew that for all of his life he would remember that bow. That particular red, that shade of green, the precise size and shape of the box in her hand.

A belated jolt went through him, from his belly to his fingertips, a silent, motionless shock curbed by sixteen years of discipline. He didn't move. Above Miss Etoile's sleeping form, his eyes met hers.

She stood still for an instant, her hand on the knob of the half-open door. From somewhere a distance away in the hall outside, the sound of male voices rose and fell in a cordial dispute.

Lady Tess looked down at the present, as if she didn't know what to do with it, and up at him.

She bit her lip, flushing like a green girl, and backed out of the room silently, drawing the door shut with her.

Twenty-six

Leda bit back panicked tears, sitting up abruptly in bed when the maid scratched on the door. She dragged the bedclothes and counterpane over herself, up to her chin. Only a few minutes before, she'd pushed off the sheets and discovered the darkened crimson that seemed to have stained everything: herself, her gown and the linens, even the counterpane was spotted with it.

So much! She didn't feel that badly injured. The stinging pain had subsided as soon as he—as he . . .

She could not even think of it coherently. Miss Myrtle's sensibilities would have been offended by the mere verbal offering of a thigh or leg or breast of chicken at table—for a person of delicacy, it was to be called simply white meat or dark. Leda had been brought up as a lady of refinement. She did not have words for what he had done.

He was gone, disappeared while she'd slept. Except for the stains, the mysterious scents and moistness, it might have been a mad dream. She had looked quickly for the glowing stone he'd dropped, but that, too, was vanished.

The maid entered without an invitation, only the usual warning scratch. The girl didn't even glance up at Leda, but only bobbed a quick curtsy and brought a tray to the bedside. "M'lady said as miss wasn't feeling well and slept late, you might wish to breakfast in bed."

"Yes. Please." Leda's voice was low and cracked, as if she hadn't spoken for days. Lady Tess' innocent solicitude made her want to weep.

There was an extra cup and saucer on the tray. The maid said nothing about that, only settled the tray over Leda's

lap, and then went to make up the fire. Usually that was
done much earlier; the quiet scrape of the coal scuttle was
what woke Leda on any normal morning. It was unthinkably fortuitous that there had apparently been some delay
in the morning routine today.

She had a horrible thought.

What if there had not been a delay? What if the girl had
looked in and seen . . .

The smell of toast and butter seemed abruptly nauseat-
ing. Surely, surely, the sound of the door opening would
have awakened her as it usually did. She had thought she
would never sleep again, this morning, after . . .

She closed her eyes, still unable to find expression for
what had happened.

The chambermaid swept the hearth, gave another swift
curtsy, and withdrew. Leda tried to remember if the girl
had been more pleasant and friendly yesterday. The maid
had never been loquacious, and Leda was content to deal
with servants at whatever level of distance they wished to
keep, but didn't this one usually smile shyly and say,
"Good morning, miss" as she entered and left?

Leda set the tray aside. She felt desperate. She felt as
if she must have a bath, but she was too mortified to ring
for one. What about the stains everywhere? What could
she say? She thought of excusing them as her monthly
illness, but that had been only a week ago, and the laundry
staff must know it quite perfectly well. She shoved back
the counterpane and ran barefoot across the room, yanking
open the drawer of the vanity, searching wildly through
the neat contents for scissors to cut herself.

A light knock sounded at the door. Leda froze.

Lady Tess slipped in, closing the door behind her.
Leda's body jerked with the beginning of a motion to fling
herself toward the bed and concealment, but as the older
woman lifted her eyes, she saw that it was useless.

Lady Tess knew.

Leda stood frozen in the middle of the floor in her
stained gown, clutching it closed at her throat.

She knew, she knew, she *knew*.

The kindest, best, most generous of ladies; the mother

of the girl he intended to marry; the family that had given Leda shelter—more than that—unreserved friendship, even a kind of affection . . .

Leda's unsteady breath began to come in gasps. She closed her eyes, pressed her hands together, holding them to her mouth. Her knees gave beneath her. The tears broke free as she sank to the floor, tears of bewilderment and shame and terror of what would happen to her now.

"Shhh. Shhh." Lady Tess' arms came around her as she huddled there on the carpet, shaking with frenzied sobs. She drew Leda's head against her breast, stroking her hair, rocking her. "Hush. It will be all right. Everything will be all right."

"I'm so—" Leda lost her voice in another tearing sob. "Oh, ma'am!"

"Hush, love." Lady Tess pressed her cheek against the top of Leda's head. "Don't try to tell me now."

Leda could not seem to lift her face, nor contain the tumult of weeping. She turned into Lady Tess' pretty, lacy blouse and cried. The quiet support, the gentle hand brushing back her damp hair only made it worse; she could not understand how Lady Tess could bear to touch her.

At last she fell into hiccoughs and sniffs, wiping her face with the handkerchief Lady Tess gave her.

"I'm so sorry!" She managed to say it, and then her face wrinkled up and she sobbed again. "I never meant— I never would have—I didn't under*stand!*" Her voice ended in a squeak.

"Come into the dressing room." Lady Tess drew her to her feet. "I've had them heat water and leave the slipper bath there. Let us have this thing off of you."

Leda looked down at her gown, and could not help fresh tears. "The bed. Everyone will know belowstairs, won't they?"

"It doesn't matter. I will take care of that."

Something in her tone made Leda look up in fright. "They already know?"

Lady Tess took her hand and squeezed it.

Leda felt the awful tears push into her eyes again. "The maid! The chambermaid came early!"

"We'll talk about this when you've dressed." Lady Tess's voice was soothing, as if she were speaking to an agitated child.

A sensation of utter numbness came over Leda. If the servants knew . . . a sign across her back could not proclaim her shame any more loudly in the house.

In a daze, she allowed Lady Tess to lead her into the adjoining dressing room, let the gown be lifted over her head, stood completely unclothed for the first time in her memory in front of someone else. The proof of what had happened marked her thighs in dark ugly smears, but Lady Tess seemed to think nothing of it: she only poured hot water as if she were a common maid, and gave Leda a washcloth and sweet soap after she stepped in.

Leda wished she could sink into the steamy bath and stay there forever. She wished she could drown herself.

She could not. Lady Tess had a robe and fresh linen for her, with a pad to prevent further stains. "You've no need to wear a corset and bustle today. Would you like to wear this skirt, or the stripe?" she asked Leda composedly.

Her quiet consideration started Leda crying once again. She could not stop herself; she just stood in the robe, weeping. Lady Tess put her arms around her while Leda sobbed into her shoulder. When the tears subsided, she coaxed Leda to the chair before the fire in her bedroom.

"Oh, ma'am—I don't know how . . . How can you be so good to me?"

Lady Tess smiled wryly. "I think—because I'd like to do this for Samuel. But I can't. So I'll do it for you."

There was no censure in her voice. Leda wiped her eyes. "You don't hate me?"

She smiled more openly and held out the blouse for Leda. "No, I don't hate you. I like you. And I expect Samuel feels much the same as you do this morning."

Leda gave a half-sobbing laugh. "He must be hysterical, then."

"Perhaps. But you won't know it to look at him."

"You've seen him?"

Lady Tess paused in her buttoning down Leda's back. She did not answer.

"Ma'am?" Leda asked with a tremble. "Was it . . . did . . . was it the maid who told you?"

The fingers at her back resumed their work. "I brought a present to hide under your bed this morning. I'm afraid I didn't wait for you to answer my knock."

Leda's heart dropped. "Oh, ma'am. Oh, ma'am."

"It was a bit of a shock."

For a long moment, Leda said nothing. She felt ill. When Lady Tess proffered the skirt, Leda stepped into it stiffly, moving like an automaton. Lady Tess began to take up the long row of buttons on the high waist.

Even in her mortification, she couldn't keep the rise of hope from her voice. "Does that mean . . . that only you know, ma'am?"

"Come and sit down."

Leda closed her eyes, understanding that answer for what it was. She took a deep breath and went to sit in the chair by the fire. Lady Tess poured a cup of tea off the tray, brought it to her; poured one for herself and sat down at the vanity.

"I'm afraid this won't be easy for you, Leda. You have to know—the chambermaid came this morning at her regular time. An hour before I did, at least. It's nearly noon now."

The cup rattled a little in Leda's hand. She put it down and folded her hands in her lap. "Everyone knows."

"Gryf told me that at breakfast, the rumor was that Tommy is yours and Samuel's, conceived when Samuel was here on business last year."

She came to her feet. "Ma'am!"

"Leda—people have remarked it as strange already—I didn't realize how much until now—that Samuel brought you to us. And Tommy . . ."

"He isn't mine! I *swear* to you! It isn't true; you can ask Inspector Ruby or Sergeant MacDonald!"

Lady Tess gave a twisted little smile toward the stained gown that lay over the bed. "No. I'm very sure that last night was your first time to be with a man."

Leda looked at her with wide, embarrassed eyes, then turned sharply away. "You'll wish me to go. I don't know what I've been thinking of—I should have been packing my things already."

"I don't wish you to go."

"Oh, ma'am! There is Lady Kai, and Mrs. Goldborough and her daughters—you cannot suffer my presence here. Not—as I am now."

"Ah . . . because you might tarnish their girlish innocence? I suppose then I must send Samuel away, too—and probably Robert and Lord Haye as well, although Mr. Curzon may still be a lily-white virgin." She toyed with a hat pin from the vanity. "One would have difficulty with that call."

"Ma'am!" In spite of herself, Leda was shocked.

"I don't wish you to go, although you may if that's what you decide." She looked at Leda very directly, her dark hair smooth and her eyes intense. "If you care what I wish . . . I wish you to be brave, Leda, dear, and stay here and face them."

Face them. Lord Ashland, Lord Robert, Mr. Curzon, all the guests . . . Lady Kai.

"I don't think—I can." Her voice almost failed her. She clutched her hands in the folds of her skirt.

Lady Tess fingered the pearl drop at the end of the hat pin. She looked up again. "If you leave, where will you go?"

Leda caught the reflection of herself in the tall pier glass between the windows. She feared that she even looked different, her hair tumbling over her shoulders, still unbrushed, her skin blotchy with tears, her eyes too large in her pale face. Did she appear fast? Could anyone see that she was unchaste?

She spread her fingers wide in the folds of her skirt, turning away from the image. "I wished to be a typist. I've saved my wages—and if I had a letter . . ."

Lady Tess did not answer the unspoken plea. She pressed the tip of the hat pin against her forefinger, as if the action were a delicate and important one. "Do you think that Samuel owes you nothing more?" she asked softly.

To her dismay, Leda felt the hot tears well up. She bit

her lip, trying to prevent them from spilling over again. "No, ma'am," she whispered.

Lady Tess laid the hat pin aside and lifted her head. "Really? I suppose it's natural that I have more faith in him than you do. I'd like to think that we brought him up to know what is right."

"I am not—his responsibility."

"Oh, Leda. Leda."

"He is to marry Lady Kai." She said it quickly, or she would not have been able to say it at all.

Lady Tess turned her teacup around on its saucer. "I'm not aware that any such engagement has been announced."

Leda remembered suddenly that Lady Tess was opposed to the marriage, that she had been most upset when Lord Gryphon had told her of Mr. Gerard's intentions. Leda began to breathe more deeply. "Ma'am—it would be very foolish—you cannot force him—he will not wish to marry me!"

"I'm afraid that's true. And you are free to go away if that's what you decide, my love, because it will be very hard for you if you stay. He will not yield to this easily."

"You want—you want me to prevent their marriage? Do you hate the match so much?"

The older woman frowned, gazing past the vanity mirror out the window. "I love my daughter. I love Samuel as well. I don't want you to misunderstand me, but in a certain sense I—have a deeper attachment to Samuel. Kai and Robert—I wish nothing would ever hurt them. They're my children. I wish happiness for them all of their lives. But Samuel . . . Samuel is the strongest . . . much, much stronger than I can tell you—" She smiled sadly, and shook her head. "—and the one whose happiness I hope for the most ferociously." Her smile tilted up on one side. "Vicky and her cubs are nothing to me as a mother, I assure you."

Leda looked down at the red-and-blue carpet at her feet.

"I don't know." Lady Tess rested her cheek on her hand. "I'm sure when I was younger, I'd have thought that by the time my children were this age, I'd fret over them less. I wonder why it seems as if I brood about them more?"

"Ma'am," Leda said shyly, "I should think it must be very wonderful to have a mother like you."

"Well." She sat up more briskly. "If I have my way, Samuel will most likely wish me at Jericho, and you, too. Will you stay, and give him a chance to do as he ought?"

The thought that Mr. Gerard would wish her at Jericho—or worse—was not soothing. The idea that he might really "do as he ought" seemed so implausible, and so painfully disheartening, that Leda's shoulders drooped. "I think I should go away, ma'am."

"Leda . . . do you not care for him at all?"

She turned away, to hide her face. "He loves your daughter."

"That is over."

"Only yesterday—the necklace—"

"Please do not make me cross by underestimating Kai. My daughter is your friend, Leda—even if she wished to do so, do you suppose she would become engaged to him, knowing that he'd failed you? If she loves him, the first thing she will expect of him is the same thing I expect— that he will do his duty by you. To believe less of him would be an insult."

"Do his duty." Leda's voice was dull.

"Yes. I suppose that isn't a very pretty way to put it." She sighed. "But this is not a dreamworld, love. However innocently you did it, you've done a real thing that has real consequences. There might be a child. Have you thought of that?"

Leda stood stock-still. She stared at Lady Tess. A tiny noise of denial escaped her.

"This is where babies come from." Lady Tess nodded toward the bed. "I'm afraid the stork and cabbage leaf are fiction."

Leda spread her fingers wide, as if she could push the idea away from her. "Are you certain?"

"About the stork, yes." She smiled briefly. "Quite certain. As to whether you will have a baby as a result of last night—no, I can't be certain of that. It's only a possibility."

"Oh, *ma'am!*" The world blurred. "How do I find out?"

"It will be several weeks. If you miss your monthly courses, that is a fair sign."

Leda began to breathe very rapidly. A darkness crept over her vision.

"Leda!" Lady Tess' sharp voice and supporting hand caught her before the dark mist engulfed her. Leda found herself in the chair, bent over her lap. "There now, there . . ." Lady Tess murmured in her ear. "Don't panic, love. Don't terrify yourself. Hush, my brave girl . . . hush now . . . don't cry. He will take care of you, Leda; you're not alone."

Samuel stared into the mirror. He should have been able to see his face as contour and shade; potential: capable of conforming to any role required of him. Falsehood and illusion were tools of his discipline. He should never be lost between what was real and what was deceptive.

Seishin. A whole heart. He kept *seishin-seii.*

He closed his eyes and opened them again. He saw no truth. No wholeness. He saw nothing but himself, his mouth set with rage, his jaw stiff, his eyes glittering in the shaft of light from the dressing-room window.

In his past, they'd called him beautiful. A beautiful amusement. A handsome, tempting cub.

After all of Dojun's brutal training, no cut had ever left a scar. No bruise remained. Nothing marred him.

He loathed his own face.

With an abrupt move, he turned away, sweeping up cuff links from the dresser. The secret things he carried always with him were already transferred to his morning coat; the discarded comfort of his Oriental clothing lay in a dark lumpy heap—his "exercise costume," as the maids called it belowstairs.

The scent of her, and himself, still clung to it. He stood over it a moment, breathing in that incense. His body grew taut.

It was worse, now that he knew. Now that there was memory, fresh and vivid, to fuel the blaze. Desire had its own life and will: the thought of her filled him with elation.

He would pay her to go away. That, at least, he knew was required. A liberal *douceur,* he'd heard it called. Cheap irony, to label a payoff "sweetness." How conveniently French.

He seized the pile of midnight gray, tossing it over the back of a chair. His hand tangled in the cloth. *Leda,* he thought, but his mind could not seem to think beyond her name.

The pleasure was like pain inside him, like a torture at the base of his throat.

He had to control this. He had to speak to her, arrange everything, find some semblance of command over the situation. How he could have slept as if he had been doped, as if he were blind and deaf, how he could have heard nothing, felt no danger, allowed . . .

Lady Tess . . .

His whole body flushed with shame.

He heard a jolting crack. He realized that he'd moved— and looked down to find the chair frame split all the way down to the floor along a fracture of raw wood. He let go of it as if it burned his hands. It tilted drunkenly on three legs.

"Chikushō." He swore softly, calling himself a beast. And he was. God. He was.

Guests were leaving, though none of them seemed to be in very much hurry about it. In the front hall, three suitcases and a trunk sat gathered in one corner. A buffet lunch had been laid out in the breakfast room. Though it was well after two in the afternoon, spirit lamps still glowed beneath the silver dishes of ham and ptarmigan, giving out a sharp bouquet as Samuel walked in. Haye and Robert pottered among the chafing dishes, filling plates.

"Gerard." Lord Haye gave him a brief nod of recognition.

Robert just held his half-filled plate and regarded Samuel, as if he couldn't quite decide who he was. Then he looked down and popped a chunk of cheese into his mouth. "Got to talk to you," he said. "Privately."

Samuel governed his motion with care. Robert never wished to talk to him privately.

The sounds of guests and servants gathering in the hall provided an excuse to turn away. The Whitberrys were taking leave; Robert grimaced, put down his plate, and went out to see them off.

Samuel served himself and sat down at the big table. He and Haye ate in silence, with the full length of the white cloth between them. There had never been more than cool courtesy between them—this morning, Samuel could not even manage the basic requirements of civilization.

The oldest Goldborough girl stood in the door of the breakfast room, bending over and peeking in. "We're come to say good-bye, and Merry Christmas."

Haye and Samuel stood up. While the other man made gracious small talk about the weather and the journey to the station, Samuel murmured the most commonplace salutation within his power. He wished them all to hell.

What did Robert want to speak to him about?

The two younger Goldborough daughters came, wrapped in thick coats, carrying rabbit muffs. He bowed to them, kissed their hands when they held them out expectantly, leaving him no choice. They looked at him with the same wide-eyed expressions of giggly awe with which they'd looked at him since he'd been introduced to them.

Haye left the breakfast room with them. Samuel stood for a moment, and then abandoned his plate unfinished, leaving by the door into the deserted drawing room instead of the hall. He wandered to the billiards room. It was empty. He went up the back stairs and stopped in the hall outside Miss Etoile's room.

No one answered his light knock. He couldn't risk lingering there. As he turned and walked on, Kai met him coming down from the nursery.

She carried Tommy on her shoulder. The baby looked red-eyed and disgruntled, as if he would rather be asleep than thrust into Samuel's arms, as he was, without ceremony.

"Kai—" Samuel said, and was cut off by a rising wail.

"There—doesn't he want you, Tittletumps?" she crooned in baby talk. "Come back to me, then. Come back to me. There, now, there." She hefted the baby. As the wail subsided to a thin sob, she gave Samuel a sideways look. "Is it true?"

Everything inside him froze.

She patted Tommy's back, watching Samuel with her eyebrows lifted.

"Is what true?" He did not know how he found the power to speak.

She hugged Tommy. "Everyone is saying that you and Miss Leda—"

She went on, but he didn't hear her words. He heard nothing but his heart pounding in his ears: the silent, impossible sound of his life disintegrating.

"No." He denied it. He would not let her believe it. The sound of that one violent syllable died away in the hall; he heard the echo, as if someone else had said it.

Tommy snuffled, wrapping his fist around her collar, snuggling his face into her shoulder. The soft sound of birds murmured from the foliage in the central hall.

She bit her lip, her face troubled. "I thought it was a terrible rumor—I told Miss Goldborough that it was. But Manō, you would not . . . you would tell *me* the truth, if it were so?"

He gazed at her.

"Manō—you would not lie to me?"

His eyes dropped. He looked away.

"Oh . . ." Dismay drifted in her voice. "Manō."

"Kai—it means nothing. It's—" His jaw grew taut. "God, you don't *know!*" he said fiercely. "You can't understand."

"It doesn't mean anything?" She stared at him.

"No."

Her voice rose. "Are you saying that it's true, and it doesn't *mean* anything?" A transformation came over her face. "What about Tommy? What about Miss Leda? You can't possibly—why, I don't believe it of you! You can't say it means *nothing!*'' Tommy began to cry again, his raspy wails rising above her vehemence, but she did not stop. ''Would you have left them in the streets? Just abandoned them? Or—or—'' Her eyes widened and her chin went up. ''I see! You are not so very cruel. You have brought them here, and expected us to wash your dirty linen for you, while you won't even acknowledge it!''

He stood rigid, with the full extent of the disaster dawning upon him as she spoke. ''There is nothing to acknowledge,'' he said tightly.

''Nothing!'' In her passion, she pushed Tommy at him. ''Does he seem like nothing?''

Samuel had to take the baby or allow it to fall; Tommy arched his spine awkwardly and screamed at the clumsy transfer, one screech after another.

''Why, he has your eyes!'' she said with scorn. ''I don't know why I never remarked it!''

''You never remarked it because it is nothing but imagination.'' That much he managed to say, barely grinding out the words. He could not reason with her now. Temper stiffened all his movements; fury at fate and at himself. He moved past her toward the nursery with the shrieking child.

She came after him; he felt her hand on his arm and turned—but her eyes were shining with furious tears. She snatched Tommy from him and whirled away, kicking out her skirts with the force of her stride as she fled up the hall toward the nursery stair.

''Samuel.'' Lord Gryphon's voice stopped him cold at the door. The evening lay in a frigid mist on the drive and lawns, swallowing the last carriage headed for the railway station.

''Yes, sir.'' Samuel did not turn around.

''Going out?'' The question was soft, almost lazy, with infinite implications.

Samuel closed his eyes briefly. ''Yes, sir.''

''I'll go with you.''

''Yes, sir.'' He yanked on his gloves. ''If you wish.''

They walked out together. Lord Gryphon moved silently alongside Samuel, his hands in his pockets, breathing frost. The gravel drive curved away from the house, leaving warmth and light behind.

Samuel had wanted isolation. He had not wished to encounter anyone, not after his confrontation with Kai. He'd secluded himself while the rest of the guests finally departed, watching from a window as Kai went out on the front steps to see Haye off. She had stood in the drive and waved until the carriage disappeared.

Samuel's hands tightened in his leather gloves at the recollection. He'd no mastery of himself, could find nothing but jealousy and outrage in his heart.

The trees showed dark shapes through the mist. They seemed to float slowly past, while the crunch of his and Lord Gryphon's footsteps filled up the quiet. A set of steps that led to the formal gardens loomed, darkly silvered with the damp.

"What do you intend to do?" Lord Gryphon asked.

He gave the question no context. Samuel stopped. He took a deep breath. "I don't know what you mean."

"The hell you don't." The words were mild. Lord Gryphon kicked a stone to the side of the drive. He looked off into the mist and smiled grimly.

Samuel's mute endurance broke. "I'll send her away," he snapped. "I'll never lay eyes on her again. I'll give her money enough to live like a princess for the rest of her natural life. I'll cut my throat—is that good enough?" He tilted his head back to the empty sky with a wordless sound of torment. "What would be good enough?"

The other man leaned against a stone pedestal, crossing his arms. "Good enough for what?"

Samuel met his cool stare.

"I'm not requiring absolute pristine virtue of you." Lord Gryphon watched him steadily. "I'm no particular saint myself, but when I found the woman I loved, I didn't lay a different one."

Samuel's throat was dry, the air cold in his lungs.

"Do you understand me?" Lord Gryphon asked softly.

Don't. Samuel closed his eyes against it. *Don't do this to me.*

The quiet voice was inexorable. "I retract my consent. I won't let you hurt my daughter. Or my wife."

Samuel turned on him, walking away. He stopped and looked back through the vapor. "I would kill myself first."

"Yes." Lord Gryphon uncrossed his arms and pushed off the stone. "So I thought."

The footman held out the note on a silver tray. Samuel recognized the handwriting before he touched it. He pulled off his gloves, reduced to such small and pointless evasions for postponing the inevitable.

Lady Tess waited in the music salon to see him.

That was all it said. Samuel had been beaten once, bludgeoned in the back by a barroom stool, in the days when he'd been learning what it meant to be hit. It had arrested his breath, centered all his consciousness on exploding pain, annihilated him—and he had had to go on, to keep fighting, to move when his body was paralyzed.

He did it now. He functioned on discipline and nerve alone. He knocked on the door, opened it in response to her voice, and closed it behind him.

White and pink orchids nodded gently from the mantelpiece and reflected from the black glaze of the grand piano. She sat on the bench, fingering a sheet of music. As he entered, she set it back on the rack.

"I was never a musician," she said. "Kai could play—" She stopped, and looked embarrassed. "Never mind that. Samuel, I . . ."

Her voice trailed off again. She stood up, smoothing her skirt awkwardly, resting her hand on the piano lid and taking it away again.

"Lord Gryphon has already spoken to me," he said.

She looked up from the keys.

"You don't have to trouble to say it again, ma'am. If seeing me makes you uncomfortable."

She pressed her lips together. "I'm sorry that—everything became common knowledge. I would not have told anyone. Not even Gryf."

A candle burned softly within a frosted globe on the instrument. He watched that, unable to look elsewhere. "You have nothing to be sorry for." He locked his hands behind his back. "Nothing. Beyond bringing me into your house. I've never—been able to tell you. I've tried to say . . . what that meant . . ." He lost authority over his voice. Finally, openly, he looked up into her face and said, "I would not be alive."

"Oh, Samuel." She turned back to the piano keys. He watched her bent head, her slim, sun-darkened hands. His chest felt too taut to breathe.

"Hell," he said stupidly, knowing he had made her cry.

"Yes." She wiped at her eyes. "That's just the way I feel, too."

He wanted it over with and plunged ahead, speaking in stiff sentences that held nothing of what he felt. "I'll be leaving tomorrow. I won't see Kai. I'd only ask—that someone tell her the baby isn't mine. That's the truth. I never saw . . . Miss Etoile—before that day at the dressmaker's. And I never—before last night—"

The words got knotted again. She stood gazing down at the piano keys.

He wished that she would look up at him. He thought that what he couldn't say must be plain in his face. But she did not. She touched one black key, running her forefinger down the length of it.

"I would wait for Kai the rest of my life," he burst out suddenly, "if you thought there might come a time when you could forget this day."

Her finger traced the shape of an ivory note. "It's not mine to forget."

"Kai doesn't know. She only heard what they said about the baby. She doesn't understand—the other."

"It's not Kai's to forget, either," she said quietly. She turned and looked up at him. "Have you not once thought of the girl you've ruined?"

His back and shoulders grew tight. "Ruined."

"I think that word might be used, yes."

"Miss Etoile will be well taken care of. I don't think she'll regret this particular 'ruin.' "

Lady Tess arched her fine eyebrows. "That isn't what she's told me."

He swore sharply. "She shouldn't have spoken to you about it. What has she said?"

"Very much what you've said. That she's betrayed our friendship. That she will leave here. That you are in love with Kai."

"What did she ask for?"

"Nothing. She told me that she isn't your responsibility. I believe that she almost asked me for a letter of character, so that she might become a typist." She tapped her fingernail against the keys. "But in the end, she didn't."

"I'll talk to her." With an abrupt move, he turned to the fireplace. He took up the poker and thrust it among the coals. "She won't have to become a damned typist."

"What will you make of her, Samuel?"

He dropped the poker and leaned both hands against the mantel. "I'll give her a house and five thousand dollars. She won't have to be a typist."

"No," Lady Tess said gently. "What will she be instead?"

He scowled hard into the fire, seeing blue flames lick among the charcoal.

"I wished you to forget where you came from," she said. "I always wished you to forget. Now—I can't believe you don't remember."

Deep inside himself, he began to shake. "I remember."

"And you don't care that she—"

With a violent push, he turned from the fire. "I remember!" he shouted. "If you think it's the same—that I'd make her into what I was—that I could—" He expelled a furious breath, controlling himself, putting the black expanse of the piano between them. "I haven't forgotten where I came from."

Her lower lip trembled. She looked down. "I'm sorry. I shouldn't have said such a thing."

"Don't cry!" He spoke through his teeth. "God help me, don't cry. I'll come apart."

She sat down abruptly on the bench. The piano made a discordant note as her elbow hit the keyboard.

Never had he said something like that to her before. Never raised his voice, never asked for anything.

His hand closed around a glass paperweight on the ebony surface, his fist reflected in the shine. With a careful command of his tone, he said, "She'll expect me to give her a liberal amount of money. A house in addition is . . . more than generous. She won't have to sell herself anymore. Unless she wishes to."

Lady Tess lifted her head. "Anymore?"

"She's far better off than she's been in the past. The Lord Bountiful who sent her that note at the dressmaker's had her living in a garret."

"Samuel—" Her face paled. "You are mistaken."

"I'm not mistaken," he said grimly. "I know the place."

"But last night . . . did you not—" She wet her lips. "Oh, Samuel."

Something in her voice drew him to her wide and dismayed eyes. His hand tightened on the glass.

She spoke slowly, as if the words were difficult to utter. "Samuel . . . did you not realize she was a virgin?"

He looked down at his hand. Inside the crystalline oval, swirls of color and circles of tiny blossoms made a gay pattern. "Did she tell you that?"

"She didn't need to tell me. I've seen her. A young woman of experience would not weep so, nor bleed."

He remembered a boy who had done both: tears and blood that a lifetime of resolution had not scoured clean. Tears and blood were all that he recognized, the only connection between what he remembered of his past and the physical joy of last night. But he could not admit that he had expected such things, and still had allowed it to happen . . . had wanted it to happen, wanted it.

The paperweight fell into his palm, heavy and cold. In the oval of glass, his body perceived a potential weapon: his muscles weighed it automatically; his hand judged and shaped the surface for possibilities. He set it down again with care.

He had wished to marry Kai, had tried to make himself

good enough, had longed for her purity to absolve him of what he was. He felt walls closing on him.

"I promised her . . . that you would do what is right."

If he looked up, he would see Lady Tess pleading, and her daughter in her, and everything he'd fought to become.

"Samuel—" The plea faded to bewilderment. "I was so sure that I knew you."

He moved his hand, curled his fingers around the paperweight.

"I never thought . . . you would not look me in the face," she whispered. "I never thought you would disappoint me."

The glass hit the marble hearth with a sound like a gunshot. He saw the colors explode before he knew he'd hurled it. Curved shards fell into the fire, sending flame and sparks sailing upward.

The flare died back. Lady Tess stood with her hands over her mouth, staring at what he had done.

All his fury, all his frustration—glittering in facets of glass amid the coals. *What's right. Do what's right.*

Kai! He could not believe it. He could not believe that everything was gone.

He turned, walking out in a haze, leaving Lady Tess alone with the razor-sharp fragments of his dreams.

Twenty-seven

⊕

Lady Tess had bade her wait alone in the room beside the nursery. Leda could not settle; she wandered amid the old scent of long-lost roses and the faded flowers on the slipcovered sofas. It had once been a lady's boudoir, high up in the house overlooking the drive and front gardens, with chintz drapes drawn now over the wide windows.

She paused a moment at the sound of voices from the nursery—but it was only the new nurse and a maid, murmuring over Tommy as they put him to bed. The nurse came to the half-open door and peered in, saw Leda, smiled, and said good night as she shut it fully.

A hush descended. Leda felt like a ghost in the boudoir full of comfortable pillows and well-used chairs. She thought that a room such as this must have known much happiness; family had sat and laughed in the welcoming hollows of the love seat; children had played on the soft rug; a grandmother had worn the bare spot beneath an old rocking chair. Leda was only a brief visitor, an unfamiliar presence come and gone and soon forgotten.

Mr. Gerard entered silently; she turned from the case of books, the copies of *Alice in Wonderland* and *Grimm's Fairy Tales,* and found him there, a cold and potent angel in mortal dress.

She'd prepared a little speech, but it deserted her. Conventional cordiality seemed impossible with—someone one had last held conversation with in one's bedroom—in one's bed—in a most unseemly embrace. She flushed and stood silent, looking at him, trying to believe that what she remembered was true. This man, wintry and golden, had kissed and held and invaded her, slept with his arms around her.

"Miss Etoile." He made no attempt at civility, either. "We'll be married after Christmas, if that is satisfactory to you."

She looked away at the impersonal words. She clasped her hands together and sat down in the rocking chair, gazing at her fingers. "Mr. Gerard—please do not feel—that you must make such an—unalterable decision. Perhaps— you would wish more time to consider."

"What would I consider?" The bitterness showed through his detachment. "The decision was made last night. And it is unalterable, Miss Etoile."

"But . . . Lady Kai . . ."

"I no longer have her parents' consent. Or her— affection."

Leda twisted her hands together. "I'm sorry," she whispered. "I am so sorry."

"Tell me one thing. Tell me the truth." His face grew taut. "I was the first?"

For a moment, she did not understand him. Then she felt the color coming into her breast and throat and face. She pressed her feet against the floor, pushing back in the rocking chair, a hopeless effort to hide herself in it. "Yes."

His eyes met hers with a flash of heat. Her face burned. The first. Did he think there would be a second? That she could bear to be touched in that way by anyone but him?

"I didn't know." He turned away. His brusque words held anger and chagrin. "I'm not—very experienced in the matter."

Leda pushed free of the rocker, drawing herself stiffly up. "Mr. Gerard, I would *never* have to do with gentlemen in such a coarsely familiar fashion."

"Wouldn't you?" He slanted an ironic look at her.

Leda had a sudden, intense recollection of his body pressed over her, his hands in her hair, the sensation of bared skin against hers. "I should not have!" she exclaimed. "It was very wrong of me!"

"I could wish you'd remembered these scruples last night."

"I thought that you were lonely! I did not know—that you meant—what you meant."

His glance raked her. She balled her hands into fists.

"I assure you, sir, that I never knew such a thing was even *possible!* I'm certain no one ever told me of it!" She lifted her chin indignantly. "I would not have believed them if they had!"

A peculiar smile traced his mouth. "I was led to expect I'd find you weeping, and pale from loss of blood."

"I'm sure anyone would weep. Out of astonishment, if nothing else. It was the most singular experience of my entire life."

"Yes," he said. "Mine, too."

She sat down again, and began rocking madly. "And now they all think—" She bit her lip. "It is so humiliating! Everyone looks at me! *Must* we marry, when you'll dislike me for it so? Lady Tess says that is how—that is—babies, you know. And I must wait several weeks to be sure!" She sprang out of the chair and turned away, squeezing her eyes shut, hugging herself. "I'm frightened!"

He didn't answer. When she opened her eyes, he was beside her, shockingly close.

"Oh!" She let out a startled gasp. "However do you do that, when the floors all squeak so abominably?"

He caught her chin, holding her as he looked down into her eyes. "You're panicking."

"No, I am not. I wasn't brought up to vulgar displays of emotion. But if I had been, I'm sure that being stared at, and whispered about, and pointed to, and expected to marry a gentleman who will hate me, gives me sufficient reason! And you needn't remind me to breathe, Mr. Gerard. I'm sure you'd be just as pleased if I didn't, and then you would be rid of me very shortly."

"No. You'd only turn blue, and faint, and afterward you'd be as alive as ever. And I'd still be obliged to marry you."

"You shan't, if you don't wish to! I tried to tell Lady Tess, if I could only have a letter of character—"

His fingers tightened on her chin. "You won't need letters," he said. "We're to be married in three weeks. I'll take care of you."

She swallowed. "Lady Tess said that you would."

"Did she?" He let go of her. "She knows me." His mouth curved in moody humor. "She knows I wouldn't disappoint her."

The wedding took place on a windy, cloudy day in January, in the private chapel at Westpark, with Lady Kai as Leda's maid of honor. It all seemed as unreal and fraudulent as the white satin gown and pristine tulle veil Leda wore, made up in haste by Madame Elise and sent down just yesterday from London, along with a personal note of congratulations from that commerce-minded lady, who wished that Miss Etoile might be pleased to honor the couturiere by allowing Madame to provide any gowns of fashion and taste that the bride-elect might require to complete her trousseau.

Leda wasn't certain who had paid for the gown, nor Lady Kai's new apricot organza with the big bow at the back, nor the dreadfully out-of-season real orange blossoms that perfumed the cool air. She feared that it had been Lord Gryphon, who was splendidly distinguished as he waited with her in the alcove, and who pressed her arm reassuringly as they started down the aisle. If he had not been there, supporting her, Leda knew that her knees would have failed her and she would have sunk to the stone floor in misery and fear.

The chapel was all light and white plaster, even on the dull day, an eighteenth-century ecstasy of carving and harmony. Leda knew that she didn't belong there—no aristocratic ancestor of hers had created this fairy-tale space.

Mr. Gerard, however, fit the elegant scene far better than his groomsman Lord Robert, who fidgeted with his boutonniere as music filled the chapel. Mr. Gerard stood unmoving, dressed in a black, close-fitting morning coat, watching while the sparse congregation rose, row by row, as Leda passed—and she thought that no one in imagination or reality could have been more precisely formed to create an image of cold, bright, ruthless perfection.

Then through her veil, she had a glimpse of Lady Cove—Lady Cove! Her eyes pricked; she had to bite her lip against the rush of feeling. They had all come from South Street: Lady Cove rose with rapt face and ready handkerchief, in a hat laden with what appeared to be a stuffed partridge—so new and fashionable as to be almost ungenteel—and there was Mrs. Wrotham, wearing her best cap, bought twenty years ago in Paris. But it was dignified Miss Lovatt, to whom tears were a weakness of the common classes, making a stern face and then plucking Lady Cove's handkerchief away to dab at her own eyes with a resentful grimace and her mouth all puckered up, who broke Leda's fragile composure. The scene went completely blurred. She clutched Lord Gryphon's arm, walking blindly ahead, with hot tears tumbling down beneath the veil.

They thought it was real. They had come all the way from London, must have taken the train, even though Mrs. Wrotham became so dreadfully ill with the motion of the cars. They were her friends; they were happy for her—and it was all a sham, even the white gown for purity.

Lord Gryphon released Leda's arm. Lady Kai took her bouquet, smiling with excitement. Then there was no choice—Leda had to turn and face him.

Through the veil and the blur, she saw only his shape, dark and gilt. She heard his voice, and it was steady, without emotion. Love, comfort, honor. How could he say it? She did not think she could make a sound.

And yet, when her turn came, the words emerged, plain and resolute. She did love him. She did. That was the one true moment in all of the ritual mockery.

In sickness and in health, as long as we both shall live.

He lifted her veil. She blinked, and saw him clearly. His eyes, dark-lashed, the gray of first light; his face so inhumanly flawless; his mouth that had tasted hers. She saw him perceive the tears. The faintest tightening came in his jaw as he bent his head and brushed his lips against her wet cheek.

Lady Tess moved about the room. She turned down the bed, twitched at pillows, tugged at the closed draperies, then smoothed the white gown that the maid had hung in the empty wardrobe. "This was my grandmother's room. You may redecorate it, if you like. I'm afraid it's sadly out of date."

"It's lovely, ma'am," Leda said.

"Call me Tess." She straightened an oval frame hanging by a ribbon from the picture rail, a photograph of a little boy fishing. Her restless motion made Leda even more nervous than she was already.

"Oh, I could not—"

"Please." She looked up. "Tess. It's short for Terese, which I must confide that I dislike immensely."

"Yes, ma'am—Tess."

An ivory box lay on the white-and-gold vanity. "This is from Samuel. He asked me to bring it to you."

Leda accepted the unadorned gift. She hesitated a moment, but Lady Tess—Tess, rather, though Leda doubted she could ever really bring herself to be so impertinent as to call Lady Tess that—watched her expectantly, so she sat down in an upholstered armchair and opened the lid. Inside, lying on pink satin, were a brush and mirror, dearly familiar, even down to the little speckled pattern in the vintage reflection that Leda had always thought looked like a tiny elf-face peeping out from the edge of the glass.

"Mr. Gerard found this?" She felt a lump rise in her throat.

"Leda!" Lady Tess sounded provoked. "I wish you will not cry again!"

"Yes, ma'am." Leda sniffed and bent her head. Then she looked up and gave a watery, squeaky half-laugh. "That's precisely what Miss Myrtle would have said to me." She touched the mirror, traced the pattern in the silver frame. "I never thought to see this again."

"Would you like me to brush out your hair?" Without waiting for permission, Lady Tess picked up the brush and began to pull combs and pins from Leda's hair.

It fell, curling heavily, onto her shoulders. Lady Tess worked silently, and none too gently, for a few moments. Leda tried not to wince.

"Well, I am going to meddle again." Lady Tess's voice had that faint exasperation that Leda was learning meant she was upset, or uncertain. "I didn't have a mother, either, when I married, but I had a friend. I'd like to be your friend, Leda. Will you mind very much if I sit down and tell you some things that I think you should know?"

"No, ma'am. Of course not."

" 'Tess,' please."

"Oh, ma'am—I just cannot. I'm sorry! It seems too pert of me."

Lady Tess sat down on the edge of the high bed, with her feet propped on the little step stool next to it, still holding Miss Myrtle's brush. "Well, Samuel has never brought himself to it, either, so I suppose it's all right. Though it makes me feel very old and stuffy. No one called me 'Lady' for the first twenty years of my life, and I think it's unkind and disagreeable of everybody to ma'am me to death now."

Leda instantly turned to her. "You aren't at all old, ma'am. Tess, I mean! I will try!"

"Thank you. I feel younger already." She tilted her head. "Now, I'm going to tell you what I learned from my friend, and you must not be shocked." She smiled. "Well, you may be shocked, if you wish—I suppose it's too much to hope I won't shock you—but after that you must promise to forget Miss Myrtle and propriety and all of that, and think about what I say."

Leda felt herself turning red. "Is it about . . ."

"Yes, that is what it's about. You and Samuel. It's all *right*, Leda—don't look away from me. You're a married woman now. You have it in your power to give your husband pleasure, or to make him miserable. It will be your choice, but I don't want you to make it out of ignorance."

"No, ma'am. Tess, I mean."

"My friend's name is Mahina Fraser. She is from Tahiti. And I can assure you, Leda, there's no one more conversant with the physical love between a man and a woman than a Tahitian."

"Oh," Leda said dubiously.

"Have you heard of Tahiti? It's an island. Mahina told

me these things on a beach. We had hot sand between our toes, and our hair loose, just as yours is. Men are a little different, but I think a woman requires relaxation to make love properly. Our hair free, and no apprehension.'' Her pretty eyes narrowed teasingly. "There—I've shocked you already, and we haven't even begun. Are you afraid of Samuel, Leda?''

The question came so suddenly that Leda only blinked.

"Did he hurt you?'' Tess asked gently.

Leda looked down at her lap, rubbing her thumb against the mirror's silver handle. "Yes.''

"Believe me, please believe me—that is only temporary. It will not hurt after a little while; if it does, there's something wrong. Don't forget that. And do not—do *not*—allow Samuel to believe differently. Because I fear that he does. I'll tell you about Samuel presently, but on this point I'm right. I'm old and I'm stuffy and I know more than either of you about it. A girl's body takes a little time to become accustomed, and that's all the hurt or pain or bleeding that there ever is. Do you understand?''

Leda swallowed. She nodded.

"Smile for me. It's not terrible. It's very nice. Have you ever had warm sand between your toes?''

"No, ma'am.''

"Think of something warm and luxurious, then. A feather comforter. A cashmere shawl.''

Leda's glance wandered to the canopied bed. Tess' quick look caught her. Leda blushed hotly.

"Are you thinking of Samuel?'' Tess wriggled as if she were a delighted child and leaned forward. "That's excellent. Now, I'm going to tell you all about what Mahina told me about men . . . and it's all true, too.''

By the time Tess had finished, Leda knew the Tahitian names for things that she'd never even imagined existed, and for places that she had only thought vaguely of as "there.'' Miss Myrtle would have fainted dead away long before Tess gave Leda a quizzical look and said, for the twentieth time, "Now I've shocked you. Don't giggle, if you please. It sounds much sillier than it really is.''

"Oh, dear," Leda said between her fingers. "If it's only half as absurd as it sounds, I don't know how one manages."

"You'll manage. And don't succumb to the giggles at the wrong moment, or you'll hurt his feelings. Men are very sensitive. And Samuel . . ." She grew pensive, spinning the brush in her hand. "I think I should tell you about him, Leda. He wouldn't wish me to, but—" Her lower lip tightened stubbornly. "But I'm a meddlesome old lady, who's convinced she knows best."

Something in the careful way she laid the brush on the bed and stood up, holding onto the bedpost, made Leda's heart beat faster.

"All these things I've been telling you—" Tess said, "—I believe they're good and right between people who care for one another. Within a marriage. I should tell you that I was married once before, a long time ago, when I was very young and extremely stupid. It was annulled, after a short time."

Leda controlled her surprise, not knowing what to say.

"The man was—a Mr. Eliot. He was—quite frightening. It worries me still, sometimes, because I never understood why he was the way he was. Why he did to me—what he did." Her fingers grew white where she held the post. "There are people who mix all these things up, Leda, and turn them inside out, and make love into something terrible. And I don't know why—I really can't explain that part, as old and wise as I am." She smiled wryly and drew a breath, as if arming herself to go on. "There are men who will pay women to do what I've been talking about, and mostly they're to be pitied, because there's no love in it. There are men who will pay other men. And there are men who will buy children."

Leda's spine straightened. She looked toward the slender woman leaning against the bedpost.

"The first night I was in Mr. Eliot's house, a boy came to my room. He was—five—perhaps six. I don't know. That was Samuel." She spoke evenly, but her voice held just the tiniest quiver. "He was very docile. He never said a word. Mr. Eliot tied his wrists and beat him. And it's very hard—it's impossible—for me to understand, or explain, or even talk about—but that was part of Mr. Eliot's method of obtaining pleasure for himself. And when I objected—forcefully—he locked me in a room, and didn't let me out for almost a year."

The quiver in her voice had become an audible shaking. She stood very still, looking off into a corner of the room.

"When you think that you're safe," she said, "when you think that everything is reasonable and logical and people are what they seem, and something like that happens to you . . . you never forget it. Never. I will *never*—"

Her voice finally broke. Leda stood up, not knowing what to do or offer. Tess turned, and met her dismayed gaze. She smiled, but there was no amusement in her eyes.

"It changed me. The world has never seemed the same. And I was lucky—I had friends who rescued me and took me away and arranged the annulment, and then I had Gryf—but I couldn't forget that little boy. We had detectives looking for almost three years. He was found in one of those places where children are sold to men."

Leda was still standing. She sat down heavily in the chair.

"I'm not—I don't wish to upset you, Leda. I only want you to be able to understand him a little. You said that he hurt you that first time—and frightened you, too, I think. Only imagine what it must be like, to be not yet eight years old, and alone in such a place."

Leda drew her knees up into the chair and rested her face in them. She thought of all his small, loving gifts to Tess, so meticulously considered; of the coin on a ribbon around her own throat; of the silver brush and mirror. And she thought, with a sudden certainty, of the strange pattern of his thefts in the city.

She thought: *He meant to close them down, those places.*

Instead of marches and hymns and ladies' campaigns, he'd simply, alone and silent, made it impossible for them to exist in the glare of public curiosity.

"How remarkable he is," she said, muffled in her gown.

"Do you think so?" Tess sounded so hopeful.

Leda nodded into her knees.

"Thank God." Tess sighed, a long and deep release of air. "I've been terrified to tell you. I was afraid—I knew I should, but I was so afraid that you wouldn't wish to marry him."

"I always wished it," Leda admitted, without lifting her face. "I'm only afraid—that he doesn't."

"But he has done it."

Leda curled her fingers in her gown. "Because he had no choice."

"No choice?" Tess' voice held a crisp note of incredulity. "I'm afraid that's giving him a bit more sympathy than he deserves. No one forced him to make love to you. No one coerced him to stay with you as he did, when he'd have known as well as you or I that the servants begin work at six. No one persuaded him that there would be no consequences. He's a grown man; he's done nothing that he hadn't perfect freedom to refrain from doing."

Leda could not look up. "I'm still afraid," she whispered.

Tess came to her, and touched her hair. "Yes. Of course you are, love. Everyone must be, when they have to look into the future and wonder what will happen. But I'll tell you something that gives me so much hope. You said—he's remarkable. If I were to tell Kai about him, she wouldn't see that he's remarkable. She'd be distressed, and she'd pity him, and he would die before he'd endure it. He's so proud, and so ashamed."

"He should not be." Leda raised her head. "What happened to him wasn't his fault."

"Oh, Leda." Tess smiled. "What a wise old woman I've turned out to be, to trust you to see that."

"Of course I see it, ma'am. Who would not?"

"Samuel," Tess said simply. She took both of Leda's hands. "And now I've tampered quite enough with you and your future. Even we interfering old ladies must be reined in at last. I'll tell Samuel he may come up. Be happy, Leda." She gave a squeeze, and went to the door. "You're quite remarkable yourself, you know."

The door closed behind her. Leda hugged her knees.

She held Miss Myrtle's mirror and looked down at herself in it. Her hair curled around her shoulders and cheeks. She thought it was a most *un*remarkable face—not wise or certain or clever at all.

Samuel played the part set for him. He accepted congratulations, smiled when he was expected to smile, sat down and stood up and did what he had to do through an interminable day. Most of the guests—the Hawaiian consul, a few business associates of his, and the trio of elderly ladies on Miss Etoile's side—knew nothing of the scandalous circumstances, although he doubted that it would be long before they found out. The prospect disturbed him; he didn't wish her to be subjected to more of the looks and whispers that tormented her.

So he made sure that he appeared to be honored by the bestowal of Miss Etoile's hand upon him, as one diminutive old lady with a gentle, fluttery voice and a dead bird on her hat put it. His smile wasn't completely feigned; these faded grande dames, with their potent scent of violets and soap, their intense interest in what would be served at the wedding luncheon, their complicated stratagems to satisfy their inquisitiveness about the household arrangements—everything from servants to the amount of coal consumed in heating such large rooms—without betraying an ill-bred curiosity, their staunch pride in "their" Miss Etoile and sincere concern for her happiness—he found them oddly touching. They made only the simplest of demands: an estimate of the number of candles in the dining room chandelier appeased them, a promise to have the cook send a recipe for lemonade gratified them, a cup of tea brought by the bridegroom put them into a delicate fuss of self-conscious delight.

He spent the afternoon mostly in their company, avoiding deeper connections, as he'd avoided them since Christmas by traveling to London and Newcastle, investigating the potential of Charles Parsons' turbine steam engines. While Samuel had been gone, Lord Haye had come back to Westpark—with a motive so obvious that Samuel wondered with a remote contempt why the engagement had not yet been announced.

He would not be here to see it when it was. Watching Kai's enthusiasm in the wedding celebrations, hearing Lady Tess talk of what might be planted in the gardens in spring, he thought: *I won't be here.*

It was like an unexpected cavern at his feet. He felt dazed with it.

But he had always been out of place. He'd simply proved it, surrendering finally to the darkness that had never left him.

He'd tried, turning and turning away. But the other was there. It was there now, inside him, springing to intense life when Lady Tess took Miss Etoile—his wife, God . . . his wife—and went upstairs with her.

Robert grinned and winked at him. He returned an austere stare. Everyone else went on talking, as if it were the most common of occasions. But he sensed the new note of distraction beneath the outward ease. No one else would look directly at him. They smiled past him and around, as if he embarrassed them by standing there.

He felt himself going numb. Was it so flagrant, what he wanted? That even now, when it had ruined him, when it had brought him to this, he still craved to lie down with her and be covered in that seductive, secret blaze?

Even Kai avoided him, contriving a sudden exhaustion, making a motion as if to reach for his hands, and then, pink-cheeked, breaking it off without touching him. "Good evening, Manō. Congratulations."

As if it were a signal, the whole company began to break up. In her mother's absence, Kai shepherded the overnight guests toward their quarters, while Robert and Haye wandered out together. Samuel was left alone in the drawing room, among the flowers that Kai had tied with white satin bows, the table of gifts, the veil that lay discarded across the embroidered cushion of a window seat.

My wife, he thought.

Even the words seemed foreign. But the slow burn of desire—that he knew: the shadow of his other self, the enemy inside him.

Twenty-eight

◈

He went to her because it would have been a defeat not to. It would have been an admission that he had no rule over himself at all.

She was curled up in a chair when he entered, clasping her knees, like a painting he'd seen once of a pensive young girl nestled in an alcove, her hair flowing loose, trailing with the ribbons on her gown. The doorknob made a click as he released it. Her head came up sharply at the sound. She looked toward him and immediately rose, snatching up the robe that lay over the back of the chair.

Her bare feet, the swing of her hair as she swept it over her collar, the curve of her cheek when she looked away shyly . . . He simply stood, mute with the strength of his response.

He failed in what he'd intended to say. He'd meant to make vows, to pledge not to touch her, but he could not.

Not now—not yet.

"You left this downstairs." He held the veil in his right hand, the yards of lace doubled between his fingers.

"Oh! You should not carry it so." She reached for the mass of white froth and smoothed it out carefully. "You might have torn the net. It's Irish—the nuns make it specially, upon hundreds of bobbins. I have a receipt for washing it in milk and coffee to give it the proper color. It should never be starched, you know, nor ironed." She glanced at him quickly and carried it away to the mirrored wardrobe. Her jade-green robe rustled along the carpet. When she turned back, skittishly, she focused her look somewhere near his elbow. "Such a lavish dress! And the fee for the rush, over Christmas—it must have been dreadfully dear! I was never so amazed; when the trunk arrived. I fear that Lord and Lady Ashland have been much too kind. How I shall ever find a way to thank them, I don't know!"

"Do you like it?"

She drew in a breath, still not looking at him. "I couldn't imagine anything more lovely."

"That's sufficient," he said. "You don't have to thank anyone."

He saw the realization dawn upon her. She met his eyes directly. "Oh, sir—did you arrange for it?"

He put his hands behind his back, leaning against the door. "Madame Elise informed me that you'd need a wardrobe of untold proportions. I've opened a bank account for you—you've only to tell me when you need a draft deposited. The initial balance is ten thousand pounds."

"Ten thousand!" She gaped at him. "That's madness!"

"You needn't spend it all at once."

"I could not spend it all in a lifetime! Dear sir!"

"You're my wife." He came to his prepared speech. "You have a rightful claim to my support. What I possess is yours."

She said nothing, but wandered a few steps, skimming her fingers over the vanity and the fringed draperies in a bewildered way, finally sitting down with a plump on the vanity bench. "Well! I am vexed." She drew the jade-green wrapper closely around herself. "You've found me Miss Myrtle's dressing set, and kindly conferred ten thousand pounds upon me, and I have not got anything at all for you."

He tried not to look at the outline of her body beneath the silky cloth. "It doesn't matter."

She rubbed one thumb back and forth over the other, staring down at her hands. "I had thought of a razor, but I didn't know; I've heard that gentlemen are especially particular about such things."

"I have a razor," he said.

"I might have made you a shirt, or given you a new silk hat."

"I also have a tailor."

She looked down at her lap, smoothing her palm over the glossy jade fabric. "Perhaps," she said in a small voice, "you would like for me to massage your back?"

Samuel leaned harder against the door. He gazed at her lowered head. With a feeling like sliding from a height, he felt the image take hold of him.

"I'm not precisely experienced at massage." She buttoned and unbuttoned a single button on her robe. "In fact, I've never been required to execute the procedure myself. But when I was twelve, and had the influenza and ached so, Miss Myrtle would rub me with camphor, and it quite comforted me. Lady Tess said that massage is something married gentlemen enjoy—only without the camphor, of course. I would be honored to try."

"No." He put his complete weight back against the door, pressing on it. "I don't think that would be wise."

"You would not like it?" She looked up at him.

His body had already gone thick and excited: he adored her upturned face, her English voice, her jade-green robe, her toes peeping from beneath the fold of white gown. She was pretty. Maidenly. Her freshness aroused him, called to the devil inside him.

He shoved away from the door, turning toward the fire screen to hide himself. "I wanted to speak with you about this connection. I've thought that the circumstances might lead you to fear that I won't view the marriage as a serious obligation. I do. You can depend on me for whatever you require."

He heard the rustle of her robe as she stood up. "Thank you. I should like to take the opportunity to say that—as you mention, the circumstances being untoward—and matrimony being a very solemn occasion, not to be entered into lightly—and myself being of—not to say perplexed, in the general way of things, as to what I ought to do—but in the present case in some uncertainty—that is to say, as to what a gentleman requires and prefers—not being very familiar with gentlemen, excepting yourself, of course—to which I feel compelled to add that I should not like—although I know that a man is troublesome in the house—'' She took a breath amid the tangle of stilted phrases. ''I wouldn't care for you to believe that I'm unhappy to be your wife!''

He stared down into the painted scene of powdered ladies and mincing gallants on the fire screen. *My wife,* he thought. *My wife, my wife.*

He found himself moving toward her instead of away, catching her wrists hard in his hands. Looking down into her startled face, into eyes wide and green and vulnerable, he felt how much larger he was; how he could hurt her; with one easy motion he could crush her, and in the same instant he wished to safeguard and please and worship her with his body.

He wanted to say something, but he did not know what. Even as he gave in to it, he wanted to promise her that he would never yield to what was burning up his heart and his body. He slowly pressed her hands together behind her back—as if he were pushing her away and bringing her closer at once.

The move caused her breasts to arch toward him. He couldn't feel it beneath his coat; he could only see the robe slide open and the white gown beneath tauten, outlining the swelling shape clearly. His chest went tight.

He kept her imprisoned against him, catching both of her hands in one of his. He'd meant differently. He'd intended to visit her, inform her that she was safe from any imposition of his, now or in the future, and go away.

But he thought: *God, only let me . . .*

She made no resistance. She lowered her eyes modestly, gazing ahead at the wing collar and white tie of his wedding clothes. He stared down at her eyelashes, the smooth contour of her face; he felt her acceptance of his hold and knew he'd lost.

''Leda,'' he whispered. He lowered his head and slowly and softly kissed her ear, the skin below it, pushing her hair back with his free hand. ''I'm not going to hurt you. I'd never hurt you.'' He wanted to show her how he felt, but it was difficult, torturously hard to keep the drive of his passion in check.

Her body held the yielding arch. He slid his fingers down the curve of her throat, awed at the delicacy of it, tasting her skin where his fingertips passed. His hands knew how to do this, like calligraphy, like shaping wood to its own spirit: move with the life in her, take it into himself and give it back.

She had the same wonderful fragrance, female heat, more stirring even than he remembered, not so chaste, not so innocent . . . a shock of pure lust rocked him as he realized what he perceived: her body's response to him.

If he could only show her that he didn't mean to harm her, that all he felt was this fervent tenderness; he only wanted to touch every part of her, taste the radiant, lovely life that scented her skin with a sensual glow. He shaped her breast with his palm, passing his thumb across the nipple.

She made a little sound, resisting his hand, pressing to free her wrists.

"No—please don't stop me." His voice was infinitely mild, shaking with what he held back. His touch was reverent as he caressed her. "I want to make you see how beautiful you are to me. I won't harm you. I swear to you."

"I'm not afraid," she whispered. "Dear sir. I only feel . . . as if I've been drinking cherry brandy."

He felt the vibration of her murmur beneath his lips. She was quivering in his hold. Where his grip on her wrists made her hips curve into him, his arousal pressed hard against her.

He lowered his other hand, sliding it down the arc of her back. His fingers spread over the swelling curve below, felt the soft reality of a female figure, without skirts or pads or distortion, only the fine layer of gown and robe between his hand and her naked form.

He let go of her wrists and caught her to him for a moment—only a moment—that was all he could bear of the explosive sensation of her buttocks in his palms, his stiff sex squeezed by the pressure. He expelled a harsh breath and released her, pushing her back against the edge of the vanity, spreading his legs to control her.

•He cherished her, stroking and fondling and kissing, everywhere he could reach, her cheeks and eyelashes, her shoulders, her breasts. She began to make small sighs in her throat, her head tilted back, her hands grasping the gilded edge of the vanity. The tips of her nipples changed, stood erect; he could feel it through the gown.

"Leda. Let me see you." He brought his mouth closer to hers, tasting her with his tongue, holding her taut nipples up in the arc of his open thumb and fingers. "I have to see you."

She lifted her lashes. He did not wait for an answer; he dropped his hand and slowly, carefully, worked the pearls free from her waist to her throat. White skin gleamed in the shadows, seductive contours, lush swelling.

Gently he pulled the gown apart. Her bared breasts were round and pale, flowering with the rich brownish-pink nubs, lifting and falling with her breath. He slipped both the gown and robe off her shoulders, allowing them to fall down to the vanity at her hips.

Leda gazed at him. The dreamlike sensation enveloped her. She was not herself, Miss Leda Etoile, standing indecently, scandalously unclothed before a man . . . she was someone else. The Leda of mythology, a woman with a god for a lover—the story Miss Myrtle had never taught her, but that Leda had learned secretly, and kept in a book beneath her bed, not understanding fully, but knowing it for a pagan and forbidden mystery.

A lover. No Zeus, no huge and magnificent swan, but a man, who looked at her as if she were a goddess, at her body as if it were precious.

Softly, he touched her breasts, so softly and sweetly that she closed her eyes against the shame and delight of it. He moved closer to her; she felt him slide downward, kneel, his legs open across her, his body holding her against the hard edge of the vanity.

His thumbs caressed the tips of her breasts. She tilted her head back. And then he touched her with his mouth, and she felt sunlight bloom inside her. His breath blew warmth; he played with her, searching and toying; his teeth and tongue closed with a tug that sent a shot of sensation down her tummy.

"Oh!" She pressed down on her arms, lifting herself toward him.

He sucked harder, pulling at her gown as she moved her hips, dragging it down below her waist.

He laid his cheek against her, sliding his hands up and down her torso. "You're lovely." He turned his face into her and laughed, a quiet, incredulous laugh, blowing his breath on her skin. "Your breasts are lovely, your shape is lovely, your skin is so beautiful."

Leda put her arms around his head, cradling him, ashamed and exhilarated with the velvety tickle of his hair against her bare skin, his cheekbone and temple firmly pressed to her. He caught her wrists again, spreading her arms open, trapping her with the heels of his hands braced on the edge of the table. He licked between her breasts, moving downward.

With her arms imprisoned against the table, Samuel caressed her with his tongue. He wanted to show her how delicious she was to him; he wanted to kiss her everywhere. He could taste the pleasure on her; he savored the hot woman-scent as he worked his way down her belly. Her calves shifted and twitched between his open thighs.

She whimpered softly. He nuzzled the soft rosy bush of hair, breathing her body deeply. Her arms were resisting his grip, shaking with the effort, but he would not let her go. Nothing in his life had impelled him like this. Nothing had ever felt like this. Her legs pressed against him just where all sensation centered. Her fragrance kindled flame.

He kissed her. Gently. So gently. He opened his mouth over that secret, silky place, pushing his tongue into the taste.

She jerked against him with a wordless sound of protest.

"Shhh." He blew a whisper. He wasn't going to stop. No power on earth was enough to make him resist the delight of stroking her. He kissed the arch where her skin disappeared beneath sweet curls. Bending his head, he licked deep, and then upward, and then the soft skin around. She was trembling all over; each time his tongue crossed upward, she shivered and gasped, her hands working against him.

He relished the sound of her agitation. He found the place that drew it most hotly and celebrated it with his tongue, over and over, until she pushed each time beneath his mouth the way that he wanted to push himself inside her.

He liberated her hands suddenly. He rose in the same motion, kissing her thighs and her belly and then her breasts. She put her arms around his shoulders and bent her head into his chest as he straightened.

"Oh, sir! Oh—sir!" She sounded faint. Each breath was a pant. She wilted against him, her cheek pressed to his heart. He held her there, throbbing in every limb, feeling her naked back beneath his sleeves, the fragile shape of her in his arms.

After a few moments, he trailed his hand down her hip. He spread his fingers, touching the place he'd kissed. It was slick and succulent, full of moisture; he bent his head and closed his teeth on her neck as he pushed his fingers in.

She whimpered again, stiffening beneath his entry. He withdrew his fingers and freed his trousers. The curls between her legs touched him; erotic, teasing; he closed his eyes in excitement, shoving slowly forward.

The abundant moisture welcomed him. Her legs spread. She clung to him, exquisite, hot, smooth and yet tight. Her head dropped back; he opened his eyes to the vivid sight of her breasts rising with the flexion, her hair falling backward off her bare shoulders.

He held her with one arm and caught her flushed nipple between his fingers. She cried out, a female cry, bashful and surprised as her hips twisted hard against him, her fingers clutching, her body closing around him with a long, desperate shudder, and then voluptuous quick pulsations.

It sent him to climax without even moving—his senses exploded in response; his muscles convulsed; unbearable pleasure washed over him as he held her impaled, trembling and winded and crushed against his chest.

* * *

Nothing that Lady Tess had told her had prepared her.

Leda felt herself wholly embraced, cradled in every part by his arms and his body. The only places that hurt were where she was pinned against the rigid edge of the vanity and a faint smarting stretch inside her, no worse than a kid glove that was too small for her hand.

She'd anticipated ''nice''—the agreeable warmth of a hot brick in bed, perhaps; that was what Lady Tess had led her to expect. Not one word of warning did Leda recall. Not one mention of the wild euphoria, the flooding sensation that had possessed her.

But she remembered Lady Tess' teasing eyes, and thought: *She knew of this.*

She hadn't tried to describe it; how could anyone? How could anyone say how it felt to be held in this way, bare skin pressed to black-and-white silk, embarrassed and not embarrassed, still feeling the tremors of his passion flowing through him.

She felt him draw a deep breath. He released a harsh sigh, as if the air had been repressed and finally burst out. He bent his head beside hers. ''I can't help myself,'' he murmured roughly. ''I can't—stop myself.''

Leda bit her lower lip, hiding her face in his coat. She traced her fingers along the lapels. ''Dear sir,'' she said. ''It's not wicked. Not now.''

A heavy shudder ran through him. His breathing grew deeper. Slower. His head drooped toward her ear, and then he twitched and straightened, like a person falling asleep on his feet.

Leda didn't feel sleepy at all. Now that her heartbeat had slowed, she felt light and clearheaded for the first time in weeks. ''We must put you to bed,'' she said, giving his collar a brisk tug.

He lifted his eyes. Leda looked up into that drowsy gray intensity and smiled, patting the black expanse of his shoulder.

''Only stand back, sir, if you please, and leave this to me.''

He didn't, right away. He leaned his arms on the vanity

and kissed her mouth. There was a taste on him like nothing she'd tasted before, like the earth on a damp day, the sea tide on the Thames, thick and salty but not disagreeable. Really rather alluring in a strange sort of way; she kept wanting to put her nose as close as possible to his skin and draw the opulent spice into her lungs.

Suddenly he moved, taking her up against him, lifting her as if she weighed nothing. She said, "Oh!" as his invasion slipped away and he set her on her feet. She glanced down, and said, "Oh," again.

That was all there seemed to be to say. She felt the abundant moisture between her legs, but none of it was blood this time. And him . . . but he passed his hand before the opening on his trousers and turned away, which rather vexed her. Lady Tess had *explained* everything, in words, but one wouldn't mind seeing with one's own eyes whether such things were perfectly possible.

She knelt and picked up her robe, pulling it around her. Dressed—more or less—she felt herself mistress of the situation, and began to issue proper orders.

"Dear sir, I'm sure when you think of it, you will find that it has been a most fatiguing day. I'm not at all tired myself; in truth I feel refreshed. You'll allow me to help you with your dress, and take your coat and just give it a brush before I lay it down."

He stood still. With the carpet under her bare feet, she went to him, reaching up to find the stiff piqué of his tie and pull it free. She laid the length of cotton over a chair and smoothed her hand down his chest, finding the buttons on his waistcoat.

"You don't have to do this," he said.

"And who else is to do it, pray? I daresay you think that I don't know anything about gentlemen's clothing— which is true, in the strictest sense, but I assure you that I understand the importance of proper care of costly fabric." She paused. "But I don't—I fear I don't know quite how to manage removing it from your person. Your coat, sir?"

For a moment, she wasn't sure that he would lend his cooperation. Then he shrugged out of the morning coat in an easy move. She caught it from his hand and took it to the wardrobe to lay down carefully in the lower drawer.

When she turned back, he'd already taken off the waistcoat and was standing at the vanity, unbuttoning the close button at the top of his collar. Leda paused a moment, admiring him. Really, he was quite the most handsome man of her acquaintance, not only in his face, but in the grace with which he moved, the admirable proportion of his shoulders and limbs.

He dropped the pearl studs from his shirt into a glass bowl on the vanity with a little clink. Miss Myrtle would have decried his sun-darkened skin as common, but Leda found it pleasing, most particularly when he loosened his cuffs, pulled the white straps from his shoulders, and removed his shirt.

He didn't see her watching him. He rested his shoe on the needlepointed vanity bench—there was a man for you—to untie the laces. He was tanned all over his back and chest, the contours of his body just like the classical statues, only alive and moving, perfectly fascinating to watch.

He looked at her over his shoulder. Leda quickly manufactured a reason for her interest. She nodded toward the straps that hung in pale loops from his waist. "What are those?"

His hands stilled. "What?" he asked curtly.

"Those white straps. I should like to begin to learn the nomenclature of gentlemen's furnishings."

An almost imperceptible tension in his back relaxed. If Leda had not been aware of every curve of muscle and bone, she would not have noticed it. "These?" He flipped one loop and went back to his shoes. "Braces."

"Oh." She picked up his waistcoat where he'd tossed it over a chair and laid it away, then lifted his shirt. The scent of him clung to it. Surreptitiously, she held it to her mouth and nose, breathing deeply for just an instant, before she put it aside to be laundered.

There was a very awkward moment, in which they both seemed to find nothing to say. He stood in his stocking feet and trousers; Leda saw no evidence that a dressing gown had been provided for him—who should have done that? Did he not have one? Surely gentlemen must.

"Would you prefer that I go somewhere else?" he asked abruptly. He walked off to a side door beyond the wardrobe and opened it, looking through. "There's a sleeping couch in here."

Of course there was. Leda had not even noted the dressing room; most probably that was where his dressing gown and all his clothes had been placed, too. When the late Lord Cove's cousin and wife had come to visit Lady Cove, Leda recalled that such had been the arrangement—and much toil and trouble it had been, endless conversation and question and flutter over the provision of coat-brushes and slippers to outfit the dressing room and obtain a borrowed cot for the gentleman, who had never used any of it.

Not even the cot, when she came to think.

From this recollection, Leda made a leap of logic. Perhaps married gentlemen did not really care to sleep in their little dressing rooms. Perhaps the unfortunate husbands were required to make the request every night, hoping that their wives would grant permission for them to sleep in a comfortable bed, but relegated to the cots if approval was not forthcoming.

"Certainly I don't wish you to go anywhere else." Leda gave him a bright and magnanimous smile. "You must feel free to sleep here in the bedroom. You needn't ask me, on any night, Mr. Gerard."

"Samuel." He sounded rather annoyed as he picked up a silver snuffer. "We're married, for God's sake. My name is Samuel." He walked to the mantel and lifted his arm to extinguish the candle in the mirrored wall sconce. Reflected light focused on his hand.

She had opened her mouth to reprimand him for his language, but she closed it.

If Lady Tess had not told her, Leda would not have instantly recognized the slight scar across his wrist. She would not even have noticed it. But the intensity of candlelight heightened the contrast, picking out an unmistakable band of paler skin across the base of his hand. When she looked at his other hand, she could see it there, too, just distinguishable.

"You should not swear, Samuel," she said, in a quieter tone than she had meant to use. She almost said nothing at all, but that seemed somehow uncomplimentary—as if, like some jungle-raised creature, he could not even be expected to conduct himself in a civilized manner.

"I beg your pardon." He gave her an ironic look.

To show a spirit of full conciliation, Leda smiled. "I'm honored that you should prefer the informal address. I would be pleased if you also would—" A sudden shyness caught her unexpectedly. She clasped her hands and turned a little. "If you would feel comfortable to—do the same—and call me Leda."

He snuffed the last candle. The room went to darkness and firelight, tinged with the faint pungency of smoke. "I already have, haven't I? In certain moments of forgetting myself." His disembodied voice seemed strangely angry still.

Leda pulled her robe around her and went to the bed, feeling with her bare toes in the chilly shadows for the step stool. The collar of her robe pulled at her as she tried to lie down, but she had no intention of removing the garment. She dragged the bedclothes up, fluffing and arranging them, and lay carefully close to the edge.

She stared up at the orange glow of the fire on the underside of the canopy. Then she closed her eyes.

It seemed a long time before he came. The motion of the bed surprised her; his touch surprised her even more. He took her in his arms, pressing himself close to her all along his body. He had nothing on; she plucked her hand away—and then had nowhere to put it.

He nuzzled his face into the curve between her shoulder and her neck. She blinked up at the canopy.

"Good night, dear sir." She barely whispered it.

"Leda," he murmured. He curled his fist in her hair. His arm lay across her, tight at first, and then slowly,

slowly relaxing. She felt every small slackening of tension in his body and easing of his breathing as he fell asleep.

"Dear sir," she whispered again, and laid her hand on his forearm. "Pleasant dreams."

Twenty-nine

❖

Lady Kai, in her friendly way, wished to go with Leda to see the South Street ladies off at the station. This required a little adjustment, as the carriage was not quite suited to five persons, and while everyone knew that Mrs. Wrotham must be seated next to a window to relieve her traveling sickness, and the younger ladies of course offered to occupy the forward seat, Miss Lovatt insisted that she would take the middle as a compliment to Lady Cove, who felt that it was not perfectly right that her elder sister should give up the more comfortable position by the window.

Lady Cove attempted to precede her sister to the lesser seat, eliciting a brisk remark to the effect that after forty-two years as a peeress, one might think that the common notion of proper precedence would have finally made an impression upon the mind of some people, who apparently still had no idea of their rank as the wives of barons. Lady Cove was no proof against such sisterly kindness, and meekly stepped aside.

Miss Lovatt settled into the middle of the seat, making certain that she appeared cramped by hunching her shoulders in a suitable way, which would have been most affecting if she might have maintained it all the way to the station. However, as soon as the carriage began to roll and Mrs. Wrotham complained of faintness, Miss Lovatt forgot to crouch, being too busy producing the smelling salts that Mrs. Wrotham had overlooked, and making certain that the rug was securely over Mrs. Wrotham's lap, and the window adjusted just to her liking, to remember to appear painfully confined to a narrow seat.

After Mrs. Wrotham regained her composure, Miss Lovatt sat back and said, "Well, Leda. I have wanted an opportunity to tell you that I am glad to see you so nicely settled. I had had some fears when I heard, I must confess. But your young gentleman is most agreeable. He has given me his personal promise to have the cook forward the receipt for the lemonade to South Street."

Before Leda could thank her for her compliment, Miss Lovatt recalled an instance of a similarly well-set-up young man, most respectable, who had married a lady of her third cousin's acquaintance, and subsequently taken an ax to the gardener and been hanged. This unfortunate story reminded her of another example of masculine character, this one not having occurred to anyone of her personal acquaintance, but issuing from that spotless source, the confectioner's wife. It appeared that a serious young lady had wed a wealthy and admirable doctor, only to find, to her dismay, that the fellow was not a real physician at all, but had smuggled himself back from deportation to Australia and posed as a medical man with such success that he'd treated upward of three hundred patients, and killed the half of them with mistaken practices, before he was found out.

Similar stories beguiled the entire ride to the station. As the carriage stopped, Miss Lovatt concluded, "I'm afraid matrimony is a very risky thing. I'm not sure that I would have your courage, Leda, if a gentleman were to take a fancy to me."

"Well, you do take a gloomy view," Lady Kai protested. "Samuel is not in the least untrustworthy!"

"Of course he is not, Lady Catherine!" Miss Lovatt's eyebrows rose. "I would not for the world suggest such a thing!"

"It seems to me that you were suggesting that very thing. I would trust Samuel with my life, and so may Miss Leda! Mrs. Gerard, rather."

"Certainly!" Miss Lovatt stiffened so much that Mrs. Wrotham and Lady Cove had to hunch to accommodate her raised feathers. "I found him most admirable, for an American."

Fortunately, the porter opened the door at that moment, and no reply was required, for Leda feared that Lady Kai's pink cheeks denoted some heat upon the subject. While Miss Lovatt was overseeing the porter's disposal of their baggage, Lady Cove laid her glove on Leda's arm, smiling at Lady Kai as she did so.

"You must not allow my sister to worry you, my dears," she said softly. "Rebecca has often felt it her duty to warn young people of matrimony, so that they do not rush into trouble, but I fancy you will find that a little innocence and trust is a very fine thing in a marriage."

"Do you think so, ma'am?" Lady Kai asked, with more anxiety than Leda had expected from her.

She took Leda and Lady Kai each by the hand. "Well, I've never been very strong-minded, as Rebecca is, but I will tell you what I think of marriage. I think that if married people, man and wife, always think of one another through their cares and heartaches, and find their joys in one another in better times, then life will proceed very well." She had a smile, and a little glitter in her eyes as she spoke. "That is what I hope for you, Leda. And for you, too, Lady Catherine."

A silence reigned in the carriage as they returned through the wintry lanes to Westpark, until Lady Kai said, "What nice friends you have. I especially liked Lady Cove."

Leda felt that she must defend Miss Lovatt a little, but had only got as far as describing how she always made quite certain that the coal man brought the right measure, when Lady Kai interrupted suddenly.

"Leda—may I call you 'Leda' now that we are as good as sisters? I must speak to you privately!"

The suppressed excitement in her tone made Leda glance at her warily. "Of course," she murmured.

"I hope . . . I suppose you may have thought that I haven't been quite . . . quite friendly, in the past few weeks! I do hope you'll forgive me!"

Leda looked down at her gloves, and then out the window. "You mustn't apologize. I hadn't noticed anything at all."

"Because you've been in a daze!"

"Yes. It's all—happened so quickly."

"Leda . . . this is very difficult to say, but—I wanted to explain . . . that is, there was the most infamous rumor just when you and Samuel became engaged, and I—I believed it, for a little while. I know it's not true! I understand now. Mother explained it to me, and I'm so ashamed that I ever even listened to such a wretched thing, and I'll never speak to Miss Goldborough again! I hope Robert isn't so stupid as to marry the silly girl, but I don't think he likes her more than half."

Leda said nothing. She only sat in mortified agony.

"I was jealous, I think," Lady Kai said matter-of-factly. "I was so afraid that you and Samuel would take Tommy away."

Leda looked up. "Tommy?"

"I want to keep him, Leda! I really do. And if it's not true that you're his mother—then he really is an orphan, and I think I have as much a right to keep him as you and Samuel! Especially since—"

"I'm not his mother!" Leda cried. "Why must everyone *believe* that?"

"No—no, Mum told me that it was impossible, even if we should think such a thing. It was only that I was upset, that I believed it even for a moment. Because Samuel had said that he would adopt him, and I hadn't thought, at that time, that things would . . . turn out . . . as they've turned out . . . ." She rubbed her gloved palms together and turned pleading eyes on Leda. "Lord Haye has asked me to marry him. And I've said yes, I would. And he's come to love Tommy, too, and said that he'd be glad to be a father to him. So you see—"

"You're engaged?" Leda drew in a quick breath. Her first thought was Samuel.

"Yes. It's going to be announced this evening. Daddy and Mum asked us to wait to say anything until you were married."

"Oh, my."

"Would you mind very much, Leda?"

"No! Of course not. Not for myself. I wish you very happy!"

"Do you think Samuel wants him so dearly?" Lady Kai gripped her hands together. "Except that he said he would adopt him, I hadn't really thought he acted as if he was very much attached to Tommy. But lately—you know him better than I do lately, I suppose."

Leda could not look her in the face. "I'm not sure I know anyone very well lately. Including myself."

"I know," Lady Kai said. "I know exactly what you mean!"

But Leda found that she knew him well enough. The moment she saw him, standing by the fire in the drawing room as she and Lady Kai came in, she knew that he'd been told.

He carried off his congratulations with the same composed bearing that he'd maintained through the wedding. Lady Kai immediately accosted him in the matter of Tommy. He wasn't so easily convinced as Leda had expected, but merely said that he would speak to her parents and Lord Haye. Leda thought that very wise, but Lady Kai was inclined to pout and protest her devotion to the child.

"You're eighteen," he said.

"I'll be nineteen in two weeks. And what has that to do with it?" she demanded.

"Everything," he said unhelpfully.

"I suppose you think I'm too young to know my own mind. I assure you, if I'm old enough to marry, I'm old enough to know that I want babies. Tommy is only a little sooner than I should have my own, anyway."

He turned away. "I'll speak to Lady Tess," he repeated.

"And what of Leda?" Lady Kai wasn't going to give up so easily. She waved a hand to where Leda had sat down and pretended to interest herself in a book of scientific monographs. "She hardly knows enough to change his napkin. If I can't manage Tommy, how is it that you expect Leda to? Your own babies will be quite enough for her to contend—"

He flashed her a look that seemed to startle her. She pressed her lips together.

"Manō," she said, in a hurt tone. "Are you angry at me?"

He hesitated, and then said, "No."

"You are! When this should be the happiest day of my life!" She grabbed her skirts and whirled, marching to the door. She paused there dramatically. "I'd hoped that you, of all people, my very best friend, would wish for everything to be perfect."

He made no answer. He only stood still, his hands locked behind his back, and Leda wondered that Lady Kai could not recognize what was in his face.

"Oh!" Lady Kai cried. "You're disagreeable, both of you! I'd wanted you to laugh, and swing me about and be truly happy for me! And you act as if—as if someone's great-aunt has just died! *Please* . . . Manō! Won't you even smile, at least?"

He looked a little to the side. Then he made a sweeping bow. "Certainly, madam." He came up smiling. "Your slightest wish—!"

Lady Kai clapped her hands with a satisfied squeal. She ran to him and gave him a hard hug. "There! *That* is my Manō. I knew you weren't truly vexed. And you'll tell Mum and Daddy that I'm perfectly, absolutely capable of keeping Tommy?"

"Yes."

She kissed him soundly on the cheek. "Good. Now—I have to go and find Lord Haye. He'll be so pleased."

The room seemed to grow very silent when she was gone, with only the hum of the fire and the small flutter of a page as Leda turned it, staring down at the Latin names and colored prints of vividly marked parrots. She did not look up as he walked to the window behind her chair.

I'm sorry, she wanted to say, *I'm sorry, I'm sorry*—even though she thought it would have been the most dreadful thing in the world if he had ever asked Lady Kai to marry him.

"We'll be leaving tomorrow," he said. "Important affairs at Honolulu." The depth of self-mockery in his voice matched the bow he'd given Lady Kai.

Honolulu. Even the exotic sound of it unnerved her. Unimaginably distant, utterly isolated, a tiny speck she'd scarcely been able to see on the globe of the world.

She took a deep breath. "I shall be honored to accompany you wherever you wish to go, dear sir."

She felt him come close behind her. He touched the nape of her neck. His finger stroked a line beneath her ear and along the angle of her chin. He spread his hand: the heat of it hovered over her skin, as the things he had done to her the night before hovered over everything she thought or did.

"Thank you," he said.

He left her. She did not even see him until dinner, where the talk was of Tommy, how little good a long trip to Hawaii would do him at such a young age, how it would be perfectly satisfactory to Lady Tess to keep him right there at Westpark until things were better settled all round, and of when the wedding would take place. Lady Kai gaily insisted that whatever business it might be that took Samuel and Leda home now, they had to return for the ceremony in July.

But late in the night, after coffee and the engagement toasts, long after the men had gone to smoke and the ladies to bed, he came silently to their room. He touched her body as he had touched her before, all sensation and hot possession—and afterward held her fast and fell asleep with his face nestled into her shoulder.

And she lay awake a long time, gazing at the fading glow of the fire reflected in the canopy above their heads, thinking of what Lady Cove had said of marriage, and hoping.

Samuel lied—"a small prevarication," as Leda put it meticulously—about their schedule, manufacturing a steamship departure within the week from Liverpool. But once they had left Westpark and arrived in London, he saw no particular reason to rush. He saw no particular reason to do anything. He lay in bed in a hotel suite the first morning in the city, dozing—the only time in his life he'd ever done it in full health.

Not precisely dozing. The muted clatter and grind of traffic beyond the closed drapes mingled with the faint chink of silver as she brought a tray of tea in from the sitting room. She wore a cream-colored dress, her hair pinned up in that intricate heavy mass, her slim waist flowing into the ornate folds around the bustle. He watched her through his lashes, as he'd watched her when she rose from the bed, a pale nymph in the semidarkness, and took up her robe where he'd dropped it last night on the floor.

She put the tray down on a marble-topped table. He saw her glance at him, her head tilted a little to one side. Then she went to the window and drew the drapes, so that a crack of foggy light crept through.

She waited. After a moment, she drew the drape a little wider.

"It must be time to get up," he said.

She jumped, and dropped the curtain closed. "I beg your pardon—I didn't realize—I thought perhaps . . . a little gentle light would not be amiss."

He pushed up in bed. It still felt strange, to be bereft of weapons and clothing, to be deep among pillows and soft encumbrances; to be more vulnerable than he had allowed himself to be for a long, long time.

"Good morning," she said. "Would you like your tea? I hope I didn't wake you. I'm afraid I was feeling too brisk to keep from stirring."

She poured as she spoke, and brought him the cup as if she fully expected he would sit up in bed and drink it there. He found that he didn't have much choice, short of ordering her out of the room so he could reach his pants. So he leaned his shoulders against the brass bed and accepted the cup and saucer. The crisp scent of tea mingled with the lingering incense of their physical intimacy, an aura that seemed to fill up the room and all his faculties.

She smiled at him, a shy and pleased expression, then

picked up her skirt and went back to the table. Pouring her own cup, she sat down and looked at him as she sipped.

He swallowed the aromatic bitterness of black tea. "You ought to think of anything you'd like to buy. Dishes, and whatever. You might as well order them here, unless you want to wait until San Francisco."

"Dishes?" She put down her cup.

"Dishes. Pictures. Furnishings. The house is finished, except for the interior. I have the plans and dimensions, for carpets and windows and so on. I guess we need everything."

"You would like me to fit up your entire house?" She sounded incredulous.

"Our house."

She turned crimson. "That's very generous of you."

He set the empty cup aside. It provoked him when she was so humbly deferential. With a kind of defiance, he swept the bedspread back and rose, although he made sure he got out of bed on the far side from her. "It's not generous of me, damn it. You're my wife."

He expected a horrified objection to his nudity; instead, in the small silence, he saw that fresh clothes had been laid out for him on a chair next to the bed. He began to dress.

"Please do not swear," she said.

"I beg your pardon." He sat down in his linen and pulled on his socks. "Please do not act as if you're my cookmaid."

When he looked up, she had her head bent and her hands clasped in her lap. For an instant he thought—but no . . . when she peeked up at him, she was pressing a smile from her lips. He felt a relaxation of something somewhere deep inside him.

"I thought ladies liked to shop," he said gruffly.

"Oh, yes. Rather."

He inclined his head. "Good."

"Is it a very large house?"

He thought a moment, buttoning his trousers. "Twenty-four rooms."

She put her hand over her breast and cleared her throat. "Well. That will require a considerable attack upon Mount Street."

"The plans are in that smaller case—the portfolio's in the bottom."

As she retrieved the leather cover, he went bare-chested into the dressing room and pulled the bell marked "Hot Water Within 1 Minute." And within forty-five seconds, the little window on the dumbwaiter showed white. He opened the door and found a steaming copper jug.

Back in the bedroom, she was poring over the spread house plans. He mixed shaving soap and tilted up the mirror on the low dresser as he rinsed and covered his face.

She rustled plans. "I shall ring for breakfast, and we can prepare our campaign as we eat."

"I'll leave the campaigning to you." He lifted his chin, bracing one arm against the dresser as he leaned, trying to see himself in the mirror.

"I'm afraid I can countenance no such cowardice as that. I shall need your expertise in regard to the battle terrain. What is to be the function of this little room to the side, for instance?"

He had to walk across to her with his face half-lathered. "That's for the electrical plant."

"Oh. Does electricity come from plants?" she asked innocently. "And this—ah—this is the house?" She pulled a photograph from the portfolio into her lap.

Samuel watched her as she bent her head over the picture of the house, with its two stories of broad lanai and tall windows. Muddy workmen stood proudly on the wide stairs that cascaded down to the lawn-to-be, saws and hammers in hand, construction scraps at their feet. "It wasn't yet painted then," he said finally, when she didn't speak.

"Oh, my," she murmured softly, as if she hadn't heard him. "Oh, gracious me." She gave her head a little shake. "That is to be . . . our house?"

He wanted to ask her if she liked it. He wanted to, but instead he walked away and picked up his shaving brush, leaning over the mirror. "There wouldn't be much point in photographing a different house."

In the reflection, he saw her shake her head again as she held the picture at arm's length. "I promise, I shall *try* not to act like a scullery maid, but really, dear sir—I am awed!"

A slow sensation of satisfaction grew in him. He began to shave his face.

For three days Samuel participated in the testing of sofas and examining of china patterns. He made lists and measured tables. He lent himself to correcting the impression of any shopmen who were not initially quite deferential enough toward Mr. and Mrs. Gerard, of Honolulu, the Kingdom of Hawaii, who had just come down from Lord and Lady Ashland's lovely country seat, having heard from Lady Ashland herself that Coote's of Bond Street had the best selection of marquetry chests, or that Mackay and Pelham were to be depended upon for excellent quality in silk and chintz; little asides which she made to Samuel in the most naturally innocent manner, and which, he had to admit, always worked to produce passionate enthusiasm among shopmen. The stratagem was effective even when he couldn't help smiling mockingly at her as she did it, for which he got himself soundly rebuked as soon as they stepped into the street.

In spite of the subversive smiling, he was found useful in several capacities; primarily as list-bearer, and occasionally as the handy receptacle for small packages, and infrequently as a consultant in matters of taste, since he thought most all of the furniture they saw was god-awfully ugly. Then of course he had to beg pardon for swearing, so in general he kept his mouth shut. She looked at pieces that were so hideously dark and heavy that his soul revolted, but in the end, the only things she bought were the things he preferred—an antique bureau-cabinet with an abundance of drawers, partitions, and secret compartments, and a set of dishes with different birds on each of the dinner plates. He wasn't so naive that he thought their tastes coincided exactly: by the time the dishes were chosen, he saw how carefully and discreetly she was judging him, and tuning her reactions to his.

He wasn't certain how he felt about that. It was a new experience; only Dojun had ever expended that intensity of awareness on him, and for entirely different reasons. Dojun drove him, demanded of him, watched for flaws and weakness. But *her* . . . he couldn't see why she would care what he thought of furniture and curtains.

A part of him seemed to turn to it, though, like a secret vine growing beneath pavement and buildings, pushing and yearning toward the light. But the very strength of the pleasure alarmed him: it was like his hunger for her body; it felt as if it might have that kind of power over him if he allowed it.

Already he walked the public streets in a mist, halfway between reality and fantasies of her. He was aroused by nothing more than the neat, straight line of her back, from her demure collar down to the curve of her hip. Knowing the real contour beneath the gathered abundance of fabric and padding stimulated him; a trace of shared scent or the sight of the tiny, tender wisps of hair at the nape of her neck when she bent her head over some glass-topped counter were electrifying.

And the sleep, heavy and dreamless, that overcame him after he had her; it scared him. In its own way, it carried more power and attraction than the act itself. To hold her close and drift into limbo while she talked in that gently animated voice of what they'd bought and seen that day— talked, for God's sake; when the lethargy took hold of him like a blanket of dusky cotton unrolling, and he could not answer, nor help himself: utterly lax, wholly vulnerable and happy—he felt it must be someone else who lay there. It could not be himself.

They had arrived at a pattern, an order of things, after three days. He rose after she did; he shaved and dressed in front of her, except for the few moments he spent alone in his dressing room in swift and concentrated rituals of weaponry and concealment, the only moments of shining hardness left in a fog of intangibles. Then he went out and shopped—an incongruity which amused and disturbed him in its depth of contrast.

After dinner in a private room—no amount of persuasion would convince her to eat in the public dining room and be labeled "fast"—she left him and went upstairs. He surmised that he was then expected to sit in solitary splendor, smoking and drinking port. Instead, he went out and walked along Piccadilly, where the whistles of doormen shrilled at intervals amid the traffic. A girl, dressed in tinsel pink, stepped out from the shadows and took a man's arm. "Come along with me, dear," she said, "and I'll toss you off."

None of those women ever approached Samuel, though he felt them look at him as he passed. They exasperated him by their open stares; their very existence embarrassed him. If one of them had ventured to take his arm that way, to touch him, he would have tossed *her*—fifteen feet, he thought darkly.

The embarrassment lingered. Finally he reached an open bookshop, where he was free to loiter unobserved. He felt hot and restless, thinking of Leda. He wished he were lying with her now, but it seemed somehow that he did not deserve to; that he was an impostor; that what he ought to do was walk until the night swallowed him up.

He stared down at the book in his hand, leafed through the pages of a translation of German philosophy, standing amid dust and books and other browsers. Novels, cookery, travel. Dictionaries. The clock in the back of the store chimed ten times.

Was that late enough? Last night, he'd waited until eleven. He'd found her fresh, her hair slightly damp; he'd turned down the lamp and kissed her, undressed them both, one garment at a time, as they stood in the dark.

If he kept remembering it, he would humiliate himself. But he didn't think he should go to her this early. He should stay here. He should walk longer. He should just keep walking, forever.

He was breathing too deeply. He put an account of sheepherding in New Zealand back on its shelf, thrust his hands in his pockets, and walked out of the shop, nodding in return to the man behind the counter.

He stood in the street. And then he turned back toward the hotel.

The light was on when he arrived at their suite; he could see it beneath the door. The ornately decorated sitting room was empty, but she said his name in a questioning tone. He identified himself and hesitated, not certain if he should go through to the bedroom.

She appeared in the doorway immediately, lush in the jade-green robe, her hair loose. "Hullo."

The way she hovered in the door, not approaching or retreating, instantly warned him that something was different. She stood with her fingers making a little basket. He wanted to ravish her. Instead he took off his hat and gloves.

She retrieved the items from where he cast them on a chair, turning the yellow kid of a glove over. "You've dirtied them."

"Book dust," he said.

"Oh, did you go to Hatchard's? I might have given you a commission if I'd known. Do you read fiction?"

"A little."

"I enjoy Mr. Verne's work," she went on brightly. "He writes of such exotic places. But you've seen all that sort of thing in person. I suppose it's nothing to you."

"Of course. Giant squids. Cannibals. Every day."

"I really meant—" She smiled down at his hat. "Well, I don't know what I meant. I found his stories most exhilarating reading, though."

He looked at her and thought, *Books? Are we going to discuss books?*

She put his gloves together and started to walk past him. He caught her arm. Her body went rigid; she stopped in his hold.

He didn't know what to do, what to say. All of her yielding was gone, the sweet concurrence that made everything bearable. His hunger burned as hot as ever.

He should not have come back. He should have kept

walking, and walking, and walking, until he walked off the edge of the earth.

He let go of her. He went to the window and held the drapes apart, leaning on the frame, shutting his eyes. His fingers closed hard on velvet and wood.

She said somberly, "I should tell you—that I'm ill."

He dropped the curtains and turned.

"Oh, no—dear sir—don't look so!" She made a fluttery, patting motion. "Don't look so! It's only . . . you see . . . every month . . . a few days . . . it's very mortifying!" She gazed at him helplessly.

The thunder in his ears slowly receded. "Jeez-us," he muttered.

"I'm sorry!" she said in a small voice. "I didn't intend to alarm you."

He let out a long breath. It took several moments to think past the rush of panic. He had only the vaguest idea of these cryptic female things, but it was pretty clear that she didn't care for him to touch her in this passing illness. "I'll sleep in the dressing room," he said.

"Oh." She looked rather glum at that.

He scowled at her. "What do you want me to do?"

"I shouldn't like you to be uncomfortable," she said diffidently.

Her wavering was enough to drive him to madness. He strode to her and took her shoulders and kissed her hard. The stiffness in her spine relaxed; she tilted her head back, opening to him as he put his arms around her. As she acquiesced, the dread of rejection in him died away. He grew gentler, exploring her lips. "Tell me what you want," he whispered.

"Well, I thought . . . perhaps you might just . . . lie down. In our bed. And I could—possibly you would find it pleasant if I should—massage your back."

"No." He let go of her.

She ducked her head.

"All right." He set his jaw. "All right. If that's what you want." He felt the shaking deep inside him, that unnerved place, but he shut it down, forced it out of his awareness.

She looked up at him. She took his hands. "If you don't wish it, dear sir, then neither do I."

Relief flooded him. He had an irrational desire to thank her. "Just—let me hold you. That's all. Hold you and go to sleep." He smoothed his thumbs over the back of her hands. "You can tell me everything about tableware."

She was silent a moment, gazing down at their hands. Then she said, "Would you like to know about holloware or flatware?"

"Flatware. Naturally, flatware."

"I shall certainly put you to sleep with that. I venture to say you'll be snoring by the time I get to the runcible spoon."

"My God. Do I snore?"

"You were decidedly snoring last night, as I was en-lightening you upon the nature and arrangement of side-boards. I'm rather a connoisseur of sideboards, but I suppose not everyone enters into my own enthusiasm. Kindly refrain from swearing, if you please."

"I beg your pardon." He kissed her nose, and slid his hand down to her hip. "Are you certain that you're ill?"

"Quite certain."

"Hell," he said. And covered her mouth with his before she could open it.

Thirty

✦

He would have liked to show America to Leda in all its
raw glory of mountains and sky—instead she saw mostly
raw and very little glory, and he imagined the United States
must look a grim and mindlessly vast place of rain and
snow and more rain; half-frozen, dripping icicles off the
eaves of shabby little clapboard stations with two horses
and one ugly yellow dog as the only evident inhabitants.

He hadn't even shared a cabin with her aboard the
steamer. Sailings had been cut back for the winter: short
of waiting another three weeks, there'd been nothing available in the best staterooms for two persons—not, at least,
on any of the steamship lines he was willing to board. So
he'd booked her into a well-appointed ladies' cabin in extra first-class, and been secretly proud of her, the way she
hadn't admitted that the sway and pitch of the ship terrified
her. She was fortunate not to be seasick, and tried hard to
appear composed, but the weather had been so bad that
Samuel finally advised her to keep to the ladies' saloon
for her meals instead of trying to make her way out to the
dining room.

He saw little of her at all until they reached New York,
and not much more of her there, where she was borne off
to the Ladies' Mile on Broadway with the wives and
daughters of the men who sat down across from him at
mahogany tables to talk gold and loans, timber and oil
stocks—and always, sugar. He let them talk, and listened,
offering only enough of his own assessment to keep the
information flowing. He did not, for instance, mention the
engineer Parsons in Newcastle who intended to manufac-

ture his steam turbines himself, and develop a design to drive a ship at thirty knots.

It was easy for Samuel to slip back into that part of his life; the wonder was how natural it seemed to smile when he walked with a businessman into some Fifth Avenue manse for dinner and heard a light English accent among the vociferous American females. Leda talked enough—to him, at any rate—but somehow she didn't gush. Her voice didn't grate, nor turn shrill with enthusiasm. It was a good voice to go to sleep to—and that was the thought that made him smile.

At night, he heard all about the lamentably vulgar objects of French manufacture, with gilt and inlay and massive curlicues, that her new American friends had urged upon her. Everyone was most kind, but it was really very sad to see how they had been taught to judge an item by its price rather than its refinement and quality, although she would admit that in New York, things in general were costly indeed. The hotel must burn coal by the hundredweight, she thought, the rooms were kept so warm. And all that plumbing in the bath!

And worse, the—what did one call them? Spittoons. Such an unpleasant word; something more recondite should be employed. She was sure he wouldn't think of acquiring the habit; tobacco was most objectionable to any person of true gentility, and particularly displeasing in that form.

It was at Denver that she mentioned the spittoons. She looked at him a little anxiously, turning her head on the pillow. He curled a lock of her hair around his finger and promised that he wouldn't take up chewing tobacco—not the most difficult promise he'd ever made in his life, but rewarding, in its own small way. He slept notably well that night.

In San Francisco, on a whim, he took her into Chinatown the foggy evening they arrived—the Chinese New Year. He didn't warn her; the expression on her face as they crossed into the land of red and gold light was worth it. She walked beside him wordlessly through the crowds of Chinese in gorgeous silks, holding onto his arm and jumping a little at the intermittent rap of firecrackers.

Everywhere red and orange paper fluttered; incense and cooking smells lay thick. Rows of splendid lanterns dangled from the balconies overhead. All the shops bore tall signs in joyous scarlet, painted in gold Chinese characters and draped with crimson cloth.

He stopped at an open table covered with ribbons and dishes of narcissus in bloom, surrounded by baskets of fruit. A shopkeeper with a black skullcap and a pigtail down to his waist bobbed in pleasant eagerness. Samuel greeted him with a wish for the New Year in Canton pidgin, which brought the eagerness to enthusiasm. With quick, energetic movements, the merchant hopped up on a stool and handed down the two colored scrolls Samuel selected from the hanging display.

"We'll put these over our door." Samuel held the scrolls up to the saffron light of a Chinese lantern and pointed to the characters on one. "These are the five blessings. Health, riches, longevity, love of virtue, and a natural death."

"Can you read that?" She looked at him as if he were something remarkable.

The merchant thrust an orange toward her. *"Kun Hee Fat Choy!"*

Samuel saw her eyebrows go up in consternation. "It's a gift, for the New Year," he said. "The orange is good fortune."

"Oh!" With a smile of scandalized delight, she thanked the merchant. The shopkeeper then presented her with a dish of the narcissus. He clasped his hands together in his sleeves and bowed again, deeply. She held the orange and the flowers and made a little curtsy. "Thank you!" she said. "Thank you very much. Happy New Year to you, too, sir."

The shopkeeper held up a string of red packets to Samuel. "Burn firecracker, mister? Dollar-quarter."

He shook his head. "No can do. Go look-see."

"Ah! Look-see, good. Big boom, ah! Missus like."

"What does the other one say?" Leda nodded to the second scroll.

He hesitated, feeling suddenly reluctant to tell her. She put her nose among the flowers and looked up at him expectantly, her lips slightly parted, half-curving in a smile. The merchant read the scroll in Chinese, nodding helpfully.

Samuel had a little Cantonese, enough to understand him. He understood the calligraphy anyway. He just felt foolish saying it out loud. He would rather have had it hang, incomprehensible to her, behind some door in their house where only he would see it.

"You can't read that one?" she asked.

"It's just a New Year's expression."

She looked at the scroll, with its painted decoration in gilt and ebony. "It's pretty. I wish I knew what it said."

He rolled it up. "It means 'Love one another.' "

Her lashes lifted.

"It's just a saying." He looked up at the other banners and read a few. " 'Longevity, Joy, Happiness, and Official Rewards.' 'May we always have rich customers.' That kind of thing."

"Oh." She buried her nose in the narcissus again and peeked up at him, her eyes shining. "I see."

He felt as if he were walking a tightrope blindfolded. Strolling off a cliff . . . and somehow, somehow, still walking on thin air, with an unthinkable depth beneath him.

The weather continues deplorable, Leda wrote to South Street, *but I cannot grieve for that, when such excitement prevails at our final departure for the Sandwich Islands. We sail at this very moment on my honoured husband's flagship, the* Kaiea. *This praiseworthy vessel enjoys—* here she consulted the notes Samuel had written down for her. *—a Gross Registered Tonnage of eighty-six hundred tons, and is built of steel with twin-screw propellers and triple-expansion engines of 17,000 horsepower, all qualities of particular excellence with regard to steamships. You will be pleased to learn that these attributes result in a service* *speed of twenty-one knots, which commendable swiftness exceeds the performance of the ship* Oregon, *present recipient of the Blue Riband of the Atlantic in honour of the most speedy passage between Liverpool and New York. There does not seem to be a Blue Riband for the Pacific, which is most unjust, I feel, as it is certain that the* Kaiea *would secure any such prize. I could write more exhaustively concerning the particulars of this admirable steamship, however Mr. Gerard has admonished me not to weight my letter with maritime "jargon."*

Leda lifted her head from the writing desk and looked about her. *We occupy the master stateroom on the topmost deck,* she continued, *which is comprised of three spacious rooms, namely, a dining room, a sitting-room, and a sleeping-cabin with bath and toilet-room adjoining. The fittings are very beautiful, of highly polished brass, Asian teak, and other exotic woods. A large gilt mirror overhangs the mantel. The walls are papered in lovely Chinoiserie of birds and blossoms, on a background of cheerful crimson, which I have learned is the color of good fortune among the Orientals, believed to be efficacious in the keeping away of evil spirits. Splendid vases full of fresh flowers, set out on the tables and in sconces on the walls, or bulkheads, as they are properly termed, greeted us upon boarding. The whole effect makes it difficult for one to imagine that one is on board ship. Mr. Gerard and myself have a steward whose sole duty it is to be at our service upon the pressing of an electrical button.*

I must now close, as the tender which is to take off these letters and convey them back to San Francisco is preparing to leave us, and we will shortly be passing through the celebrated Golden Gate, an experience, I am told, which is not to be omitted even in the roughest weather. As you may note by my handwriting, our cabin is an excellent retreat from the general motion of the ship, placed as it is to take advantage of a particular design factor, which I must confess is not perfectly clear to me. However, it is true that the extreme pitching characteristic of such disagreeable weather is reduced to a more gentle roll in this location.

*I remain, as always, your respectful and devoted friend
. . . Leda Gerard.*

She admired her married name for a moment, and then
sealed up the sheet, adding it to her other last-minute answers to the letters which had overtaken them at San Francisco, one for her from Lady Tess, another from Lady Kai,
and the last from Miss Lovatt, writing on behalf of all the
South Street ladies. She rang for the steward, who materialized instantly: a tall, spindly man by the name of Mr.
Vidal, very decent and respectful. He took her letters and
helped her into the rubber slicker and floppy hat that had
been provided upon boarding the *Kaiea* in a downpour.

Besides a door to the inside passageway, the parlor gave
out onto a sort of private balcony that overlooked the bow
of the ship, but as this offered no protection from the
weather, Mr. Vidal suggested—by raising his voice to a
bellow over the driving rain—that she descend from the
balcony to join Mr. Gerard on the captain's deck. She was
quite glad of the steward's steady hand to help her on the
outside stairs that led to the command quarters and the
decks below.

The rain did not abate, and her view of the Golden Gate
proved a dim one. Somehow, she felt completely safe
aboard a ship that her husband had built, as she hadn't on
the Atlantic crossing, although she thought perhaps her
ease was partially due to her becoming a more intrepid
sailor. In point of fact, she felt that she might attain the
status of "old salt" with only a little effort.

She found it vastly interesting to sit snuggled in her
"sou'wester" in a corner of the heaving glass-fronted hur-
ricane deck, her hands wrapped around a mug of hot co-
coa, while the ship's captain gave orders and the engineer
shouted into his mouthpiece, and the ship met the huge
waves of the Pacific . . . . "Pacific" evidently being an op-
timistic misnomer, as she mentioned to Samuel when a
surge threw her off her stool and heavily against him.

He grinned and wrapped his arms around her, leaning
back against the bulkhead. She thought it rather an improper pose, but no one paid them any mind, everyone
else being busy with their seafaring business.

Once the tugboat dropped away and the course was set, the deck settled into a quieter routine. As Samuel had business with the captain, Leda decided to take advantage of Mr. Vidal's offered escort to the first-class lounge. From the shelter of Samuel's balancing embrace, she shook the captain's hand and complimented him upon his work, to which he responded, "Well, you're a sailor, ma'am! That you are."

Flushed with this commendation, she made her way down the treacherous outside stairs, and in the lounge found out just how true the statement was. All the rest of the hundred-odd passengers had confined themselves to their cabins. There was no one in the saloon at all but one seasick schoolboy, who sat in a plush velvet chair with his shoulders hunched and his mouth squeezed into an awkward line.

Mr. Vidal asked him if he didn't wish to join his parents in their cabin, and was informed in a miserable whisper that the boy was traveling alone, and he'd been sick in the basin in his cabin, and it smelled so awfully that he couldn't stand it. And then he began to cry.

Leda took his hand. "Come up to my stateroom directly," she said. "It doesn't roll so there. You may lie down, and in a little while you'll feel better."

His fingers curled around hers gratefully. Shepherded by Mr. Vidal, they made their way by the inside stairs to the master stateroom, with the boy's hand growing tighter and tighter on hers, his tearstained face growing whiter and whiter as they went. Just as they reached the parlor, and Leda sat him down on the sofa, he leaned over his lap and vomited into his trousers.

"Oh, my!" Leda wrinkled her nose. "Let us take those off instantly, and you may lie down."

But the boy sobbed and pushed her hand away. "I can't—I can't . . . you're a lady!"

"All right, dear. Don't worry a moment. Mr. Vidal!" She stood up and turned. "Please see to his trousers. I'll wait in the passage—hand them through the door and I'll take them away."

"Yes, ma'am. Just drop them down the stairway for the time being. I'll get him a blanket."

Leda stepped into the hall and took the offending trousers when he thrust them out the door. She grabbed the railing and made her way to the stairs. She couldn't quite bring herself just to pitch the soiled garment, so she only rolled it up and tucked it at the top step before she turned back to the cabin.

Outside the door, she was startled to hear Samuel's sharp voice inside—unintelligible—with a ferocity in it that jolted her. She started to push open the door, just as something slammed into it from the other side. Leda seized the passageway railing; the door bounced wide with Mr. Vidal hanging onto it. He stumbled back, grabbing the handle for balance.

Samuel stood in his dripping rain gear, just inside the outer door, staring at the steward. "Keep your stinking hands off him." His words grated, like an animal's warning. Cold poured past him from the open door. "Get out of here. Before I kill you."

A gust of wind banged the outer door shut. Leda blinked at him, and at Mr. Vidal. The steward's blue jacket was ripped at the collar. The boy lay propped up in the corner of the couch, wide-eyed, his mouth half-open and a blanket clutched over his bare knees. He looked as if Samuel were some unexpected monstrosity from the deep.

"Samuel! What on earth—" Leda clung to the door frame with the roll of the ship. The steward's ripped collar and the expression on Samuel's face frightened her.

"What did I do?" Mr. Vidal stood rubbing his shoulder, utterly bewildered. "Sir, I—what did I do?"

Samuel didn't move. She could see the pulse beating in his throat from where she stood.

And it dawned upon her, with a slow falling together of one thought after another—the boy half-dressed and weeping, the other man, Samuel's rigid face . . .

"Oh, Samuel! It's not what you think," she exclaimed. "I asked him here. I asked them both. The child was seasick; he ruined his trousers. Mr. Vidal was helping me."

The ship swayed. On the sofa, the boy worked himself upright, dragging the blanket fully across his bent knees. She saw the crystallizing of reason in Samuel's eyes: a moment of comprehension, and then a rush of deep color in his throat. He glanced at the boy, and at Mr. Vidal.

He looked at Leda. And then: distance. All trace of emotion left him.

With a methodical motion, he began to take off his wet gear. Just as if nothing had happened, he handed the oil-skins toward Mr. Vidal. The steward hesitated.

"Are you hurt?" Samuel asked, in a quiet voice.

Mr. Vidal's jaw twitched. "No, sir."

"Will you accept my regret?"

"Sir." The other man stood to his spindly height. "What did I do?"

"Nothing." Samuel's face was stony. "I'll speak to the captain about compensation to you, if you wish."

"Well, if I've done something to deserve—"

"Thank you, Mr. Vidal," Leda interrupted. "That will be all, except that you may bring a fresh set of the boy's trousers back. What is your name, dear, and your cabin number?"

"Dickie, ma'am. B-5." The boy spoke in a small, hoarse voice. "Ma'am? Could I have my own pillow? It's on my bed."

"And his pillow," Leda said. She turned back to him. "Are you feeling better?"

He snuggled down into the blanket, still gazing in awe at Samuel. "Some. But my mouth tastes awful. And my nose burns. And I'm thirsty. How come he threw him at the door, if he didn't do anything wrong?"

"It was a misunderstanding," Leda said.

"I'll bring a pitcher of lemonade, ma'am," Mr. Vidal said. He gave a stiff bow, little more than a nod, and left the cabin.

"It was an awful big lick," the boy said. "He flew all the way from here to there."

Leda took a breath. "I'm sorry you were startled, but it was an unfortunate error."

"I don't think it was, ma'am. He just come in here and

grabbed him and there he went! And he said he'd kill him.
Did you hear that?"

She pressed her lips together.

Samuel said nothing. He grasped the handle on the door
and opened it into the wind. The gale took it and slammed
it behind him—shutting him out, leaving Leda and Dickie
alone in the parlor.

Rain matted his coat against the back of his neck. He
thought only of the stairs beneath his feet, the wind at his
back, the roll of the ship as she crashed down through the
next wave. The empty deck stretched in front of him with
rain swash sweeping along it, white ripples over silvered
wood.

In a door bay, he took shelter. He leaned back against
the steel surface, gripping the handrail on either side of
the door, his fingers already aching in the wet and chill.

For a long time, an endless time, he watched the sea
surge past. He began to shake, uncontrollably.

It was the cold; he told himself he was shaking with the
cold.

"Oh, shit," he mumbled. "Oh, shit."

He dropped his head back hard against the door, welcoming the pain of it. He ground his teeth and slammed
his head back again. It hurt; it hurt all down his chest and
arms and legs.

How could she know?

He'd looked right in her eyes and he'd seen it. Nobody
sane would have done what he'd done; nobody normal.
Jesus, Vidal hadn't even caught it; Samuel had hurled the
man across the room by the collar, and the steward couldn't
figure out why.

Leda had.

Chikushō. Beast. Beast! He wasn't even rational. Why
hadn't he stopped for the instant it would have taken to
realize there was nothing wrong? How could he betray
himself like that?

*Oh, Leda, oh, Leda, you shouldn't know, you can't
know, you can't.*

The ship rose and fell, a slow pendulum working against

the blow. Three quarters of a million dollars of engine and steel; he owned every inch of her: his name was on the papers. Six hundred people got paid every month with checks drawn on his accounts; profits of four hundred thousand a year went right back into a bank with his name on the door of the biggest office.

His name—that he'd had to choose out of a book.

The Origin of Norman Surnames. He remembered it; it had been all he could find in the school library for a source. So he'd made himself a Norman, looked into the mirror and decided he had a Germanic nose, and his gray eyes were Norse; he'd imagined a family and a past, how his ancestors had come with the Conquest, how his real grandfather had been killed in the charge of the Light Brigade, had lived in an ancient and noble castle, but a crooked land agent had cheated him of all his money, and someday, someday, a letter would come that would say it had all been a mistake; that what Samuel remembered had been the fiction, none of it had happened; Lady Tess and Lord Gryphon kept him safe until his real parents could find him again.

Fantasies. Dreams and smoke. Leda! In his heart he'd felt how he hung in thin air, with safe ground yards behind him. The same way he'd known, at fourteen, or fifteen, or thirteen—who knew how old he'd been, or was?—that no real family looked for him.

His arms were shuddering, his muscles hard with holding on. His hands and the brass rail felt as if they'd become the same thing.

She shouldn't know.

She shouldn't! He stared at the sea, with cold moisture dripping down inside his collar. It wasn't possible that she knew, that from her own experience she could comprehend. She'd married him, bound herself to him, let him touch her. She could not have known.

God—there on the bridge, he'd felt it and not understood—the way she'd stiffened against his arms around her.

Oh, Jesus. Leda. He dropped his head back, clenching his jaw.

And an intuition came to him. The guess became a foreboding . . . then a certainty so terrible that he wanted to howl with the anguish of it. She hadn't known.

She'd been told.

Those letters that had come. Tess had written her, and told her.

For an instant, it seemed a treachery too deep to conceive. But then he realized. It was him, his own fault; Lady Tess would never have betrayed him if he hadn't given in to what he was. If he hadn't forgotten everything that Dojun had taught him and gone to Leda and lain down with her and let the darkness have him.

His fault.

He had done this, as he'd lost Kai, and lost everything he'd worked to become.

The way that kid had looked at him in the cabin. At *him,* as if he were the one to be afraid of.

He smashed his head back against the steel. Black sparks of pain danced in his eyes.

He had to drag the pieces of his soul back together. He hadn't admitted to himself how much he'd let go, floundering in this sea of emotion. Dojun would perceive it instantly. Samuel couldn't arrive in Hawaii like this.

You're a warrior, he thought. *Your heart is a blade.*

He pressed his head back against the door, freezing cold, breathing hard, shaking and laughing.

Dojun. Samuel had to find his balance. The frigid wind cut him—clean and mindless and pure. In the gale and the waves was the impersonal justice of the universe. Dojun had given him eyes to see it, resolve to endure it, strength to ride it. Patience, endurance, perseverance—and a thousand ways to hide in shadow.

Thirty-one

⊕

Leda.

The soft voice said her name, and in her dream she felt a wave of pleasure and relief—he'd come back, and everything would be all right now.

He said it again. She opened her eyes, coming awake to the ceaseless roll of the ship. A dark, cool breeze flowed over her, relief from the stuffy warmth of her nightgown. She could just see his shape as he stood over her berth; he wore white, a barely visible ghost in the blackness.

"Come with me," he whispered, and she remembered Dickie in the upper berth, remembered that Samuel had not approached her for seven days, remembered what was real and why the sound of his voice had soothed her so in her dream.

She realized that the constant rumble of the engines had stopped. The roar of the wind was gone. The cabin seemed silent, only the muffled sound of the ship's surge through the waves marking a slow time in the distance.

"Samuel." She sat up, reaching out her hand.

"Come with me," he murmured. "I want to show you something."

He drifted back out of reach. Squinting, Leda pushed the sheet away and set her feet on the carpet, searching for her slippers in the netting at the foot of the berth. She rose and made her way through the dark to the sitting room, shutting the door softly so as not to wake poor Dickie now that he finally slept sound after enduring seven unrelenting days of foul weather and motion sickness.

Samuel was a pale outline in the dimness by the open

354

door. The light breeze came from there, carrying a fresh scent. As she went to him, he held her robe out to her. She couldn't really see his expression, but his hands were impersonal as he laid the garment around her shoulders.

She ducked her head and stepped out onto the little semicircle of the private deck. The wind was stronger there, blowing her hair around her face. Overhead, the steamship's empty masts had blossomed with sails. The vast arch of the sky flowed from midnight to a glowing blue at the zenith, a color she'd never seen before, vivid tint and transparency at once, blending down to a sapphire-tinged ivory in the east.

She hugged her robe around her and leaned against the teak rail. Before them, the dark water was flushed with the colors of the sky, an infinity of rushing mirrors that formed and broke and formed again, while the ship's wake trailed off in lines of dim phosphorescence.

The height of their deck and the curve of a small sail hid everything but the very bow of the ship. She felt as if they were floating alone in a crystal world, where the silver undersides of clouds on the horizon turned to pink towers at their height—a pink that ripened to orange as she watched, color as soft as the warm wind that caught her gown and hair.

"Look." He stood a little behind her, his own hair a golden disorder in the breeze. He nodded toward the vista ahead.

Leda looked. At the base of the clouds, the growing light revealed a shadowy form on the sea, a dark, steady shape at the horizon.

"Oahu," he said. Then he pointed off toward the left-hand distance, where Leda could barely see a gray hump beneath another spire of billowing clouds that held gold in their uppermost turrets. "That's Molokai."

She stared at them. She bit her lip. "They're very small."

"They'll get bigger. We're still twenty miles out."

Leda would have thought the islands no more than a few miles away, for already she could make out peaks and hollows as the dawn blossomed. She curled her fingers around the rail, waiting for him to speak again, afraid to break this moment of simple connection. But for a long time he said nothing. He stayed outside the circle of contact, one hand resting where the rail curved sharply round the deck.

"I just thought you'd like to see it," he said at last, rather stiffly.

"It's beautiful."

He made no answer, but he didn't leave.

Leda wished to say many things to him, but they were beyond saying. Even when all had been going straight and well, she could not have found words to tell him how she cherished his quiet company, how she treasured the way he had held her and fallen asleep at night. And her feelings about what had come before falling asleep—she could no more have spoken of that in words than she could have taken wing and flown from here to the distant rocks at the edge of the sky.

She missed him. Poor seasick Dickie had seemed to move into the master stateroom by some universal consent, his pillow and his clothes slowly making their way to the sleeping cabin while he occupied the upper berth. The child was so miserable and trusting and guilelessly confident in her solicitude that she could not have wished to do else, but she wished also that it had not meant she wouldn't see Samuel through the whole voyage.

She remembered his face when he'd realized his mistake with the steward—and thought, wistfully, that perhaps Samuel might need her, too, a little.

"I hadn't realized that the sky was so tall." She looked up at the steeples and heights of clouds. "It never seemed so at—" She almost said "home." But this was to be her home, these gloomy lumps of rock on the horizon. "At London," she finished, pushing her hair from her eyes.

Still he didn't speak, nor take his leave. She watched a small and lacy cloud drift past, glowing as if it carried its own pink light within it.

"Do you suppose that it will continue a fine day?" she asked.

"I can't say." He spoke in a formal tone, as if she were

someone to whom he'd only just been introduced at an evening party.

"But you have a supposition?"

"It rains off and on, this time of year."

Leda began to feel somewhat dismayed at his stiffness. "Why are the sails up?"

"We've got a fair wind. We're sailing."

"Oh. I thought perhaps the engine was broken."

"It isn't broken."

The seed of anxiety grew. He was so cool, as if she had done something that he hadn't liked. Tentatively, just to keep the conversation open, she remarked, "I should think it would be faster with the engine and sails, too."

"Are you in a hurry?" he asked dryly.

"No. Not precisely. But it seemed that everyone was. I thought speed was the great thing about steamships."

He paused. "I asked them to shut down the boilers. For a little while. I thought—you might enjoy it."

He was still behind her as he said it; she couldn't see his face. She felt shy, and perplexed, and wished that she could think of something more eloquent to do and say than looking down at her hands and murmuring, "Thank you. That was very kind."

She saw his tanned fingers drum quickly on the rail. He released it.

"I have paperwork," he said abruptly. "Good morning to you."

Leda turned, but he was already gone, disappeared by the cabin door that swung gently back and forth with the rock of the waves.

Somehow, Leda had got the notion that Hawaii would look rather like Scotland. Not that she'd ever seen Scotland, but she knew it for a bleak place of barren mountains and tiny villages—and the gray-and-white dry-plate photographs of Honolulu, with stark black masts on the sailing ships in harbor, the dingy buildings and hazy mountains in the background, had seemed to fit that description. She had not expected the color.

It was color beyond imagination. As if someone had

spilled a giant box of watercolor in the sea: indigo flowed into cobalt, into azure, turquoise, jade, advancing in brilliant wreaths to the shore. Behind the black and reddish-tan slopes of Diamond Head, clouds caressed green mountains, glowing and dissolving as they passed. Another crater, clothed in intense volcanic red and vermilion, stood in perfect symmetry at the base of the mountains, rising from a fringe of palms and forest.

Even the air seemed vivid, soft and yet full of sweetness. As they steamed along the narrow, twisting channel into Honolulu Harbor, where one could see right down into the edge of the coral jungle, the dull thunder of surf mingled and faded into strains of music. On the dock, amid hundreds—thousands—of people, an excellent brass band in red coats and golden epaulets played exuberant tunes.

Leda stood with Dickie, as amazed and enchanted as the twelve-year-old at this fantasy land, while the crowd from the dock streamed aboard the *Kaiea* by the dozens, every shade of nationality, sweeping loose gowns, scarlet and yellow, green, white, pink—and all, every one, male and female, adorned with garlands and strands of flowers and leaves.

It was all Leda could do to keep Dickie from running down the stairs and into the lively confusion, or leaping over the rail to join the brown sprites swimming and splashing in the clear water below. Mr. Vidal had told them both to wait on the private deck, while he located the boy's parents. Leda could see why. Dickie tugged and pleaded "just to go down and see—", filling in whatever caught his eye for the instant, until finally he leaped up and down and yelled, "There they *are! Daddy! Mum!*"

He broke free of her hand and tore down the stairs, tumbling into the flower-loaded arms of a couple dressed all in white. In a moment, he was twined and decorated with blossoms, and the next, he was gone amid the crowd surging and flowing on the deck below.

Leda watched the greetings. She really had no reason to feel doleful, she thought. She really had every reason to feel cheered. The city seemed no more than a sleepy town, dirt streets, a few church spires and roofs amid the greenery, but what a smiling face it had. She found herself searching among the numerous white-suited men wearing straw boaters and thinking: *If only . . .*

Which was a very foolish thing to think. It was certainly a sign of weak character and want of self-control. She'd built up a large castle of air in the past month; there was nothing to be gained by living in it. Miss Myrtle had always said that things that came too easily were not be relied upon.

This was her new home. She was the wife of the owner of this noteworthy vessel. She would not be so misguided as to weep because she was afraid that he had renewed regrets of his marriage, or because he did not turn to her—because he avoided her—in matters that troubled him deeply. One proved oneself deserving of trust. One held up one's head and overlooked the ship with a smile and was truly, sincerely, unreservedly proud and pleased to be Mrs. Samuel Gerard at this moment.

She saw Mr. Vidal at the foot of the stairs and picked up her skirts to follow him. But before she could, he was halfway up, at the head of a column of ladies and gentlemen all trooping up and thronging onto the private deck and into the master stateroom.

"Aloha!" A fragrant wreath of flowers went over her head and dangled down her shoulders. Another "Aloha! Welcome to Hawaii, Mrs. Gerard!" and another wreath, and more, as perfect strangers greeted her by name and bestowed trails of blooms and took her hand, calling out their names and laughing over the noise. Tropical flowers of shapes and perfumes unknown piled one atop the other, up to her collar, and then her chin. At last she was standing on tiptoes, trying to respond to the greetings over the cool brush of petals at her mouth. A giggling lady, not very old, but quite old enough to be more reserved, twined a length of blossoms around Leda's hat, and a bearded young gentleman pushed a bouquet of red carnations into her hands.

"Aloha! Best wishes, ma'am! Walter Richards, your general manager. I've already telephoned the hotel and got you the king's own suite. Mrs. Richards and I'll see y' settled.''

Mrs. Richards was the giggling lady. The others crowded along, guiding Leda down the stairs wrapped in her flowers as if she were a player at blindman's bluff. As she came to the gangplank, the whole crew was lined up along the deck. The captain awaited her. He took off his hat; Leda shook his hand and thanked him cordially for a safe and pleasant trip. As she walked down, the crew waved their caps and cheered, an acclaim that was taken up by the remaining crowd below.

Samuel stood at the base of the ramp. Among all the smiling and welcoming faces, his was the only one without expression. He held a trailing cascade of flowers over his arm: purple, red, white.

Leda hesitated, daunted for a moment by his remoteness. Then she thought: I shall *not* disgrace him. No one here is going to think that I'm not splendidly happy.

She smiled, and lifted her hand to the crowd, and felt rather like the dear Queen herself as she walked down and set foot for the first time in Hawaii. She blinked and swallowed, surprised to find that solid ground didn't seem quite as steady as she'd anticipated.

Samuel reached out and caught her arm. She saw him frowning at her, but as the illusion of motion passed away, his grip loosened. ''Rubber legs?'' he asked.

She'd forgotten; the same few moments of deceptive dizziness had plagued her when she'd disembarked in New York, too. She held onto his arm. ''Oh, dear. I should so dislike to fall down in front of all your friends.''

He loaded his flowers overtop the ones she already had on, right up to her eyes, so that she couldn't see a thing but blossoms. The onlookers renewed their cheer, as if it were some sort of holiday.

''What a very ebullient company,'' she remarked.

He held her by both shoulders. Though she could only see him through the blind of petals and leaves, she felt him bend close to her ear. ''Aloha, Leda,'' he said softly. ''Welcome—'' He stopped, as if he'd lost the tail of his sentence. Then he stepped back. ''Welcome to Hawaii.''

Leda had a wild moment. She burrowed her fingers among the coil of flowers around her hat, pulled it off, and lifted it. Finding a peephole through the floral tribute, she reached up and tossed the pink and purple wreath over his head. It caught on his hat, and then fell onto his shoulders.

The onlookers seemed to find that quite a pleasing gesture, for the men yelled and whistled enthusiastically, and all the ladies laughed. Samuel turned dark beneath the golden skin at the collar of his linen suit.

"Aloha, dear sir," she said, although she doubted anyone could hear her, muffled as she was in flowers.

Mrs. Richards and Leda sat in rocking chairs of white wicker on the wide veranda, where the ruby flame of a trailing bougainvillea hid them from the greater part of the Hawaiian Hotel. The hotel was an easy, busy place, open to the air all the way through its broad corridors, overlooking a shaded lawn with the brilliant blue sky and the mountains beyond.

Officers of the British and American navies abounded in their crisp summer uniforms, along with tourists and planters and ship captains, finding amusement in everything, as everyone seemed to do here. Indeed, it was impossible not to be pleased with life in such a place; it was difficult to feel worried; she could not brood. Not that she wished to do so, but she hadn't seen Samuel since yesterday, when the Richards had swept her off to the hotel from the ship.

He had sent a message by telephone that he was delayed at his dockside office. So delayed, it ensued, that he had never come at all.

Leda told herself that she was overly anxious. He'd been gone from his business for months; certainly he would have much to occupy him. And by no means had he neglected her; he'd instructed Mr. and Mrs. Richards to make her welcome, as they had done admirably. When she found herself looking at the huge stately columns of palms, the cascades of clematis and passionflower, the laughing faces all around, and thinking again: *If only . . .* she gave herself a good mental shake.

Mrs. Richards sipped at her fruit ice. "I know I've said so a hundred times, but you can't imagine what a shock— a delightful surprise!—it is to us that Mr. Gerard should marry. You've no notion of how the girls here have moped themselves to death over him, and he never looked at anyone of them twice!"

She had indeed said so a hundred times. Leda hadn't known quite how to reply, and finally did no more than smile and nod in as gracious a manner as she could manage each time this never-ending wonder was mentioned.

"That was such a sweet thing, to give him your lei. Everyone says you must have a Hawaiian heart. And you tell me that Lady Kai is engaged. To a lord! She's very young, don't you think? Not yet twenty. Of course, I married Mr. Richards when I'd just turned seventeen, but that was different."

She didn't explain why it was different. The spirit of benign curiosity seemed to be a guiding force among the European and American ladies—and gentlemen—of Hawaii, with everyone's business carefully investigated, relayed, and commented on freely. Leda had already been called upon by six females and seven gentlemen, including Dickie's parents, who wished to thank her for her care of him.

Just now, she wasn't being interviewed for all available information in her possession on any topic whatsoever because Samuel had telephoned again. He was on his way to take her on a tour of her new home, and while they waited, Mrs. Richards had found her this hiding place behind the bougainvillea.

"This way," she said, "you'll get off more speedily when he arrives, because if there's someone here visiting you, you'd never be able to move for an hour or two, you know, and I know how keen you must be to see it. It's away up the valley—three showers up, that's what we say, because no doubt it will rain on you that many times before you get there. But you mustn't mind—you'll dry out before you know it. Ah! There he is!" She sat back with a sigh as Samuel walked out through the open lobby, carrying his summer straw under his arm. "He is the most romantically dashing man! It's positively indecent to be that good-looking. Not that anyone blames *him;* he never encouraged any girl in the slightest, I assure you, but you can't imagine how many hearts he's broken, Mrs. Gerard."

Leda half-suspected that Mrs. Richards' heart might be one of them, but she only smiled and nodded.

He greeted her so pleasantly that her spirits rose on the instant. No one wore gloves, on account of the tropical climate, and it felt strange and yet familiar to have his bare hand beneath hers as she stood up. For the time that it took to pass with him down the curving stairs to the lawn and waiting fringe-topped carriage, held by a barefoot Hawaiian in an otherwise immaculate uniform, Leda walked on air.

As Samuel drove them out of the hotel grounds, though, a delicate silence prevailed between them. Leda gazed at the king's palace across the avenue, a handsome, modern building with towers at each corner and deep stone verandas. They plunged into the shade of overarching trees, with the sunlight flashing down through.

"What is that?" Leda asked, staring at a tree that looked as if it had dozens of white trumpets hanging downward from all its branches.

"A trumpet tree," he said.

"Oh." She fiddled with her closed parasol, and then pointed at a tree covered with gorgeous clusters of golden blossoms. "What's that one?"

"It's called a gold tree."

"Oh." Somehow, the obviousness of the names made her feel foolish for asking. He didn't expand on the information. Obviously, his earlier friendliness had been for Mrs. Richards' benefit—naturally he wouldn't like it to appear to his manager's wife that there was anything irregular about his marriage.

He would be thinking now that it should have been Lady Kai whom he was escorting to her first view of her new home. He would be thinking of his plans and dreams. He would be wishing that it was not Leda in this carriage with him.

The air held all the scents of gardenias and lilies and roses. Beyond the somewhat tipsy white fences, houses lay in deep shade, under bowers of flowering vines. She caught glimpses of open rooms beyond the ubiquitous wide verandas.

"Is everything satisfactory?" he asked abruptly. "The hotel is all right?"

"Oh, yes."

"You have a decent suite?"

"It is an excellent suite. Perfect."

"Mrs. Richards is taking good care of you."

"Indeed, she has been everything that's kind. It's all lovely!"

He clucked to the horse. It picked up a quicker trot, splashing through a mud puddle. Leda pretended to watch the raindrops that suddenly cascaded from nowhere out of a blue sky, bright drops with sunlight glistening through them.

Lovely, she thought dismally. *Perfect.*

It was the shower that caused the watery shimmer in her vision. She was not undignified. She was *not* weeping.

"This is the upstairs parlor," Samuel said. He glanced back to see that Leda had reached the top of the stairs. His footsteps echoed on the polished wood of the central hall.

"Oh, no." She shook her head as she walked past him through the doorway where he'd stopped. Light filtered in the shuttered French doors, laying bars of white glitter across the floor. "No, on the plan, you told me it was to be your study. You remember that we measured the partners' desk, to see that it would not interfere with these doors."

"I can put the desk in my office downtown."

He watched her stop, the light blue dress she wore trailing out behind her on the wood. She'd already abandoned the padded bustle. Few women wore that kind of thing here—because of the heat, he supposed. She held her white parasol tip propped on the floor. With her wide-brimmed hat and pensive downward look, she seemed something out of an elegant painting.

He felt a need to sound decisive, so that she could not see how this cost him. "The desk was all you'd already ordered for my use, wasn't it? Just furnish the room as a parlor. I won't—need it. You don't have to make it a study."

She remained looking away at some spot on the floor for a moment, then picked up her parasol and walked slowly toward the opposite door. He couldn't tell what she thought, if she understood what he was trying to offer her.

"It's not necessary that I spend a lot of time here," he said.

She passed into the next room. He heard her measured footfalls.

He followed her, found her standing before a door, the shutters opened onto the second-floor lanai. She stood looking out at the view.

He walked behind her, stopping in the middle of the empty room. Beyond her figure, he saw the tops of trees on the slope below, then the vast sweep of the island and the sea. The *Kaiea* lay in her berth, her white decks toy-like at this distance. A half-formed rainbow hung in the air over the lower slopes and the red crater of the Punch-bowl.

"Do you like it?" he asked.

For a long time she didn't speak. Then she said, without turning, "It is the most beautiful place I have ever seen."

He felt relief—and pain, slow and deep inside him. He could not look at her without thinking of touching her.

This room, at the corner, with a breeze flowing down from the green cliffs and the waterfalls behind the house—it was marked on the plans as Kai's bedroom. When they'd been building the place, he'd never even imagined himself in it, only thought of how to make it pleasant for Kai.

But now—now all he thought of was what it would be like to sleep here with Leda in a broad bed, with the cool air of the mountains on his back and her body warm beneath him.

"You might like to plant fruit trees," he said. "Mangoes, or something."

"I had a mango last night." She made a small sound that might have been a laugh. "It was messy."

"Papaya, then. Or maybe just something with flowers." He would have liked her to commit to a tree, as a sign that she saw a future here. "Plumerias grow fast."

"Do you like them?"

"They bloom a lot. The flowers have a nice scent."

She looked at him over her shoulder. "Yes, but do you *like* them?"

He didn't give a damn about them one way or the other. He wondered—if he went closer to her, would she move away? They were alone now, with no appearances to keep up. There was nothing to stop her from avoiding him.

He felt paralysis start at his feet and spread up through his body: his arms and hands, his throat.

And at the same time, a violent desire.

She still looked at him, over her shoulder, an inquiry on some topic that he'd forgotten already. Powder-blue and white, with the deeper sky behind her. Faintly, so faintly that he didn't know if it was his imagination, he saw the lithe outline of her legs beneath the muslin. And her breasts, the rosy aureoles—he knew that was fantasy—

"Sir?" she murmured.

He could not move. He saw her with her hair falling back, her shoulders bare and her throat exposed. She turned toward him—a supple, feminine sway of her hips beneath the dress.

He could not move. He could not; he would not. His body had turned rock-hard.

And then he did; he caught her shoulder; he pressed her to the bare whitewashed wall. She had no chance to shun him; he didn't give her time. The hat, with its ribbons and feathers, fell askew between her shoulders and the wall.

He kissed her. He imprisoned her against the surface. He couldn't look at her as he did it. He buried his face in her neck, pulling her skirts up, hating himself, loving her, the sensation of her, the softness.

Thrust to the wall by his urgency, she made a faint gasp,

like a wordless sob. Petticoats, lace, mysteries, everything she was to him: fresh muslin, sweet bared skin beneath, his hands finding the round supple shape of her buttocks, the eyelet that released intricate female garments. The fire came over him like a fountain as he felt her soft hips, her waist, the light fabric crushed in his fingers.

He didn't stop to caress her. He was afraid; afraid that as she spread her hands against his shoulders she would push him away. He kissed her roughly: no words, he wouldn't let her say it. He caught her hands, shoved them off. Amid the yards of cotton he jerked at his strained buttons; he lifted her against the wood, sinking between her thighs, gripping her with his hands beneath her, his mouth and his tongue at her throat. She inhaled sharply as he entered her.

He couldn't open his eyes. He just did it, forced himself on her with her hips against the wall and her body crammed to his. The position drove him deep. In hard thrusts he took her. She made no sound; there was nothing but his impassioned breathing and the impact of the solid wall and the rising thrill, the crisis.

He came to the peak with a visceral groan that echoed in the empty room.

Pleasure and guilt, release.

Ruin.

He knew it the instant he knew anything. For once the dizzy relaxation of climax did not roll over him. Instead, it was wholesale loathing.

He leaned against her, his forehead resting on the wall, drinking air and fresh paint and the light salt of perspiration below her ear. Slowly, he released his hands from their tight grip on her, realizing at the same time that she held his shoulders just as tightly, as if she were afraid of falling.

Her feet touched the floor. The tangle of dress and petticoat was still between his fingers, her lacy linen a disorder that slid out of his hands.

He shoved away. He didn't look at her face. The white parasol lay spread in a feather-edged triangle on the floor.

He picked it up, using that and his coat as cover to adjust his clothing, hide himself, his back to her.

He stared out at the vista.

After a moment, he heard faint rustlings behind him. He imagined her restoring her skirts and linen, smoothing and brushing, trying to erase the vestiges of what he'd done. He closed his eyes, expelling a long breath.

"I'm sorry." It came out harshly, nothing of what he felt, the despair, the dread of having to turn and see what was in her face.

She didn't speak. He heard a footfall. He thought she was leaving; he had to turn at last, but she only stood leaning against the wall, holding her hat over her flattened skirt like a little girl, her face lowered. She plucked at the brim.

"I'll take you back to the hotel." He bent and retrieved his own hat. "You may wish to know—the *Kaiea* sails tomorrow afternoon for San Francisco."

She looked up, with shock in her face.

He shrugged. "We're efficient. The turnaround for this load is fifty-two hours."

Still she looked at him, as if the very thought of it dismayed her.

"I've promised you that you have my support. If you want to go, you still have it. Your account is open in London. You only have to tell me what you need beyond that."

The hat fell from her fingers. It settled at her hem, feathers nodding gently. "You wish me to go back?"

"I don't wish anything." He walked to another door, unlatched it, flung it wide. A brisk breeze carried the scent of water past his hot face. Around the edge of the lanai, the steep rise of the mountain showed a drift of mist across the green. "It's your decision. If you would rather stay, and live in this house, and—keep up a conventional appearance, I promise you that I won't—make any demands on you." His mouth curled. "I've been trying to say that, but—" A curt laugh escaped him. "God! I suppose I can hardly expect to convince you now."

"You should not swear," she said in a very small voice.

"I'm sorry." He leaned his hand on the door frame.

Then he lifted his face to the mountains. "So goddamned sorry," he said through his teeth.

When he looked at her again, she was standing straight. She had picked up her hat. She took two steps, to the middle of the empty room.

"It is my decision?"

He could hear the tears behind her shaky words. Tears. He had a burn in his throat and chest that seemed to suffocate him. "Certainly," he said in a tight voice.

"Then I wish to stay here," she said. "And live in this house. And keep up a conventional appearance."

Thirty-two

When you bow, Dojun had taught him, you must not bow casually, as if it were some aimless gesture. The beauty of it must be complete, the motion whole: the two hands, palms open, placed together smoothly and slowly, fingertips raised to the proper zenith. The whole body bending from the waist, powerfully: form and force—mind composed, back straight, weight even and firm on the ground—then rise with hands still together and stand naturally.

In this way, Dojun said, you show respect. For your master, for your opponent, for life.

In the light from a single oil lamp in his office, at three A.M., Samuel bowed to Dojun. He prevented his shadow from falling on the window shade. The encounter was unusual in its place and timing—that Dojun would seek him out, set a meeting on Samuel's territory, was unprecedented.

Dojun came dressed in shabby clothes, as any plantation laborer might dress, carrying nothing that was visible to an untrained glance. He returned Samuel's bow with a slight one, and said, in Japanese, "You've been with a woman."

Thus was Samuel's shower, his scrubbing of himself, rendered futile.

"I'm married," he said.

There was a deep silence, with only the obscure, endless sound of the surf far off over the reef beyond the harbor. Samuel couldn't even hold Dojun's dark gaze, but

370

looked at the barren shadows in the corner beyond his desk.

"Ah. The Lady Catherine would have you?"

Of course. Of course, Dojun would know what he'd planned for years, though never once had Samuel spoken of it. It was the faint sense of disapproving surprise in Dojun, of an invisible eyebrow raised at the idea that Kai would accept his proposal, that brought blood to Samuel's face.

"I never asked Kai." He felt hideously exposed, unable to keep his mind free enough, attentive enough, to cope with an attack should Dojun launch one. "I married no one of importance. She's English." He moved to change the atmosphere, nodding toward the fragrant pot on his stove. "I've warmed *sake* for you. It's nothing special, but please accept it anyway."

He spoke of it that way, politely, even though it was the best *tokubetsuna* grade available, and both he and Dojun knew it.

"Itadakimasu." Dojun received the drink as Samuel poured it for him from its little ceramic carafe. They sat together on the floor, sipping from the miniature wooden boxes that he'd prepared by placing salt on the lips.

"You know that there are questions asked about you," Dojun said.

"Yes." Samuel had already heard that report. For several weeks, apparently, there had been particular inquiries into who and what he was in both Honolulu and San Francisco. The source was vague, not traceable beyond talk in Chinatown so far. "I don't know who."

"Nihonjin desu," Dojun said, looking at him over the fumes rising from his drink.

Japanese. Japanese investigating him. Samuel thought instantly of the sword mounting sealed beneath his stove.

"Why are they asking, Samua-san?" There was a coolness in Dojun's voice. Samuel knew his own rapid connection had been detected—Dojun was that good, that he might read Samuel's mind if he allowed it. Too late to say that he had no idea why Japanese might be interested in him. Too late to appear as if he had nothing to hide.

He stood up, brought the tiny carafe to Dojun and offered it, bowing deeply again. After Dojun had held up his cup to be refilled, Samuel spoke in English. "With my apologies, Dojun-san. It's my problem."

Dojun regarded him. He sipped slowly at his *sake*. "You're too thoughtful. I'm an old man, and you think to indulge me. But we'll share this problem, *nē?*" He kept to his own language in spite of Samuel's switch, indicating many things—his position, that he would direct the conversation, that what he wished to speak of was subtle and not to be misunderstood. "Tell me why these men ask about you."

"I stole something." Samuel kept his back straight as he sat cross-legged. "From the Japanese embassy in London. Perhaps they're looking for it."

Dojun gazed at him. Unfathomable.

"I'll see that they get it back," Samuel added.

Dojun's face had changed indefinably. His eyes were black and potent. "What do you have, little *baka?*"

Samuel did not allow his body to stiffen at being called a fool. "A *kazaritachi.*"

Dojun made a sound like a controlled tempest. Not anger, but a sound of pure energy. He stared at Samuel. "Where is it?"

There was no need to tell him in words. Samuel had only to think it, and Dojun looked directly at the place where Samuel's careful seal of horsehair lay unbroken over his secret cache beneath the stove.

"You might have done worse." Dojun shook his head, smiling strangely. "You don't know what you're dealing with."

Samuel waited. He would get no explanation if he asked. Or if he didn't. Only if Dojun chose to give him one.

"Tell me the names of the five great swords," Dojun demanded.

"The Juzu-maru," Samuel said. "Dōjigiri, the Dōji-Cutter. Mikazuki, the Sickle Moon. O-Tenta, Mitsuyo's Masterpiece. Ichigo Hitofuri, called Once in a Lifetime."

"Five is the highest number, according to tradition. It's

written in the *Meibutsuchō* that there is another sword with a name among the five.''

''There cannot be another. There are five names, and five blades.''

''But you read it, didn't you? That among the *meitō*, there are the five great swords, and another sword among the five?''

''I read that. I never understood it. I'm accustomed to that when I try to decipher Japanese writing.''

Dojun smiled a little. ''Well, it's only a foolish puzzle anyway. The monks might make something philosophical of it, but the truth is that there's a sixth great sword, and the appraisers who compiled the *Meibutsuchō* were just afraid to write down its name.''

He picked up the pitcher of *sake,* holding it over Samuel's wooden *masu.* He poured gracefully, and set the carafe down again.

''Better,'' he said, ''if they'd just left it out entirely, instead of telling nothing to someone who doesn't know, and hiding nothing from someone who does.''

Samuel sipped his warmed wine.

Dojun watched him. A trace of humor still lingered at his mouth. ''Patience!'' he said. ''You ask too many questions.''

Samuel waited. The old sense of focused calm was flowing back as he listened, not to Dojun's words as much as to his certainty. Samuel felt his own significance in that certainty, knew that nothing Dojun told him was without purpose.

''*Gokuakuma.* That would be the name of this sword, if it existed. The Highest Demon. Someone told me they went to the Christian school and heard about the angel who became the devil. That is the spirit of this sword.''

''If it existed.''

''The blade is two *shaku* and five *sun* in length. Six inches under an American yard. It's a wide blade, to balance the length, with grooves on each side at the back of the curve. Below the tang, it's engraved with the demon called the *tengu,* long claws, wings, and a savage beak. The tang isn't signed. It's only marked with those characters—*Goku, aku, ma*. There is not a sword-maker in all history who went by such a name."

Samuel recognized the inventory of attributes that typified the descriptions from the *Meibutsuchō*, the catalog of the famous swords of Japan. It only needed a history of ownership and daring deeds to be complete, though there was no such record, no such sword, described in what he'd read. "Is it lost?"

"No. It is not lost. It is . . . potential."

In the lamplight, Dojun's face looked timeless, no older, no younger than what he had always seemed to Samuel. Only his black hair was different, cut years ago to the short Western manner. While everyone and everything else changed around him, Dojun remained.

He held up his hand, closing it into a fist. "Without a hilt, a good blade is merely dangerous. You cut your fingers if you aren't careful when you handle it. Given luck, you might kill someone with an unmounted blade. You might just as easily kill yourself. But mounted, with a hilt made for a man's hand, a guard to protect him and a sheath to be carried—potential becomes its own truth. The spirit in the blade is now the spirit in the man."

Samuel thought of the ceremonial sword he'd stolen, the dull iron stem within the gorgeous mounting. He began to sense what was coming.

"Gokuakuma is a beautiful thing, and terrible. It's older than anyone knows. The first certain record is from seven hundred years ago, when a sword with a golden hilt appeared in the hands of Minamoto Yoritomo as he swept away the Taira clan from the capital and destroyed the boy emperor. But to be in power is not enough—the Gokuakuma demands more. Yoritomo rid himself of his own brother and slaughtered those in his family who hindered him. At his death, his wife's family, the Hō-jō, came to own the sword—and the demon in it possessed them. They killed Yoritomo's heirs, assassinated the clan down to the last main line, and took control. Still the danger of the blade was not recognized, only the power. A masterless samurai made a plan to obtain it, stealing the blade and leaving another in the mounting. This *rōnin*, whose infamous name is erased from history, at first appeared successful, gathering other *rōnin* to follow him, and coaxing the Hō-jō vassals to his will, but when he tried to use it in combat, the blade failed him, flying from the hilt he'd forced on it, causing him to fall from his horse and impale himself.''

Dojun stopped. Samuel watched him steadily.

''The Gokuakuma fits only one mount: one hilt and one scabbard—only the real blade will seat true in the golden hilt.'' Dojun's voice took on a dreamlike, chanting quality. ''It was Ashikaga Takauji who reunited the true mount with the blade, attacked the Hō-jō, and forced them to cut their bellies in *seppuku*. Sixty years of war ensued, until the grandson of Takauji came into possession of the Gokuakuma and its strength. But he was wise, and separated the blade from the hilt again. He placed the mount in his Golden Pavilion, where it could be enjoyed for the beauty of the craftsmanship, and the blade in the care of monks in the mountains of Iga. While it lasted, the country enjoyed peace, the golden age of the Ashikaga, but the Gokuakuma has its own pattern. The sword calls out to be made whole, and it calls most strongly to the ones who are . . . 'not-quite'—those who are in great power but not at the peak. The brother of the shōgun Yoshimasa burned down the monastery to obtain the blade, reunited it with the mount, and initiated civil war. For centuries the sword passed from one hand to another, amid wars and chaos, until Nobunaga obtained it, entering then into the hands of a man of military genius.

''Nobunaga conquered central Japan, but was murdered in his prime by an ambitious vassal. His general Hideyoshi, with both genius and the Gokuakuma, eliminated his rivals, united all the country, and declared war on China and Korea. He ordered all swords confiscated, or registered, to be carried only by samurai. It was his successor Ieyasu who claimed the Gokuakuma and destroyed the remnants of Hideyoshi's family. But this Ieyasu took warning from the fate of the heirs of Nobunaga and Hideyoshi, and made a profound dedication to separate the Gokuakuma again. He asked the divine emperor to consecrate the protection of the blade to a single family, whose duty it was to hide and guard it. And for two hundred and seventy-three years, the Gokuakuma has been kept from being made whole.''

''I have the Gokuakuma's mounting.'' It wasn't even a question. Samuel knew it, without having heard a description of it, without an explanation of how it was possible.

''You have the mounting.'' Dojun inclined his head and shoulders. ''And I have the blade.''

The dry irony in his expression slowly sank into Samuel's consciousness. ''You!''

''I've guarded it for twenty-one years. I've kept it hidden, and apart from the mounting that makes it complete. When I yield my life, the trust will pass to you.''

Samuel gazed at him, with certainties sliding.

''It's what you're trained to,'' Dojun said simply.

The empty *masu* sat in Samuel's hands, a small square shape. Silence, silence . . . he felt bewildered.

''Knowledge passes like a stream from heart to heart. The duty came to me from my own blood clan; when I was a child I was cultivated as you have been, in the art I've taught you, and more. In peace, we kept alert and ready; but it's in the time of change that the Gokuakuma is most lethal, that possession of it breeds aggression in the spirit; that it is hunted most zealously for the power it brings. I was given this task, when the samurai revolted against the Shōgun—to escape with the Gokuakuma, to hide and wait. In those days Japan was under seclusion; it was death to leave the country without permission, and those who sought the Gokuakuma hated the Western barbarians most fanatically of all. I was one of a single shipload of men who, during the turmoil of civil unrest, signed contracts to come here as laborers. We were already on the ship when the government fell to the rebels, who took stronger control of the country. Our passports were canceled. But Americans held the contracts—'' He smiled suddenly, an unexpected humor springing from his dispassionate recital. ''—and Americans really care nothing for emperors and shōguns and demon swords. They'd paid good money for this ship and these workers, and so they sailed with us out of Yokohama Bay before dawn, without lights.'' He looked down into his interlocked hands, his mouth curved, as if the memory still amused him.

Samuel didn't move. He sat staring at the man who had dominated three-quarters of his life.

He felt as if the last leg of a chair had been kicked out from under him.

"For this sword?'' he said. "Everything you've taught me; it's all been—for a sword blade?''

Dojun watched him. Samuel heard the incredulity in his own voice.

"In my clan,'' Dojun said, "one who does what I've done is called a *katsura*-man. I'm like a *katsura* tree planted on the moon, cut off from those who sent me. Here I must shed my own seed, foster it, so that it will survive when I'm gone. You I chose when I first came. Shōji, the boy who sweeps—he is the next.''

That, somehow, was the deepest shock of all—that Dojun had begun to train someone in Samuel's place, and he had not even known it. Not suspected it. Never looked at Shōji and seen anything but a broom and bashful boy.

After a silence, Dojun said, "Recently I received word that the mounting had been sent to this English queen, in an attempt to render it permanently out of reach of those who would militarize Japan for their own ambitions.'' He met Samuel's eyes. "Fate, it would seem, has not collaborated.''

Samuel took a breath and rose, going to the stove to heat more wine. In the ritual action, he sought evenness. Balance. He could not, for the moment, think farther than that.

Dojun sat quietly.

"Forgive me!'' Samuel broke the ceremony, speaking in a rigidly controlled voice. "I'm stupid, Dojun-san. I'm not Japanese. I don't believe in demons.'' He turned and faced Dojun, still standing by the stove.

"Don't you?''

"No.''

"Ah. Then I suppose it's angels that haunt you. Angels

make you spend your life trying to become strong, and fast, and smart, and safe.''

Samuel lowered his eyes. He poured warm *sake* into the carafe.

''What are you trying to make yourself safe from, Samua-san, if you don't believe in demons?''

He had no answer. He had thought . . . God, what he had thought humiliated him.

The effort of it, the endless commitment—and Samuel had never wondered why.

Want too much, you. Dojun had said that to him, warned him, over and over. And he had never heard.

Hadn't wished to hear. Had only driven himself to the farthest limits of his strength and spirit for Dojun's recognition, and Dojun's regard, and Dojun's friendship.

''There was a time when I wondered myself about the Gokuakuma,'' Dojun said. ''I doubted. I thought—I'm spending my life in exile, and for what? Because someone made a joke, maybe, and chiseled the word for 'demon' in the tang of an admirable blade. If I had lived all my life in Japan, such a notion might never have occurred to me, but it's different here.'' He held up his *masu* for the wine that Samuel poured. ''Here in the West, one questions everything. And that goes nowhere, Samua-san. You can think until your mind becomes a spinning top, and find no answer. In the end, it makes no difference whether there's a real demon in the sword. History says that a nation will rise to the command of the Gokuakuma. Men read history, and they'll kill for that power. That I know to be the truth, because I've seen my own family die to keep the blade separate from the mounting that makes it whole.'' He sipped slowly. ''Perhaps that's the nature of demons, that they live asleep in the minds of men, until a sword blade reflects the light that wakes them.''

Samuel scowled down at his hands. ''Then destroy the sword.''

''Do you know of the starfish, that kills the oyster reefs? In the old days, when a fisherman caught one, he cut it in half and threw it back.'' Dojun lowered his wine, set it on the floor. "And down in the reef, with no one watching, the halves grew into two starfish."

Samuel stood up, his body stiff. "And this is it? This is why you taught me everything? All that time—my God—so much time!" His clenched hands throbbed; he forced open his fists. "Tell me why you never told me!"

A pencil-thin throwing blade appeared in Dojun's hand. Samuel made a slight evasion; his body recognized the direction of the strike before his mind did; the *bo shurukin* struck the wooden wall with a crack.

"When form and force are flawless, the motion that follows will be flawless." Dojun's gaze was level, unblinking. "Draw the bow, think without thinking, aim exactly right, and let go." He lifted his wine in both hands and nodded. "That is what I've done. You are my arrow. I have let go."

With a harsh exhalation, Samuel turned. He knelt and broke the seal, shoving the stove a half-inch aside in spite of the heat against his palms. The space he revealed held darkness. He plunged his hand deep inside.

It was empty. Empty. The Gokuakuma's mounting was gone.

Leda had noticed a number of respectable ladies eating in the hotel dining room, which hardly seemed a dining room at all, but more like a veranda, with open windows that looked on the mountains on one side and the tops of tropical trees on the other. Everything was so relaxed—she decided that it might not be improper to take breakfast there, and indeed, the Hawaiian steward made her so welcome, and the Chinese servants in their coiled pigtails and spotless white linen were so smiling and good-natured, if not very fluent in English, that she forgot to feel uncomfortable. No one stared at her, but several of the naval officers and residents she'd met yesterday stopped to speak kindly before they went to their own tables and sat down to place settings decorated with piles of bananas, limes, oranges, and guavas.

Outside, birds clamored in the trees. A light breeze flowed in the window next to her. She looked dubiously

at the fried fish—it appeared to be a large goldfish of the
variety found in common household aquariums—that the
Chinese waiter had brought her instead of the toast that
she'd ordered. She was in the midst of attempting to explain the mistake to the obliging but puzzled servant, when
Samuel walked up behind him.

He appeared quite tall next to the little Chinaman. "Take
i'a go." He spoke abruptly to the waiter. "Say cookee,
fire the bread side *'ula'ula* some good, catchee coffee me."

"Ah!" The waiter whisked away her goldfish with an
apologetic bow.

Leda's heart was pumping in quite an uncertain manner.
He sat down across from her, not looking at her, gazing
out the window and saying nothing. She curled her napkin
in her lap, twisting it around her finger under the table.

"Good morning," she ventured at last.

His coffee arrived. They both watched the waiter pour.
The pleasant scent drifted to Leda as she raised her eyes
from the servant's crisp white sleeve and looked at Samuel's face.

He was staring down into the black liquid, his mouth
set in a brooding line. When the waiter retired, he met her
eyes with a metallic lack of expression. "I want you to
leave," he said.

It was not a suggestion, as it had been yesterday, when
it had cut her to the heart. It was an order.

"I'll have a man here for your trunks at twelve
o'clock." Again he looked away, down at the flower-laden
trees outside. "The ship sails at two."

A tiny bird flew in the window and landed on the edge
of their table. The waiter arrived with her toast, set it
down, and waved. "Go! Go bird!"

The bird blithely stole a crumb directly from Leda's
plate, and then hopped across the cloth and took off,
sweeping out the window.

Leda had no appetite for toast. She felt sick. She could
not even find the breath to speak. She sat, watching the
butter in the toast congeal.

She wished to ask if she had done something wrong.
But if she had, she didn't want to hear it, if it was so

terrible that she must be sent away. And she knew, in her heart, that it was nothing she'd done. He didn't want her here. He'd made it clear yesterday. He'd touched her roughly, as if she disgusted him, as if he could drive her away by making something that had been so intimate and special between them into a coarse assault.

In an empty room. Against a wall.

She bit her lip, pressed her napkin and her fingers over her mouth. This was worse even than that—to be told in a public place, where it would humiliate her beyond reason to burst into tears.

His voice was utterly without emotion. "The captain will handle whatever arrangements you need. He'll have a check to be drawn in San Francisco for the rest of your trip. Feel free to go wherever you like, but I would prefer to be . . . kept informed of where you are. If you would send a telegram to my office in San Francisco once a week, it would assure me that you're—" He scowled out the window. "That you're safe and well."

The bird came back. It had brownish-orange feathers and a white band around its bright eye. It seemed almost tame, so bold was it in hopping up to pick at Leda's toast.

"Will you do that for me?" he asked.

"Yes."

It was all she could manage, that one syllable.

"I'll wish you *bon voyage* now. I don't think—it will be possible for me to come to the ship."

She swallowed with an effort and rose hastily. "Of course. There is no need."

He stood up. For one instant she allowed herself to look at him, to impress on her memory what was beyond remembering. Once he was gone, it wouldn't be possible to create an image bright enough, or perfect enough, because when she looked at him she couldn't seem to see the man Mrs. Richards had called indecently good-looking. She couldn't see the potent, flawless, angel-Gabriel fascination that caused the ladies at the far table to slide glances over their menus at him. She knew it was there, before her eyes, but in her heart she only saw Samuel—saw the unhappiness in him, saw that his set expression was a mask.

"Is there anything else I can do?" he asked.

She bent her head and shook it, wordlessly.

"Good-bye, Leda," he said. "Good-bye."

She could not say it. Her throat would not open and let the words out. Without lifting her head, she turned quickly and found her way among the tables, walking out of the room.

Thirty-three

❖

Dojun drifted through Samuel's house, inspecting it.
Samuel stood on the second-floor lanai, leaning against
the rail, watching past the open doors as Dojun probed
and scrutinized, evaluating the strength of the defenses.

Samuel felt a certain bitter satisfaction each time Dojun
missed something, though it wasn't often. The trapdoors,
and the windows that would only open to a piece of paper
slipped into the right place—those Dojun found. The natural lava tube that provided an underground entrance and
exit into the mountain behind, he already knew. It was
one reason Samuel had chosen this property. But Dojun
finally had to ask how to spring the panel that led to it.

Samuel walked through the echoing house, locking and
unlocking the precise combination of doors on the floor
above that allowed the panel to move.

Then he went back out on the lanai. He stood there,
watching, as the *Kaiea* steamed to sea.

How easily she'd agreed to go. No hesitation, no questions. She hadn't even said good-bye.

He supposed that after a night to think about it, she'd
found that she didn't wish to keep up a conventional appearance after all. He supposed that if he could have kept
himself in check—

He closed his eyes, his jaw tightening.

Better that she'd left. She would distract him. She would
be vulnerable. The men who'd taken the Gokuakuma's
mounting, entering his office, finding and removing the
kazaritachi without disturbing any of his seals—they
would have been at this house, too. He had to assume they would

have found everything Dojun could find. He had to assume they would strike at any weakness—and Leda was his.

She was his weakness even as he stood there, watching.

Below him, he could hear the soft voices of three of his "gardeners," hand-picked from both his and Dojun's networks. To turn a house into a stronghold, quickly, without appearing to do so, required choices. Samuel knew his own people, native *kanakas*, Chinese, and a scattering of *haoles*—Americans and Europeans of various stripes; he selected for loyalty and caliber, and lack of Japanese contacts, to lessen the chance of subversion.

Dojun had his own clansmen. Samuel still felt the interior shock of finding that the friendly connections Dojun had made among the new immigrants were actually family ties—older and stronger than anything between himself and his teacher. Shōji, with his broom and his respectfulness, turned out to be a nephew, sent especially to be instructed, to be raised and trained and dedicated to guardianship of the Gokuakuma.

In the years when Dojun had been alone, when Japan would allow no immigration, he'd made do with what he found. He'd trained Samuel. And Samuel felt like a fool to care, to be resentful of a boy with a broom.

He leaned his shoulder against the white pillar, scanning the city among its thick trees; Honolulu Harbor, and the broad sheen of Pearl Harbor far to the west, with fish ponds and taro patches between. Somewhere, they were there—an unknown number—outside of their native territory, and in his. Dojun would protect the blade; prepare the house to be safe, withdraw and adapt: the strength of *in*. Samuel would go out, turn the tables and seek the hunters: the energy of *yo*.

That was all he knew of Dojun's intentions. All that Dojun had confided to him.

A "demon" blade. He wanted to roll his eyes. He had his directions, he would give whatever Dojun demanded of him as he always had. But this time, for the first time, there was a small, cold, sullen place; a reservation in his heart.

He didn't say the obvious: that if he'd been told, if he'd

been trusted to understand, that he would not have precipitated this crisis. He wouldn't have stolen a *kazaritachi* in
ignorance, for his own ends, and brought it here so close
to the blade—and God knew, he would never have brought
Leda near it.

But he remembered the empty cache beneath his stove,
and the duplicate mounting that had been so conveniently
"found" to replace the sword he'd stolen in London. Dojun's adversaries had been going after the Gokuakuma's
mount before Samuel ever touched it; there was no other
ready explanation for the existence of a duplicate. It must
have been made to replace the real mounting before the
presentation to the Queen. Samuel's theft had forestalled
the switch, and set the pursuit. And it had taken the pur-
suers months, but they'd managed to do what half the force
of Scotland Yard hadn't—identified and tracked him.

Whoever hunted the Gokuakuma had been trained as
he'd been, only better. If they believed in it, then it was
as Dojun said—the demon was as real as the hunters, and
whatever they were capable of doing.

He studied the land. Three years ago it would have been
easy—there had been so few *Nihonjin* in the islands. Samuel had known every one in Honolulu by name. But there
were thousands of Dojun's countrymen now, on the plantations and beginning to set up business in the city. Thousands of faces to hide behind.

It was, possibly, an advantage that he did not believe in
the Gokuakuma the way Dojun and his opponents must
believe.

To win, Dojun said, *it is essential not to wish to win.*

Samuel watched the *Kaiea* move in slow stateliness behind Diamond Head, her smokestacks trailing as she took
the heading for Makapu'u Point—beyond sight, beyond
reach of the signal that would call her back.

It had seemed such a sensible idea on the dock. It had
seemed very clear and exact. Leda was certain that when
the moment had arrived for her to put her foot upon the
gangplank, and she had not done it, that she had been in

possession of an entirely persuasive and reasonable train of thought in support of the decision.

That it had something to do with obedience and wifely duty, she was sure, but now that she was reinstalled at the Hawaiian Hotel, with the sound of the *Kaiea*'s departing horn long since faded from the air, she could not seem to perfectly reconstruct the logic which had required a direct defiance of her husband's expressed wish in order to present herself in an obedient, respectful, and salutary light.

Manalo, the Hawaiian driver Samuel had sent to take her to the ship, helped her into the buggy. He was a strapping young man, formidable in his height and athleticism, but he seemed perfectly content to wear most of the flower leis that he'd brought to pile over Leda's head, although he insisted on adorning her with at least one trailer of hibiscus and gardenias. " 'As for you—come stay already. Haku-nui, number-one man, he like, yeah, you no go down California. Good thing stay Hawai'i.'' Manalo grinned. "Got trunks all set, take you up d' place, *wiki-wiki.*''

He gave the horse a lash, so that it careened at a wild trot out of the grounds of the hotel, neatly missing the mule-drawn trolley and turning on two wheels in the direction of the mountains.

Leda wasn't quite so anxious to bucket up the hill as Manalo. Nor was she so perfectly sanguine about "Haku-nui" and his reception of the news that she hadn't boarded the ship after all. She had hoped to be able to prepare a small speech in defense of her decision, but between the fluster of having her trunks retrieved at the last moment from the deck, and then the congenial surprise at her unexpected return to the hotel, and a certain amount of prolonging—possibly deliberate on her part—of rambling conversations and greeting of people she had only taken leave of an hour or two before, and now, having to cling for dear life to the buggy's supports as they maintained a dashing pace through the mud streets of Honolulu—she really had no idea at all of what she was going to say to Samuel, and wasn't precisely looking forward to the moment.

The poor horse was steaming by the time they reached the cooler heights. Samuel's house—*our* house, she thought stubbornly—stood in white elegance against the rise of the mountain, with the red slash of bared soil around it. As Manalo reined the horse up the steep cinder-paved drive, two gardeners stepped out from where they appeared to have been clearing brush. They had something of a brooding air, standing with their hoes and sickles in silence until Manalo shouted in Hawaiian and gestured at Leda. Then the dark faces broke into grins. They picked up their woven hats and swept wide bows to her as the buggy passed.

She inclined her head in a cordial manner. The horse swung around the final rising curve. The buggy clattered to a halt at the base of the steps, where other workmen were still laying cream-colored stones to complete the pavement.

Leda held on to the panel of the vehicle for a moment. There was no sign of Samuel. An Oriental man dressed in plain, sober clothes appeared at the open doorway and came down the steps.

"Aloha!" Manalo leaped from the buggy. "Dojun-san! *Wahine*-lady, she no wanna leave—she went d'*Kaiea*. Where number-one Haku-nui?"

The other man bowed deeply, his palms on his thighs. "Ah, Mrs. Samua-san. Aloha!" His greeting had a courtly air. As Manalo helped her from the carriage, he bowed again and raised his hand upward. "Samua-san on top."

Leda followed his gesture. On the veranda above, leaning against one of the tall fluted pillars, with his arms crossed, Samuel watched them. His soft *aloha* drifted down on a decidedly ironic note. "What the hell are you doing here?"

"With due consideration," she began, "and upon most earnest reflection, the fact was borne in upon me as I was about to step upon the gangplank of the excellent *Kaiea*, that it is . . . ah . . . unfitting that I leave." She was aware of the eyes of all the workers on her. "That is, so soon. Without justification. People will think it very odd. Perhaps, if you would—if we might discuss this with more privacy."

"There's not much to discuss. The boat's gone."

"Yes, I . . . I believe that may be so."

"Seventeen miles past Makapu'u Point by now, I'd estimate."

"I would have come sooner, and mentioned the—change of plan, you see, but Manalo and I felt that—it would be expedient to convey the trunks back to the hotel."

"There's nothing else for two weeks."

"Is there not?" She looked down, with the fragrance of gardenia enfolding her. "How unfortunate!"

Even from her position below him, she could hear the slow sigh he exhaled. The sound of footsteps on wood reverberated into distance.

She peeked up at the front door, where the Oriental man observed her with an apologetic demeanor.

"Ey, number-one man make *huhū.*" Manalo put on a terrific scowl, then grinned in high good humor and shook his head sorrowfully. *"Pilikia! Ho'opilikia* you!"

Leda had heard *pilikia*, the native word that seemed to be applicable to trouble of all sorts and sizes. She gave Manalo's golden, laughing face a subduing frown, but he only sank into the background—as much as his six-foot-plus frame could sink—when Samuel came down the open hall and onto the lower veranda.

He stopped at the top of the steps. Leda could see the trace of temper around his eyes, but he said nothing beyond: "What do you plan to do now?"

"Well, I . . . thought that I should begin work."

"What work?"

She summoned up her courage. "It's my place to make your house comfortable for you."

He looked at her silently.

His lack of response goaded her into quicker speech. "I can see that we've not done nearly enough in London. We've hardly ordered sufficient to furnish one room, and it may not arrive for some time. Mrs. Richards told me that furniture could be got here in Honolulu, and fittings."

"Furnita make," the Oriental man said, bobbing eagerly. "I make, Mrs. Samua-san! Tomorrow you come back, look-see house, all room, need this, need this. I stop—make measure. Table. Chair. What you like.''

"No," Samuel said. "I don't want her up here."

Leda flushed. She moistened her lips and took a step backward.

The little man looked mournfully at him. "Samua-san got wife. Furnita need. Chair, bed, all that.''

Samuel's jaw flexed. "No." He glanced at her. "You can go back to the hotel and stay put there." He sent a cold stare beyond her toward Manalo. "I'll take her. Since it looks like I can't trust anyone else with a simple order."

The Hawaiian, adorned with his red and yellow flowers and trailing leaves, managed to look hurt and lugubrious at once. "Ey, what I can do? She no wanna go ship. You no say me, 'Eh, Manalo, t'row her on, any way!' ''

"Certainly not," Leda said. "It isn't Manalo's fault.''

"You like chair here, Mrs. Samua-san?" The Oriental man spread his hands, indicating a corner of the veranda. "Nice place. Pretty. Sit. Look-see ocean, mountain, everything. All kind wood got, koa, ohia, paulownia wood. What kind, eh?''

Samuel spoke to him curtly in his own language. The servant made a humble bow, and replied. As Samuel's mouth grew tighter, the bows grew lower and lower and the murmured salutations longer.

Suddenly Samuel made a foreign-sounding exclamation and turned away. "Furnish the place, then! Enjoy yourself! Take all the time you like!" He stalked back into the interior of the house, as if the rest of them didn't exist.

"OK! OK, Samua-san." The Oriental man bowed after him, and then at Leda. He pointed to his nose. "Dojun name. Carpenta. Good table, good chair. You tell what want already.''

She had rather anticipated further discussion with Samuel, but Mr. Dojun looked at her expectantly, as if she were to present him with a list at once. "Well—I suppose—a table will be necessary. For the breakfast room. And chairs. Really, two would be sufficient, to start with. How long would that take?''

"Got table. Got dine chair. Got—" He held up his palm

and folded down his thumb and forefinger, and then each of his fingers one at a time until only his little finger was left standing straight. "One-two-three-four. Four dine chair on hand been make. I bring. You like—no time."

"It's already made, do you mean?"

"Hai! Been make."

"I see. Do you have other pieces on hand, Mr. Dojun?"

"Chest." He outlined a large, squarish shape in the air, much taller than himself. "Bookcase, Chinese long chair. Rocky chair. Small-little table. Big table. All kind furnita on hand. Dojun furnita, *tansu* chest, no same buy somebody else. More better. Japan, say *shibui*—no ugly, no fancy too much. Beauty, yes. Fancy hybolic, no. Savvy? I bring all this house, you look-see, what you like."

"Oh, you mustn't go to so much trouble. I can come to your shop and see it."

"No, no! I bring! You say me, put there, put there, look-see, you no like, take-go."

"Well, that's most kind of you. I should like to see how it would look in place, I imagine."

Mr. Dojun bobbed. "Tomorrow, *nē?* You come this house. I bring."

Leda hesitated. With this sudden cornucopia of furniture, was it not possible . . .

She would make everything look very handsome—and Samuel liked Japanese things; she remembered Lady Kai saying that he did his own woodwork in the Japanese style. But she didn't know—she acknowledged herself sadly deficient in the comforts that might tempt a man to run tame about the house.

In the accustomed way of things, feminine delicacy would not have endured a discussion with strangers of something so personal as her husband's tastes. However, experience taught that a familiar retainer, a maid or even a cook, often would be more conversant with her mistress' private inclinations than the closest family relations. It seemed likely that the same would hold true of gentlemen. She looked shyly at Mr. Dojun and Manalo. "I wonder— if you don't think me impertinent for asking—is it possible that you and Mr. Manalo have known Mr. Gerard for some time?"

"Time?" Mr. Dojun repeated.

"Some years? You, and Mr. Manalo, work for Mr. Gerard a long time?"

"Ah. Much year. Sixteen, eighteen year. Before, twenty year, work my lady—work my lady Ashlan', she been take-care Samua-san."

"Ah, Lady Ashland!" She lost her last reservations about Mr. Dojun. If Lady Tess had employed him, Leda felt that she could be assured of his excellent character.

"Manalo-kun, he more young. No full thirty year, eh?" Mr. Dojun bowed slightly toward the Hawaiian. "Maybe, six, seven year work Samua-san."

Manalo grinned good-naturedly. "Too much time. No swim, no ride, no sing. *Auwē!* All work!" He passed his hand over his brow.

"Perhaps . . . if you know him well—" She lowered her voice. "I'm rather in a quandary, you see, as to how a gentleman would prefer the house to be done up. I wonder if you might have some suggestions for the primary choices."

They both looked at her blankly.

"What particular furnishings a man would prefer—" She saw that she was making no progress. "What furniture a man likes," she exclaimed at last. "What man like in house?"

"Bed," Manalo said. And positively winked at her.

"Ah!" Mr. Dojun nodded. "Number-one thing, bedstead. Husband like!"

Leda felt herself blushing to her ears. While Manalo laughed himself silly at her confusion, Mr. Dojun began an intricate and indecipherable description of a bedstead that he happened to have "on hand."

For all Manalo's vulgarity—and she would have been surprised if he wouldn't eat raw onions in a front parlor—he seemed quite sincere. It was his opinion that tables, chairs, what-nots, and chests of drawers were of no consequence. Mat of palm or feather tick, a bed was the first article of furniture that a husband required.

"I suppose," she said to Mr. Dojun at last, "you should be certain to bring the bedstead."

"Bring bed." Mr. Dojun bowed. "Got bed, make home."

"Well, yes," Leda agreed. "That's rather what one hopes."

"And Mr. Dojun tells me that he has a particularly handsome bedstead of fiddlestick wood," she said, making a swirl in her ice cream with a spoon. "I'm not precisely sure what that is."

"Fiddleback wood. It's a top-grain koa." Samuel watched her. She wouldn't look up at him; she hadn't met his eyes once since he'd handed her into the buggy to return her to the hotel. "Expensive."

Her spoon stopped its aimless circle. "You think it too extravagant?"

"Spend whatever you like."

The spoon went back to its slow swirl. She took a small bite. He didn't know why he was sitting here. He had work, Dojun's and his own, but he just kept sitting, gazing at her hands, her neatly parted hair, her pink-and-white striped skirt: drinking in her presence.

"I thought, perhaps, an Oriental motif would be attractive," she said. "Would you like that?"

"Anything you want. I don't care."

He was aware of the churlishness of his reply. For her to be present now, at a risk he couldn't calculate, couldn't believe in and couldn't discount—he didn't want it. He didn't want her at the house in particular. His instincts shouted at him to lock her into a room and mount ten guards at the door; his reason and his training agreed with Dojun's terse advice: that any guard at all, any indication that she was of interest or value, would be mistaken.

He didn't want her here, and he sat losing himself in the sound of her voice, the sweet drift of inconsequential talk: what colors did he think might be attractive in the curtains, was it going to be possible to find an experienced cook at reasonable wages, did he know whether it was likely that wallpaper would not stick in the climate, as Mrs. Richards had warned her?

He felt the pull of it. The gentle seduction of her interest in his opinions. The delicate beguilement, the simple affinity. She was staying. All she spoke of was a future, in his house, as his wife.

The ice cream had melted in her dish. Outside the dining room, a sunset blazed and faded in the soft air that flowed through the open windows. Still she trifled with the spoon, her conversation gradually dwindling, until they sat silently amid the clink of glasses and murmur of other voices.

"Perhaps, if you have no business this evening—" She looked at him from under her lashes. "—you might like to take coffee in our suite?"

He thought it unlikely that she was in any jeopardy. And he thought: if he stayed, he would know she was safe. He nodded briefly and stood, pulling out her chair.

The suite was the largest in the hotel, with high ceilings and a sitting room suitable for a royal reception. Huge bouquets of flowers in Chinese vases adorned every table. The coffee had mysteriously arrived ahead of them on a silver tray—the boy poured and served, and vanished.

Samuel prowled along the floor-length windows that opened onto the lanai. Anyone could walk in here, with no effort whatsoever. It wouldn't require the stealth of a baboon.

Leda sat with her coffee, illuminated only by the light from a red paper lantern filtering through the half-closed Venetian blinds. It gave a rose tint to the cream-colored gardenias in her lei, and left her skirt in shadow.

"Why did you come back?" he asked.

She stirred sugar around and around in her cup. "Because it would be wrong of me to leave."

"I told you that you were free to go."

Her mouth took on a small, stubborn curve. "That does not make it right and proper that I do so."

"You should have gone." The blinds rattled as he snapped them closed and open. "Damn it, I'm not—I can't promise—" He tilted his head back. "God, you saw what it would be like! Get out of here, go away, you don't have to stay with me.''

"Marriage is a solemn vow," she said, with a trace of defiance. "I don't see how I am to comfort, honor, and keep you in sickness and in health if I am not in the reasonably near vicinity.''

"It was a farce!" He swung to face her. "Would you have made any vows if you'd known?''

She stood up. "It was not a farce. I will not have you say so!''

"You're too admirable! A regular saint."

"I daresay that you mean to be sarcastic. I daresay you've forgotten common cordiality in your regret that I'm not the person whom you hoped to wed.''

"I don't regret that," he muttered.

"Do you not? I suppose I'm to believe that you've only been treating me to an ingenious imitation of the fact. And there,'' she exclaimed, turning away, "you've made me lose my temper and lower myself to mockery also. I hope you may be satisfied!''

He gazed at the distorted reflection of himself in a convex pier mirror. He could see her warped image behind him. "I don't regret it," he repeated. He stared at the spiral of colors in the mirror until his vision seemed to go dim. "I don't regret it. I love you.''

Blood suddenly began pumping hard through his body. He felt himself hanging in midair, ten feet off that bottomless cliff, no footing underneath him.

"I know that doesn't change anything," he uttered sharply, throwing himself back toward solid ground. "I don't want you on this island. I don't want you in my house. Do you understand? *Is that clear?*''

The mirror reflected immobility. Impossible to see her expression. The palm trees in the grounds outside made a clattering rustle in the breeze that stole through the transoms and the blinds.

She spoke gently. "Dear sir—I've never thought of you as muddleheaded, but it seems a very muddleheaded thing to say.''

"Forget it," he said. "Just forget it." He walked

through to the bedroom, intending to check there for points of entry.

As he stood in the dusky rays of lantern light, scowling at the mosquito-netted bed and the same ludicrously vulnerable floor-length windows, she came up behind him. "I really don't think I shall be able to promise that."

"Forget it! Stay. Go. Do anything you like."

"I never wished to leave at all. I love you very much also, you see."

He shot her a glance. "My God, your manners are impeccable, aren't they? 'When a gentleman declares his affection,' " he mimicked her aphorisms ruthlessly, " 'a lady should instantly respond with a suitable lie—pardon me—a suitable "prevarication," in order to save him looking a complete ass.' "

She gazed at him, and then lowered her head. "You think—that what I said—isn't true?"

"I think that knowing what you know about me, it's impossible."

She remained looking at the carpet. "Everything I know of you is admirable."

He laughed out loud, fiercely. "Right."

"Everything," she said.

"You know, don't you? She told you."

She lifted her eyes. He waited for her to say something, braced himself for it, but she only looked at him with a tender, patient gravity.

The shaking was there in his gut, just below the edge of feeling. He stood still, forcing it out of his muscles, fighting it. His throat held onto words.

"I love you, dear sir."

"That's impossible."

"It is not impossible."

Air seemed to come hard, as if he had to think, to remember to draw each breath into his chest. "You don't have to say this. I've told you; I've told you that you don't have to say it."

Her chin tilted up. "Nevertheless, I do say it."

He made a furious move away. "You're wrong. You're lying. You—cannot."

"I do not wish to grow heated upon the subject with you." She kept her chin lifted obstinately. "On our wedding night, Lady Tess mentioned to me several things which she felt were relevant to our—to our union. She said that you would not like it, and I see that you don't. I'm very sorry if you feel that it is a character defect in me, but I found, and still find, that nothing of what she said—and nothing that I have learned in my acquaintance with you—nothing, dear sir!—could make me feel anything but—" Her voice began to lose its steadiness. "But a deep regard and respect for you. My very dear sir!"

The shudder inside him threatened violently; to shut it out he reached for her. He dragged her close to him. "Even this?" He brought his mouth down on hers, kissed her hard, gripping her arms with a force he knew would hurt.

The crushed gardenias in her fading lei filled the air with heavy fragrance as he held her tight to him. He slid his hand downward and molded her body. His fingers found the provocative valley at the base of her spine. He rubbed his thumb and fingers up and down in it, pressing deep through the pink-and-white skirt, pulling her lasciviously against his already turgid sex.

Deliberate crudity and instant passion, his tongue in deep penetration . . . he pushed her away as suddenly as he'd seized her.

In the rosy shadows, she was tousled and pretty, her eyes wide.

"Yes." She turned away and smoothed at her cuffs. "Even that. Because—I am half-French, you see." She bent her head over her hand. "And I know it would grieve you to hurt me on purpose."

It grieved him. It revolted him. He wished to cradle her and smooth her hair, but he did not dare touch her. She wouldn't want it; she couldn't; what being half-French had to do with it he didn't hope to understand. It was just Leda, she would say such things, nonsense and innocence—stubborn, gentle, resolute, oblivious innocence, to know what was inside him, what he had been and what he was, and call him admirable.

To say she loved him.

He felt afraid when he thought of it.

What if I'm afraid? he'd asked Dojun once, a long, long time ago. And Dojun had said: *Afraid?* as if he did not know the word. *Fear comes of fighting* against. *Always go* with, *not against.*

And long ago, he'd understood it. In a fight, become the situation; be with the adversary.

He didn't understand now. He looked at Leda and felt everything inside him flame and fuse and flow away, flow out the cracks in himself, until there was going to be nothing left.

She looked over her shoulder at him. "I wish, dear sir, that you would stay here with me tonight."

Too vulnerable, this hotel room was too vulnerable. He glared at the window blinds. "I'll wait in the parlor while you change."

A glad smile spread on her lips. She ducked her head. "Of course. I won't—that is—you need not—I'll only be a few moments!"

He walked into the parlor. At the door, he stepped outside into the lantern light. The paper lamps swung softly, alternately, shedding circles of illumination along the length of the wide lanai. At the far end, a couple stood looking over the fairy-like lights of the grounds. Samuel appraised them: *haole* and innocuous, residents from one of the other islands on holiday. New bars of light fell on the lanai floor as the electric lamp came on in Leda's bedroom.

He watched the white drift of waiters over the lawn, looking for a certain essence of movement, a telltale balance, like the animal grace of Dojun's natural stance. He saw nothing but a Chinese server scolded for bringing an ice water instead of a lemon ice.

Sometimes he thought that keeping *zanshin* was like dying calmly. It was like dying to give up desire, and doubt, and self. To become a shadow, and move freely in the dark.

Tonight, it was like drowning deliberately in a frozen ocean. The slow burn of ice, from his fingertips to his limbs to his brain, until sensation was gone. Until he felt nothing.

The bedroom lamp went out, leaving only the swaying rings of lantern light.

He moved back into the suite and closed the door, not bothering to lock it. He went silently to the bedroom. She'd drawn the mosquito netting all around the bed, a pale canopy falling from the ceiling.

He used that as camouflage for his white linen. He leaned against the wall where his clothes would blend with the netting from the angle of the door and windows.

"Sir?" Her voice came softly from the bed.

"Go to sleep. I'll be here. I won't leave."

A dark shape sat up within the gauzy tent. "Are you not . . . you're not going to come to bed?"

"Go to sleep, Leda. Just go to sleep."

For a long time, she sat up. His eyes adjusted to the darkness, but he could never really see her face. Finally, she lay down amid the pillows. It was two hours later, and the soft laughter and talk from the lawn and the verandas had all died away, replaced by white moonlight that crept in laddered strips across the floor, before her even breathing told him that she'd fallen asleep.

Thirty-four

Leda woke to the sound of the surf, very clear in the early morning when no wind moved the trees. The endlessly sweet air of Hawaii kissed her skin; outside the open blinds, the blazing scarlet spikes of a poinciana tree waved gently against deep green shade. She felt happy and bewildered, a little dazed, gazing up at the gathered netting above her head.

The bedroom was empty, but she heard someone moving in the parlor, and the faint chink of china. Without stopping to put up her hair or even find her slippers, she pushed aside the netting and went to the door in her gown.

"Good morning!" she said warmly, before she saw that it was not Samuel.

"Aloha." Manalo's mellow voice greeted her. He rose, a self-composed giant next to the pig-tailed Chinese who was just setting out the breakfast tray. "Aloha! You eat, bumbye, I gonna take you up house. Haku-nui, he say come."

"Oh. Oh, dear!" Leda realized she was standing in the doorway barefoot and undressed—not that the typical dress of the Hawaiian ladies was much different from her nightgown, except more colorful. She popped the door shut and padded to the bathroom. She began to wash her face, as if it were any normal day.

As if, when she looked in the mirror, she could keep herself from smiling, her cheeks pink from scrubbing and pleasure. As if it were not the day after the night when he'd said that he loved her.

He loved her. He had said so, quite audibly. She was certain that she was not mistaken.

And then, in the next breath, just as certainly, had said that he wanted her gone. Proud and bitter, wounded.

She gazed at her reflection.

Miss Lovatt had perhaps been right to warn her. Decidedly, matrimony was a risky thing. A most painful, joyful, perplexing institution.

To find his quarry, Samuel followed the trail backward, extending gentle feelers: nothing too anxious or ardent, simply expressing a mild interest in who was interested in him. It was only what he'd have done in any case. In the golden, twilight world of Chinatown, it would have been considered strange—and stupid—if he'd ignored the thing.

It had taken only a few days for the path to lead to this wide-beamed water barge anchored off a low, scrub island in the expansive harbor of Pearl River. That the trail hadn't led into the plantations, where he might have lost it so easily among the streams of new laborers, was lucky, and indicated that these men lacked ties among the Japanese who came on contract, to make ends meet, to feed and clothe families at home. Their connection was with another echelon of society entirely, one that had no need or desire to leave Japan.

Silence was a tangible element on Pearl; silence, aquamarine and silver in the angle of light on the smooth water. Samuel's companion, a half-Hawaiian, half-Portuguese fisherman who could be trusted to hire out his boat and keep his mouth shut, sat with his bare feet elevated and his hat pulled down over his eyes, emitting a gentle snore every few minutes.

Beyond that, the only noise was the occasional carillon of old tin cans strung in a manifold network across the rice paddies, jerked by some small boy stationed in a lookout shack in order to frighten plundering sparrows. Samuel kept his own face in the shadow of his hat, fishing diligently, looking less at the barge than at the situation; the angles and avenues of approach.

His adversaries hadn't worked too hard to conceal themselves—but then, they didn't need to. It was a good position, an easy lookout on all sides, hard to breach even with a nighttime attempt. There were four men on the barge; he knew of three more in the city; beyond that—it was questionable how many there were. The men onshore reported to one "Ikeno" on the boat. Pointless to speculate whether that was his true name or not. Japanese tended to change names anyway, with a frequency that baffled foreigners, bestowing on themselves a new identity for anything from the assumption of some new post to the attainment of a life goal.

No doubt Ikeno had his new name all picked out for when he reunited the Gokuakuma. And he, or whoever he worked for, had tinder for the flame in Japan: proposed treaty revisions that gave more rights to the West and enraged the nationalistic sentiment, while the government teetered back and forth debating the unprecedented concept of a constitution.

High stakes, and a trump card in a demon sword.

The obvious routes of departure were covered by Ikeno's men; for Dojun to move off the island with the blade as he planned would require a backcountry exit—through the mountains and off some secluded beach in a native canoe; then interception of a larger vessel. Luck and complexities.

Dojun's problem, he thought. Samuel didn't know where the blade was hidden; when or how Dojun intended to move it. He only provided cover and protection, and a concealed exit beneath his house to the mountains.

His house, where Leda was happily pottering in and out, furnishing things, while Dojun played houseboy.

Everything was quiet. At suspension. It could last a day. Or a year. Sometime, somehow, Dojun would make his move; transfer the blade from its hiding place to Rising Sea—and escape.

Samuel stared beneath his hat at the barge. The resentment still moved in him, cracking the ice of *zanshin.* He cared nothing for the safety of the sword; he cared only that the hunters had every reason to believe that he as well as Dojun knew where the blade was located: his London theft could only have appeared to them an aggressive maneuver to possess the mounting.

He shouldn't have done it. Action and unseen consequence, like Dojun's starfish. Two threats grew from one cut in half. Their adversaries would be looking for weakness, leverage. Dojun had none. Samuel had it all. Leda's mere existence gave it to them. Everything he did to protect her would make her appear more important to him. The house was not absolutely safe; the hotel was impossibly worse. And if Dojun got away with the blade in secret—then where was the end of it? Would the hunters ever know for sure that the blade was gone? Would they ever be certain enough to leave here completely, to believe Samuel had no knowledge of it, to cease to be a threat to what he'd tangled his heart with?

American thoughts, Dojun would say. *Western fears. Your life is no more than an illusion. When you're buried, no one will go with you, no one will love you. Death comes between one moment and the next; you must live every day as if you will die this night.*

He didn't want to die tonight. He'd had enough illusions in his life, but Leda was not one of them.

Because of her, he entertained a thought worse than all the rest. He thought that if the hunters had the blade and the mounting, his part in it—and Leda's—would be finished.

Betrayal. He turned it over in his mind. And as he thought of it, he knew that Dojun would have thought of it. And he knew why Dojun didn't trust him with the location of the Gokuakuma now.

Seventeen years.

The Japanese said, *Okage sama de*—Because of what you've done for me, I have become what I am.

I owe you.

Dojun, he thought, closing his eyes in pain.

Leda could never have made so much progress so quickly without the help of Mr. Dojun and Manalo. The Hawaiian driver took her everywhere, carried chairs and potted plants, drove her to the teas and luncheons to which she was invited almost daily. After a week, she had even coaxed and scolded him into keeping to a reasonable pace in the buggy.

And Mr. Dojun had been very helpful in the decoration of Rising Sea. Leda would not have thought, herself, that furniture of such simple lines could be so surprisingly attractive, but when she looked over the study and bedroom, she felt that nothing could be cooler or more handsome than the simple, textural cross-weave of the *lauhala* mats in place of heavy carpets, the cane-backed rocker or the beautiful honeyed wood grain of the unadorned *tansu,* a chest with sliding doors above and smooth drawers below that made a soft musical note each time they were pulled— an innovation Mr. Dojun seemed quite proud of.

"New wife chest," he said. "Japan all new wife bring chest home husband house. You like, Mrs. Samua-san?"

"Oh, yes. It's lovely. And the bedstead is magnificent."

He leaned over and traced a callused finger over the headboard, outlining the inlaid medallion of a spread-winged, slender bird. "Good fortune wish. Japan, we say *Tsuru wa sennen.* Crane live thousand year."

"Is that what it means? It's a good-wish symbol?"

"Good wish. Long live. *Tsuru wa sennen; kame wa mannen.* Crane live thousand year, turtle live ten thousand. Wedding-time, born-day, festival—friend make thousand paper crane, all hang up, happy thousand-thousand year, *nē?*"

Leda looked at him, smiling a little. "What a pleasant custom." She touched a smooth, tapered bedpost and sighed. "I wish I'd known of that last Christmas. The only idea I could find in the book for Mr. Samua-san was a present of dried fish."

"Dry fish, *hai.* Crane. Turtle. Rice cake. Bamboo good fortune beside. Bamboo got bend, no break, say faithful devotion. Fix bamboo in *tansu,* make drawer sing."

"Do you think he understands these things? About the cranes and the bamboo and the turtles?"

"Samua-san? *Hai,* understand."

"Do you think—he might like it if I put some paper cranes about?"

"Like good. Maybe come home house more, *nē?*"

It wasn't the first time Leda had found Mr. Dojun somewhat startling in his perceptiveness. "Well, he's very busy, you know. His business requires a large amount of attention."

"Ah." Mr. Dojun bowed, as if she had just provided the answer to a baffling question.

"It would be pleasant, though. That is, if he . . ." She leaned her cheek against the cool wooden post. "I should like him to feel happy and at home here."

"Know lady make paper crane. You buy?"

"Oh, yes. Yes, I would buy some. A thousand?"

"Thousand, *hai.* All hang down, string, eh? Pretty. Turtle, few maybe. I write, say Obāsan make." He pulled a notebook and pencil from some hidden pocket and made Oriental marks upon a sheet. He tore it out, folded it carefully, and handed it to her. "Good."

"Yes, and perhaps some bamboo in pots for greenery."

He bobbed in agreement. "Manalo take Mrs. Samua-san downtown, go Obāsan, she read, all buy, paper crane and all that. Bamboo pot, go greenhouse."

"Thank you."

With a deft move, he tucked the notebook away and pushed the bell for Manalo. As Leda slid his note into her pocket, he said, "Say you secret, Mrs. Samua-san. I happy. You good wife him." He bowed to her. "Crane bed gift—you, he. I give."

"Oh," Leda said softly. "Thank you!" She felt shy under his exotic gaze. "I'm really trying to be a good wife. But I don't seem entirely to have the proper knack of it yet."

"Got bed. Got *tansu.* Only need *hanayome-taku.*"

"What is that?"

He made a circular gesture with his hands. "Small-little table. Boy make, give mother. Samua-san been make *hanayome-taku,* oh, long time. Been boy. Give Lady Ashlan'. New wife—what word you say? New wife?"

"Bride."

"Ah. Bride go mother house, take *hanayome-taku* husband house. Good marriage, after bring house."

Leda tilted her head in interest. "Mr. Samua-san made one of these—whatever?"

"*Hanayome-taku.* Bride-table. I been help make. Been make, oh, fifteen year maybe. Mrs. Samua-san go down Lady Ashlan' house, you see table." He lifted his eyebrows. "Ah! You go down, bring Samua-san bride-table here this house, *nē?* All OK then. Make good marriage. Samua-san, he come home, all right."

She smiled. "I'm sure that's a very good idea, but—"

"Good! I draw." He pulled his notebook out again and made a sketch that at first glance appeared to be a larger version of the Japanese characters that he'd written on the note he'd given her. When she looked, she could see that it must be something rather like a plant stand, with three splayed legs, a square top, and a single round shelf nearer the bottom. "You go Ashlan' house, bring table."

"I don't think I—"

"All fifteen year, Lady Ashlan' bedroom. You look lady bedroom, see *hanayome-taku.* Bring here."

"Mr. Dojun, I'm afraid I couldn't just take something out of their house."

"No, no. Belong you!" He thrust his hand out emphatically. "You Samua-san bride. No keep Lady Ashlan' this table, she know."

"Still, I—"

"Samua-san, he like see *hanayome-taku.* He see, know you honor, got respect him."

Leda bit her lip.

He bowed. "He see, he know sure. No need word."

It seemed a large accomplishment for a small-little table. But Leda looked sadly around the newly fitted room, that Samuel had not so much as expressed a desire to inspect in the few taciturn evening meals he'd taken with her, and found herself willing to give anything a try. "Perhaps you could bring it from the Ashlands'. I should feel like a housebreaker."

Mr. Dojun waved his palm in front of his face in a negative manner. "No can do. New wife, she bring. She no use own hands—got no fortune, no good marriage. Small-little furnita. No heavy, eh?"

Leda sighed. "Well, I shall consider it."

And she did consider it. That night as she lay in the new crane bed, listening to the rustle of red paper cranes that hung in long drifts from bamboo canes suspended at the ceiling, she considered. It was the first night she'd spent at Rising Sea, and she was alone.

Not alone, precisely. The several gardeners lived-in: now and then, through the open shutters, she heard them speak to one another quietly from the grounds below, and Mr. Dojun slept in the butler's room downstairs.

But Samuel wasn't there.

At the hotel, he had at least come at night, though he always sat up awake until long after she was asleep and left before she woke. Last evening, he hadn't come at all in spite of having given permission—through Manalo—for her to move into the house.

In the morning, she decided to go to the Ashlands' house and bring the bride-table, and hoped she would not be arrested for burglary. Manalo didn't seem to think she would be. He didn't seem to think much of anything when he arrived with the buggy, sunk in gloom because his wife had left him and moved in with a man from Wahiawa.

Leda tried to hide her shock at this story, which was freely admitted and meticulously detailed. She was to attend a garden breakfast at General Miller's; all the way, Manalo regaled her with the sad facts of the breach and asked mournfully for advice. In all honesty, she felt she had none to give, but what little she did suggest seemed to slide right off the Hawaiian's broad and drooping shoulders. He didn't even drive at his usual mad pace, and they arrived at the breakfast a full quarter-hour late.

When she left the gathering, Manalo had fallen from garrulity into strange and silent gloom. He wore a lei of yellow hibiscus and tiny red berries nestled among fragrant leaves. Leda herself wore a wreath of white carnations that Mrs. Miller had given her, but in spite of the flowers' scent, she noticed a peculiar, sweet odor about Manalo.

His driving regressed back to its worst in speed and recklessness. Leda several times had to hang onto the buggy and speak sharply for him to slow down, and he got lost on the way to the Ashlands' house, driving around the same block three different times. But finally he turned the horse into a shady gate, where a lovely white two-story house, surrounded by verandas like Rising Sea, stood in a fine lawn, the emerald dappled by black-green shade from huge, stooping trees and tall palms.

Orchids hung down from the trees in profusion, hot-house plants blooming wild: purple, white, pink. It seemed a magically spooky place, beautiful but utterly silent, and yet manicured as if the family might step out onto the grass at any moment. Manalo did not jump down to help her out, but sat slumped in his seat. Leda glanced at his funereal, half-masted expression, and gathered her skirts, stepping down alone.

Mr. Dojun and Manalo had both said the house would not be locked. No one locked anything here, apparently. Still, Leda would not have minded Manalo's company as she slipped inside the dim interior.

The furniture was all covered with white duck, and the floors were bare of any mats or carpet. She tiptoed through the wide hall and up the stairs, finding Lord and Lady Ashland's bedroom by the glass-fronted case that Lady Kai had given her mother and described to Leda.

Beside the bed, she carefully lifted the covering from a tall, narrow stand. The moment she saw the table beneath, she knew it was Samuel's *hanayome-taku*. The austere, outward curve of the legs was like nothing English; it was completely *shibui*, as Dojun would say, astringently elegant and Japanese in its simplicity, the wood showing an intense grain from black to golden-red, almost as if an artist had brushed arcs of colored ink across it.

A small collection of mementos lay on the polished top: a homely brown stone in a black bowl, a wooden calabash, and a sweet-smelling box that she recognized as sandal-wood. As she looked at them, she felt very certain that she should not take the table, that it was unforgivably impertinent of her.

But she set the items carefully beneath the covering on the dressing table, hoping that Mr. Dojun was quite cor-

rect, and Lady Tess would understand. She folded the
muslin and laid it on the bed. The table itself was much
heavier than she'd expected, and an unwieldy shape, as
tall as her waist, with a tendency to tilt in an awkward
manner when she picked it up.

She carried it downstairs with exquisite care. Working
her way through the front door required extra effort, while
Manalo just sat there, apparently half-asleep in the buggy.
He didn't respond to her low calls, and she didn't care to
shout and rouse the neighborhood. She bore the table
painstakingly out to the carriage, but she didn't dare try
to lift it inside herself, for fear of scratching it.

"Manalo!" she hissed. "Do wake up and forget your
troubles for one moment!"

He turned his head and looked at her drowsily. Then he
hauled himself up, looped the reins around the buggy post,
although the poor horse looked in no mood to travel, and
ambled around to her side.

"If you would just lift it to me, please, after I've got
in—"

Before she finished her instructions, he'd hoisted the
table out of her hands and stood swaying in a very odd
manner. Just as it struck her that the strange, non-floral
odor about him was that of strong spirits, the horse decided to take a closer look at the lawn grass. The trailing
leg of the table caught on the edge of the buggy panel.
Manalo stumbled forward.

Leda cried out in dismay as the table bounced off the
carriage and hit the brick-paved drive with a horrible crack.

"Oh, *look!* How could you?" She pushed him away
with a hand on his chest. He tripped backward, landing in
the grass with a grunt, but Leda had no time to worry over
his well-being—she was too busy staring in consternation
at the table leg that was fractured down its length and
hanging loose from the top. "Oh, no!" she whispered.
"Oh, dear; oh, no!"

Gingerly, she bent and turned the table slightly. A flat
metal bar with Oriental calligraphy carved into it stuck out
of the end of the leg, a joint of some sort. As she tilted it

farther, the whole leg came off in her hand. She gave a little moan as she held it up.

With a strange sizzling sound, the metal bar began to slide free. She sucked in her breath and tried to right the leg, but the weight of the metal was already beyond resisting. Leda jumped back, saving her feet from a yard of curved and glistening steel with a wicked point that caught the sunlight through the trees and sent a spark of multicolored light into the atmosphere as it fell.

For an instant, she thought: *What a strange fastening for a table.* But no sooner had that crossed her mind than she knew it was no fastening, nor furniture joint. It was nothing to do with furniture at all. She was gazing at a sword blade, a beautiful, viciously sharp blade, with an intricate carving of some sort of unpleasant-looking beast along the upper length.

"Oh, good God, look at this!" she exclaimed, and then clapped her hand over her mouth as she heard her own language. She glanced over her shoulder at Manalo. He was lying still in the grass. With another exclamation, she knelt next to him, but he only lifted his eyelids and closed them again, and began to snore, his breath redolent of something like cherry brandy. She dropped his limp hand on his chest. "*Pilikia* you!" she said in disgust. "What am I to do now?"

She turned back to the table, gingerly lifting the blade by the blunt, squared-off end. She attempted to slide it back into the leg, and dropped both with a gasp, clutching at her fingers to staunch the cut while tears sprang to her eyes. Laying the broken leg flat on the ground, she nudged the sword toward it, angling the point into the raw, cracked end of the hollowed-out slot. When she finally got the blade back in place, she upended the whole table and tried to fit the leg back on, hoping against hope that it might be possible to fix.

What a sword blade was doing in Samuel's table, it seemed pointless to ponder. No doubt it had something to do with Japanese tradition. Probably all bride-tables had them, and it was the worst sort of luck for a bride to break the thing, and expose the sword—most likely it meant future disaster of unimaginable proportions.

The present disaster was awful enough. How was she going to tell Samuel? Or Mr. Dojun? Or Lady Tess?

She didn't realize she was muttering to herself, trying to fit the leg back into place, until someone answered her. Then she jumped a foot, and looked up at the toothless grin of a straw-hatted, barefoot kau-kau man who seemed to have appeared from nowhere at all, with his pole over his shoulder weighted down by two huge baskets of fruit hanging at the ends.

"Need help, missy?" he asked in a genial way. "Broke de table?"

"He broke it," she said crossly. "But it's my fault. I never should have touched it. Oh, what shall I *do?* I wouldn't have seen it scratched for the world, and here it is damaged beyond repair!"

"Want fix, missy? Got grandson fix. All fix, never know broke."

Leda looked up, hope flooding her, and then back down at the table. "I don't see how it could possibly be fixed."

"Fix yes! Yes, yes! My grandson, Ikeno, he best cabinet-maker in island. Dat special table, yes? Not everybody know how fix. My grandson know."

"Does he?"

"Special sword table. Japanese, ey? My grandson only one can fix. He live way out, Ewa, Aiea, closer the plantations."

"Way out?" Leda felt dubious and desperate. "How far?"

"Take buggy, maybe hour."

"Is there nothing closer? In the city? Surely the better woodworking shops would be here?"

"Huh. Too many *haole,* Chinese. Don't know nothing for Japanese sword table. My grandson come over last year Japan."

"Do you think he might be able to do it on the spot? Right away, so that I could wait and take it home with me?"

"Yes, yes! I take you, he fix. Big sign say, 'While You Wait,' yes. Fix while you wait.''

Leda turned to Mañalo. She bent down and shook at his shoulder. "Oh, do get up! Wake up! We must go!''

He opened his eyes and mumbled. With much coaxing, she got him to sit up. He stared blearily past her at the fruit seller.

"We must go right away, Manalo. I'm sorry that you're not feeling your best, but he's going to get the table fixed, and I want to see that it's done. Come along. Come *along!*'' The last plea was made as he shook his head and pushed her away, slumping down again on the grass. A small brown flask slid from his shirt pocket. She stood up and stamped her foot, turning to the vendor in desperation. "Can you drive? Can you take me there and back? I would be glad to pay you."

"No pay, no pay! I drive.'' He heaved his fruit baskets into the back of the buggy and went to where the horse was grazing placidly off the edge of the drive. "You come with me. No cry, missy! We get table fix. No cry, no cry!''

Five days of careful work, not too much eagerness, showing just a degree more impatience rather than less in the cautious contacts he made with Ikeno's men, and Samuel was aboard the water barge in Pearl Harbor. He was there as a traitor to his own—as Dojun's *gyaku fukuro,* a sack turned inside out.

Fukurogaeshi no jutsu—to go deep, to appear to change sides completely—a method effective in exact proportion to the risk of the technique. It would have been impossible without the conveniently incriminating background of Samuel's London theft. He could see nothing of Ikeno's doubts as the man sat cross-legged on the cabin floor, lifting rice on his slender, enameled *hashi* from a bowl, as delicate and graceful as a girl in his movements, and yet with a power hidden, as his suspicions must be.

But Samuel, too, could use chopsticks with refinement. He knelt barefoot in his Western clothes and ate little, quickly, enough to satisfy politeness and calculated to show at the same time his own discipline. Eating, like sleeping, was a pleasure to be leisurely indulged in times of relaxation. This was not one of them; he wished Ikeno to see that he understood it.

He wished, in fact, to keep Ikeno baffled as to what he understood and did not. The man spoke an awkward and schooled English, painfully accented; Samuel deliberately addressed him as superior, refusing to use English, answering persistently in the humble forms of Japanese to any English question. He knew that he was outside all experience: an elephant taught to waltz, not expected to be anything but Western and clumsy, and yet with training that must be as obvious to them as theirs was to him.

He would make mistakes, that he knew. Dojun had rebuked him often enough for transgressing some obscure line of correct behavior, for embarrassing himself with Western ignorance. But his mistakes, perhaps, would win him more credit for what he did correctly. A perfectly trained talking dog might arouse suspicion; an imperfect but willing one had an opportunity to draw the spectators into sympathy.

"You wish to give me fidelity, hmmm?" Ikeno had a soft face, soft eyes, lashes like a woman's, but an aristocratic hook to his nose and an upward slash to his brows that caught the savagery of the Japanese paintings of ancient warriors. He looked young, not much older than Samuel by *haole* standards. Which meant he was likely forty or more. "I don't understand you."

He'd finally given in to speaking Japanese, but he was rude in his tone. Samuel bowed deeply, ignoring it. "With fear and respect, this insignificant person begs Ikeno-sama to deign to spare a few moments of attention. I've little to offer that you need, a poor business and few leaking ships, but perhaps you might condescend to make some use of my education at the hands of Tanabe Dojun Harutake."

"And perhaps I should cut your head off, if the Tanabe has sent you."

Samuel bowed again, then raised his head and stared

into Ikeno's eyes. "May you pardon my impudence, but I have not been sent. I owe *giri* to Tanabe Dojun no longer."

"Do you not? That isn't what I've heard about you. I've heard that you visit him in his house, and take *sake* with him. I've heard that he is a father to you. Even now he lives in your new house, and plays the servant to your wife."

"With respect, he is not my father. I share neither name nor family with him." Samuel lifted a thumb toward his hair, a quick motion of self-mockery. "As the honored Ikeno-sama may see with his own eyes."

Ikeno smiled a little. "And he's instructed you anyway. He has told you, perhaps, of the method called *fukurogaeshi,* and sent you here to make fools of us. He's done you no favor. When I send your head back to him, I'll turn the bag inside out. Maybe then he'll realize that we are not *baka.*"

Samuel lowered his gaze. "He's told me of this *fukurogaeshi no jutsu.* He didn't ask me to execute it here. He has asked nothing of me lately, beyond the sanctuary of my deplorable house. Perhaps—" He allowed a note of bitterness into his voice. "—he didn't think I was capable of accomplishing it."

Ikeno said nothing. Samuel felt one of the other men move closer behind him.

"Deign to order your honored retainer to swing his sword," Samuel said quietly, "if my impertinence in asking to assist displeases you."

"Are you ready to die?"

"If the respected Ikeno-sama does not think me worthy of his service, I am ready."

"*Iie!* Worthy!" he snarled. "I think the Tanabe sent you here to make a fool of me!"

He jerked his chin at the swordsman. In the whistle of the blade Samuel's body recognized intention; he heard his executioner exhale with the effort of the swing; the sword flashed in the edge of his vision, light glittering along a horizontal plane.

He didn't move.

That much, every muscle and cell in him knew, like breathing—the difference between a killing strike and one that would fall short. He knelt relaxed as the blade struck, sliced his collar: the sudden sting of a light cut and the scent of blood revealing how close this slash had come.

Ikeno's face was expressionless. A little too indifferent. The long silence might have been interpreted as detachment, but Samuel rather thought it was surprise.

He bowed all the way to the floor, touching his forehead against the back of his hands. "With reverent thanks for my worthless life."

"You wish to betray your master." Ikeno's voice was a sudden snap. "Not even a dog betrays its master."

Samuel's jaw grew taut. "I've kept faith." With his posture rigid, he made as if to speak, and broke off. Then in a low, passionate voice, he said, "Tanabe Dojun has tested me in all ways. I've not failed him."

"You are here."

"He's made a mockery of me. He holds my competence in contempt."

The echo of Samuel's words died away in the still cabin. There was that deep anger beneath the ice in him; he allowed himself to feel it; to let Ikeno see it in his spirit. *Giri*—righteous duty. A man owed that blood-duty to his master; but he owed too a powerful *giri* to his own name. In a hundred old legends of Japan, warrior-heroes who would have done *seppuku*—slit their own bellies at an order from their lord—turned about and spent their lives in taking vengeance on the same lord for a far lesser insult than disdain and mockery. It was correct behavior. It was a thing Ikeno would understand.

"With my body I still bow to Tanabe Dojun Harutake," Samuel said. "But in my heart, I'm masterless. I've come to the honorable Ikeno-sama to offer my miserable aid in his praiseworthy quest. I stole the Gokuakuma's mounting in London, but I'd not yet been able to reach the blade." He made a short, jeering laugh. "Respected Ikeno-sama had no need to break into my office—I'd have given the mounting in gladness if I'd known who wanted it. This is *giri* that I owe to my name."

"On what terms, this *giri?*"

Samuel didn't speak at once. He looked at each of the other three men in the cabin in turn. Ikeno made no move to dismiss them. In English, Samuel said slowly, "Dojun-san trained me for the Gokuakuma. I loved him. I honored him. I have not failed at any test. None! And he puts me aside, only because—" His mouth curled in scorn. "—I am . . . what I am. Not *Nihonjin*. White. I'm not to be given the trust. He has taken a boy—a boy of fourteen!—in my place, now that immigration is again allowed." Slowly, he turned his head aside and spit at the floor. "I will not wear this shame he gives me."

One of the other men growled, but Ikeno moved his hand in a slight, soothing gesture. In Japanese, he said, "You assert a stain on your honor? I thought there was nothing important but money to a barbarian."

Samuel came to his feet. The man behind him with the sword reached out. In a backward strike and block, Samuel trapped him against his own blade. They stood locked, while Samuel deliberately made no further move, only held the man so that if he shifted in any direction, he was cut.

"Most feared and respected Ikeno-sama." Samuel let the other man go, thrusting him off, and turned with a bow from the waist. "Forgive my poor ears and blind eyes. I didn't hear the wise and honorable words just spoken."

He straightened. Ikeno stared meditatively at him. Samuel looked back beneath lowered eyelids, holding his deferential posture with a visible defiance.

"What assistance," Ikeno asked slowly, "does the barbarian Jurada-san offer in particular?"

Samuel recognized the elevation of his surname to an honorific. "Respected Ikeno-sama is in possession of the Gokuakuma's mounting. The blade is required."

Ikeno inclined his head, acknowledging the obvious.

"Dojun is aware of the theft of the mounting. He assumes that those who seek the Gokuakuma have it; he does not suspect that I myself stole it. He knows of your presence here, and surmises that the mount is in your hands. So he proposes to take the blade off the island; go into hiding elsewhere.'' Samuel shrugged. "I don't know where it's hidden or where he intends to go, but I'll know when he makes his move, and how.''

"The Tanabe trusts you with this?''

"He trusts me with nothing of importance. But he depends on my devotion. I know him well. And I know the island. I can do what I say.''

"And what return for your honored contribution?''

"Only to see the Gokuakuma whole, Ikeno-sama. To see it with my own eyes, and know that it's out of the hands of Tanabe Dojun, who has spent his life in guarding it from being made complete—as I've spent my life in preparing to take his place . . . until he chose to supplant me.''

"Perhaps, in your eagerness for this reprisal, you wish the Tanabe to see it, too?''

"That isn't necessary. It would be dangerous. For me to see it, for me to know that the defilement of my honor has been cleansed in a proportionate manner—that is enough.''

Ikeno nodded. "I compliment you. When the world is tipped, it should be balanced. Your design seems a precise vengeance for the indignity offered.''

Samuel returned to his most formal demeanor. "The undeservedly generous praise of honored Ikeno-sama causes a heavy weight of gratitude.''

His enemy regarded him with austere, intelligent eyes. "What of the weight of gratitude, then? Your teacher has made a man of you. You owe him.''

"I owe him. And he has taken from me the means of repayment.''

"*Giri* is hardest to bear when it is two sides of the same heart. What will you do to pay your debt to him, Juradasan?''

Samuel returned the fathomless look, unflinching. "To betray Dojun-san is shame beyond enduring. When it's done, when I give you the Gokuakuma . . . there's nothing left to me but what honor requires.''

Ikeno inclined in a bow that recognized equality. ''If it must be so. Bring me the blade—and you may use the Gokuakuma with honor on yourself.''

Thirty-five

※

Leda had become quite uncomfortably doubtful by the time they reached the little pier that stretched like a tipsy ribbon out into the still harbor. "Are you certain this is the correct direction? It seems overly far. There isn't a residence in sight."

It was at least the twentieth time she'd suggested some mistake had been made. The air seemed dustier here, hotter, the profuse and shadowed greenery of the city having long since given way to flooded paddies and dry brush, interrupted only by palms that looked as inviting as ragged and stooping dustmops.

The kau-kau man jumped down and lifted the table from behind the buggy seat. "Right way, missy! Only got boat now. Take boat, go there chop-chop."

"Boat?" Leda looked dubiously at the small craft tied not far along the dock, just out of the mud-flats. She brushed away a mosquito. "I really don't think I'd like to take a boat."

"Only way get there, missy! Come, Ikeno fix table, you want, eh?"

"No," she said, taking the decision that had been creeping upon her for the last half hour. She picked up the horse's reins. "No, I certainly don't wish to go a step farther."

"No want go?" He shook his head, and then broke into a grin. "I take table, then. Get fix, bring back you house tonight, OK?"

Before she could protest, he bore the broken table off down the pier and set it carefully into the boat. Leda frowned. She had recently come to the conclusion that she was being kidnapped, and the present time appeared ripe to make her escape. However, as the man seemed genuinely kind, in the manner of all of these islanders, and more interested in the table than in her person, the kidnapping conjecture appeared to be an overstatement of the case. The table was of considerable value to herself, of course, but she could not see that it held any serious prospect of ransom sums.

She also realized, as the horse began to move purposefully toward the nearest bush, that she was not much hand at driving. In point of fact, she'd never gone so far as to touch the reins before. She tugged on the bit, trying to discourage the browsing, and found the buggy moving rapidly backward toward the water.

"Ho!" she cried. "Ho, ho—please, stop! Do stop!"

The kau-kau man came pelting back up the pier. He grabbed the horse by the bridle just as the rear wheels sank into the tiny waves lapping against the mud. After Leda became convinced that in order to prevent the horse from moving backward it was counterproductive to hang onto the reins, he coaxed the animal back on shore.

"You drive town by you self, missy?" he asked skeptically. "Maybe more better you wait here."

She gathered her skirts. "Tie him up, if you will. I'll go with you."

"Good thing, missy!" He quickly unhooked the horse from the traces and set it free. Immediately the animal swished its tail and began to amble back the way they'd come.

"Won't it wander off?" Leda asked in alarm.

"No, no. No wander. Stay there—grass, you see? Horse always like grass. Come along boat, missy."

Leda didn't see any grass. In another moment, she didn't see any horse. There was nothing to be seen but bushes and tall canes and the sandy two-wheeled track that ended at the pier. Everything seemed silent, except for a strange tuneless clatter that sounded like a hundred children banging on distant cookpots. It came on the wind and drifted away, leaving quiet again.

"Come along boat, missy. Ikeno fix table."

She pressed her lips together. But the little kau-kau man wasn't forcing her, nor doing anything brutish, as one imagined kidnappers must do. He just leaned over the pier, holding the boat up close, grinning cheerfully at her as he told her to watch her step.

A few hundred feet out onto the water, her suspicions revived in force. She had expected the kau-kau man to row for the nearest finger of land, readily in view off to the left. Instead, he seemed headed for the low, desolately empty-looking island in the middle of the lake. "Where are we going?" she demanded. "I insist that you point out where you're taking me!"

He pulled steadily at the oars, not answering. Leda craned to see over his shoulder. As they passed a sandy point, the masts of a stubby fishing vessel came into view, and she realized with a shock that he was heading for it.

"I shall leap overboard!" she declared. "Unless you turn about at once!"

"Sharks," the kau-kau man said succinctly.

Leda drew in a breath and closed her eyes. She gripped the sides of the boat, and then snatched her fingers in and held them in her lap. "You won't get any money. My husband won't descend to paying you a farthing."

"This place got shark-goddess," he said conversationally. "She name Kaahupahau. *Kanakas* say she live here this harbor."

"How quaint," Leda murmured.

Be brave, she said to herself. *You must not panic.* She held the table against her knee and thought that if he tried to attack her, she could fight him off with the sword.

He remained congenial, though, and when they reached the larger boat, he called out, and seemed much more interested in handing the table safely on board than in seeing to her. She sat in the rocking dinghy as he transferred the table, all too close to the shark-infested greenish-blue water that was clear enough to see well down under the encrusted hull of the fishing boat.

A shout of surprise and elation came from above, then instantly a scuffle and babble of foreign voices broke out.

As the dinghy rocked, she looked about anxiously for any telltale fins.

"Leda!"

Samuel's voice seemed to come out of nowhere. She jerked her head up. He was leaning over the rail, looking down at her.

"Oh, thank the good Lord!" She almost leaped to her feet in the tiny boat, but the violent motion of it made her sit back down hastily. "Samuel!" She put her hand to her throat in relief. "Oh, Samuel—what—is it a surprise party? My gracious, you very nearly—"

"Stay there," he hissed, in a barely intelligible tone.

"There are sharks," she protested, but he was gone from the rail. She heard him speaking in Japanese, a sharp and urgent tone, and then an answer from someone else.

Two Oriental men came to the rail and lowered a paltry rope ladder. They looked at her expectantly. When she hesitated, one of them spoke to her, and gestured for her to come up.

"Samuel?" she asked uncertainly.

A third man looked down at her. "Jurada wife-san, you are to come up. Many gratitude due."

Leda really felt rather confused. "Gratitude?"

"This Ikeno," the kau-kau man said, holding the dinghy up close to the ladder. "You go up, missy."

"I'm sorry. Mr. Gerard asked me to stay in the boat."

The man above spoke over his shoulder. After a moment, she heard Samuel's voice. "Do as he says. It's all right."

He sounded—not quite himself. She gathered her skirt and delicately, gingerly took hold of the ladder, pulling herself up. With the help of the kau-kau man and the Oriental men above, and only one terrifying moment when she caught her foot in her skirt and the dinghy rocked madly, she got on deck and took a deep breath of relief. The kau-kau man pounded twice on the hull, shouted "Aloha," and then pushed his boat away, manning the oars again.

Samuel stood barefoot in his white suit, with a shocking bloodstain at his collar. She almost tripped over the table in her relief as she went toward him. One of the Oriental men held the blade that had been inside the leg. Another had a complete sword in his hand, hilt and all. There did not seem to be any ladies present.

She stopped. She bit her lip. In a very small voice, she said, "Is it—perhaps—a costume party?"

"You've done well, Leda. The correct act. I thank you." Samuel spoke in an odd way, emphatic and slow. Then he added, without emotion, "It's business. Leda, do whatever I tell you. Instantly. Don't argue. The one speaks some English but when we run words together he won't understand. For God's sake do what I tell you."

It was peculiar to hear him say she'd done well so clearly, and then such forceful things in an utterly dispassionate voice. She swallowed, and bent her head. "Oh, yes. Of course. I was rather afraid that it wasn't a costume party." She looked up at him. "Are you hurt?"

"No." He smiled, and nodded, as if congratulating her. "Tell me how you got here with that blade."

"Oh, the sword? This sword? Samuel, I'm so dreadfully sorry I broke your bride-table! I only wanted to do as Mr. Dojun recommended, and take it from Lady Ashland's house to ours as the Japanese tradition says—so that we would have a good marriage, and you'd know I honor and respect you, but then Manalo's wife left him, and he over-indulged in strong spirits, and he broke it, and fell asleep, and it's all gone wrong!"

"Bride-table?" he echoed in a strange way.

"Yes, you know—this one that you made for Lady Tess, the table a bride is to take to her new home with her own hands—had you forgotten? _Hano—hana_—something. It begins with an 'h' in Japanese. But it broke! Does that mean ill luck? I meant to fix it—I was coming to have it fixed. That little man happened along—is he a friend of yours? He said that Mr. Ikeno could fix it and no one would know the difference. Mr. Dojun told me you'd be pleased with me for fetching it to Rising Sea, so I did. Or rather, I was trying to—"

"Christ." The single word was a snarl. "_Dojun_ brought you into this?"

Leda moistened her lips, aware of the way no one moved, and yet everyone watched her with a new intensity. "Well, he suggested that I fetch the table. I'd not have known of it otherwise."

Samuel closed his eyes. For an instant there was such a static fury in him that it almost seemed as if it passed through her like a wave of heat and ice. He opened his eyes, his face without expression, and turned away from her. Bowing toward Mr. Ikeno, he spoke in measured English. "Tanabe Dojun takes me for a fool once again," he said, with bitter emphasis on each word. "My wife is a foolish and inferior person, with value only to myself. As for her deed in providing the blade, nothing could be more surprising. The act is worthless, but accept the benefit it brings."

While Samuel's aspersions seemed somewhat overstated, Leda supposed that having broken the table, she was not precisely high in his estimation at the moment. She glanced at Mr. Ikeno, and found him watching her.

He bowed to her. "Jurada wife-san."

His alien eyes, so dark and unblinking, made her uncomfortable in a way that Mr. Dojun never had. She smiled slightly and nodded. "Good afternoon, sir. I'm pleased to meet you."

"Pray good will," he said. Then he gave a sharp order, and one of his crew ducked inside the low arch of the deckhouse. In a few moments, the man returned with a flat, enameled box and a felt bag, of a shape and length that Leda found dismayingly familiar. Mr. Ikeno took the bag and drew forth the weapon—the ceremonial sword of the golden bird hilt and mother-of-pearl inlaid in red lacquer, a sword that Leda would have recognized if she hadn't seen it for decades.

She looked up at Samuel, but he only watched Mr. Ikeno and the sword. Wild uncertainties flew through her mind: that he'd stolen the Jubilee gift to sell Mr. Ikeno, that he was a spy or a traitor or a sordid thief after all.

"How Jurada-wife possess?" Mr. Ikeno nodded toward the carved blade from the broken table and looked at her.

"It was in the—the limb." She found that she couldn't

bring herself to say anything so coarse as "leg" aloud,
even to a foreigner.

"Pardon, Wife-san. Rim?"

"Limb. Leg! This part. It was inside this part, as you
can see."

"See, yes. Inside know you, Wife-san?"

"I didn't know. It broke, and I saw the sword." She
resisted an urge to chew her lip. With all of these
dangerous-looking strangers, she had no idea what was
best to say. "So—here it is!"

Mr. Ikeno glanced at Samuel. "You are not fool, hope
to cheat me with false blade, no?"

Samuel only stared at him, unmoving.

Mr. Ikeno motioned at the deck, and a woven mat was
unrolled at his feet, the box placed precisely above center,
its contents of folded cloth, obscure jars, and small tools
set out in a neat pattern. With a somber air, Mr. Ikeno
knelt and laid the golden scabbard on the mat. He drew
the hilt partially out. Selecting an instrument that appeared
to be a wooden pick from the box, he tapped lightly at a
spot on the hilt. A small pin fell onto the folded cloth.

Then he drew the coarse blade completely free of the
scabbard and hit his fist lightly against his forearm. The
bar, already unsteady, loosened completely. He pulled it
from the hilt and flung the crude iron over the rail.

As the splash died away, the man bearing the carved
blade stepped forward, offering it with a deep bow. Mr.
Ikeno took the sword, holding it above the cutting edge.
He raised it upright and fitted the hilt to the new blade. It
did not seem to suit. The tang stuck halfway in, not quite
adjusting to the opening in the hilt.

Mr. Ikeno looked up at Samuel.

Leda had never seen a stillness in her husband's face
like the unreadable stillness there now.

The Japanese man lowered his eyes again to the sword.
He gripped the hilt of the upright sword and struck the
end down into his open palm. The blade seemed to shudder, and then seated firmly into place.

"*Iza!*" Mr. Ikeno's soft exclamation seemed to break a
spell. The men around shifted and murmured, grinning.

Mr. Ikeno bent over the hilt and tapped the pin back into place. He lifted the sword aloft to the sunlight. *"Banzai!"*

"Banzai!" The other men's shout echoed across the silent bay.

"May we go home now?" Leda asked.

Samuel smiled. "Listen to me, Leda," he said approvingly, in that smooth flow of English that he'd said Mr. Ikeno wouldn't understand, "no matter what happens, do as I say. Bow to this man, and to me."

She hesitated, and then obeyed him, copying the motion she'd seen him and Mr. Dojun do a hundred times.

Mr. Ikeno ignored her. He looked at Samuel and made a nod, the sword held across his chest, his shoulders stiff. "This honorable Jurada wife, may Kwannon favor. Petition ask, Ikeno petition grant. Future, honorable wife-san not alone while lifetime of Ikeno."

"Sumimasen," Samuel said. "For this, my debt to you will never end." He looked at Leda, and she remembered to bow to him. Softly, before she raised her head, he said in a slurred and tender voice, "Leda, when I tell you, the instant I tell you, you get off this boat. Overboard."

She straightened up abruptly. "Pardon me?"

"Do as I tell you. Whatever happens." His mouth grew hard. "Whatever happens."

"But—"

"Silence!" He strode to her suddenly, shoving her by the shoulder into a place against the rail, with his back to the others. "Listen to me, wife," he said fiercely through his teeth, "I'm telling you that if you don't do exactly what I say, you won't get home alive, and neither will I. This is no costume party. If I tell you to go over the rail, you go. Understand?" He shook her by the collar. "Now—start to cry. Do it!"

Leda was already halfway to weeping with shock. She didn't understand; it made no sense. She squeezed her eyes shut and opened them again. "Samuel—"

"They can't leave until the tide turns. Four hours. No matter what happens, Leda. Into the water when I tell you. Do as I say no matter what happens."

Real tears of fright began to fill her eyes. "What's going to happen?"

He made a rough sound and pushed away. He faced Mr. Ikeno with his back straight, the bloodstain at his collar dark against the creamy linen. "*Yōi shiyō.*"

The Japanese man responded at length in his own language, with a gesture toward the sword and toward himself. Samuel hesitated, then inclined his head, as if assenting to a decision.

Mr. Ikeno issued orders to his men. Everyone's demeanor had become grave, every move deliberate. Another mat was laid before the first, a second, shorter sword with a plain hilt placed on it. Samuel knelt at the point of the second sword, a graceful folding of his body. He touched his forehead to the back of his palms on the mat and straightened.

Mr. Ikeno also knelt. He sat facing Samuel, and picked up the shorter sword. With ritual deliberation, he drew it out of the sheath and released the blade from the hilt as he'd done to the other. He wiped the blade with a cloth, slowly, in silence, the only sound the gentle, watery swash of tiny waves against the island.

Leda was not certain that she liked this. She watched Mr. Ikeno pat over the blade a little pillow, like a powder puff, leaving a light dust. With another cloth, he wiped the white powder away, even more slowly, more carefully.

The clean steel gleamed. Mr. Ikeno turned it over and over in his hands, examining it. Then he extended it, bared tang first, toward Samuel.

Leda held onto the low iron rail of the fishing boat. Her cheeks felt hot. The summer straw hat gave her little shade from the mid-afternoon sun. Samuel wore no hat at all; his hair caught light, concentrated it, as the blade in his hand rippled sun along its length. He studied it, observing the edge, and then handed it back to Mr. Ikeno.

Samuel sat motionless while the Japanese man oiled a cloth and applied it to the sword as carefully as he'd wiped it clean. He reseated the blade in its stark hilt and replaced it on the mat, without the sheath, with the naked point directed toward Samuel.

Then he picked up the sword with the golden hilt and began the same ritual.

Leda drew in a breath. They were going to have a sword fight. She could see that this was some kind of ceremonial preparation. Her heart thumped in her throat. "Samuel," she said in a quavery voice. "I would like us to go home."

Mr. Ikeno looked up at her, as if a sea gull had spoken. He ceased his cleansing of the sword.

For a moment, Samuel was silent. Then he said to Mr. Ikeno, "*Gomen nasai.*"

Mr. Ikeno held the long blade. He nodded. "*Sō.*"

Samuel sheathed the shorter sword, laid it down, rose and came toward her. He touched her arm and leaned close to her ear. "We can't go home. Listen to me, do what I say; that's all I ask."

"What's going to happen?"

He rested the tips of his fingers against her cheek. "Please, Leda."

"What's going to *happen?*"

He only looked into her eyes. Leda swallowed in a dry throat, frightened. She caught his coat.

"Samuel—I won't have this! I won't have it."

"Do you love me?"

Her lips parted. "Yes!"

"Then depend on me. Do what I tell you. Cry if you want, scream if you want. Just listen for what I tell you, and do it."

"This is a nightmare."

He drew his fingers down her jaw. "I love you, Leda. Don't forget."

She stared at the bloodstain on his collar. Her throat was tight with terror. Her mouth opened on protests that wouldn't come.

He smiled faintly. "And don't forget to breathe."

"Samuel! If anything happens to you—!"

"Don't forget," he whispered.

Samuel left her. He faced Ikeno and the short, unadorned *harakiri-gatana*, with its double edge and workmanlike hilt wrapped in black silk thread. He knelt, with proper salute, and focused his attention on the Gokuak-uma.

Ikeno had offered him a backhanded honor: *kaishaku*, to act his second, to stand as a relation, finishing off the ritual suicide with the demon blade. To save Samuel the full pain of the act, and retain the noble principle—as he grasped the sword and plunged it into himself, Ikeno would strike off his head.

It was a kindness, and a tacit assumption that a Westerner couldn't take it; wouldn't have the discipline to cut himself left to right, up and down, and then thrust the blade in his own throat, as a true warrior.

Samuel watched the hands that polished the Gokuak-uma. Loving hands, like a mother caressing a child, smoothing the cloth lengthwise to purify the blade. Ikeno took his time. A Japanese sword was tested by noting how many bodies of dead enemies it could cut through at one stroke. This blade, unused for centuries, would be verified on Samuel.

Ikeno inspected the Gokuakuma inch by inch. He extended the blade to Samuel, allowed him to look at it without touching it, to judge the razor edge and the burnished steel, unrusted, shining without flaw in a blaze that brought the carved *tengu* to life, made the beak and claws seem to writhe as the sword moved.

Samuel bowed in acknowledgment. Ikeno placed the blade in its golden hilt and tapped the pin in place. He sheathed the Gokuakuma and stood up, taking his position behind Samuel.

In his mind, Samuel chanted the *kuji*, and conjured the strength of the nine symbols that his hands did not form. He listened, hearing nothing, and felt, experiencing nothing, and breathed the void, until there was nothing but earth, water, wind, fire, and the unremarkable sword in front of him.

Time, and the sword. Infinite time.

The moon shines on the water, and the water slips past, and past, and past, while the moon's reflection never moves.

The boat drifted on the incoming tide, and then the turn, the horizon creeping past.

He thought, and did not think, of Leda. Of Dojun.

It was like dying, *zanshin*.

The old song came to him, the first song, the shark's song.

And sometime, in that endless time, he heard the sound of tuneless bells. One carillon. Two. Three.

Leda, he thought. *Leda!*

He reached for the blade and lifted it.

Thirty-six

⊕

Leda felt a trickle of perspiration slide from her nape to her collar. It was hours—she knew it had been hours, because she'd watched as Mr. Ikeno stood behind Samuel, holding the red-and-gold sword in both hands, by the hilt and the scabbard, his shadow lengthening, crawling across the deck with immeasurable slowness as the boat turned.

Everyone waited. It was like a dream. All the silence, the endless silence, this place, these men; Samuel, with the bloodstain on his collar and the swords that drew light from everywhere and turned it to gold and silver and steel.

It was because it was a dream that she didn't move when the shadow caught her eye, sweeping beneath the rail and the boat. Then she turned her head slightly, unwilling to look away from Samuel. It drifted past again.

She jerked.

Her body seemed to lose every nerve, everything that held her in place. She twitched once, all over, and froze. The edge of her vision darkened.

Breathe.

She gasped for air. And then she turned right around and looked down—and it had to be a dream. It was a hideous, unthinkable dream, a dark nightmare half as long as the fishing boat, moving streamlined and slow, now nosing at the hull, now floating beneath, and now disappearing into the depths with one sudden flick of the tail.

She opened her mouth. No sound at all emerged. She began to weep silently, staring around at the others who seemed oblivious to anything but Samuel and Mr. Ikeno.

Through the quiet, she heard tinny bells, the tuneless

clatter from the rice paddies onshore—such a mundane, earthly sound that it didn't seem to fit anything. She felt as she'd felt in dreams, as if she were trying to cry out and couldn't move, as if everything happened like slow honey from a jar.

She saw Samuel bow before the blade on the mat. With a sound of wind, of a chanted whisper, Mr. Ikeno drew his sword.

He spread his legs and lifted the golden hilt, grasping it in both hands. The sword ate up the sun, spawning a bead of fire at the point.

The image froze in her eyes. She stared at the dazzle of the steel poised over Samuel's head.

No, she thought. *No!*

She heard a scream: she felt hard hands on her arms, holding her back; she watched Samuel lift the sword from the mat. He raised it in one fist.

As he drove it toward himself, the other blade came sweeping down.

And the screaming was her own: *No, no, no!*

Samuel's body collapsed like a boneless doll, like a cab horse she'd seen fall dead in the street. Mr. Ikeno pitched over him, and Samuel was dead, butchered, crumpled on the deck with his killer, but he was yelling at her *Now, in the water now!*

In the water.

Samuel came out of a roll with both swords in his hands. He pivoted, driving his foot into Mr. Ikeno's chin with a force that hurled the man backward, his head slamming into the cabin wall. His crewman released her arms, lunging for a hooked spear from the deck.

"Leda!" Samuel shouted. *"Go!"*

His voice was a tangible agent, a force that pushed her. She gripped the rail, and looked down, and there was the shark gliding out from beneath the hull, breaking the surface with a horrible fin.

As she turned, Samuel evaded the wicked point of the spear, a step sideways and in, past the hook. He smashed down with the plain hilt onto his attacker's hand and drove his elbow up under the man's arm, sent knee into kneecap with a force that Leda heard crack bone. The man endured it without a sound, swinging the hook as he went down. The fierce slash made a low whirling note in the air. It cut open Samuel's cheek, a bright line of instant crimson.

He scrambled back, like a cat half-falling from a tree. His short sword flickered, slicing fingers from the spear as the injured man twisted away, trailing blood when Samuel kicked it overboard.

"He manō!" Another cry came across the water. One of the Japanese blocked Samuel, while the other swung a fishing net. Mr. Ikeno pushed himself up, staggering against the cabin wall. Beyond them all Leda saw a native canoe, paddles flashing, driving toward the boat with a spreading wake behind it on the still water. The shark's fin appeared, made its own wake, a curve and then submersion as it turned away.

Samuel backed from the Japanese attackers and threw a leg over the rail. Leda shrieked as he pitched himself outward, but he didn't jump; he ducked the net flung over him, swinging under the rail by his arms and legs. The net slid past with no purchase, weights rattling across the metal rail. As he came around, he let go with one arm and brought the long sword in a powerful sweep over the calf and shin of the closest man, exposing flesh and bone. The man stumbled and stood, but his legs failed him in a step forward.

Samuel wheeled up, straddling the rail with the golden hilt in his hand. Blood smeared over half his face, still welling from the cut; blood from his attackers stained the mats on the deck and thickened the air with scent. He shouted in Japanese, and the last man checked suddenly, the only one of them standing uninjured.

"He manō! He manō!" A bark of frantic warning came from the canoe. *"Auwe,* Haku-nui! No! No leap!"

Leda recognized Manalo and Mr. Dojun in the native craft, but she had no time to think of it. Mr. Ikeno lunged toward her. She recoiled from him, but he caught her arm, jerking her back. The railing collided painfully with her hips. Her straw hat flew off. Her feet came off the deck.

He shoved her, and she tilted so far over that she caught a flashing image of her hat twirling to the water.

Mr. Ikeno held her there by one arm, her fingers slipping on the round metal rail, a scream jammed in her throat. Then he pulled her upright just enough to keep her frantically kicking feet from finding the deck.

Samuel was staring at them, breathing hard. The canoe thumped into the hull of the fishing boat, below him.

Mr. Ikeno spoke. His voice was soft, but Leda gasped against his tightened grip. She couldn't wriggle from the brutal hold. And he was pushing her again; he was tipping her backward so that if he let her go, she would topple over the rail and into the water.

She tried to curl her hand in his sleeve, around his arm, her fingernails digging into whatever she could catch. Her feet found the deck, slid and slipped helplessly, and lost contact. It was only Mr. Ikeno's grip that held her balanced.

"Fuka!" Samuel bellowed. *"Same!* Do you see it, Ikeno? *That's my shark."* He thrust the short sword through his belt and swung off the rail. *"I called it!"* He sounded crazy, shouting in Japanese and English at the fierce limit of his lungs. He hit his chest with his fist. *Boku-no,* Ikeno, *wakarimasu ka?"*

Suddenly he wielded the golden sword in a two-handed swipe at Ikeno's man. His target sprang upward, a superb leap that should have cleared the blade, but Samuel halted the momentum in mid-pivot, and the man came down with the point at his throat. As he arched backward into the rail, Samuel kicked his feet from under him, so that he teetered over it for a moment in the same way Leda did.

The man threw his legs upward and back, vaulting the bar like a circus performer. He held on by his hands, his feet dangling over the water.

"Onaka ga sukimashita ka! Are you hungry, shark?" Samuel brought the blade of the sword flat on the iron rail. It rang like a cracked bell. Leda felt the vibration under her fingers. He hit it again. "Come here, *fuka!* I'll feed you!"

"You *lōlō?*" Manalo shouted from the canoe. "No call shark!"

"He won't hurt me. Or what's mine." He swept the sword over the dangling man's hands, a breath from cutting them. "He might eat this if I gave it to him."

Mr. Ikeno shouted, abrupt and guttural in his own language. Leda gave a little shriek and scrabbled for a purchase as he pushed her further out of balance over the rail.

Samuel stepped back, allowing the man to pull himself up and clear the rail. At the same moment, Mr. Dojun hiked aboard from the canoe.

Mr. Ikeno kept her at a perilous angle, calling out sharply in Japanese.

Samuel stood still in the middle of the deck and the matting streaked with blood. He reached down and picked up the red lacquered sheath and rammed the blade inside it.

"Ikeno-san! Dojun-san!" He held the sword aloft, shouting. "Who wants it?"

No one moved; no one said anything.

"Dojun-san! My master, my teacher, my friend! My *friend!*" His furious voice echoed back from the island and the water. "Here's your sword, Dojun-san!" He swept a deep bow and extended it, the sheath shining crimson and gold.

Mr. Ikeno growled a warning and tipped Leda a degree further backward. She shrieked, fighting to hold onto his arm, the slick rail, whatever she could clutch.

"Why, Dojun-san!" Samuel said in vicious mockery. "Look what happens if I give the Gokuakuma back to honorable master."

Mr. Dojun stared at him, unblinking.

Samuel shrugged, lowered the sword. "So. Get another wife, *nē?* You bastard. You bastard, you don't care; you conned me; you screwed me; you've used me for seventeen *years*, you bastard, *why's she here?*" He was breathing harshly, a loud sound through his teeth. *"Look at her!"* he howled, holding the sword over his head. *"Do you know how fast I'd kill you both?"*

"You got weakness, Samua-san," Mr. Dojun said quietly. "Want too much."

Samuel stared at him. He lowered the sword. "Want too much," he repeated, in a disbelieving voice. "*I* want too much!"

The drying blood on his face was like war paint. He shook his head, as if the idea bewildered him, as if Mr. Dojun dumbfounded him.

He turned suddenly, pounded the sword on the iron rail again. "*Do you hear him, shark? I* want *too much!*"

Leda sucked in air as she looked sideways and saw the ghastly shape shoot out from beneath the boat, blunt-nosed and tremendous, so huge that when its head was even with the end of the boat, the triangular fin was right below her. It bumped the hull, and the whole vessel rocked.

Samuel said, "I don't want too much." He turned with the sword toward Leda and Mr. Ikeno.

Mr. Dojun made a noise. It began as a drawn-out, growling shout and rose. It ran through her with a paralyzing shock; she felt her captor's hold on her tighten.

Samuel stopped as if a wall had sprung up in front of him. Leda squeezed her free hand frantically, trying to cling to the rail, fighting, feeling her balance slipping as Mr. Ikeno tilted her.

"Samuel!" she whimpered.

He moved. With a sound that was no sound, an explosion of air and force that sent everything else to silence, he hurled the sword in the air.

Mr. Ikeno shoved away from her, leaping to intercept it on the upward arc. Leda screamed and scrabbled for equilibrium, half over the rail, water and boat pitching wildly in her vision. Something caught her arm, jerking her savagely forward onto her feet. Samuel dragged her against his chest, stumbling backward with the force of his haul. Mr. Ikeno didn't even glance at them; he was staring up at the sword that tumbled end over end in a high arc and came hurtling down.

It struck the water point first, ten feet from the boat. It barely made a splash, and seemed to catch the sun along its full length beneath the clear water. From a distance, the shark turned with feline quickness. The sword sank like a leaf falling, leisurely, the golden hilt dimming and flashing. As the creature shot toward the weapon, its huge head seemed to swell. The body rolled, showing white belly and gaping mouth, a macabre instant of nightmare teeth and the sword sliding in as if sucked by a siphon.

"Iya!" Mr. Ikeno murmured.

The gray fin broke the surface. The shark swept past the fishing boat, rocking it with the surge of its passage.

"He manō," Manalo called from the canoe, with awe in his voice. *"Ka waha ō Kaahupahau!"*

No one else spoke. The shark turned away to the open harbor. Its fin slipped beneath the water. The appalling shape grew indistinct, and sank out of sight in the depths.

Samuel held Leda against him, his back pressed to the low deckhouse. He felt the shudders running through her, one after another, each time she tried to speak or move. Her hair had come loose and was dragging in her eyes; he smoothed it back, looking over her head toward the others.

Ikeno stood motionless, gazing after the shark. *"Aiya!"* he muttered. "Buddha and all the gods secure us. What has the Tanabe done here?"

"I know not," Dojun said softly.

Ikeno didn't turn at his voice. "Is he a madman or holy? What have you done, Tanabe-san? What have you made?"

"I have no answer. It happened."

Ikeno pulled an *omamori* charm from beneath his clothes and held it in his fist. "The god of war speaks, *nē?"* he suggested uneasily. "Perhaps Hachiman of the bow and feathered shaft is ill at ease, and slips from beneath his temple stone to fly abroad. *Namuamidabutsu; namuamidabutsu."* He made a little chant beneath his breath.

"What will you do?" Dojun's voice was even.

Ikeno let go of the charm. His eyes narrowed, and he shrugged, as if shaking off the superstitious dread. "Fish for shark,'' he said, with a jerk of his chin. But beneath the defiance, there was a weight of gloom in his voice.

"Hopeless," Dojun said. "Your *rōtō* bleed."

Ikeno looked over his shoulder, where his one uninjured man was binding up the others. "We'll all bleed from a bellyache. *Kuso!* I should have gone in after it."

"A dog's death. A pointless death."

"You're a traitor! You've betrayed our country. The Gokuakuma is needed now. We're kneeling with our foreheads to the floor before the West."

"Then let us stand upright, and not give our trust to demons!" Dojun snapped. "I don't believe the god of war lives beneath a temple stone. I've been in the West too long. Hachiman lives elsewhere, Ikeno-san—in the bellies of politicians and priests and men like you and me."

Ikeno snorted. *"Nihonjin no kuse ni!* The Tanabe has indeed been in exile too long. He is not Japanese."

Dojun whirled on him, with a look of more emotion than Samuel had ever seen in his face. Ikeno stood with his legs apart, head lifted, welcoming a fight.

A voice rose in emphatic pidgin above the murmurs of the bloodied fighters by the cabin. Manalo had come aboard; with island artlessness, he tied bandages, lending himself to helping men who would have killed him without conscience a quarter hour before.

Dojun turned his head. He watched them. After a moment he met Samuel's eyes. With a sardonic smile, he said, "Perhaps honored Ikeno-san speaks more than he knows."

Samuel couldn't interpret that look. He realized that he'd never really known anything of Dojun's true emotions. Even now he didn't, having filtered it all through the sieve of his own yearning, his own anger and hurt. Always—always—Dojun had pulled his strikes, except for that one trial in Haleakala, and even then—even then . . . Samuel had sometimes wondered.

Dojun was a master. He always had been. He always would be.

But this time, Samuel had challenged the adamantine wall of his intention and broken it with his own.

Dojun bowed toward him with rigid pride. "A Western friendship is a potent and difficult thing, I find. But there are things that can't be avoided in this cycle of existence."

Samuel heard the accusation—and admission. He held the look defiantly. "He didn't get your demon sword, did he?"

"No." Dojun gazed out at Pearl Harbor. "He did not." He smiled faintly. "But remember the starfish, Samua-san."

Samuel held Leda's body to him and put his face into the curve of her neck. She clutched at his hand. A long shudder ran through her.

"If you please," she said, in a small and ordinary English voice, "may we go home now?"

Samuel called to Manalo, who instantly raised his hand in acknowledgment and dropped down into the canoe. When Leda saw that, she stiffened in Samuel's embrace.

"Must we go in that small boat?"

He tightened his arms around her. "The shark's gone."

She shivered. She took a deep breath. "Well. Yes! I'm sure that you must be right." With a little push, she stood straight. Without looking at Ikeno, or Dojun, or the mess on the deck, she set her face into the stern resignation of a martyr and stepped gingerly over the bloody mats. At the rail, she stopped. "I should like to take the bride table, Mr. Dojun. If you would kindly bring it. Perhaps it can be fixed, and another sword found to replace the one that was—swallowed."

Dojun didn't blink. He bowed and said, "*Sayō.* I fix, Mrs. Samua-san. All good luck."

"Excellent. And I must thank you and Mr. Manalo for your rescue. As you saw, Mr. Gerard had the situation well in hand, but your courage and kind aid were most obliging."

"*Kin doku.* Too much honor." Dojun bowed, a deep bow of respect. "Good wife. Good wife, Samua-san. *Kanshin, kanshin.*" He changed to Japanese. "Take her now. I mean what I say. She is admirable. I respect her. She wishes very much to do you credit."

Samuel hesitated. It was praise beyond anything he'd ever heard from Dojun. "You're not coming?"

"Send Manalo back for me." He smiled wryly. "I'll bring your bride table."

Samuel flickered a glance toward Ikeno and the others.

"I wish to persuade this ill-advised person of his folly in thinking I am not Japanese," Dojun said lightly.

Ikeno pushed back from where he'd been gazing out over the far rail and grunted. His scowl was like one of the devil-faced warriors of the woodblock prints, as if he'd enjoy killing someone.

Anger at Dojun still rode deep in Samuel's blood, but some perverse fusion of loyalty and habit and obligation made him say, "Need help?"

Dojun passed his hand in front of his face, a negative gesture. *"Chigaimasu.* What do you think, little *baka?"*

Samuel looked sideways at Ikeno's ready stance. He smiled caustically. "All right," he said in English. "Have fun."

Leda sat in front of him in the canoe, rigid, with her hands and elbows pulled in close to her body. They reached shore without any sign of threat from sharks. The boy Shōji, who'd manned the rice-paddy tin cans to communicate with Samuel while he was aboard the fishing boat—a single ring to alert him that one of Ikeno's men was coming, two for a stranger, three for Dojun—stood waiting. He jumped to help drag the canoe onto the muddy beach. Samuel, his linen trousers plastered to his knees, waded up onto dry land to hand her out. She gathered her skirts as if she were exiting a carriage in Park Lane.

Shōji had the horses tied to the buggy. Leda waited while they put one in the traces. She looked like a street waif, with her hair flying around her face and her hat gone.

Samuel wanted to go to her and drag her into his arms and hold her, hold her, tight and close. But instead he worked with Manalo and the boy, hiding the awkwardness that came on him. He finished fastening a buckle and stood there, staring at it.

Shōji gave him an anxious look, and he realized that the boy was worried about Dojun. "He's all right," Samuel said shortly. "Just keep watch."

Shōji slipped silently onto the path among the bushes and vanished.

Manalo headed back to the canoe. When Leda vigorously protested the danger of it, the Hawaiian only shrugged. "Got go back, pick up that Dojun-san sometime."

"But the shark—"

He grinned. "Manalo too much bad taste. Shark no like."

"Maybe relish for the whiskey flavor, eh, *blad?*" Samuel muttered. "You get drunk next time, I call shark here, rip off you *laho.*"

Manalo's grin lost its easy polish. He gave Samuel an uncomfortable look.

"Mahope aku," Samuel said, with a jerk of his head. "Later, brother. We talk."

The Hawaiian made a wry face and bent over the outrigger, wading in as he shoved off. "Maybe Manalo go fish few days." He leaped aboard, lifting his paddle in the air. "Aloha *nui.*"

Leda stood and watched intently until the canoe was out of sight around the island in the harbor. "Well!" she said. "I hope he may know whereof he speaks concerning sharks."

Samuel leaned his hand on the horse's flank. He saw her shiver, but she didn't look at him. She hugged herself and stared at the water, blinking rapidly.

"Leda—"

She turned her head, with a bright, blank look. Then her gaze moved over the bloodstains on his collar and lapels. Her breath became a sob. She hugged herself tighter and swallowed, panting, making desperate little noises in her throat. "I don't want to cry! I'm not going to cry!"

He took a step, and halted. "It's all right." He stood stiff, gripping a support bar of the buggy top. "You can cry."

She shook her head violently. "I won't! It's so—undigni—" A loud, sharp, hiccuping sob interrupted her. "Undignified!" Her hair came free and tumbled across her shoulder as the tremor in her broke, going to dry sobs that jarred her body, deep and shrill with delayed hysteria. "I don't—*like* . . . sharks! I don't *wish* to be held over sharks!"

"No more sharks," he said. "No more swords." He kept his hand clamped on the buggy pole, squeezing it.

"And that—and that is anoth-th—another thing! That was the most un—*sports*manlike sword fight I ever saw!" She clutched her arms tight around herself. "Even if I've never seen *any!*" she added vehemently. "It was preposterous! Why did you have to begin by sitting *down?* Mr. Ikeno had *all* the advantage! And with that mah-huh—mah-huh . . . *monstrously* insufficient—sword they gave you! You might have been—you might—have been—" She lost her voice in squeaky gasps. "Oh—*Samuel!*"

He let go of the pole. He grabbed her hard into his arms. She was shaking so much that her knees kept crumpling beneath her. She clutched him by the sleeves, burying her face in his chest. He stroked her and held her, and rocked her, with a strange, fierce laughter welling up inside him. "My brave lady. It's all right. My brave girl. My sweet, brave lady."

She wept against him. He cradled her, took all her weight on himself. He rested his torn cheek against her hair, welcoming the sting of it.

"Oh, God—Leda," he whispered, with his hand in her hair, her body pressed to his.

Her trembling began to subside. She stood leaning on him, making smaller and smaller sobs. "I wish—I wish I would have thought of something very sharp and cutting to say to those men!" She took a breath and exhaled with a huff. "To be sure I will tomorrow, when it will be too late! I don't see what there is in it for you to laugh about."

"Don't leave me." He shook her. "Leda! Don't ever go away and leave me."

She pushed back from him. "Well, what a nonsensical thing to say! When you've done your best to drive me off!" Abruptly she flung herself away and marched to the buggy. She stopped there, her lips quivering, her dress and hair in wild disorder. "I daresay that if I were not a person of character, I would have gone!"

He took a deep breath. All that empty air beneath him, all the long fall—but he wasn't going to ask, and hope, and work, and bleed, and slice his heart to shreds any longer. He wanted this; he was going to take it. "You've lost your chance to go."

Her chin lifted. "I have never wished to *have* a chance, you impossible man! I suppose it is incomprehensible to you, as a male, to be told that I've loved you since you retrieved a pair of scissors for me when I was a showroom woman! That will mean nothing to you; I daresay you've forgot it entirely, but men are known to be the most hopeless creatures alive when it comes to a subject of any consequence whatsoever. And I must say, it is certainly beneath feminine delicacy to have to continue to insist upon one's affection in such brazen terms!"

"Is it? What if I want to hear it?"

She tucked her chin and blinked at his sudden intensity.

"What if I need to hear it?" he asked fiercely. "What if I need to wake up every goddamned morning of my life and hear you say you love me?" His voice began to grow louder. "What if that's all that means any fucking thing to me?"

She drew in a scandalized breath. "That is a bad word, isn't it? That is *most* indecent language!"

"So what?" he shouted. "What if I fucking want it, Leda? Every morning! You love me. *What if I want to hear it?"*

She stared at him. He was breathing hard, as if he'd been fighting. The echo of his words went over the water and came back again and again.

She moistened her lips. Then she gathered her skirts

and wiped her hand across her wet cheeks. Her petticoat made a rustling flourish as she stepped up into the buggy. She pulled pins from her hair and coiled and tucked it into a semblance of order.

"Well, then, sir." She sent a prim look back at him beneath her lashes. "To be sure, you shall hear it!"

Thirty-seven

Leda felt quite shy, and Samuel was no help. Mr. Dojun was not even there to smooth over the delicacy of the moment with an idle conversation in pidgin. The gardeners had all seemed to vanish from the premises. Rising Sea was deserted, with the tall white pillars catching the late-afternoon light and casting sharp shadows across the lanai.

She wriggled her bare toes against the polished wood, having learned to leave her shoes and stockings by the threshold after Mr. Dojun had advised her that it wasn't polite to wear one's shoes indoors. She waited in the hall, just within the open front doors, while Samuel took the horse around to turn it into the paddock.

The house seemed stark and stately and lonely, white walls against the deep reddish-gold gleam of the koa door frames and tall shutters. There was no furniture in the hall, nor anywhere else except in the bedroom and study upstairs, where she had concentrated all her initial efforts.

She hoped that he would like it. She was hoping so hard that she couldn't hear anything but her heart in her ears. He made her jump when he appeared, moving silently on bare feet. She'd suggested that he drop his hopelessly stained coat and shirt in the horse trough until the laundress could take it; he'd evidently washed his face there, too, for his hair was damp and the war-marks of blood were gone, leaving only an angry slash from his jaw to his temple.

She frowned at him. "Your poor face! I still believe that we should have reported this incident to the police."

444

"Maybe I'll develop a rakish scar." A corner of his mouth tilted. "Not that it's ever happened yet."

"A doctor should see to it."

"Not tonight." He leaned on the door frame, crossing his arms over his chest. In bare feet, muddy trousers, and no shirt, he looked as sun-bronzed and disreputable as Manalo, only without all the flowers.

She clasped her hands, feeling self-conscious. He hadn't spoken much on the drive back, only informed her that the police would be of no assistance in this matter; that it had not been a kidnapping for ransom after all, but just some rather rough business associates of his. She made a mental note to deliver an address upon the wise and proper choice of one's commercial colleagues in the very near future.

But not now. Gentlemen were known to be inclined to resent any implication that they were not perfect masters of their own enterprise. She didn't wish to discuss it with him now.

"Well!" She gave him a bright company smile. "I would invite you to sit down in the parlor, but I'm afraid there's no furniture."

"I thought you'd done nothing but haul furniture up here for the past week."

"I have. I began with the upstairs chambers." She felt herself blushing. "I thought—"

Samuel watched her.

"Manalo . . . he and Mr. Dojun recommended—"

He moved his shoulders back a little, a shadow of combativeness in his easy bearing. "You listen to me, not those two."

"I shall be most happy to do so. It's been rather difficult of late, as you weren't here to be listened to."

He was silent a moment. "Now I'm here."

It seemed altogether too forward to just brazenly invite him up to the bedroom. She considered various modes of working it into the conversation, but since there was no conversation, or very little of it, and that only marginally civil, she felt helpless and somewhat ill-used. He was the most singularly provoking man of her acquaintance.

"Do you love me, Leda?" he demanded.

"Decidedly."

"I want to—" He exhaled sharply and turned his head. The cut on his face grew white at the edges.

Belatedly, she realized what he meant—and what was happening to him. He muttered something too low for her to hear. She bit her lip, the corners of her mouth curving upward, but the abruptness with which he pushed himself off the door frame and came toward her made her turn and press her back against the wall.

He stopped short. His face went taut.

Then he swung away, walking past her to the staircase. "So. I want to go look at your damned furniture."

He went up the hand-burnished stairs two at a time, past the elegant curve where the staircase bent back upon itself. He stopped there. She couldn't see his face, but she saw him seize the carved rail.

"Leda!" His yell echoed through the vacant house. "God damn it! You said you loved me. *And that's me!* I can't help it; I can't stop it; I want to touch you; I want to lie down with you; I want to be inside you. Christ, as soon as I got you out of that bastard's hands I wanted it! On the deck, in the buggy, against a wall. I don't care! It doesn't make any damned difference to me!"

She looked down at her toes peeking from beneath the sandy hem of her skirt. "I prefer a bed."

"Fine! I understand there's one up here."

"Well, yes—I've been wondering how I might genteelly allude to the topic."

Her voice resonated back in a soft murmur and died away.

His hand was motionless on the stair rail.

"You were?" he asked slowly.

"Yes."

A very long silence passed. The light breeze through the hall cooled the warmth of her face and neck.

"Then why the hell are you still down there?" he asked in an agonized voice.

She rubbed her toes together. "Because—I don't wish

to be there when you see—how everything is done up. In case you shouldn't like it.''

"For God's sake. It's only furniture.''

"There are . . . a few other things as well.''

He said nothing. Leda tapped her fingers nervously against the wall. After a few moments, the hand on the polished rail vanished.

She knew that he moved silently. She thought that she should be starting to become accustomed to it. But the way he disappeared, and the lack of any sound for such a long time from the floor above, unnerved her.

Finally she went to the stairs. She mounted them softly. In the upper hall there was no one to be seen, no sound. She padded through the study to the bedroom.

He was standing there, among the ten-times-one-thousand red paper cranes of long life and happiness.

They hung from their suspended bamboo arcs in cascades, in streamers of twenty and thirty and fifty, spinning slowly from the twelve-foot ceiling. Some of them trailed almost to the floor, drifting an inch or two above it in the breeze from the open doors. Most strands were high enough that Leda and Mr. Dojun had walked beneath them easily. She had forgotten how much taller Samuel was; they brushed his face and rested on his hair, dangled over his bare shoulders, moving with his breath, like a canopy of crimson willows.

He raised his arms outward and upward, gathering a rustling quantity toward him. He closed his eyes and let them fall away across his upturned face.

Leda hung in the doorway. She didn't know if he even knew she was there.

"Did you do this?''

He asked without opening his eyes, with his still face turned toward the ceiling.

"It was—my notion. The lady—Mrs. Obāsan—she made them all. Mr. Dojun said that the custom is one thousand cranes, but I thought—I thought that perhaps, as she had them already made up and in hand, that ten thousand would be an advantageous investment.''

"An advantageous investment,'' he repeated.

"In good luck and happiness. In the manner of stocks, and bank shares, and so forth. I trust that cranes work upon the same principles. I don't see why they shouldn't. And one has the benefit of a discount when buying in quantity. Have you seen the turtle?"

"No," he said in an odd voice. "I haven't seen the turtle."

"It's in your study. On the writing table, in a very handsome black lacquered bowl, with some white rocks and a little water. It's only a box turtle. Dickie has lent it us, until our own can be imported."

"You're importing a turtle?"

"Mr. Richards is to arrange for it. He thinks it will arrive within the month."

"Why?"

"It's a gift. My wedding gift for you. Mr. Dojun said that you would understand."

He just looked at her.

"And there is something else, too, from me. But I— I'll show you that in a moment. First I must tell you that Mr. Dojun has given us this bed, with the crane on it. And the drawers on the chest sing a little note when one opens them. He did that, too."

Samuel touched one of the two bamboo plants at the foot of the bed.

"And bamboo is a lucky plant," she added. "Constant, devoted, flexible."

He pulled a leaf downward and let it go. " 'Be as the bamboo leaf bent by the dew.' " He shook his head slightly. "Dojun's always saying things like that."

"Is he? I shall have to listen to him more closely."

"Don't listen to him. Don't touch any more 'bride-tables' on his account."

"I am so sorry about the table!"

"Forget the table. It's nothing. One hundred percent nothing. He made up that bride rubbish." He lifted his face. "But this—" He shook his head again, with a dazed smile. "I can't believe you did this. And a turtle, for God's sake. You awe me. I'm—awed."

"You are?"

He lifted his hand and let a streamer of cranes slide across it. He grinned.

"Oh! I'm so glad. Then perhaps you will like the fish."

He gave a laugh. "Jesus—not dried fish? Leda!"

"No, no. I think dried fish would have an odor, don't you? Come here." She caught his hand, drawing him through the door into the bath. It was fitted up in the most modern style, with hot and cold plumbing and a white marble tub two feet deep and six feet in length, the present occupants of which were two ivory-and-golden fish, regal and slow in their circling progress, trailing translucent mists of tail and fins. *"This* is my real present. This is what I've been planning since—" She touched her upper lip with her tongue. "That is, since—the first night—when you came to—when you came . . . that is, when we . . ." Her embarrassed voice fell into silence. "Do you remember?"

He took his hand from hers.

"They'll have to stay here until a place can be made in the garden. Mr. Dojun says they must be sunned for an hour every day, to keep their color. I hope you don't mind. I hope—"

He slid his fingers up the side of her throat, forcing her to turn, to lift her face. He kissed her ruthlessly. His tongue searched her mouth. He held her tight up against him.

"I hope you like them!" she said breathlessly, when she had a chance.

"Tomorrow—" He tasted the corners of her lips. "Tomorrow I'll like them. Tonight . . . Leda . . ."

He began to unbutton her dress.

She submitted to it graciously. It was a well-known fact that gentlemen must be provided with all due encouragement in such circumstances, so as not to hurt their feelings. As her dress fell away, Leda closed her eyes, lifted her arms around his shoulders and her mouth to his, and set about encouraging in a most correct and cheerful manner.

The Passion and Romance
of Bestselling Author

Laura Kinsale

THE SHADOW AND THE STAR
76131-9/$4.99 US/$5.99 Can

Wealthy, powerful and majestically handsome Samuel
Gerard, master of the ancient martial arts, has sworn to
love chastely…but burns with the fires of unfulfilled
passion. Lovely and innocent Leda Etoile is drawn to
this "shadow warrior" by a fevered yearning she could
never deny.

Be Sure to Read

THE HIDDEN HEART 75008-2/$4.50 US/$5.50 Can
MIDSUMMER MOON 75398-7/$3.95 US/$4.95 Can
THE PRINCE OF MIDNIGHT
76130-0/$4.95 US/$5.95 Can
SEIZE THE FIRE 75399-5/$4.50 US/$5.50 Can
UNCERTAIN MAGIC 75140-2/$4.95 US/$5.95 Can

The Passion and Romance of

KATHERINE SUTCLIFFE

SHADOW PLAY

75941-1/$4.95 US/$5.95 Can

A lusty adventurer whose courage was renowned, the handsome Morgan Kane was in truth a rogue and a charlatan. Beautiful Sarah St. James left the glitter of London behind to seek justice in a lush and savage wilderness. Bound by ties of vengeance, together they found a passionate ecstasy beyond dreams.

A FIRE IN THE HEART

75579-3/$4.50 US/$5.50 Can

She fled the horrors of a British workhouse, seeking refuge with a dark, moody aristocrat. Begrudgingly he sheltered her, fighting the fascination of her saucy innocence. But never did he imagine she would force his surrender to the exquisite torment of a love that denied all reason.

RENEGADE LOVE   75402-9/$3.95 US/$4.95 Can